THE CRASHING WAVES FAR BELOW

Driven by fierce and frigid winds that had them leaning far forward just to prevent being blown over, icy, stinging snow crashed against them more than fell over them. That driving wind shifted constantly among the alternating cliff faces, swirling and changing direction, denying them any chance of finding a shielding barricade, and always seeming to put snow in their faces no matter which way they turned. They each tried to formulate a plan and had to shout out their suggestions at the top of their lungs, putting lips right against the ear of the person with whom they were trying to communicate.

In the end, any hope of a plan for achieving some relief had to rely completely upon luck—the companions needed to find a cave, or at least a deep overhang with walls shielding them from the most pressing winds.

Drizzt bent low on the white trail and placed his black onyx figurine on the ground before him. . . .

FORGOTTEN REALMS

FORGOTTEN REALMS

SEA OF SWORDS

THE LEGEND OF DRIZZT®

BOOK XIII

R. A. SALVATORE

THE LEGEND OF DRIZZT
BOOK XIII
SEA OF SWORDS

©2001, 2009 Wizards of the Coast LLC

Cover art by Todd Lockwood
Map by Todd Gamble
This Edition First Printing: June 2009
Originally Published in Hardcover in October 2001

9 8 7 6 5 4 3 2 1

ISBN: 978-0-7869-5121-5
620-24021740-001-EN

U.S., CANADA,
ASIA, PACIFIC, & LATIN AMERICA
Wizards of the Coast LLC
P.O. Box 707
Renton, WA 98057-0707
+1-800-324-6496

EUROPEAN HEADQUARTERS
Hasbro UK Ltd
Caswell Way
Newport, Gwent NP9 0YH
GREAT BRITAIN
Save this address for your records.

Visit our web site at www.wizards.com

H e worked his scimitars in smooth, sure circular motions, bringing them through delicate and deceiving arcs. When the opportunity presented itself he stepped ahead and slashed down at a seemingly exposed shoulder with one blade. But the elf, bald head shining in the sunlight, was faster. The elf dropped a foot back and raised a long sword in a solid parry, then

PROLOGUE

came forward in a straight rush, stabbing with a dirk, then stepping ahead again to thrust with the sword.

He danced in perfect harmony with the elf's fluid movements, twirling his twin scimitars defensively, each rolling down and over to ring against the thrusting sword. The elf stabbed again, mid-torso, then a third time, aiming low.

Over and down went the scimitars, the classic, double-block-low. Then up those twin weapons came as the agile, hairless elf tried to kick through the block.

The elf's kick was no more than a feint, and as the scimitars came up, the elf fell into a crouch and let fly the dagger. It sailed in before he could get the scimitars down low enough to block, before he could set his feet and dodge aside.

A perfect throw for disembowelment, the devilish dagger caught him in the belly.

✕ ✕ ✕ ✕ ✕

"It's Deudermont, to be sure," the crewman called, tone growing frantic. "He's caught sight of us again!"

"Bah, but he's no way to know who we are," another reminded.

"Just put us around the reef and past the jetties," Sheila Kree instructed her pilot.

Tall and thick, with arms rock-hard from years of hard labor and green eyes that showed resentment for those years, the red-headed woman stared angrily at the pursuit. The three-masted schooner forced a turn from what would certainly have proven to be a most profitable pillaging of a lightly armed merchant ship.

"Bring us a fog to block their watchin'," the nasty pirate added, yelling at Bellany, *Bloody Keel*'s resident sorceress.

"A fog," the sorceress huffed, shaking her head so that her raven-black hair bounced all about her shoulders.

The pirate, who more often spoke with her sword than with her tongue, simply did not understand. Bellany shrugged and began casting her strongest spell, a fireball. As she finished, she aimed the blast not at the distant, pursuing ship—which was long out of range, and which, if it was *Sea Sprite*, would have had no trouble repelling such an attack anyway—but at the water behind *Bloody Keel*.

The surf sizzled and sputtered in protest as the flames licked at it, bringing a thick steam up behind the fast-sailing ship. Sheila Kree smiled and nodded her approval. Her pilot, a heavyset woman with a big dimpled face and a yellow smile, knew the waters around the western tip of the Spine of the World better than anyone alive. She could navigate there on the darkest of nights, using no more than the sound of the currents splashing over the reefs. Deudermont's ship wouldn't dare follow them through the dangerous waters ahead. Soon enough *Bloody Keel* would sail out beyond the third jetty, around the rocky bend, and into open waters if she chose, or turn even closer inland to a series of reefs and rocks—a place Sheila and her companions had come to call home.

"He's no way to know 'twas us," the crewman said again.

Sheila Kree nodded, and hoped the man was right—believed he probably was, for while *Sea Sprite,* a three-masted schooner, had such a unique signature of sails, *Bloody Keel* appeared to be just another small, unremarkable caravel. Like any other wise pirate along the Sword Coast, though, Sheila Kree had no desire to tangle with Deudermont's legendary *Sea Sprite* or his skilled and dangerous crew, whoever he thought she was.

And she'd heard rumors that Deudermont was looking for her, though why the famous pirate-hunter might be singling her out, she could only guess. Reflexively, the powerful woman reached back over her shoulder to feel the mark she'd had branded upon herself, the symbol of her new-found power and ambition. As with all the women serving in Kree's new sea and land group, Sheila wore the mark of the mighty warhammer she'd purchased from a fool in Luskan, the mark of Aegis-fang.

Was that, then, the source of Deudermont's sudden interest? Sheila Kree had learned a bit of the warhammer's history, had learned that its previous owner, a drunken brute named Wulfgar, was a known friend of Captain Deudermont. That was an connection, but the pirate woman couldn't be certain. Hadn't Wulfgar been tried in Luskan for attempting to murder Deudermont after all?

Sheila Kree shrugged it all away a short while later, as *Bloody Keel* worked dangerously through the myriad of rocks and reefs to the secret, sheltered Golden Cove. Despite the expert piloting, *Bloody Keel* connected more than once on a jagged shelf, and by the time they entered the bay, the caravel was listing to port.

No matter, though, for in this pirate cove, surrounded by towering walls of jagged rock, Sheila and her crew had the means to repair the ship. They took *Bloody Keel* into a large cave, the bottom of a system of tunnels and caverns that climbed through this westernmost point of the Spine of the World, natural tunnels now smoky from torches lining the walls, and rocky caverns made comfortable by the plunder of what was fast becoming the most successful pirate band anywhere along the northern reaches of the Sword Coast.

The small-framed, black-haired sorceress

gave a sigh. She likely knew that with her magic she'd be doing most of the work on these latest repairs.

"Damn that Deudermont!" Bellany remarked.

"Damn our own cowardice, ye mean," one smelly sea dog remarked as he walked by.

Sheila Kree stepped in front of the grumbling man, sneered at him, and decked him with a right cross to the jaw.

"I didn't think he even saw us," the prone man protested, looking up at the red-haired pirate with an expression of sheer terror.

If one of the female crew of *Bloody Keel* crossed Sheila, they'd likely get a beating, but if one of the men stepped too far over the vicious pirate's line, he'd likely find out how the ship got its name. Keel-hauling was one of Sheila Kree's favorite games, after all.

Sheila Kree let the dog crawl away, her thoughts more focused on the latest appearance of Deudermont. She had to admit it was possible that *Sea Sprite* hadn't really even seen them, and likely, if Deudermont and his crew had spotted the distant sails of *Bloody Keel*, they didn't know the ship's true identity.

But Sheila Kree would remain cautious where Captain Deudermont was concerned. If the captain and his skilled crew were indeed determined to find her, then let it be here, at Golden Cove, the rocky fortress Sheila Kree and her crew shared with a formidable clan of ogres.

✕ ✕ ✕ ✕ ✕

The dagger struck him squarely—

—and bounced harmlessly to the floor.

"Drizzt Do'Urden would never have fallen for such a feint!" Le'lorinel, the bald-headed elf, grumbled in a high and melodic voice. His eyes, blue flecked with gold, shone with dangerous intensity from behind the black mask that Le'lorinel always wore. With a snap of the wrist, the sword went back into its scabbard. "If he did, he would have been quick enough a'foot to avoid the throw, or quick enough a'hand to get a scimitar back down for a block," the elf finished with a huff.

"I am not Drizzt Do'Urden," the half-elf, Tunevec, said simply. He moved to the side of the roof and leaned heavily against a crenellation, trying to catch his breath.

"Mahskevic enchanted you with magical haste to compensate," the elf replied, retrieving the dagger and adjusting his sleeveless light brown tunic.

Tunevec snorted at his opponent. "You do not even know how Drizzt Do'Urden fights," he reminded. "Truly! Have you ever seen him in battle? Have you ever watched the movements— impossible movements, I say!—that you so readily attribute to him?"

If Le'lorinel was impressed by the reasoning, it did not show. "The tales of his fighting style and prowess are common in the northland."

"Common, and likely exaggerated," Tunevec reminded.

Le'lorinel's bald head was shaking before Tunevec finished the statement, for the elf had many times detailed the prowess of Drizzt to his half-elf sparring partner.

"I pay you well for your participation in these training sessions," Le'lorinel said. "You would do well to consider every word I have told you about Drizzt Do'Urden to be the truth and to emulate his fighting style to the best of your meager abilities."

Tunevec, who was naked to the waist, toweled off his thin and muscular frame. He held the towel out to Le'lorinel, who just looked at him with contempt, which was usual after such a failure. The elf walked past, right to the trapdoor that led down to the top floor of the tower.

"Your enchantment of stoneskin is likely used up," the elf said with obvious disgust.

Alone on the roof, Tunevec gave a helpless chuckle and shook his head. He moved to retrieve his shirt but noted a shimmering in the air before he ever got there. The half-elf paused, watching as old Mahskevic the wizard materialized into view.

"Did you please him this day?" the gray-bearded old man asked in a voice that seemed pulled out of his tight throat. Mahskevic's somewhat mocking smile, full of yellow teeth, showed that he already knew the answer.

"Le'lorinel is obsessed with that one," Tunevec

answered. "More so than I would ever have believed possible."

Mahskevic merely shrugged, as if that hardly mattered. "He has labored for me for more than five years, both to earn the use of my spells and to pay you well," the wizard reminded. "We searched for many months to even find you, one who seemed promising in being able to emulate the movements of this strange dark elf, Drizzt Do'Urden."

"Why waste the time, then?" the frustrated half-elf retorted. "Why do you not accompany Le'lorinel to find this wretched drow and be done with him once and for all. Far easier that would seem than this endless sparring."

Mahskevic chuckled, as if to tell Tunevec clearly that he was underestimating this rather unusual drow, whose exploits, as Le'lorinel and Mahskevic had uncovered them, were indeed remarkable. "Drizzt is known to be the friend of a dwarf named Bruenor Battlehammer," the wizard explained. "Do you know the name?"

Tunevec, putting on his gray shirt, looked to the old human and shook his head.

"King of Mithral Hall," Mahskevic explained. "Or at least, he was. I have little desire to turn a clan of wild dwarves against me—bane of all wizards, dwarves. Making an enemy of Bruenor Battlehammer does not seem to me to be an opportunity for advancement of wealth or health.

"Beyond that, I have no grudge against this

Drizzt Do'Urden," Mahskevic added. "Why would I seek to destroy him?"

"Because Le'lorinel is your friend."

"Le'lorinel," Mahskevic echoed, again with that chuckle. "I am fond of him, I admit, and in trying to hold my responsibilities of friendship, I often try to convince him that his course is self-destructive folly, and nothing more."

"He will hear none of that, I am sure," said Tunevec.

"None," agreed Mahskevic. "A stubborn one is Le'lorinel Tel'e'brenequiette."

"If that is even his name," snorted Tunevec, who was in a rather foul mood, especially concerning his sparring partner. " 'I to you as you to me,' " he translated, for indeed Le'lorinel's name was nothing more than a variation on a fairly common Elvish saying.

"The philosophy of respect and friendship, is it not?" asked the old wizard.

"And of revenge," Tunevec replied grimly.

⚔ ⚔ ⚔ ⚔ ⚔

Down on the tower's middle floor, alone in a small, private room, Le'lorinel pulled off the mask and slumped to sit on the bed, stewing in frustration and hatred for Drizzt Do'Urden.

"How many years will it take?" the elf asked, and finished with a small laugh, while fiddling with an onyx ring. "Centuries? It does not matter!"

Le'lorinel pulled off the ring and held it up before his glittering eyes. It had taken two years of hard work to earn this item from Mahskevic. It was a magical ring, designed to hold enchantments. This one held four, the four spells Le'lorinel believed it would take to kill Drizzt Do'Urden.

Of course, Le'lorinel knew that to use these spells in the manner planned would likely result in the deaths of both combatants.

It did not matter.

As long as Drizzt Do'Urden died, Le'lorinel could enter the netherworld contented.

PART ONE

It is good to be home. It is good to hear the wind of Icewind Dale, to feel its invigorating bite, like some reminder that I am alive.

That seems such a self-evident thing— that I, that we, are alive—and yet, too

HINTS OF DARKNESS

often, I fear, we easily forget the importance of that simple fact. It is so easy to forget that you are truly alive, or at least, to appreciate that you are truly alive, that every sunrise is yours to view and every sunset is yours to enjoy.

And all those hours in between, and all those hours after dusk, are yours to make of what you will.

It is easy to miss the possibility that every person who crosses your path can become an event and a memory, good or bad, to fill in the hours with experience instead of tedium, to break the monotony of the passing moments. Those wasted moments, those hours of sameness, of routine, are the enemy, I say, are little stretches of death within the moments of life.

Yes, it is good to be home, in the wild land of Icewind Dale, where monsters roam aplenty and rogues threaten the roads at every turn. I am more alive and more content than in many years. For too long, I struggled with the legacy of my dark past. For too long, I struggled with the reality of my longevity, that I would likely die long after Bruenor, Wulfgar, and Regis.

And Catti-brie.

What a fool I am to rue the end of her days without enjoying the days that she, that we, now have! What a fool I am to let the present slip into the past, while lamenting a potential—and only potential—future!

We are all dying, every moment that passes of every day. That is the inescapable truth of this existence. It is a truth that can paralyze us with fear, or one that can energize us with impatience, with the desire to explore and experience, with the hope—nay, the iron will!—to find a memory in every action. To be alive, under sunshine or under starlight, in weather fair or stormy. To dance every step, be they through gardens of bright flowers or through deep snows.

The young know this truth so many of the old, or even middle-aged, have forgotten. Such is the source of the anger, the jealousy, that so many exhibit toward the young. So many times have I heard the common lament, "If only I could go back to that age, knowing what I now know!" Those words amuse me profoundly, for in truth, the lament should be, "If only I could reclaim the lust and the joy I knew then!"

That is the meaning of life, I have come at last to understand, and in that understanding, I have indeed found that lust and that joy. A life of twenty years where that lust and joy, where that truth is understood might be more full than a life of centuries with head bowed and shoulders slumped.

I remember my first battle beside Wulfgar, when I led him in, against tremendous odds and mighty giants, with a huge grin and a lust for life. How strange that as I gained more to lose, I allowed that lust to diminish!

It took me this long, through some bitter losses, to recognize the folly of that reasoning. It took me this long, returned to Icewind Dale after unwittingly surrendering the Crystal Shard to Jarlaxle and completing at last—and forever, I pray—my relationship with Artemis Entreri, to wake up to the life that is mine, to appreciate the beauty around me, to seek out and not shy away from the excitement that is there to be lived.

There remain worries and fears, of course. Wulfgar is gone from us—I know not where—and I fear for his head, his heart, and his body. But I have accepted that his path was his own to choose, and that he, for the sake of all three—head, heart, and body—had to step away from us. I pray that our paths will cross again, that he will find his way home. I pray that some news of him will come to us, either calming our fears or setting us into action to recover him.

But I can be patient and convince myself of the best. For to brood upon my fears for him, I am defeating the entire purpose of my own life.

That I will not do.

There is too much beauty.

There are too many monsters and too many rogues.

There is too much fun.

—Drizzt Do'Urden

I

BACK TO BACK

His long white hair rolled down Catti-brie's shoulder, tickling the front of her bare arm, and her own thick auburn hair cascaded down Drizzt's arm and chest.

The two sat back to back on the banks of Maer Dualdon, the largest lake in Icewind Dale, staring up at the hazy summer sky. Lazy white clouds drifted slowly overhead, their white fluffy lines sometimes cut in sharp contrast as one of many huge schinlook vultures coasted underneath. It was the clouds, not the many birds that were out this day, that held the attention of the couple.

"A knucklehead trout on the gaff," Catti-brie said of one unusual cloud formation, a curving oblong before a trailing, thin line of white.

"How do you see that?" the dark elf protested with a laugh.

Catti-brie turned her head to regard her black-skinned, violet-eyed companion. "How do ye not?" she asked. "It's as plain as the white line o' yer own eyebrows."

Drizzt laughed again, but not so much at what the woman was

saying, but rather, at how she was saying it. She was living with Bruenor's clan again in the dwarven mines just outside of Ten-Towns, and the mannerisms and accent of the rough-and-tumble dwarves were obviously again wearing off on her.

Drizzt turned his head a bit toward the woman, as well, his right eye barely a couple of inches from Catti-brie's. He saw the sparkle there—it was unmistakable—a look of contentment and happiness only now returning in the months since Wulfgar had left them, a look that seemed, in fact, even more intense than ever before.

Drizzt laughed and looked back up at the sky. "Your fish got away," he announced, for the wind had blown the thin line away from the larger shape.

"It is a fish," Catti-brie insisted petulantly—or at least, the woman made it sound as if she was being petulant.

Smiling, Drizzt didn't pursue the argument.

⚔ ⚔ ⚔ ⚔ ⚔

"Ye durn fool little one!" Bruenor Battlehammer grumbled and growled, spittle flying as his frustration increased. The dwarf stopped and stamped his hard boot ferociously on the ground, then smacked his one-horned helmet onto his head, his thick orange hair flying wildly from beneath the brim of the battered helm. "I'm here thinkin' I got a friend on the council, and there ye go, letting Kemp o' Targos go and spout the price without even a fight!"

Regis the halfling, thinner than he had been in years and favoring one arm from a ghastly wound he'd received on his last adventure with his friends, just shrugged and replied, "Kemp of Targos speaks only of the price of the ore for the fishermen."

"And the fishermen buy a considerable portion of the ore!" Bruenor roared. "Why'd I put ye back on the council, Rumblebelly, if ye ain't to be making me life any easier?"

Regis gave a little smile at the tirade. He thought to remind Bruenor that the dwarf hadn't put him back on the council, that the folk of Lonelywood, needing a new representative since the last one had wound up in the belly of a yeti, had begged him to go, but he wisely kept the notion to himself.

"Fishermen," the dwarf said, and he spat on the ground in front of Regis's hairy, unshod feet.

Again, the halfling merely smiled and sidestepped the mark. He knew Bruenor was more bellow than bite, and knew, too, that the dwarf would let this matter drop soon enough—as soon as the next crisis rolled down the road. Ever had Bruenor Battlehammer been an excitable one.

The dwarf was still grumbling when the pair rounded a bend in the path to come in full view of Drizzt and Catti-brie, still sitting on the mossy bank, lost in their cloud-dreams and just enjoying each other's company. Regis sucked in his breath, thinking Bruenor might explode at the sight of his beloved adopted daughter in so intimate a position with Drizzt—or with anyone, for that matter—but Bruenor just shook his hairy head and stormed off the other way.

"Durned fool elf," he was saying when Regis caught up to him. "Will ye just kiss the girl and be done with it?"

Regis's smile nearly took in his ears. "How do you know that he has not?" he remarked, for no better reason than to see the dwarf's cheeks turn as fiery red as his hair and beard.

And of course, Regis was quick to skitter far out of Bruenor's deadly grasp.

The dwarf just put his head down, muttering curses and stomping along. Regis could hardly believe that boots could make such thunder on a soft, mossy dirt path.

⚔ ⚔ ⚔ ⚔ ⚔

The clamor in Brynn Shander's Council Hall was less of a surprise to Regis. He tried—he really did—to stay attentive to the proceedings, as Elderman Cassius, the highest-ranking leader in all of Ten-Towns, led the discussion through mostly procedural matters. Always before had the ten towns been ruled independently, or through a council comprised of one representative of each town, but so great had Cassius's service been to the region that he was no longer the representative of any single community, even that of Brynn Shander, the largest town by far and Cassius's home. Of course, that didn't sit well with Kemp of Targos, leader of the second city of Ten-Towns. He and Cassius had often been at odds, and with the elevation of Cassius and the appointment of a new councilor from Brynn Shander, Kemp felt outnumbered.

But Cassius had continued to rise above it all, and over the last few months even stubborn Kemp had grudgingly come to admit that the man was acting in a generally fair and impartial manner.

To the councilor from Lonelywood, though, the level of peace and community within the council hall in Brynn Shander only added to the tedium. The halfling loved a good debate and a good argument, especially when he was not a principal but could, rather, snipe in from the edges, fanning the emotions and the intensity.

Alas for the good old days!

Regis tried to stay awake—he really did—when the discussion became a matter of apportioning sections of the Maer Dualdon deepwaters to specific fishing vessels, to keep the lines untangled and keep the tempers out on the lake from flaring.

That rhetoric had been going on in Ten-Towns for decades, and Regis knew no rules would ever keep the boats apart out there on the cold waters of the large lake. Where the knucklehead were found, so the boats would go, whatever the rules. Knucklehead trout, perfect for scrimshaw and good eating besides, were the staple of the towns' economy, the lure that brought so many ruffians to Ten-Towns in search of fortune.

The rules established in this room so far from the banks of the three great lakes of Icewind Dale were no more than tools councilors could use to bolster subsequent tirades, when the rules had all been ignored.

By the time the halfling councilor from Lonelywood woke up, the discussion had shifted, thankfully, to more concrete matters, one that concerned Regis directly. In fact, the halfling only realized a moment later, the catalyst for opening his eyes had been Cassius's call to him.

"Pardon me for disturbing your sleep," the Elderman of Ten-Towns quietly said to Regis.

"I-I have been, um, working many days and nights in preparation for, uh, coming here," the halfling stammered, embarrassed. "And Brynn Shander is a long walk."

Cassius, smiling, held his hand up to quiet Regis before the halfling embarrassed himself even more. Regis didn't need to make excuses to this group, in any case. They understood his shortcomings and his value—a value that depended upon, to no small extent, the powerful friends he kept.

"Can you take care of this issue for us, then?" Kemp of Targos, who among the councilors was the least enamored of Regis, asked gruffly.

"Issue?" Regis asked.

Kemp put his head down and cursed quietly.

"The issue of the highwaymen," Cassius explained. "Since this newly sighted band is across the Shaengarne and south of Bremen, we know it would be a long ride for your friends, but we would certainly appreciate the effort if once again you and your companions could secure the roads into the region."

Regis sat back, crossed his hands over his still ample—if not as obviously as before—belly, and assumed a rather elevated expression. So that was it, he mused. Another opportunity for him and his friends to serve as heroes to the folk of Ten-Towns. This was where Regis was fully in his element, even though he had to admit he was usually only a minor player in the heroics of his more powerful friends. But in the council sessions, these were the moments when Regis could shine, when he could stand as tall as powerful Kemp. He considered the task Cassius had put to him. Bremen was the westernmost of the towns, across the Shaengarne River, which would be low now that it was late summer.

"I expect we can be there within the tenday, securing the road," Regis said after the appropriate pause.

He knew his friends would agree, after all. How many times in the last couple of months had they gone after monsters and highwaymen? It was a role Drizzt and Catti-brie, in particular, relished, and one that Bruenor, despite his constant complaining over it, did not truly mind at all.

As he sat there, thinking it over, Regis realized that he, too, wasn't upset to learn that he and his friends would have to be out on the adventurous road again. Something had happened to the halfling's sensibilities on the last long road, when he'd felt the piercing agony of a goblin spear through his shoulder—when he'd nearly died. Regis hadn't recognized the change back then. At that time, all the wounded halfling wanted was to be back in his comfortable little home in Lonelywood, carving knucklehead bones into beautiful scrimshaw and fishing absently from the banks of Maer Dualdon. Upon arriving at the comfy Lonelywood home, though, Regis had discovered a greater thrill than expected in showing off his scar.

So, yes, when Drizzt and the others headed out to defeat this newest threat, Regis would happily go along to play whatever role he might.

✖ ✖ ✖ ✖ ✖

The end of the first tenday on the road south of Bremen seemed to be shaping up as another dreary day. Gnats and mosquitoes buzzed the air in ravenous swarms. The mud, freed of the nine-month lock of the Icewind Dale cold season, grabbed hard at the wheels of the small wagon and at Drizzt's worn boots as the drow shadowed the movements of his companions.

Catti-brie drove the one-horse wagon. She wore a long, dirty woolen dress, shoulder to toe, with her hair tied up tight. Regis, wearing the guise of a young boy, sat beside her, his face all ruddy from hours and hours under the summer sun.

Most uncomfortable of all was Bruenor, though, and by his own design. He had constructed a riding box for himself, to keep him well-hidden, nailing it underneath the center portion of the wagon. In there he rode, day after day.

Drizzt picked his path carefully about the mud-pocked landscape, spending his days walking, always on the alert. There were far greater dangers out in the open tundra of Icewind Dale than the highwayman band the group had come to catch. While most of the tundra yetis were likely farther to the south now, following the caribou herd to the foothills of the Spine of the World, some might still be about. Giants and goblins often came down from the distant mountains in this season, seeking easy prey and easy riches. And on many occasions, crossing areas of rocks and bogs, Drizzt had to quick-step past the deadly, gray-furred snakes, some measuring twenty feet or more and with a poisonous bite that could fell a giant.

With all of that on his mind, the drow still had to keep the wagon in sight out of one corner of his eye, and keep his gaze scanning all about, in every direction. He had to see the highwaymen before they saw him if this was to be an easy catch.

Easier, anyway, the drow mused. They had a fairly good description of the band, and it didn't seem overwhelming in numbers or in skill. Drizzt reminded himself almost constantly, though, not to let preconceptions garner overconfidence. A single lucky bow shot could reduce his band to three.

So the bugs were swarming despite the wind, the sun was stinging his eyes, every mud puddle before him might conceal a gray-furred snake ready to make of him a meal or a tundra yeti hiding low in waiting, and a band of dangerous bandits was reputedly in the area, threatening him and his friends.

Drizzt Do'Urden was in a splendid mood!

He quick-stepped across a small stream, then slid to a stop, noting a line of curious puddles, foot-sized and spaced appropriately for a man walking swiftly. The drow went to the closest and knelt to inspect it. Tracks didn't last long out there, he knew, so this one was fresh. Drizzt's finger went under water to the second knuckle before his fingertip hit the ground beneath—again, the depth consistent with these being the tracks of an adult man.

The drow stood, hands going to the hilts of his scimitars under the folds of his camouflaging cloak. Twinkle waited on his right hip, Icingdeath on his left, ready to flash out and cut down any threats.

Drizzt squinted his violet eyes, lifting one hand to further shield them from the sunlight. The tracks went out toward the road, to a place where the wagon would soon cross.

There lay the man, muddy and lying flat out on the ground, in wait.

Drizzt didn't head toward him but stayed low and circled back, meaning to cross over the road behind the rolling wagon to look for similar ambush spots on the other side. He pulled the cowl of his gray cloak lower, making sure it concealed his white hair, then came up into a full run, his black fingers rubbing against his palms with every eager stride.

✠ ✠ ✠ ✠ ✠

Regis gave a yawn and a stretch, then leaned over against Catti-brie, nestling against her side and closing his big brown eyes.

"A fine time to be napping," the woman whispered.

"A fine time to be making any observers think that I'm napping," Regis corrected. "Did you see them back there, off to the side?"

"Aye," said Catti-brie. "A dirty pair."

As she spoke, the woman dropped one hand from the reins and slid it under the front lip of the wagon seat. Regis watched her fingers close on the item, and he knew she was taking comfort that Taulmaril the Heartseeker, her devastating bow, was in place and ready for her.

In truth, the halfling took more than a little comfort from that fact as well.

Regis reached one hand over the back of the driver's bench and slapped it absently, but hard, against the wooden planking inside the wagon bed, the signal to Bruenor to be alert and ready.

"Here we go," Catti-brie whispered to him a moment later.

Regis kept his eyes closed, kept his hand tap-tapping, at a quicker pace now. He did peek out of his left eye just a bit, to see a trio of scruffy-looking rogues walking down the road.

Catti-brie brought the wagon to a halt. "Oh, good sirs!" she cried. "Can ye be helpin' me and me boy, if ye please? My man done got hisself killed back at the mountain pass, and I'm thinking we're a bit o' the lost. Been days going back and forth, and not knowing which way's best for the Ten-Towns."

"Very clever," Regis whispered, covering his words by smacking his lips and shifting in his seat, seeming very much asleep.

Indeed, the halfling was impressed by the way Catti-brie had covered their movements, back and forth along the road, over the last few days. If the band had been watching, they'd be less suspicious now.

"But I don't know what I'm to do!" Catti-brie pleaded, her voice taking on a shrill, fearful edge. "Me and me boy here, all alone and lost!"

"We'll be helping ye," said the skinny man in the center, red-headed and with a beard that reached nearly to his belt.

"But fer a price," explained the rogue to his left, the largest of the three, holding a huge battle-axe across his shoulders.

"A price?" Catti-brie asked.

"The price of your wagon," said the third, seeming the most refined of the group, in accent and in appearance. He wore a colorful vest and tunic, yellow on red, and had a fine-looking rapier set in his belt on his left hip.

Regis and Catti-brie exchanged glances, hardly surprised.

Behind them they heard a bump, and Regis bit his lip, hoping Bruenor wouldn't crash out and ruin everything. Their plans had been carefully laid, their initial movements choreographed to the last step.

Another bump came from behind, but the halfling had already draped his arm over the bench and banged his fist on the backboard of the seat to cover the sound.

He looked to Catti-brie, at the intensity of her blue eyes, and knew it would be his turn to move very, very soon.

✖ ✖ ✖ ✖ ✖

He'll be the most formidable, Catti-brie told herself, looking to the rogue on the right, the most refined of the trio. She did glance to the other end of their line, though, at the huge man. She didn't doubt for a moment that he could cut her in two with that monstrous axe of his.

"And a bit o' the womanflesh," the rogue on the left remarked, showing an eager, gap-toothed smile. The man in the middle smiled evilly, as well, but the one on the right glanced at the other two with disdain.

"Bah, but she's lost her husband, so she's said!" the burly one argued. "She could be using a good ride, I'd be guessing."

The image of Khazid-hea, her razor-sharp sword, prodding the buffoon's groin, crossed Catti-brie's mind, but she did well to hide her smile.

"Your wagon will, perhaps, suffice," the refined highwayman explained, and Catti-brie noted that he hadn't ruled out a few games with her completely.

Yes, she understood this one well enough. He'd try to take with his charms what the burly one would grab with his muscles. It would be more fun for him if she played along, after all.

"And all that's in it, of course," the refined highwayman went on. "A pity we must accept this donation of your goods, but I fear that we, too, must survive out here, patrolling the roads."

"Is that what ye're doing, then?" Catti-brie asked. "I'd've marked ye out as a bunch o' worthless thieves, meself."

That opened their eyes!

"Two to the right and three to the left," Catti-brie whispered to Regis. "The dogs in front are mine."

"Of course they are," Regis replied, and Catti-brie glanced over at him in surprise.

That surprise lasted only a moment, though, only the time it took for Catti-brie to remind herself that Regis understood her so very well, and had likely followed her emotions through the discussion with the highwayman as clearly as she had recognized them herself.

She turned back to the halfling, smiling wryly, and gave a slight motion, then turned back to the highwaymen.

"Ye've no call or right to be taking anything," she said to the thieves, putting just enough of a tremor in her voice to make them think her bold front was just that, a front hiding sheer terror.

Regis yawned and stretched, then popped wide his eyes, feigning surprise and terror. He gave a yelp and leaped off the right side of the wagon, running out into the mud.

Catti-brie took the cue, standing tall, and in a single tug pulling off her phony woolen dress, tossing it aside and revealing herself as the warrior she was. Out came Khazid-hea, the deadly Cutter, and the woman reached under the lip of the wagon seat, pulling forth her bow. She leaped ahead, one stride along the hitch and to the ground beside the horse, pulling the beast forward in a sudden rush, using its bulk to separate the big man from his two partners.

✕ ✕ ✕ ✕ ✕

The three thugs to the left hand side of the wagon saw the movement and leaped up from the mud, drawing swords and howling as they charged forward.

A lithe and quick-moving form rose up from a crouch behind a small banking to the side of them, silent as a ghost, and seeming almost to float, so quick were its feet moving, across the sloppy ground.

Shining twin scimitars came out from under the folds of a gray cloak, and a white smile and violet eyes greeting the charging trio.

" 'Ere, get him!" one thug cried and all three went at the drow. Their movements, two stabbing thrusts and a wild slash, were uncoordinated and awkward.

Drizzt's right arm went straight out to the side, presenting Icingdeath at a perfect angle to deflect the sidelong slash way up high, while his left hand worked over and in, driving the back, concave side of Twinkle down across both stabbing blades. Down came Icingdeath as Twinkle retracted, to slam against the extended swords, and down and across came Twinkle, to hit them both again. A subtle dip and duck backward had the drow's head clear of the outraged thug's backhand slash, and Drizzt snapped Icingdeath up quickly enough to stick the man in the hand as the sword whistled past.

The thug howled and let go, his sword flying free.

But not far, for the drow was already in motion with his left hand. He brought Twinkle across to hook the blade as it spun free. What followed was a dance that mesmerized the three thugs. A swift movement of the twin scimitars had the sword spinning in the air, over, under, and about, with the drow playing a song, it seemed, on the weapon's sides.

Drizzt finished with an over and about movement of Icingdeath that perfectly presented the sword back to its original owner.

"Surely you can do better than that," the smiling drow offered as the hilt of the sword landed perfectly in the hand of the stunned thug.

The man screamed and dropped his weapon to the ground, turning around and running off.

"It's the Drizzit!" another of them shouted, similarly following.

The third, though, out of fear or anger or stupidity, came on instead. His sword worked furiously, forward in a thrust then back, then forward higher and in a roundabout turn back down.

Or at least, it started down.

Up came the drow's scimitars, hitting it alternately, twice each. Then over went Twinkle, forcing the sword low, and the drow went into a furious attack, his blades smashing hard, side to side against the overmatched thug's sword, hitting it so fast and with such fury that the song sounded as one long note.

The man surely felt his arm going numb, but he tried to take advantage of his opponent's furious movements by rushing forward suddenly, an obvious attempt to get in close and tie up the drow's lightning-fast hands.

He found himself without his weapon, though he did not know how. The thug lunged forward, arms wide to capture his foe in a bear hug, to catch only air.

He must have felt a painful sting between his legs as the drow, somehow behind him, slapped the back side of a scimitar up between his legs, bringing him up to tip-toe.

Drizzt retracted the scimitar quickly, and the man had to leap up, then stumble forward, nearly falling.

Then Drizzt had a foot on the thug's back, between his shoulder-blades, and the dark elf stomped him facedown into the muck.

"You would do well to stay right there until I ask you to get up," Drizzt said. After a look at the wagons to ensure that his friends were all right, the drow headed off at a leisurely pace to follow the trail of the fleeing duo.

⚔ ⚔ ⚔ ⚔ ⚔

Regis did a fine impression of a frightened child as he scrambled across the muck, arms waving frantically, and yelling, "Help! Help!" all the way.

The two men Catti-brie had warned him of stood up to block his path. He gave a cry and scrambled out to the side, stumbling and falling to his knees.

"Oh, don't ye kill me, please misters!" Regis wailed pitifully as the two stalked in, wicked grins on their faces, nasty weapons in their hand.

"Oh, please!" said Regis. "Here, I'll give ye me dad's necklace, I will!"

Regis reached under the front of his shirt, pulled forth a ruby pendant, and held it up by a short length of chain, just enough to send it swaying and spinning.

The thugs approached, their grins melting into expressions of curiosity as they regarded the spinning gemstones, the thousand, thousand sparkles and the tantalizing way it seemed to catch and hold the light.

⚔ ⚔ ⚔ ⚔ ⚔

Catti-brie let go of the trotting horse, dropped her bow and quiver to the side of the road, and skipped out to the side to avoid the passing wagon and to square up against the large rogue and his huge axe.

He came at her aggressively and clumsily, sweeping the axe across in front of him, then back across, then up and over with a tremendous downward chop.

Nimble Catti-brie had little trouble avoiding the three swipes. The miss on the third, the axe diving into the soft ground, left her the perfect opportunity to score a quick kill and move on. She heard the more refined rogue's voice urging the horse on and saw the wagon rumble past, the other two highwaymen sitting on the driver's bench.

They were Bruenor's problem now.

She decided to take her time. She hadn't appreciated this one's lewd remarks.

⚔ ⚔ ⚔ ⚔ ⚔

"Durn latch!" Bruenor grumbled, for the catch on his makeshift compartment, too full of mud from the wheels, would not budge.

The wagon was moving faster now, exaggerating each bump, bouncing the dwarf about wildly.

Finally, Bruenor managed to get one foot under him, then the other, steadying himself in a tight, tight crouch. He gave a roar that would make a red dragon proud, and snapped up with all his might, blasting his head right through the floorboards of the wagon.

"Ye think ye might be slowin' it down?" he asked the finely dressed highwayman driver and the red-headed thug sitting beside him. Both turned back, their expressions quite entertaining.

That is, until the red-headed thug drew out a dagger and spun about, leaping over the seat in a wild dive at Bruenor, who only then realized he wasn't in a very good defensive posture there, with his arms pinned to his sides by splintered boards.

⚔ ⚔ ⚔ ⚔ ⚔

One of the rogues seemed quite content to stand there stupidly watching the spinning gemstone. The other, though, watched for only a few moments, then stood up straight and shook his head roughly, his lips flapping.

" 'Ere now, ye little trickster!" he bellowed.

Regis hopped to his feet and snapped the ruby pendant up into his plump little hand.

"Don't let him hurt me!" he cried to the entranced man as the other came forward, reaching for Regis's throat with both hands.

Regis was quicker than he looked, though, and he skittered backward. Still, the taller man had the advantage and would easily catch up to him.

Except that the other rogue, who knew beyond any doubt that this little guy here was a friend, a dear friend, slammed against his companion's side and drove him down to the ground. In a moment, the two rolled and thrashed, trading punches and oaths.

"Ye're a fool, and he's a trickster!" the enemy yelled and put his fist in the other one's eye.

"Ye're a brute, and he's a friendly little fellow!" the other countered, and countered, too, with a punch to the nose.

Regis gave a sigh and turned about to regard the battle scene. He had played out his role perfectly, as he had in all the recent exploits of the Companions of the Hall. But still, he thought of how Drizzt would have handled these two, scimitars flashing brilliantly in the sunlight, and he wished he could do that.

He thought of how Catti-brie would have handled them, a combination, no doubt, of a quick and deadly slice of Cutter, followed by a well-aimed, devastating lightning arrow from that marvelous bow of hers. And again, the halfling wished he could do it like that.

He thought of how Bruenor would have handled the thugs, taking a smash in the face and handing out one, catching a smash on the side that might have felled a giant, but rolling along until the pair had been squashed into the muck, and he wished he could do it like that.

"Nah," Regis said. He rubbed his shoulder out of sympathy for Bruenor. Each had their own way, he decided, and he turned his attention to the combatants rolling about the muck before him.

His new pet was losing.

Regis took out his own weapon, a little mace Bruenor had crafted for him, and, as the pair rolled about, gave a couple of well-placed *bonks* to get things moving in the right direction.

Soon his pet had the upper hand, and Regis was well on his way to success.

To each his own.

✗ ✗ ✗ ✗ ✗

She came ahead with a thrust, and the thug tore his axe free and set it into a blocking position before him, snapping it this way and that to intercept, or at least deflect, the stabbing sword.

Catti-brie strode forward powerfully, presenting herself too far forward, she knew, at least in the eyes of the thug.

For she knew that this one would underestimate her. His remarks when first he'd seen her told her pretty much the way this one viewed women.

Taking the bait, the thug shoved out with his axe, turning it head-out toward the woman and trying to slam her with it.

A planted foot and a turn brought her right by the awkward weapon, and while she could have pierced the man's chest with Khazid-hea, she used her foot instead, kicking him hard in the crotch.

She skittered back, and the man, with a groan, set himself again.

Catti-brie waited, allowing him to take the offensive again. Predictably, he worked his way around to launch another of those mighty—and useless—horizontal slashes. This time Catti-brie backed only enough so the flying blade barely missed her. She turned as she came forward past the man's extended reach, pivoting on her left foot and back-kicking with her right, again slamming the man in the crotch.

She didn't really know why, but she just felt like doing that.

Again, the woman was out of harm's way before the thug could begin to react, before he had even recovered from the sickening pain that was likely rolling up from his loins.

He did manage to straighten, barely, and he brought his axe up high and roared, rushing forward—the attack of a desperate opponent. Khazid-hea's hungry tip dived in at the man's belly, stopping him short. A flick of Catti-brie's wrist sent the deadly blade snapping down, and a quick step had the woman right up against the man, face to face.

"Bet it hurts," she whispered, and up came her knee, hard.

Catti-brie jumped back then leaped forward in a spin, her sword cutting across inside the angle of the downward-chopping axe, the fine blade shearing through the axe handle as easily as if it was made of candle wax. Catti-brie rushed back out again, but not before one last, well-placed kick.

The thug, his eyes fully crossed, his face locked in a grimace of absolute pain, tried to pursue, but the down cut of Khazid-hea had taken off his belt and all other supporting ties of his pants, dropping them to the man's ankles.

One shortened step, and another, and the man tripped up and tumbled headlong into the muck. Mud-covered, waves of pain obviously rolling through his body, he scrambled to his knees and swiped at the woman as she stalked in. Only then did he seem to realize he was holding no more than half an axe handle. The swing fell way short and brought the man too far out to the left. Catti-brie stepped in behind it, braced her foot on the brute's right shoulder, and pushed him back down in the muck.

He got up to his knees again, blinded by mud and swinging wildly.

She was behind him.

She kicked him to the muck again.

"Stay down," the woman warned.

Sputtering curses, mud, and brown water, the stubborn, stunned ruffian rose again.

"Stay down," Catti-brie said, knowing he would focus in on her voice.

He threw one leg out to the side for balance and shifted around, launching a desperate swing.

Catti-brie hopped over both the club and the leg, landing before the man and shifting her momentum into one more great kick to the crotch.

This time, as the man curled in the fetal position in the muck, making little mewling sounds and clutching at his groin, the woman knew he wouldn't be getting back up.

With a look over at Regis and a wide grin, Catti-brie started back for her bow.

⚔ ⚔ ⚔ ⚔ ⚔

Desperation drove Bruenor's arm and leg forward, hand pushing and knee coming up to support it. A plank cracked apart, coming up as a shield against the charging dagger, and Bruenor somehow managed to free his hand enough to angle the plank to knock the dagger free of the red-haired man's hand.

Or, the dwarf realized, maybe the thug had just decided to let it go.

The man's fist came around the board and slugged him good in the face. There came a following left, and another right, and Bruenor had no way to defend, so he didn't. He just let the man pound on him while he wriggled and forced both of his hands free, and finally he managed to come forward while offering some defense. He caught the man's slugging left by the wrist with his right and launched his own left that seemed as if it would tear the thug's head right off.

But the ruffian managed to catch that arm, as Bruenor had caught his, and so the two found a stand-off, struggling in the back of the rolling and bouncing wagon.

"C'mere, Kenda!" the red-headed man cried. "Oh, we got him!" He looked back to Bruenor, his ugly face barely an inch from the dwarf's. "What're ye gonna do now, dwarfie?"

"Anyone ever tell ye that ye spit when ye talk?" the disgusted Bruenor asked.

In response, the man grinned stupidly and snorted and hocked, filling his mouth with a great wad to launch at the dwarf.

Bruenor's entire body tightened, and like a singular giant muscle, like the body of a great serpent, perhaps, the dwarf struck. He smashed his forehead into the ugly rogue's face, snapping the man's head back so that he was staring up at the sky, so that, when he spit—and somehow, he still managed to do that—the wad went straight up and fell back upon him.

Bruenor tugged his hand free, let go of the man's arm, and clamped one hand on the rogue's throat, the other grabbing him by the belt. Up he went, over the dwarf's head, and flying off the side of the speeding wagon.

Bruenor saw the composure on the face of the remaining ruffian as the man set down the reins and calmly turned and drew out his fine rapier. Calmly, too, went Bruenor, pulling himself fully from the compartment and reaching back in to pick up his many-notched axe.

The dwarf slapped the axe over his right shoulder, assuming a casual stance, feet wide apart to brace him against the bouncing.

"Ye'd be smart to just put it down and stop the stupid wagon," he said to his opponent, the man waving his rapier out before him.

"It is you who should surrender," the highwayman remarked, "foolish dwarf!" As he finished, he lunged forward, and Bruenor, with enough experience to understand the full measure of his reach and balance, didn't blink.

The dwarf had underestimated just a bit, though, and the rapier tip did jab in against his mithral chest-piece, finding enough of a seam to poke the dwarf hard.

"Ouch," Bruenor said, seeming less than impressed.

The highwayman retracted, ready to spring again. "Your clumsy weapon is no match for my speed and agility!" he proclaimed, and he started forward. "Hah!"

A flick of Bruenor's strong wrist sent his axe flying forward, a single spin before embedding in the thrusting highwayman's chest, blasting him backward to fall against the back of the driver's seat.

"That so?" the dwarf asked. He stomped one foot on the highwayman's breast and yanked his weapon free.

⚔ ⚔ ⚔ ⚔ ⚔

Catti-brie lowered her bow, seeing that Bruenor had the wagon under control. She had the rapier-wielding highwayman in her sights and would have shot him dead if necessary.

Not that she believed for a moment that Bruenor Battlehammer would need her help against the likes of those two.

She turned to regard Regis, approaching from the right. Behind him came his obedient pet, carrying the captive across his shoulders.

"Ye got some bandages for the one Bruenor dropped?" Catti-brie asked, though she wasn't very confident that the man was even alive.

Regis started to nod, but then shouted, "Left!" with alarm.

Catti-brie spun, Taulmaril coming up, and noted the target. The man Drizzt had dropped to the mud was starting to rise.

She put an arrow that streaked and sparked like a bolt of lightning into the ground right beneath his rising head. The man froze in place, and seemed to be whimpering.

"Ye would do well to lie back down," Catti-brie called from the road.

He did.

⚔ ⚔ ⚔ ⚔ ⚔

More than two hours later, the two escaping rogues crashed through the brush, the one break through the ring of boulders that concealed their encampment. Still stumbling, still frantic, they pushed past the horses and moved around the stolen wagon, to find Jule Pepper, their leader, the strategist of the outfit and also the cook, stirring a huge caldron.

"Nothing today?" the tall black-haired woman asked, her brown eyes scrutinizing them. Her tone and her posture revealed the truth, though neither of the rogues were smart enough to catch on. Jule understood that something had happened, and likely, nothing good.

"The Drizzit," one of the rogues spurted, gasping for breath with every word. "The Drizzit and 'is friends got us."

"Drizzt?" Jules asked.

"Drizzit Dudden, the damned drow elf," said the other. "We was takin' a wagon—just a woman and her kid—and there he was, behind the three of us. Poor Walken got him in the fight, head up."

"Poor Walken," the other said.

Jule closed her eyes and shook her head, seeing something that the others apparently had not. "And this woman," she asked, "she merely surrendered the wagon?"

"She was puttin' up a fight when we runned off," said the first of the dirty pair. "We didn't get to see much."

"She?" Jule asked. "You mean Catti-brie? The daughter of Bruenor Battlehammer? You were baited, you fools!"

The pair looked at each other in confusion. "And we're payin' with the loss of a few, don't ye doubt," one finally said, mustering the courage to look back at the imposing woman. "Could'a been worse."

"Could it?" Jule asked doubtfully. "Tell me, then, did this dark elf's panther companion make an appearance?"

Again the two looked at each other.

As if in response, a low growl reverberated through the

encampment, resonating as if it was coming from the ground itself, running into the bodies of the three rogues. The horses at the side of the camp neighed and stomped and tossed their heads nervously.

"I would guess that it did," Jule answered her own question, and she gave a great sigh.

A movement to the side, a flash of flying blackness, caught their attention, turning all three heads to regard the new arrival. It was a huge black cat, ten feet long at least, and with muscled shoulders as high as a tall man's chest.

"Drow elf's cat?" one of the dirty rogues asked.

"They say her name is Guenhwyvar," Jule confirmed.

The other rogue was already backing away, staring at the cat all the while. He bumped into a wagon then edged around it, moving right before the nervous and sweating horses.

"And so you ran right back to me," Jule said to the other with obvious contempt. "You could not understand that the drow *allowed* you to escape?"

"No, he was busy!" the remaining rogue protested.

Jule just shook her head. She wasn't really surprised it had ended like this, after all. She supposed that she deserved it for taking up with a band of fools.

Guenhwyvar roared and sprang into the middle of the camp, landing right between the pair. Jule, wiser than to even think of giving a fight against the mighty beast, just threw up her hands. She was about to instruct her companions to do the same when she heard one of them hit the ground. He'd fainted dead away.

The remaining dirty rogue didn't even see Guenhwyvar's spring. He spun around and rushed through the break in the boulder ring, crashing through the brush, thinking to leave his friends behind to fight while he made his escape, as he had done back on the road.

He came through, squinting against the slapping branches, and did notice a dark form standing to the side and did notice a pair of intense violet eyes regarding him—just an instant before the hilt of a scimitar rushed up and slammed him in the face, laying him low.

2

CONFLICTED

The wind and salty spray felt good on his face, his long blond hair trailing out behind him, his crystal blue eyes squinting against the glare. Wulfgar's features remained strong, but boyish, despite the ruddiness of his skin from tendays at sea. To the more discerning observer, though, there loomed in Wulfgar's eyes a resonance that denied the youthful appearance, a sadness wrought of bitter experience.

That melancholy was not with him now, though, for up there, on the prow of *Sea Sprite*, Wulfgar, son of Beornegar, felt the same rush of adrenaline he'd known all those years growing up in Icewind Dale, all those years learning the ways of his people, and all those years fighting beside Drizzt. The exhilaration could not be denied. It was the way of the warrior, the proud and tingling anticipation before the onset of battle.

And battle would soon be joined, the barbarian did not doubt. Far ahead, across the sparkling waters, Wulfgar saw the sails of the running pirate.

Was this *Bloody Keel*, Sheila Kree's boat? Was his warhammer, mighty Aegis-fang, the gift of his adoptive father, in the hands of a pirate aboard that ship?

Wulfgar winced as he considered the question, at the myriad of feelings that the mere thought of once again possessing Aegis-fang brought up inside him. He'd left Delly Curtie and Colson, the baby girl they'd taken in as their own daughter, back in Waterdeep. They were staying at Captain Deudermont's beautiful home while he had come out with *Sea Sprite* for the express purpose of regaining the warhammer. Yet, the thought of Aegis-fang, of what he might do once he had the weapon back in his grasp, was, at that time, still beyond Wulfgar's swirling sensibilities. What did the warhammer mean, really?

That warhammer, a gift from Bruenor, had been meant as a symbol of the dwarf's love for him, of the dwarf's recognition that Wulfgar had risen above his stoic and brutal upbringing to become a better warrior, and more importantly, a better man. But had Wulfgar, really? Was he deserving of the warhammer, of Bruenor's love? Certainly the events since his return from the Abyss would argue against that. Over the past months Wulfgar hadn't done many things of which he was proud and had an entire list of accomplishments, beginning with his slapping Catti-brie's face, that he would rather forget.

And so this pursuit of Aegis-fang had come to him as a welcome relief, a distraction that kept him busy, and positively employed for a good cause, while he continued to sort things out. But if Aegis-fang was on that boat ahead, or the next one in line, and Wulfgar retrieved it, where would it lead? Was his place still waiting for him in Icewind Dale among his former friends? Would he return to a life of adventure and wild battles, living on the edge of disaster with Drizzt and the others?

Wulfgar's thoughts returned to Delly and the child. Given the new reality of his life, given those two, how could he return to that previous life? What did such a reversion mean regarding his responsibilities to his new family?

The barbarian gave a laugh, recognizing that it was far more than responsibilities hindering him, though he didn't often admit it, even to himself. When he had first taken the child from Auckney, a minor kingdom nestled in the eastern reaches of the Spine of the World, it had been out of responsibility, it had been because the person he truly was—or wanted to be again—demanded of him that he not let the child suffer the sins of the mother or the cowardice and stupidity of the father.

It had been responsibility that had taken him back to the Cutlass tavern in Luskan, a debt owed to his former friends, Arumn, Delly, and even Josi Puddles, whom he had surely let down with his drunken antics. Asking Delly to come along with him and the child had been yet another impulse wrought of responsibility—he had seen the opportunity to make some amends for his wretched treatment of the poor woman, and so he had offered her a new road to explore. In truth, Wulfgar hadn't given the decision to ask Delly along much thought at all, and even after her surprising acceptance, the barbarian had not understood how profoundly her choice would come to affect his life. Because now . . . now his relationship with Delly and their adopted child had become something more. This child he had taken out of generosity—and, in truth, because Wulfgar had instinctively recognized that he needed the generosity more than the child ever would—had become to him his daughter, his own child. In every way. Much as he had long ago become the child of Bruenor Battlehammer. Never before had Wulfgar held even a hint of the level of vulnerability the new title, father, had brought to him. Never had he imagined that anyone could truly hurt him, in any real way. Now all he had to do was look into Colson's blue eyes, so much like her real mother's, and Wulfgar knew his entire world could be destroyed about him.

Similarly, with Delly Curtie, the barbarian had come to understand that he'd taken on more than he'd bargained for. This woman he'd invited to join him, again in the spirit of generosity and as a denial of the thug he'd become, was now something much more important than a mere traveling companion. In the months since their departure from Luskan, Wulfgar had come to see Delly Curtie in a completely different light, had come to see the depth of her spirit and the wisdom that had been buried beneath the sarcastic and gruff exterior she'd been forced to assume in order to survive in her miserable existence.

Delly had told him of the few glorious moments she had known—and none of those had been in the arms of one of her many lovers. She told him of the many hours she'd spent along the quiet wharves of Luskan before having to force herself to begin her nights at the Cutlass. There she'd sit and watch the sun sinking into the distant ocean, seeming to set all the water ablaze.

Delly loved the dusk—the quiet hour, she called it—when the daytime folk of Luskan returned home to their families and the nighttime crowd had not yet awakened to the bustle of their adventurous but ultimately empty nights. In the months he'd known Delly at the Cutlass, in the nights they'd spent in each others' arms, Wulfgar had never begun to imagine that there was so much more to her, that she was possessed of hopes and dreams, and that she held such a deep understanding of the people around her. When men bedded her, they often thought her an easy target, tossing a few words of compliment to get their prize.

What Wulfgar came to understand about Delly was that none of those words, none of that game, had ever really meant anything to her. Her one measure of power on the streets was her body, and so she used it to gain favor, to gain knowledge, to gain security, in a place lacking in all three. How strange it seemed to Wulfgar to recognize that while all the men had believed they were taking advantage of Delly's ignorance, she was, in fact, taking advantage of their weakness in the face of lust.

Yes, Delly Curtie could play the "using" game as well as any, and that was why this blossoming relationship seemed so amazing to him. Because Delly wasn't using him at all, he knew, and he wasn't using her. For the first time in all their history together, the two had merely been sharing each others' company, honestly and without pretense, without an agenda.

And Wulfgar would be a liar indeed if he couldn't admit that he was enjoying it.

A liar Wulfgar would be indeed, and a coward besides, if he couldn't admit that he'd fallen in love with Delly Curtie. Thus, the couple had married. Not formally, but in heart and soul, and Wulfgar knew that this woman, this unlikely companion, had completed him in ways he had never known possible.

"Killer banner up!" came a call from the crow's nest, meaning that this was indeed a pirate vessel ahead of *Sea Sprite,* for in her arrogance, she was flying a recognized pirate pennant.

With nothing but open water ahead, the ship had no chance of escape. No vessel on the Sword Coast could outrun *Sea Sprite*, especially with the powerful wizard Robillard sitting atop the back of the flying bridge, summoning gusts of wind repeatedly into the schooner's mainsail.

Wulfgar took a deep breath, and another, but found little in them to help steady his nerves.

I am a warrior! he reminded himself, but that other truth, that he was a husband and a father, would not be so easily put down.

How strange this change in heart seemed to him. Just a few months before, he had been the terror of Luskan, throwing himself into fights with abandon, reckless to the point of self-destructive.

But that was when he had nothing to lose, when he believed that death would take away the pain. Now, it was something even greater than those things he had to lose, it was the realization that if he perished out here, Delly and Colson would suffer.

And for what? the barbarian had to ask himself. For a warhammer, a symbol of a past he wasn't even sure he wanted to recapture?

Wulfgar grabbed tight to the line running back to the foremast, clenching it so tightly his knuckles whitened from the press, and again took in a deep and steadying breath, letting it out as a feral growl. Wulfgar shook the thoughts away, recognizing them as anathema to the heart of a true warrior. Charge in bravely, that was his mantra, his code, and indeed, that was the way a true warrior survived. Overwhelm your enemies, and quickly, and you will likely walk away. Hesitation only provided opportunity for the enemy to shoot you down with arrows and spears.

Hesitation, cowardice, would destroy him.

⚔ ⚔ ⚔ ⚔ ⚔

Sea Sprite gained quickly on the vessel, and soon it could be seen clearly as a two-masted caravel. How fast that pirate insignia pennant came down when the ship recognized its pursuer!

Sea Sprite's rear catapult and forward ballista both let fly, neither scoring a hit of any consequence, and the pirate responded with a catapult shot of its own, a meager thing that fell far short of the approaching hunter.

"A second volley?" Captain Deudermont asked his ship's wizard. The captain was a tall and straight-backed man with a perfectly trimmed goatee that was still more brown than gray.

"To coax?" Robillard replied. "Nay, if they've a wizard, he is too cagey to be baited, else he would have shown himself already. Move into true range and let fly, and so will I."

Deudermont nodded and lifted his spyglass to his eye to better see the pirate—and he could make out the individuals on the deck now, scrambling every which way.

Sea Sprite closed with every passing second, her sails gathering up the wind greedily, her prow cutting walls of water high into the air.

Deudermont looked behind, to his gunners manning the catapult on the poop deck. One used a spyglass much like the captain's own, lining up the vessel with a marked stick set before him. He lowered the glass to see the captain and nodded.

"Let fly for mainsail," Deudermont said to the crewman beside him, and the cry went out, gaining momentum and volume, and both catapult and ballista let fly again. This time, a ball of burning pitch clipped the sails and rigging of the pirate, who was bending hard into a desperate turn, and the ballista bolt, trailing chains, tore through a sail.

A moment later came a brilliant flash, a streak of lightning from Robillard that smacked the pirate's hull at the water line, splintering wood.

"Going defensive!" came Robillard's cry, and he enacted a semitranslucent globe about him and rushed to the prow, shoving past Wulfgar, who was moving amidships.

A responding lightning bolt did come from the pirate, not nearly as searing and bright as Robillard's. *Sea Sprite's* wizard, considered among the very finest of sea-fighting mages in all Faerûn, had his shields in place to minimize the damage to no more than a black scar on the side of *Sea Sprite's* prow, one of many badges of honor the proud pirate hunter had earned in her years of service.

The pirate continued its evasive turn, but *Sea Sprite*, more nimble by far, cut right inside her angle, closing even more rapidly.

Deudermont smiled as he considered Robillard, the wizard rubbing his fingers together eagerly, ready to drop a series of spells to counter any defenses, followed by a devastating fireball that would consume rigging and sails, leaving the pirate dead in the water.

The pirates would likely surrender soon after.

⚔ ⚔ ⚔ ⚔ ⚔

A row of archers lined *Sea Sprite*'s side rail, with several standing forward, as obvious targets. Robillard had placed enchantments on these few, making them impervious to unenchanted arrows, and so they were the brave ones inviting the shots.

"Volley as we pass!" the group leader commanded, and every man and woman began checking their draw and their arrows, finding ones that would fly straight and true.

Behind them, Wulfgar paced nervously, anxiously. He wanted this to be done—a perfectly reasonable and rational desire—and yet he cursed himself for those feelings.

"A pop to steady yer hands?" one greasy crewman said to him, holding forth a small bottle of rum, which the boarding party had been passing around.

Wulfgar stared at the bottle long and hard. For months he had hidden inside one of those seemingly transparent things. For months he had bottled up his fears and his horrible memories, a futile attempt to escape the truth of his life and his past.

He shook his head and went back to pacing.

A moment later came the sound of twenty bowstrings humming, the cries of many pirates, and of a couple from *Sea Sprite*'s crew, hit by the exchange.

Wulfgar knew he should be moving into position with the rest of the boarding party, and yet he found he could not. His legs would not walk past conjured images of Delly and Colson. How could he be doing this? How could he be out here, chasing a warhammer, while they waited back in Waterdeep?

The questions sounded loudly and horribly in Wulfgar's mind. All he had once been screamed back at him. He heard the name of Tempus, the barbarian god of war, pounding in his head, telling him to deny his fears, telling him to remember who he was.

With a roar that sent those men closest to him scurrying in fear, Wulfgar, son of Beornegar, charged for the rail, and though no boarding party had been called and though Robillard was even then preparing his fiery blast and though the two ships were still a dozen feet apart, with *Sea Sprite* fast passing, the furious barbarian leaped atop that rail and sprang forward.

Cries of protest sounded behind him, cries of surprise and fear sounded before him.

But the only cry Wulfgar heard was his own. "Tempus!" he bellowed, denying his fears and his hesitance.

"*Tempus!*"

⚔ ⚔ ⚔ ⚔ ⚔

Captain Deudermont rushed to Robillard and grabbed the skinny wizard, pinning his arms to his side and interrupting his spellcasting.

"The fool!" Robillard shouted as soon as he opened his eyes, to see what had prompted the captain's interference.

Not that the wizard was surprised, for Wulfgar had been a thorn in Robillard's side ever since he'd joined up with the crew. Unlike his old companions, Drizzt and Catti-brie, this barbarian simply did not seem to understand the subtleties of wizardly combat. And, to Robillard's thinking, wizardly combat was all-important, certainly far above the follies of meager warriors.

Robillard pulled free of Deudermont. "I will be throwing the fireball soon enough," he insisted. "When Wulfgar is dead!"

Deudermont was hardly listening. He called out to his crew to bring *Sea Sprite* about and called to his archers to find angles for their shots that they might lend aid to the one-man boarding party.

⚔ ⚔ ⚔ ⚔ ⚔

Wulfgar clipped the rail as he went aboard the pirate ship, tripping forward onto the deck. On came pirate swordsmen, rolling like water to cover him—but he was up and roaring, a long length of chain held in each hand.

The closest pirate slashed with a sword and scored a hit against the barbarian's shoulder, though Wulfgar quickly got his forearm up and pressed out, stopping the blade from doing more than a surface cut. The barbarian pumped out a right cross as he parried, hitting the man hard in the chest, lifting him from his feet and throwing him across the deck, where he lay broken on his back.

Chains snapping and smashing, roaring to his god, the barbarian went into a rampage, scattering pirates before him. They had never seen anything like this before, a nearly seven-foot-tall wild man, and so most fled before his thunderous charge.

Out went one length of chain, entwining a pair of legs, and Wulfgar gave a mighty jerk that sent the poor pirate flying to the deck. Out went the second length of chain, rolling about the shoulder of a man to Wulfgar's left, going completely around him to snap up and smack him in the chest. Wulfgar's tug took a considerable amount of skin from that one, and sent him into a fast-descending spin.

"Run away!" came the cries before him. "Oh, but a demon he is!"

Both his chains were entangled quickly enough, so Wulfgar dropped them and pulled a pair of small clubs from his belt. He leaped forward and cut fast to the side, catching one pirate, obviously the leader of the deck crew and the most heavily armored of the bunch, against the rail.

The pirate slashed with a fine sword, but Wulfgar jumped back out of reach, then reversed stride with another roar.

Up came a large, fine shield, and that should have been enough, but never before had this warrior faced the primal fury of Wulfgar.

The barbarian's first smash against the shield numbed the pirate's arm. Wulfgar's second blow bent in the top of the shield and drove the blocking arm low. His third strike took the defense away all together, and his fourth, following so quickly his opponent hadn't even found the opportunity to bring his sword back in, smacked the pirate on the side of his helmet and staggered him to the side.

Wulfgar bore in, raining a series of blows that left huge dents in the fine armor and that sent the pirate stumbling to the deck. He had barely hit the planking though, before Wulfgar grabbed him by the ankle and jerked him back up, feet first.

A twist and a single stride had the mighty barbarian standing at the rail, the armored pirate hanging in midair over the side. Wulfgar held him there, with hardly any effort, it seemed, and with only one arm. The barbarian eyed the rest of the crew dangerously. Not a man approached, and not an archer lifted a bow against him,

From the flying bridge, though, there did indeed come a challenge, and Wulfgar turned to see the pirate wizard, staring at him while in the throes of spellcasting.

A flick of Wulfgar's wrist sent his remaining club spinning at the man, and the wizard had to dodge aside, interrupting his own spell.

But now Wulfgar was unarmed, and the pirate crew seemed recovered from the initial shock of his overwhelming charge. The pirate captain appeared, promising a horde of treasure to the one who brought the barbarian giant down. The wizard was back into casting.

The sea scum approached, murder in their eyes.

And they stopped and stood straighter, and some dropped their weapons, as *Sea Sprite* glided alongside their ship right behind the barbarian, archers ready, boarding party ready.

Robillard let fly another lightning bolt that smashed the distracted pirate wizard, driving him right over the far rail of the ship and into the cold sea.

One pirate called for a charge, but was stopped short as a pair of arrows thudded into his chest.

Sea Sprite's crew was too well trained, too disciplined, too experienced. The fight was over before it had even really begun.

"You can probably bring him back over the rail," Deudermont said to Wulfgar a short while later, with the barbarian still standing there, holding the armored pirate upside-down above the short expanse of water between the ships, though Wulfgar was now using two hands, at least.

"Yes, do!" the embarrassed pirate demanded, lifting the cage visor of his expensive helm. "I am the Earl of Taskadale Manor! I demand—"

"You are a pirate," Deudermont said to him, simply.

"A bit of adventure and nothing more," the man replied haughtily. "Now please have your ogre friend put me down!"

Before the captain could say a word, Wulfgar went into a half spin and sent the earl flying across the deck, to smack the mainmast with a great clang and roll right around it, crumbling down in a noisy lump.

"Earl of Taskadale, whatever that might be," Deudermont remarked.

"Not impressed," Wulfgar replied, and he started away, to the plank that would take him back to *Sea Sprite*.

A fuming Robillard was waiting for him on the other side.

"Who instructed you to board?" the furious wizard demanded. "They could have been taken with a single spell!"

"Then cast your spell, wizard," Wulfgar grumbled at him, striding right past, having no time to explain his emotions and impulses to another when he hadn't even sorted them out for himself.

"Do not think that next time I shan't!" Robillard yelled at him, but Wulfgar just went on his way. "And pity Wulfgar when burning pieces of sail rain down upon his head, lighting his hair and curling his skin! Pity Wulfgar when—"

"Rest easy," Deudermont remarked, coming up behind the wizard. "The pirate is taken and not a crewman lost."

"As it would have been," Robillard insisted, "with less chance. Their magical defenses were down, their sails exposed. I had—"

"Enough, my friend," Deudermont interrupted.

"That one, Wulfgar, is a fool," Robillard replied. "A barbarian indeed! A savage to his heart and soul, and with no better understanding of tactics and advantage than an orc might hold."

Deudermont, who had sailed with Wulfgar before and who knew well the dark elf who had trained this warrior, knew better. But he said nothing, just let the always-grumpy Robillard play out his frustration with a string of curses and protests.

In truth, Captain Deudermont was beginning to rethink the decision to allow Wulfgar to join *Sea Sprite*'s crew, though he certainly believed he owed that much to the man, out of friendship and respect. Wulfgar's apparent redemption had struck well the heart of Captain Deudermont, for he had seen the man at his lowest point, on trial before the vicious magistrates of Luskan for attempting to assassinate Deudermont.

The captain hadn't believed the charge then—that was the only reason Wulfgar was still alive—though he had recognized that something terrible had happened to the noble warrior, that some unspeakable event had dropped Wulfgar to the bottom of the lowest gutter. Deudermont had been pleased indeed when Wulfgar had arrived at the dock in Waterdeep, asking to come aboard and join the crew, asking Deudermont to help him in retrieving the mighty warhammer that Bruenor Battlehammer had crafted for him.

Now it was clear to the captain, though, that the scars of Wulfgar's pain had not yet fully healed. His charge back there had been reckless and foolish and could have endangered the entire crew. That, Captain Deudermont could not tolerate. He would have to speak with Wulfgar, and sternly.

More than that, the captain decided then and there that he would make finding Sheila Kree and her elusive ship a priority, would get Wulfgar back Aegis-fang, and would put him back ashore in Waterdeep.

To the benefit of all.

3
BELLS AND WHISTLES

Great gargoyles leered down from twenty feet above. A gigantic stone statue of a humanoid lizard warrior—a golem of some sorts, perhaps—guarded the door, which was set between its wide-spread legs. Just inside that dark opening, a myriad of magical lights danced and floated about, some throwing sparks in a threatening manner.

Le'lorinel was hardly impressed by any of it. The elf knew the schools of magic used by this one, studies that involved illusion and divination, and feared neither. No, E'kressa the Seer's guards and wards did not impress the seasoned warrior. They were more show than substance. Le'lorinel didn't even draw a sword and even removed a shining silver helmet when crossing through that darkened opening and into a circular corridor.

"E'kressa diknomin tue?" the elf asked, using the tongue of the gnomes. Le'lorinel paused at the base of a ladder, waiting for a response.

"E'kressa diknomin tue?" the elf asked again, louder and more insistently.

A response drifted through the air on unseen breezes.

"What adventures dark and fell, await the darker side of Le'lorinel?" came a high-pitched, but still gravelly voice, speaking in the common tongue. "When dark skin splashes blade with red, then shall insatiable hunger be fed? When Le'lorinel has noble drow dead, will he smile, his anger fled?"

Le'lorinel did smile then, at the display of divination, and at the obvious errors.

"May I—?" the elf started to ask.

"Do come up," came a quick interruption, the tone and abrupt manner telling Le'lorinel that E'kressa wanted to make it clear that the question had been foreseen.

With a chuckle, Le'lorinel trotted up the stairs. At the top, the elf found a door of hanging blue beads, a soft glow coming from behind them. Pushing through brought Le'lorinel into E'kressa's main audience chamber, obviously, a place of many carpets and pillows for sitting, and with arcane runes and artifacts: a skull here, a gigantic bat wing there, a crystal ball set on a pedestal along the wall, a large mirror, its golden edges all of shaped and twisted design.

Never had Le'lorinel seen so many trite wizardly items all piled together in one place, and after years of working with Mahskevic the elf knew indeed that they were minor things, window dressing and nothing more—except, perhaps, for the crystal ball.

Le'lorinel hardly paid them any heed, though, for the elf was watching E'kressa. Dressed in robes of dark blue with red swirling patterns all about them, and a with a gigantic conical hat, the gnome seemed almost a caricature of the classic expectations of a wizard, except, of course, that instead of being tall and imposing, E'kressa barely topped three feet. A large gray beard and bushy eyebrows stuck out from under that hat, and E'kressa tilted his head back, face aimed in the general direction of Le'lorinel, but not as if looking at the elf.

Two pure white orbs showed under those bushy eyebrows.

Le'lorinel laughed out loud. "A blind seer? How perfectly typical."

"You doubt the powers of my magical sight?" E'kressa replied, raising his arms in threat like the wings of a crowning eagle.

"More than you could ever understand," Le'lorinel casually replied.

E'kressa held the pose for a long moment, but then, in the face of Le'lorinel's relaxed posture and ridiculing smirk, the gnome finally relented. With a shrug, E'kressa reached up and took the phony white lenses out of his sparkling gray eyes.

"Works for the peasants," the illusionist seer explained. "Amazes them, indeed! And they always seem more eager to drop an extra coin or two to a blind seer."

"Peasants are easily impressed," said Le'lorinel. "I am not."

"And yet I knew of you, and your quest," E'kressa was fast to point out.

"And you know of Mahskevic, too," the elf replied dryly.

E'kressa stomped a booted foot and assumed a petulant posture that lasted all of four heartbeats. "You brought payment?" the seer asked indignantly.

Le'lorinel tossed a bag of silver across the expanse to the eager gnome's waiting hands. "Why not just use your incredible powers of divination to get the count?" Le'lorinel asked, as the gnome started counting out the coins.

E'kressa's eyes narrowed so that they were lost beneath the tremendous eyebrows. The gnome waved his hand over the bag, muttered a spell, then a moment later, nodded and put the bag aside. "I should charge you more for making me do that," he remarked.

"For counting your payment?" Le'lorinel asked skeptically.

"For having to show you yet another feat of my great powers of seeing," the gnome replied. "For not making you wait while I counted them out."

"It took little magic to know that the coins would all be there," the elf responded. "Why would I come here if I had not the agreed upon price?"

"Another test?" the gnome asked.

Le'lorinel groaned.

"Impatience is the folly of humans, not of elves," E'kressa reminded. "I foresee that if you pursue your quest with such impatience, doom will befall you."

"Brilliant," came the sarcastic reply.

"You're not making this easy, you know," the gnome said in deadpan tones.

"And while I can assure you that I have all the patience I will need to be rid of Drizzt Do'Urden, I do not wish to waste my hours standing here," said Le'lorinel. "Too many preparations yet await me, E'kressa."

The gnome considered that for a moment, then gave a simple shrug. "Indeed. Well, let us see what the crystal ball will show to us. The course of your pursuit, we hope, and perhaps whether Le'lorinel shall win or whether he shall lose." He rambled down toward the center of the room, waddling like a duck, then veered to the crystal ball.

"The course, and nothing more," Le'lorinel corrected.

E'kressa stopped short and turned about slowly to regard this curious creature. "Most would desire to know the outcome," he said.

"And yet, I know, as do you, that any such outcome is not predetermined," Le'lorinel replied.

"There is a probability . . ."

"And nothing more than that. And what am I to do, O great seer, if you tell me I shall win my encounter with Drizzt Do'Urden, that I shall slay him as he deserves to be slain and wipe my bloodstained sword upon his white hair?"

"Rejoice?" E'kressa asked sarcastically.

"And what am I to do, O great seer, if you tell me that I shall lose this fight?" Le'lorinel went on. "Abandon that which I can not abandon? Forsake my people and suffer the drow to live?"

"Some people think he's a pretty nice guy."

"Illusions do fool some people, do they not?" Le'lorinel remarked.

E'kressa started to respond, but then merely sighed and shrugged and continued on his waddling way to the crystal ball. "Tell me your thoughts of the road before you," he instructed.

"The extra payment insures confidentiality?" Le'lorinel asked.

E'kressa regarded the elf as if that was a foolish question indeed. "Why would I inform this Drizzt character if ever I met him?" he asked. "And why would I ever meet him, with him being halfway across the world?"

"Then you have already spied him out?"

E'kressa picked up the cue that was the eagerness in the elf's voice, and that anxious pitch made him straighten his shoulders and puff out his chest with pride. "Might that I have," he said. "Might that I have."

Le'lorinel's answered with a determined stride, moving to the crystal ball directly opposite the gnome. "Find him."

E'kressa began his casting. His little arms waved in high circles above his head while strange utterances in a language Le'lorinel did not know, and in a voice that hardly seemed familiar, came out of his mouth.

The gray eyes popped open. E'kressa bent forward intently. "Drizzt Do'Urden," he said quietly, but firmly. "The doomed drow, for there can be but one outcome of such tedious and careful planning.

"Drizzt Do'Urden," the gnome said again, the name running off his lips as rhythmically and enchantingly as had the arcane words of his spell. "I see . . . I see . . . I see . . ."

E'kressa paused and gave a "Hmm," then stood straighter. "I see the distorted face of an over-eager bald-headed ridiculously masked elf," he explained, bending to peer around the crystal ball and into Le'lorinel's wide-eyed face. "Do you think you might step back a bit?"

Le'lorinel's shoulders sagged, and a great sigh came forth, but the elf did as requested.

E'kressa rubbed his plump little hands together and muttered a continuance of the spell, then bent back in. "I see," he said again. "Winter blows and deep, deep snows. I hear wind . . . yes, yes, I hear wind in my ears and the running hooves of deers."

"Deers?" Le'lorinel interrupted.

E'kressa stood up straight and glared at the elf.

"Deers?" Le'lorinel said again. "Rhymes with 'ears,' right?"

"You are a troublesome one."

"And you are somewhat annoying," the elf replied. "Why must you speak in rhymes as soon as you fall into your divining? Is that a seer's rule, or something?"

"Or a preference!" the flustered gnome answered, again stamping his hard boot on the carpeted floor.

"I am no peasant to be impressed," Le'lorinel explained. "Save yourself the trouble and the silly words, for you'll get no extra coins for atmosphere, visual or audible."

E'kressa muttered a couple of curses under his breath and bent back down.

"Deers," Le'lorinel said again, with a snort.

"Mock me one more time and I will send you hunting Drizzt in the Abyss itself," the gnome warned.

"And from that place, too, I shall return, to repay you your favor," Le'lorinel replied without missing a beat. "And I assure you, I know an illusion from an enemy, a guard of manipulated light from that of substance, and possess a manner of secrecy that will escape your eyes."

"Ah, but I see all, foolish son of a foolish son!" E'kressa protested.

Le'lorinel merely laughed at that statement, and that proved to be as vigorous a response as any the elf might have offered, though E'kressa, of course, had no idea of the depth of irony in his boast.

Both elf and gnome sighed then, equally tired of the useless exchange, and with a shrug the gnome bent forward and peered again into the crystal ball.

"Word has been heard that Gandalug Battlehammer is not well," Le'lorinel offered.

E'kressa muttered some arcane phrases and waggled his little arms about the curve of the sphere.

"To Mithral Hall seeing eyes go roaming, to throne and curtained bed, shrouded in gloaming," the gnome began, but he stopped, hearing the impatient clearing of Le'lorinel's throat.

E'kressa stood up straight and regarded the elf. "Gandalug lays ill," the gnome confirmed, losing both the mysterious voice and the aggravating rhymes. "Aye, and dying at that."

"Priests in attendance?"

"Dwarf priests, yes," the gnome answered. "Which is to say, little of any healing powers that might be offered to the dying king. No gentle hands there.

"Nor would it matter," E'kressa went on, bending again to study the images, to absorb the *feel* of the scene as much as the actual display. "It is no wound, save the ravages of time, I fear, and no illness, save the one that fells all if nothing kills him sooner." E'kressa stood straight again and blew a fluffy eyebrow up from in front of one gray eye.

"Old age," the gnome explained. "The Ninth King of Mithral Hall is dying of old age."

Le'lorinel nodded, having heard as much. "And Bruenor Battlehammer?" the elf asked.

"The Ninth King lies on a bed of sorrow," the gnome said dramatically. "The Tenth King rises with the sun of the morrow!"

Le'lorinel crossed arms and assumed an irritated posture.

"Had to be said," the gnome explained.

"Better by you, then," the elf replied. "If it had to be."

"It did," said E'kressa, needing to get in the last word.

"Bruenor Battlehammer?" the elf asked.

The gnome spent a long time studying the scene in the crystal ball then, murmuring to himself, even at one point putting his ear flat against the smooth surface to better hear the events transpiring in the distant dwarf kingdom.

"He is not there," E'kressa said with some confidence soon after. "Good enough for you, too, for if he had returned, with the dark elf beside him, would you think to penetrate a dwarven stronghold?"

"I will do as I must," came the quiet and steady response.

E'kressa started to chuckle but stopped short when he saw the grim countenance worn by Le'lorinel.

"Better for you, then," the gnome said, waving away the images in the scrying ball and enacting another spell of divination. He closed his eyes, not bothering with the ball, as he continued the chant—the call to an otherworldly being for some sign, some guidance.

A curious image entered his thoughts, burning like glowing metal. Two symbols showed clearly, images that he knew, though he had never seen them thus entwined.

"Dumathoin and Clangeddin," he mumbled. "Dumathoin and Moradin."

"Three dwarf gods?" Le'lorinel asked, but E'kressa, standing very still, eyes fluttering, didn't seem to hear.

"But how?" the gnome asked quietly.

Before Le'lorinel could inquire as to what the seer might be speaking of, E'kressa's gray eyes popped open wide. "To find Drizzt, you must indeed find Bruenor," the gnome announced.

"To Mithral Hall, then," Le'lorinel reasoned.

"Not so!" shrieked the gnome. "For there is a place more urgent in the eyes of the dwarf, a place as a father and not a king."

"Riddles?"

E'kressa shook his hairy head vehemently. "Find the dwarf's most prized creation of his hands," the gnome explained, "to find the dwarf's most prized creation of the flesh—well, one of two, but it sounded better that way," the gnome admitted.

Le'lorinel's expression could not have been more puzzled.

"Bruenor Battlehammer made something once, something powerful and magical beyond his abilities as a craftsman," E'kressa explained. "He crafted it for someone he treasured greatly. That creation of metal will bring the dwarf more certainly than will the void on Mithral Hall's stone throne. And more, that creation will bring the dark elf running."

"What is it?" Le'lorinel asked, eagerness now evident. "Where is it?"

E'kressa bounded to his small desk and pulled forth a piece of parchment. With Le'lorinel rushing to join him, he enacted another spell, this one transforming the image that his previous spell had just burned into his thoughts to the parchment. He held up his handiwork, a perfect representation of the jumbled symbols of the dwarven gods.

"Find this mark, Le'lorinel, and you will find the end of your long road," he explained.

E'kressa went into his spellcasting again, this time bringing forth lines on the opposite side of the parchment.

"Or this one," he explained, holding the new image, one that looked very much like the old, up before Le'lorinel.

The elf took the parchment gently, staring at it wide-eyed.

"One is the mark of Clangeddin, covered by the mark of Dumathoin, the Keeper of Secrets Under the Mountain. The other is the mark of Moradin, similarly disguised."

Le'lorinel nodded, turning the page over gently and reverently, like some sage studying the writings of some long-lost civilization.

"Far to the west, I believe," the gnome explained before Le'lorinel could ask the question. "Waterdeep? Luskan? Somewhere in between? I can not be sure."

"But you believe this to be the region?" the elf asked. "Did your divination tell you this, or is it a logical hunch, considering that Icewind Dale is immediately north of these places?"

E'kressa considered the words for a while, then merely shrugged. "Does it matter?"

Le'lorinel stared at him hard.

"Have you a better course to follow?" the gnome asked.

"I paid you well," the elf reminded.

"And there, in your hands, you have the goods returned, tenfold," the gnome asserted, so obviously pleased by his performance this day.

Le'lorinel looked down at the parchment, the lines of the intertwining symbols burned indelibly into the brown paper.

"I know not the immediate connection," the gnome admitted. "I know not how this symbol, or the item holding it, will bring you to your obsession. But there lies the end of your road, so my spells have shown me. More than that, I do not know."

"And will this end of the road prove fruitful to Le'lorinel?" the elf asked, despite the earlier discounting of such prophecy.

"This I have not seen," the gnome replied smugly. "Shall I wager a guess?"

Le'lorinel, only then realizing the betrayal of emotions presented by merely asking the question, assumed a defensive posture. "Spare me," the elf said.

"I could do it in rhyme," the gnome offered with a superior smirk.

Le'lorinel thought to mention that a rhyme might be offered in return, a song actually, sung with eagerness as a delicate elven dagger removed a tongue from the mouth of a gloating gnome.

The elf said nothing, though, and the thought dissipated as the image on the parchment obscured all other notions.

Here it was, in Le'lorinel's hands, the destination of a life-time's quest.

Given that, the elf had no anger left to offer.

Given that, the elf had too many questions to ponder, too many preparations to make, too many fears to overcome, and too many fantasies to entertain of seeing Drizzt Do'Urden, the imitation hero, revealed for the imposter he truly was.

⚔ ⚔ ⚔ ⚔ ⚔

Chogurugga lay back on five enormous pillows, stuffing great heaps of mutton into her fang-filled mouth. At eight and a half feet, the ogress wasn't very tall, but with legs the girth of ancient oaks and a round waist, she packed more than seven hundred pounds into her ample frame.

Many male attendants rushed about the central cavern, the largest in Golden Cove, keeping her fed and happy. Always they had been attentive of Chogurugga because of her unusual and exotic appearance. Her skin was light violet in color, not the normal yellow of her clan, perfectly complimenting her long and greasy bluish-black hair. Her eyes were caught somewhere between the skin and hair in hue, seeming deep purple or just a shade off true blue, depending on the lighting about her.

Chogurugga was indeed used to the twenty males of Clan Thump fawning over her, but since her new allegiance with the human pirates, an allegiance that had elevated the females of the clan to even higher stature, the males practically tripped over one another rushing to offer her food and fineries.

Except for Bloog, of course, the stern taskmaster of Golden Cove, the largest, meanest, ugliest ogre ever to walk these stretches of the Spine of the World. Many whispered that Bloog wasn't even a true ogre, that he had a bit of mountain giant blood in him, and since he stood closer to fifteen feet than to ten, with thick arms the size of Chogurugga's legs, it was a rumor not easily discounted.

Chogurugga, with the help of Sheila Kree, had become the brains of the ogre side of Golden Cove, but Bloog was the brawn, and, whenever he desired it to be so, the true boss. And he had become even meaner since Sheila Kree had come into their lives and had given to him a gift of tremendous power, a crafted warhammer that allowed Bloog to expand caverns with a single, mighty blow.

"Back again?" the ogress said when Sheila and Bellany strode into the cavern. "And what goodzies did yez bring fer Chogurugga this time?"

"A broken ship," the pirate leader replied sarcastically. "Think ye might be eating that?"

Bloog's chuckle from the side of the room rumbled like distant thunder.

Chogurugga cast a glower his way. "Me got Bathunk now," the female reminded. "Me no need Bloog."

Bloog furrowed his brow, which made it stick out far beyond his deep-set eyes, a scowl that would have been comical had it not been coming from a beast that was a ton of muscle. Bathunk, Chogurugga and Bloog's vicious son, was becoming quite an issue between the couple of late. Normally in ogre society, when the son of a chieftain was growing as strong and as mean as the father, and that father was still young, the elder brute would beat the child down, and repeatedly, to secure his own place in the tribe. If that didn't work, the son would be killed, or put out at least. But this was no ordinary group of ogres, Clan Thump was a matriarchy instead of the more customary patriarchy, and Chogurugga would tolerate none of that behavior from Bloog—not with Bathunk, anyway.

"We barely hit open water when a familiar sight appeared on our horizon," explained an obviously disgusted Bellany, who had no intention of witnessing another of Chogurugga and Bloog's legendary "Bathunk" battles.

"Chogurugga guesses three sails?" the ogress asked, taking the bait to change the subject and holding up four fingers.

Sheila Kree cast a disapproving glance Bellany's way—she didn't need to have the ogres' respect for her diminished in any way—then turned the same expression over Chogurugga. "He's a persistent one," she admitted. "One day, he'll even follow us to Golden Cove."

Bloog chuckled again, and so did Chogurugga, both of them reveling in the thought of some fresh man-flesh.

Sheila Kree, though she surely wasn't in a smiling mood, joined in, but soon after motioned for Bellany to follow and headed out the exit on the opposite side of the room, to the tunnels leading to their quarters higher up in the mountain.

Sheila's room was not nearly as large as the chamber shared by the ogre leaders, but it was almost hedonistic in its furnishings, with ornate lamps throwing soft light into every nook along the uneven walls, and fine carpets piled so high that the women practically bounced along as they crossed the place.

"I grow weary o' that Deudermont," Sheila said to the sorceress.

"He is likely hoping for that very thing," Bellany replied. "Perhaps we'll grow weary enough to stop running, weary of the run enough to confront *Sea Sprite* on the open waters."

Sheila looked at her most trusted companion, gave an agreeing smile, and nodded. Bellany was, in many ways, her better half, the crusty pirate knew. Always thinking, always looking ahead to the consequences, the wise and brilliant sorceress had been the greatest addition to *Bloody Keel*'s crew in decades. Sheila trusted her implicitly—Bellany had been the very first to wear the brand once Sheila had decided to use the intricate design on the side of Aegis-fang's mithral head in that manner. Sheila even loved Bellany as her own sister, and, despite her overblown sense of pride, and the fact that she was always a bit too merciful and gentle-hearted toward their captives for Sheila's vicious tastes, Sheila knew better than to discount anything Bellany might say.

Three times in the last couple of months, Deudermont's ship had chased *Bloody Keel* off the high seas, though Sheila wasn't even certain *Sea Sprite* had seen them the first time and doubted that there had been any definite identification the other two. But perhaps Bellany was right. Perhaps that was Deudermont's way of catching elusive pirates. He'd chase them until they tired of running, and when they at last turned to fight. . . .

A shudder coursed Sheila Kree's spine as she thought of doing battle with *Sea Sprite* on the open waters.

"Not any bait we're soon to be taking," Sheila said, and the answering expression from Bellany, who had no desire to ever tangle with *Sea Sprite*'s devastating and legendary Robillard, was surely one of relief.

"Not out there," Sheila Kree went on, moving to the side of the chamber, to one of the few openings in the dark caverns of Golden Cove, a natural window overlooking the small bay and the reefs beyond. "But he's chasin' us from profits, and we've got to make him pay."

"Well, perhaps one day he'll be foolish enough to chase us into Golden Cove. We'll let Chogurugga's clan rain heavy stones down on his deck," Bellany replied.

But Sheila Kree, staring out at the cold waters, at the waves where she and *Bloody Keel* should now be sailing in pursuit of greater riches and fame, wasn't so certain she could maintain that kind of patience.

There were other ways to win such a personal war.

4

THE BRAND

Now, this was the kind of council meeting Regis of Lonelywood most enjoyed. The halfling sat back in his cushioned chair, hands folded behind his head, his cherubic face a mask of contentment, as the prisoners taken from the road south of Bremen were paraded before the councilors. Two were missing, one recovering, perhaps, from a newly placed crease in his chest, and the other—the woman whom the friends had believed to be the leader of the rogue band—held in another room to be brought in separately.

"It must be wonderful having such mighty friends," Councilor Tamaroot of Easthaven, never a fan of the Lonelywood representative, said cynically and quietly in Regis's ear.

"Those two," the halfling replied more loudly, so that the other three councilors on his side of the room certainly heard him. The halfling paused just long enough to ensure that he had the attention of all four, and of a couple of the five from across the way, as well as the attention of Elderman Cassius, then pointed to the two thugs he'd battled—or that he'd forced to battle each other. "I took them both, without aid," the halfling finished.

Tamaroot bristled and sat back in his seat.

Regis smoothed his curly brown locks and put his hands behind his head again. He could not contain his smile.

After the introductions, and with no disputes from any of the others, Cassius imposed the expected sentence. "As you killed no one on the road—none that we know of, at least—so your own lives are not forfeit," he said.

"Unless the wound Bruenor's axe carved into the missing one puts him down," the councilor from Caer-Konig, the youngest and often crudest of the group, piped in. Despite the poor taste of the remark, a bit of muffled chortling did sound about the decorated room.

Cassius cleared his throat, a call for some solemnity. "But neither are your crimes dismissed," the elderman went on. "Thus you are indentured, for a period of ten years, to a boat of Councilor Kemp's choosing, to serve on the waters of Maer Dualdon. All of your catch shall be forfeited to the common fund of Ten-Towns, less Kemp's expenses for the boat and the guards, of course, and less only enough to see that you live in a measure of meager sustenance. That is the judgment of this council. Do you accept it?"

"And what choice are we given?" said one of the thugs, the large man Catti-brie had overwhelmed.

"More than you deserve," Kemp interjected before Cassius could reply. "Had you been captured by the Luskan authorities, you would have been paraded before Prisoner's Carnival and tortured to death in front of a screaming crowd of gleeful onlookers. We can arrange something similar, if that is your preference."

He looked to Cassius as he finished, and the elderman nodded his grim approval of the Targos councilor's imposing speech.

"So which shall it be?" Cassius asked the group.

The answer was rather predictable, and the grumbling group of men was paraded out of the room and out of Brynn Shander, on the way to Targos where their prison ship waited.

As soon as they had gone, Cassius called for the cheers of the council, a salute to Regis and the others for a job well done.

The halfling soaked it in.

"And I fear we may need the group, the Companions of the Hall, yet again, and soon enough," Cassius explained a moment later, and he motioned to the chamber's door sentries. One exited and returned with Jule Pepper, who cut a regal figure indeed, despite her capture and imprisonment.

Regis looked at her with a fair amount of respect. The tall woman's black hair shone, but no more than did her intelligent eyes. She stood straight, unbroken, as if this entire episode were no more than a nuisance, as if these pitiful creatures who had captured her could not really do anything long-lasting or devastating to her.

The functional tunic and leggings she had worn on the road were gone now, replaced by a simple gray dress, sleeveless and, since it was too short for a woman of Jule's stature, worn low off the shoulder. It was a simple piece really, nearly formless, and yet, somehow, the woman beneath it managed to give it quite an alluring shape, bringing it down just enough to hint at her shapely and fairly large breasts. The dress was even torn on one side—Regis suspected that Jule had done that, and purposely—and through that slot, the woman did well to show one smooth and curvaceous leg.

"Jule Pepper," Cassius said curiously, and with a hint of sarcasm. "Of the Pepper family of . . . ?"

"Was I to be imprisoned in the name my parents chose for me?" the woman answered, her voice deep and resonant, and with a stiff eastern accent that seemed to shorten every word into a crisp, accentuated sound. "Am I not allowed to choose for myself the title I shall wear?"

"That would be the custom," Cassius said dryly.

"The custom of unremarkable people," Jule confidently replied. "The jewel sparkles, the pepper spices." She ended with a devastating grin, one that had several of the councilors—ten males, including the elderman, and only one woman—shifting uneasily in their seats.

Regis was no less flustered, but he tried to look beyond the impressive woman's obvious physical allure, taking even greater interest in Jule's manipulative cunning. She was one to be wary of, the halfling knew, and still, he could not deny he had more than a little curiosity about exploring this interesting creature more fully.

"May I ask why I am being held here against my choice and free will?" the woman remarked a moment later, after the group had settled again, with one even tugging at his collar, as if to let some heat out of his burning body.

Cassius snorted and waved a dismissive hand her way. "For crimes against Ten-Towns, obviously," he replied.

"List them then," Jule demanded. "I have done nothing."

"Your band——" Cassius started to respond.

"I have no band," Jule interrupted, her eyes flashing and narrowing. "I was on my way to Ten-Towns when I happened to cross paths with those rogues. I knew not who they were or why they were in that place at that time, but their fire was warm and their food acceptable, and any company seemed better than the murmuring of that endless wind."

"Ridiculous!" one of the councilors asserted. "You were speaking with them knowingly when the terrified pair returned to you—on the word of Drizzt Do'Urden himself, and I have come to trust in that dark elf!"

"Indeed," another councilor agreed.

"And pray tell me what I said, exactly," the woman answered, and her grin showed that she didn't fear any answers they might give. "I spoke to the fools knowingly about Drizzt and Catti-brie and Bruenor. Certainly, I am as versed on the subject as any wise person venturing to Icewind Dale would be. Did I not speak knowingly that the fools had done something stupid and had then been baited by the drow and his companions? No stretch of intelligence there, I would say."

The councilors began murmuring among themselves and Regis stared hard at Jule, his smile showing his respect for her cunning, if nothing else. He could tell already that with her devastating posture and shapeliness, combined with more than a measure of cunning and careful preparedness out on the road, she would likely slip through these bonds unscathed.

And Regis, knew, too, whatever she might say, that this one, Jule Pepper, was the leader of the highwayman band.

"We will discuss this matter," Cassius said soon after, the private conversations of the councilors escalating into heated debate, divisions becoming apparent.

Jule smiled knowingly at Cassius. "Then I am free to go?"

"You are invited to return to the room we have provided," the older and more comprehending elderman replied, and he waved to the guards.

They came up on either side of Jule, who gave Cassius one last perfectly superior look and turned to leave, swaying her shoulders in exactly the right manner to again set off the sweat of the male councilors.

Regis grinned at it all, thoroughly impressed, but his smile dropped into an open-mouthed stare a moment later, as Jule completed her turn, as he noticed a curious marking on the back of her right shoulder, a brand the halfling surely recognized.

"Wait!" the halfling cried and he hopped up from his seat and ducked low to scramble under the table rather than take the time to go around it.

The guards and Jule stopped, all turning about to regard the sudden commotion.

"Turn back," the halfling instructed. "Turn back!" He waved his hand at Jule as he spoke, and the woman just stared at him incredulously, her gaze shifting from curiosity to withering.

"Cassius, turn her back!" the halfling pleaded.

Cassius looked at him with no less incredulity than had Jule.

Regis didn't wait for him. The halfling ran up to Jule, grabbed her right arm and started pulling her around. She resisted for a moment, but the halfling, stronger than he appeared, gave a great tug that brought her around enough, briefly, to show the brand.

"There!" Regis said, poking an accusing finger.

Jule pulled away from him, but it was out now, the councilors all leaning in and Cassius coming forward, motioning for Jule to turn around, or for the guards to turn her if she didn't willingly comply.

With a disgusted shake of her head, the raven-haired woman finally turned.

Regis went up on a nearby chair to better see the brand, but he knew before the inspection that his keen eyes had not deceived him, that the brand on the woman's shoulder was of a design unique to Bruenor Battlehammer, and more than that, a marking Bruenor had used only once, on the side of Aegis-fang. Moreover, the brand was exactly the right size for the warhammer's marking, as if a heated Aegis-fang had been pressed against her skin.

Regis nearly swooned. "Where did you get that?" he asked.

"A rogue's mark," Cassius remarked. "Common enough, I'd say, for any guild."

"Not common," Regis answered, shaking his head. "Not that mark."

"You know it?" the elderman inquired.

"My friends will speak with her," Regis answered. "At once."

"When we are done with her," Councilor Tamaroot insisted.

"At once," Regis insisted, turning to face the man. "Else you, good Tamaroot, can explain to King Bruenor the delay when his adopted son's life may likely hang in the balance."

That brought a myriad of murmurs in the room.

Jule Pepper just glared down at Regis, and he got the distinct feeling that she had little idea what he was talking about, little idea of the significance of the mark.

For her sake, the halfling knew, that better be the truth of it.

⚔ ⚔ ⚔ ⚔ ⚔

A few nights later, Drizzt found Bruenor atop a quiet and dark place called Bruenor's Climb, in the small rocky valley the dwarves mined to the northeast of Brynn Shander, between Maer Dualdon and the lake called Lac Dinneshire. Bruenor always had such private places as this, wherever he was, and he always named them Bruenor's Climb, as much to warn any intruders as out of any personal pride.

This was the dwarf's spot for reflection, his quiet place where he could ponder things beyond the everyday trials and tribulations of his station in life. This was the one place where practical and earthy Bruenor, on dark nights, could let go of his bonds a bit, could let his spirit climb to some place higher than the imagination of a dwarf. This was where Bruenor could come to ponder the meaning of it all and the end of it all.

Drizzt had found Bruenor up on his personal climb back at Mithral Hall, looking very much the same as he did now, when the yochlol had taken Wulfgar, when they had all believed that his adopted son was dead.

Silent as the clouds flying beneath the stars, the drow walked up behind the dwarf and stood patiently.

"Ye'd think losin' him a second time would've been easier," Bruenor remarked at length. "Especially since he'd been such an orc-kin afore he left us."

"You do not know that you have lost him," the drow reminded.

"Ain't no mark in the world like it," Bruenor reasoned. "And the thief said she got it from a hammer's head."

Indeed, Jule had willingly surrendered much information to the imposing friends when they had spoken with her right after the confrontation in the council hall. She'd admitted that the brand was intentional, a marking given by a woman ship's captain. When pressed, Jule had admitted that this woman, Sheila Kree, was a pirate and that this particular brand was reserved by her for those most trusted within her small band.

Drizzt felt great pity for his friend. He started to remark on the fact that Jule had stated that the only physically large members of the pirate band were a clan of ogres Sheila Kree kept for tacking and steering. Wulfgar had not fallen in with the dogs, apparently. The drow held back the remarks, though, because the other implication, a clear one if Wulfgar was not in league with the pirates, was even more dire.

"Ye think this dog Kree killed me boy?" Bruenor asked, his thoughts obviously rolling along the same logic. "Or do ye think it was someone else, some dog who then sold the hammer to this one?"

"I do not think Wulfgar is dead at all," Drizzt stated without hesitation.

Bruenor turned a curious eye up at him.

"Wulfgar may have sold the hammer," Drizzt remarked, and Bruenor's look became even more skeptical. "He denied his past when he ran away from us," the drow reminded. "Perhaps relieving himself of that hammer was a further step along the road he saw before him."

"Yeah, or maybe he just needed the coin," Bruenor said with such sarcasm that Drizzt let his argument die silently.

In truth, the drow hadn't even convinced himself. He knew Wulfgar's bond with Aegis-fang, and knew the barbarian would no sooner willingly part with the warhammer than he would part with one of his own arms.

"Then a theft," Drizzt said after a pause. "If Wulfgar went to Luskan or to Waterdeep, as we believe, then he would likely find himself in the company of thieves."

"In the company of murderers," Bruenor remarked, and he looked back up at the starry sky.

"We can not know," Drizzt said to him quietly.

The dwarf merely shrugged, and when his shoulders came back down from that action, they seemed to Drizzt lower than ever.

The very next morning dark clouds rumbled up from the south off the winds of the Spine of the World, threatening to deluge the region with a torrent of rain that would turn the thawed ground into a quagmire. Still, Drizzt and Catti-brie set out from Ten-Towns, running fast for Luskan. Running fast for answers all four of the friends needed desperately to hear.

5

THE HONESTY OF LOVE

Wulfgar was the first off *Sea Sprite* when the pirate hunter returned to her berth at Waterdeep's long wharf. The barbarian leaped down to the dock before the ship had even been properly tied in, and his stride as he headed for shore was long and determined.

"Will you take him back out?" Robillard asked Deudermont, the two of them standing amidships, watching Wulfgar's departure.

"Your tone indicates to me that you do not wish me to," the captain answered, and he turned to face his trusted wizard friend.

Robillard shrugged.

"Because he interfered with your plan of attack?" Deudermont asked.

"Because he jeopardized the safety of the crew with his rash actions," the wizard replied, but there was little venom in his voice, just practicality. "I know you feel a debt to this one, Captain, though for what reason I cannot fathom. But Wulfgar is not Drizzt or Catti-brie. Those two were disciplined and understood how to play a role as part of our crew. This one is more like . . . more like

Harkle Harpell, I say! He finds a course and runs down it without regard to the consequences for those he leaves behind. Yes, we fought two successful engagements on this venture, sank a pirate, and brought another one in—"

"And captured two crews nearly intact," Deudermont added.

"Still," the wizard argued, "in both of those fights, we walked a line of disaster." He knew he really didn't have to convince Deudermont, knew the captain understood as well as he did that Wulfgar's actions had been less than exemplary.

"We always walk that line," Deudermont said.

"Too close to the edge this time," the wizard insisted. "And with a long fall beside us."

"You do not wish me to invite Wulfgar back."

Again came the wizard's noncommittal shrug. "I wish to see the Wulfgar who took *Sea Sprite* through her trials at the Pirate Isles those years ago," Robillard explained. "I wish to fight beside the Wulfgar who made himself so valuable a member of the Companions of the Hall, or whatever that gang of Drizzt Do'Urden's was called. The Wulfgar who fought to reclaim Mithral Hall and who gave his life, so it had seemed, to save his friends when the dark elves attacked the dwarf kingdom. All these tales I have heard of this magnificent barbarian warrior, and yet the Wulfgar I have known is a man consorting with thieves the likes of Morik the Rogue, the Wulfgar who was indicted for trying to assassinate you."

"He had no part in that," Deudermont insisted, but the captain did wince even in denial, for the memory of the poison and of the Prisoner's Carnival was a painful one.

Deudermont had lost much in granting Wulfgar his reprieve from the vicious magistrate that day in Luskan. By association, by his generosity to those the magistrates believed were truly not deserving, Deudermont had sullied *Sea Sprite*'s reputation with the leaders of that important northern port. For Deudermont had stolen their show, had granted so unexpected a pardon, and all of that without any real proof that Wulfgar had not been involved in the attempt on his life.

"Perhaps not," Robillard admitted. "And Wulfgar's character on this voyage, whatever his shortcomings, has borne out your decision to grant the pardon, I admit. But his discretion on the open waters has not borne out your decision to take him aboard *Sea Sprite*."

Captain Deudermont let the wizard's honest and fair words sink in for a long while. Robillard could be a crotchety and judgmental sort, a curmudgeon in the extreme, and a merciless one concerning those he believed had brought their doom upon themselves. In this case, though, his words rang of honest truth, of simple and undeniable observation. That truth stung Deudermont. When he'd encountered Wulfgar in Luskan, a bouncer in a seedy tavern, he recognized the big man's fall from glory and had tried to entice Wulfgar away from that life. Wulfgar had denied him outright, had even refused to admit his own true identity to the captain. Then came the assassination attempt, with Wulfgar indicted while Deudermont lay unconscious and near death.

The captain still wasn't sure why he'd denied the magistrate his murderous fun at Prisoner's Carnival that day, why he'd gone with his gut instinct against the common belief and a fair amount of circumstantial evidence, as well. Even after that display of mercy and trust, Wulfgar had shown little gratitude or friendship.

Deudermont had been pained when they parted outside of Luskan's gate that day of the reprieve, when Wulfgar had again refused him his offer to sail with *Sea Sprite*. The captain had been fond of the man once and considered himself a good friend of Drizzt and Catti-brie, who had sailed with him honorably those years after Wulfgar's fall. Yes, he had dearly wanted to help Wulfgar climb back to grace, and so Deudermont had been overjoyed when Wulfgar had arrived in Waterdeep, at this same long wharf, a woman and child in tow, announcing that he wished to sail with Deudermont, that he was searching for his lost warhammer.

Deudermont had correctly read that as something much more, had known then as he did now that Wulfgar was searching for more than his lost weapon, that he was searching for his former self.

But Robillard's observations had been on the mark, as well. While Wulfgar had not been a problem in any way during the routine tendays of patrolling, in the two battles *Sea Sprite* had fought, the barbarian had not performed well. Courageously? Yes. Devastating to the enemy? Yes. But Wulfgar, wild and vicious, had not been part of the crew, had not allowed the more conventional and less risky tactics of using Robillard's wizardry to force submission from afar, the chance to work. Deudermont wasn't sure why Wulfgar had gone into this battle rage. The seasoned captain understood the inner heat of battle, the ferocious surge that any man needed to overcome his logical fears, but Wulfgar's explosions of rage seemed something beyond even that, seemed the stuff of barbarian legend—and not a legend that shone favorably on the future of *Sea Sprite*.

"I will speak with him before we sail," Deudermont offered.

"You already have," the wizard reminded.

Deudermont looked to him and gave a slight shrug. "Then I will again," he said.

Robillard's eyes narrowed.

"And if that is not effective, we will put Wulfgar to duty on the tiller," the captain explained before Robillard could begin his obviously forthcoming stream of complaints, "belowdecks and away from the fighting."

"Our steering crew is second to none," Robillard did say.

"And they will appreciate Wulfgar's unparalleled strength when executing the tightest of turns."

Robillard snorted, hardly seeming convinced. "He will probably ram us into the next pirate in line," the wizard grumbled quietly as he walked away.

Despite the gravity of the situation, Deudermont could not suppress a chuckle as he watched Robillard's typical, grumbling departure.

✕ ✕ ✕ ✕ ✕

Wulfgar's surprise when he burst through the door to find Delly waiting for him was complete and overwhelming. He knew the woman, surely, with her slightly crooked smile and her light brown eyes, and yet he hardly recognized her. Wulfgar had known Delly as a barmaid living in squalor and as a traveling companion on a long and dirty road. Now, in the beautiful house of Captain Deudermont, with all his attendants and resources behind her, she hardly seemed the same person.

Before, she had almost always kept her dark brown hair pinned up, mostly because of the abundant lice she encountered in the Cutlass, but now her hair hung about her shoulders luxuriously, silken and shining and seeming darker. That, of course, only made her light brown eyes—remarkable eyes, Wulfgar realized—shine all the brighter. Before, Delly had worn plain and almost formless clothing, simple smocks and shifts, that had made her thin limbs seem spindly. But now she was dressed in a formed blue dress with a low-cut white blouse.

It occurred to the barbarian, just briefly—for other things were suddenly flooding his thoughts—how much an advantage the wealthy women of Faerûn held over the peasant women in terms of beauty. When first he and Delly had arrived, Deudermont had thrown a party for many of Waterdeep's society folk. Delly had felt so out of place, and so had Wulfgar, but for the woman, it was much worse, as her meager resources for beauty had been called to attention at every turn.

Not so now, Wulfgar understood. If Deudermont held another of his many parties on this stay in port, then Delly Curtie would shine more beautifully than any woman there!

Wulfgar could hardly find his breath. He had always thought Delly comely, even pretty, and her beauty had only increased for him in their time on the road from Luskan, as he had come to appreciate the depth of the woman even more. Now, combining that honest respect and love with this physical image proved too much for the barbarian who had spent the last three months at sea.

He fell over her with a great, crushing hug, interrupting her words with kiss after kiss, lifting her with ease right from the ground and burying his face in that mane of brown hair, biting gently at her delicate—and now it seemed delicate and not just skinny—neck. How tiny Delly seemed in his arms, for Wulfgar stood a foot and a half taller than her and was nearly thrice her body weight.

With hardly an effort, Wulfgar scooped her more comfortably into his arms, spinning her to the side and sliding one arm under her knees.

He laughed, then, when he noted that she was barefoot, and even her feet looked prettier to him.

"Are ye making fun o' me?" Delly asked, and Wulfgar noted that her peasant accent seemed less than he remembered, with the woman articulating the "g" on the end of the word "making."

"Making fun of you?" Wulfgar asked, and he laughed again, all the louder. "I am making love to you," he corrected, and he kissed her again, then launched into a spinning dance, swinging her all about as he headed for the door of their private room.

They almost got past the threshold before Colson started crying.

⚔ ⚔ ⚔ ⚔ ⚔

The two did find some time alone together later that night, and made love again before the dawn. As the first slanted rays of morning shone through the eastern window of their room, Wulfgar lay on his side beside his lover, his hand gently tracing about her neck, face, and shoulders.

"Sure that it's good to have ye home," Delly said quietly, and she brought her small hand up to rub Wulfgar's muscular forearm. "Been a lonely time with ye out."

"Perhaps my days out with Deudermont are at their end," Wulfgar replied.

Delly looked at him curiously. "Did ye find yer hammer, then?" she asked. "And if ye did, then why'd ye wait for telling me?"

Wulfgar was shaking his head before she ever finished. "No word of it or of Sheila Kree," he answered. "For all I know, the pirate went to the bottom of the sea and took Aegis-fang with her."

"But ye're not knowing that."

Wulfgar fell to his back and rubbed both his hands over his face.

"Then how can ye be saying ye're done with Deudermont?" Delly asked.

"How can I not?" Wulfgar asked. "With you here, and Colson? This is my life now, and a fine one it is! Am I to risk it all in pursuit of a weapon I no longer need? No, if Deudermont and his crew hear of Sheila Kree, they'll hunt her down without my help, and I hold great faith that they will return the warhammer to me."

Now it was Delly's turn to come upon her elbows, the smooth sheets falling from her naked torso. She gave a frustrated shake to toss her tangled brown hair out of her face, then fixed Wulfgar with a glare of severe disapproval.

"What kind of a fool's words are spilling from yer mouth?" she asked.

"You would prefer that I leave?" Wulfgar asked, a bit of suspicion showing on his square-jawed face.

For so many years that face had held a boyish charm, an innocence that reflected in Wulfgar's sky blue eyes. No more, though. He had shaved all the stubble from his face before retiring with Delly, but somehow Wulfgar's face now seemed almost out of place without the blond beard. The lines and creases, physical manifestation of honest emotional turmoil, were not the markings of a young man, though Wulfgar was only in his twenties.

"And more the fool do ye sound now!" Delly scolded. "Ye know I'm not wanting ye to go—ye know it! And ye know that no others are sharing me bed.

"But ye must be going," Delly continued solemnly, and she fell back on the bed. "What's to haunt ye, then, if Deudermont and his crew go out without ye and find the pirate and some o' them die trying to get yer hammer back? How're ye to feel when they bring ye the hammer and the news, and all the while, ye been sitting here safe while they did yer work for ye?"

Wulfgar looked at Delly hard, studying her face and recognizing that she was indeed pained to be speaking to him so.

"Stupid Josi Puddles for stealing the damn hammer and selling it out to the pirate," the woman finished.

"Some could die," Wulfgar agreed. "Sheila Kree is known to be a fierce one, and by all accounts she has surrounded herself with a formidable crew. By your own reasoning, then, none of us, not Deudermont and not Wulfgar, should go out in search of her and Aegis-fang."

"Not me own reasoning at all," Delly argued. "Deudermont and his crew're choosing the road of pirate hunting—that's not yer doing. It's their calling, and they'd be going after Sheila Kree even if she'd ne'er taken yer hammer."

"Then we are back where we started," Wulfgar reasoned with a chuckle. "Let Deudermont and his fine crew go out and find the hammer if they—"

"Not so!" Delly interrupted angrily. "Their calling is to go and hunt the pirates, to be sure, and yer own is to be with them until they're finding yer hammer. Yers is to find yer hammer and yerself, to get back where ye once were."

Wulfgar settled back on the bed and ran his huge, callused hands over his face again. "Perhaps I do not wish to be back there."

"Perhaps ye don't," said Delly. "But that's not a choice for ye to make until ye do get back there. When ye've found out again who ye were, me love, only then will ye be able to tell yerself honestly where ye're wanting to go. Until ye get it to where all is for the taking, then ye'll always be wondering and wanting."

She went quiet then, and Wulfgar had no response. He sighed many times and started to repudiate her many times, but every avenue he tried to explore proved inevitably to be a dead end.

"When did Delly Curtie become so wise in the course of life?" a defeated Wulfgar asked a short while later.

Delly snickered and rolled to face him. "Might that I always been," she answered playfully. "Or might not be at all. I'm just telling ye what I'm thinking, and what I'm thinking is that ye got to get back to a certain place afore ye can climb higher. Ye need to be getting yerself back to where ye once were, and ye'll find the road ye most want to walk, and not just the road ye're thinking ye have to walk."

"I was back to that place," Wulfgar replied in all seriousness, and a cloud passed over his face. "I was with them in Icewind Dale again, as it had been before, and I left, of my own choice."

"Because of a better road calling?" Delly asked. "Or because ye weren't yet ready to be back? There's a bit o' difference there."

Wulfgar was out of answers, and he knew it. He wasn't sure that he agreed with Delly, but when the call from Deudermont and *Sea Sprite* came the next day, he answered it.

6
THE PATHS OF DOOM

Le'lorinel worked defensively, as always, letting the opponent take the lead, his twin scimitars weaving a furious dance. The elf parried and backed, dodged easily and twirled aside, letting Tunevec's furious charge go right past.

Tunevec stumbled, and cursed under his breath, thinking the fight lost, thinking Le'lorinel would surely complain and moan about his deficiencies. He closed his eyes, waiting for the slap of a sword across his back, or his rump if Le'lorinel was feeling particularly petty this day.

No blow came.

Tunevec turned about to see the bald elf leaning against the wall, weapons put away.

"You do not even bother to finish the fight?" Tunevec asked.

Le'lorinel regarded him absently, as if it didn't matter. The elf stared up at the lone window on this side of the tower, the one to Mahskevic's study. Behind that window, Le'lorinel knew, the wizard was getting some more answers.

"Come!" Tunevec bade, and he clapped his scimitars in the air before him. "You paid me for one last fight, so let us fight!"

Le'lorinel eventually got around to looking at the impatient warrior. "We are done, now and forever."

"You paid for the last fight, and the last fight is not finished," Tunevec protested.

"But it is. Take your coins and be gone. I have no further need of your services."

Tunevec stared at the elf in abject disbelief. They had been sparring together for many months, and now to be dismissed so casually, so callously!

"Keep the scimitars," Le'lorinel remarked, not even looking at Tunevec anymore, but rather, staring up at that window.

Tunevec stood there for a long while, staring at the elf incredulously. Finally, having sorted it all out, the reality of the dismissal leaving a foul taste in his mouth, he tossed the scimitars to the ground at Le'lorinel's feet, turned about, and stormed off, muttering curses.

Le'lorinel didn't even bother to retrieve the scimitars or to glance Tunevec's way. The fighter had done his job—not very well, but he had served a useful purpose—and now that job was done.

In a matter of moments, Le'lorinel stood before the door of Mahskevic's study, hand up to knock, but hesitating. Mahskevic wasn't pleased by all of this, Le'lorinel knew, and had seemed quite sullen since the elf's return from E'kressa.

Before Le'lorinel could find the nerve to knock, the door swung open, as if of its own accord, affording the elf a view of Mahskevic sitting behind his desk, his tall and pointy blue wizard's cap bent halfway up and leaning to the left, several large tomes open on the oaken desk before him, including one penned by Talasay, the bard of Silverymoon, detailing the recent events of Mithral Hall, including the reclamation of the dwarves' homeland from the duergar and the shadow dragon Shimmergloom, the anointing of Bruenor as King, the coming of the dark elves bearing Gandalug Battlehammer—Bruenor's grandfather—and finally, after the great victory over the forces of the Underdark, Bruenor's abdication of the throne to Gandalug and his reputed return to Icewind Dale. Le'lorinel had paid dearly for that tome and knew every word in it very well.

Between the books on the wizard's desk, and partially beneath one of them, was spread a parchment that Le'lorinel had written out for the wizard, recounting the exact words E'kressa had used in his divination.

"I told you that I would call to you when I was done," Mahskevic, who seemed very surly this day, remarked without looking up. "Can you not find a bit of patience after all of these years?"

"Tunevec is gone," Le'lorinel answered. "Dismissed and departed."

Now Mahskevic did look up, his face a mask of concern. "You did not kill him?" the wizard asked.

Le'lorinel smiled. "Do you believe me to be such an evil creature?"

"I believe that you are obsessed beyond reason," the wizard answered bluntly. "Perhaps you fear to leave witnesses behind, that one might alert Drizzt Do'Urden of the pursuit."

"Then E'kressa would be dead, would he not?"

Mahskevic considered the words for a moment, then shrugged in acceptance of the simple logic. "But Tunevec has left?"

Le'lorinel nodded.

"A pity. I was just growing fond of the young and able warrior. As were you, I had thought."

"Not so fine a fighter," the elf answered, as if that was all that truly mattered.

"Not up to the standards you demanded of your sparring partner who was meant to emulate this notable dark elf," Mahskevic replied immediately. "But then, who would be?"

"What have you learned?" Le'lorinel asked.

"Intertwined symbols of Dumathoin, the Keeper of Secrets under the Mountain, and of Clangeddin, dwarf god of battle," the wizard explained. "E'kressa was correct."

"The symbol of Bruenor Battlehammer," Le'lorinel stated.

"Not really," Mahskevic answered. "A symbol used only once by Bruenor, as far as I can tell. He was quite an accomplished smith, you know."

As he spoke, he waved Le'lorinel over to his side, and when the elf arrived, he pointed out a few drawings in Talasay's work: unremarkable weapons and a breastplate.

"Bruenor's work," Mahskevic remarked, and indeed, the picture captions indicated that very thing. "Yet I see no marking similar to the one E'kressa gave to you. There," he explained, pointing to a small mark on the bottom corner of the breastplate. "There is Bruenor's mark, the mark of Clan Battlehammer with Bruenor's double 'B' on the mug."

Le'lorinel bent in low to regard the drawing and saw the foaming mug standard of the dwarven clan and Bruenor's particular brand, as Mahskevic had declared. Of course, the elf had already reviewed all of this, though it seemed Mahskevic was drawing clues where Le'lorinel had not.

"As far as I can tell, Bruenor used this common brand for all his work," the wizard explained.

"That is not what the seer told to me."

"Ah," the wizard remarked, holding up one crooked and bony finger, "but then there is this." As he finished, he flipped to a different page in the large tome, to another drawing, this one depicting in great detail a fabulous warhammer, Aegis-fang, set upon a pedestal.

"The artist copying the image was remarkable," Mahskevic

explained. "Very detail-minded, that one!"

He lifted a circular glass about four inches in diameter and laid it upon the image, magnifying the warhammer. There, unmistakably, was the mark E'kressa had given to Le'lorinel.

"Aegis-fang," the elf said quietly.

"Made by Bruenor for one of his two adopted children," Mahskevic remarked, and that declaration made E'kressa's cryptic remarks come into clearer focus and seemed to give credence to the overblown and showy seer.

"Find the dwarf's most prized creation of his hands to find the dwarf's most prized creation of the flesh," the gnome diviner had said, and he had admitted that he was referring to one of two creations of the flesh, or, it now seemed obvious, children.

"Find Aegis-fang to find Wulfgar?" Le'lorinel asked skeptically, for as far as both of them knew, as far as the tome indicated, Wulfgar, the young man for whom Bruenor had created Aegis-fang, was dead, killed by a handmaiden of Lolth, a yochlol, when the drow elves had attacked Mithral Hall.

"E'kressa did not name Wulfgar," Mahskevic replied. "Perhaps he was referring to Catti-brie."

"Find the hammer to find Catti-brie, to find Bruenor Battlehammer, and to find Drizzt Do'Urden," Le'lorinel said with a frustrated sigh.

"Difficult crew to be fighting," Mahskevic said, and he gave a sly smile. "I would enjoy your continued company," he explained. "I have so much work yet to be done, and I am not a young man. I could use an apprentice, and you have shown remarkable insight and intelligence."

"Then you will have to wait until my business is finished," the stubborn elf said sternly. "If I live to return."

"Remarkable intelligence in most matters," the old wizard dryly clarified.

Le'lorinel snickered and took no offense.

"This group of friends surrounding Drizzt has earned quite a reputation," Mahskevic stated.

"I have no desire to fight Bruenor Battlehammer, or Catti-brie, or anyone else other than Drizzt Do'Urden," said the elf. "Though perhaps there would be a measure of justice in killing Drizzt's friends."

Mahskevic gave a great growl and slammed Talasay's tome shut, then shoved back from the desk and stood tall, staring down hard at the elf. "And that would be an unconscionable act by every measure of the word," he scolded. "Is your bitterness and hatred toward this dark elf so great that you would take innocent life to satisfy it?"

Le'lorinel stared at him coldly, lips very thin.

"If it is, then I beg you to reconsider your course even more seriously," the wizard added. "You claim righteousness on your side in this inexplicable pursuit of yours, and yet nothing—nothing I say—would justify such unrelated murder! Do you hear me, boy? Do my words sink through that stubborn wall of hatred for Drizzt Do'Urden that you have, for some unexplained reason, erected?"

"I was not serious in my remark concerning the woman or the dwarf," Le'lorinel admitted, and the elf visibly relaxed, features softening, eyes glancing downward.

"Can you not find a more constructive pursuit?" Mahskevic asked sincerely. "You are more a prisoner of your hatred for Drizzt than the dark elf could ever be."

"I am a prisoner because I know the truth," Le'lorinel agreed in that melodic alto voice. "And to hear tales of his heroism, even this far from Mithral Hall or Ten-Towns stabs profoundly at my heart."

"You do not believe in redemption?"

"Not for Drizzt, not for any dark elf."

"An uncompromising attitude," Mahskevic remarked, stroking

a hand knowingly over his fluffy beard. "And one that you will likely one day regret."

"Perhaps I already regret that I know the truth," the elf replied. "Better to be ignorant, to sing bard songs of Drizzt the hero."

"Sarcasm is not becoming."

"Honesty is oft painful."

Mahskevic started to respond but just threw up his hands and gave a defeated laugh and a great shake of his shaggy head. "Enough," he said. "Enough. This is a circular road we have ridden far too often. You know that I do not approve."

"Noted," the uncompromising Le'lorinel said. "And dismissed."

"Perhaps I was wrong," Mahskevic mused aloud. "Perhaps you do not have the qualities necessary to serve as an appropriate apprentice."

If his words were meant to wound Le'lorinel, they seemed to fail badly, for the elf merely turned around and calmly walked out of the room.

Mahskevic gave a great sigh and dropped his palms that he could lean on his desk. He had come to like Le'lorinel over the years, had come to think of the elf as an apprentice, even as a son, but he found this self-destructive single-mindedness disconcerting and disheartening, a shattering reality against his hopes and wishes.

Mahskevic had also spent more than a little effort in learning about this rogue drow that so possessed the elf's soul, and while information concerning Drizzt was scarce in these parts far to the east of Silverymoon, everything the wizard had heard marked the unusual dark elf as an honorable and decent sort. He wondered, then, if he should even allow Le'lorinel to begin this hunt, wondered if he would then be morally compromised through his inaction against what seemed a grave injustice.

He was still wondering that very thing the next morning, when

Le'lorinel found him in his little spice garden on the small balcony halfway up his gray stone tower.

"You are versed in teleportation," the elf explained. "It will be an expensive spell for me to purchase, I presume, since you do not approve of my destination, but I am willing to work another two tendays, from before dawn to after dusk, in exchange for a magical journey to Luskan, on the Sword Coast."

Mahskevic didn't even look up from his spice plants, though he did stop his weeding long enough to consider the offer. "I do not approve, indeed," he said quietly. "Once again I beseech you to abandon this folly."

"And once again I tell you that it is none of your affair," the elf retorted. "Help me if you will. If not, I suspect I will easily enough find a wizard in Silverymoon who is willing to sell a simple teleport."

Mahskevic stood straight, even put his hand on the back of his hip for support and arched his back, stretching out the kinks. Then he turned, deliberately, and put an imposing glare over the confident elf.

"Will you indeed?" the wizard asked, his glare going to the elf's hand, to the onyx ring he had sold to Le'lorinel and into which he had placed the desired magical spells.

Le'lorinel had little trouble in following his gaze to discern the item that held his attention.

"And you will have enough coin, I expect," the wizard remarked. "For I have changed my mind concerning the ring I created and will buy it back."

Le'lorinel smiled. "There is not enough gold in all the world."

"Give it over," Mahskevic said, holding out his hand. "I will return your payment."

Le'lorinel turned around and walked off the balcony, moving right to the stairs and heading down.

An angry Mahskevic caught up just outside the tower.

"This is foolishness!" he declared, rushing around and blocking the smaller elf's progress. "You are consumed by a vengeance that goes beyond all reason and beyond all morality!"

"Morality?" Le'lorinel echoed incredulously. "Because I see a drow elf for what he truly is? Because I know the truth of Drizzt Do'Urden and will not suffer his glowing reputation? You are wise in many things, old wizard, and I am better for having tutored under you these years, but of this quest I have undertaken, you know nothing."

"I know you are likely to get yourself killed."

Le'lorinel shrugged, not disagreeing. "And if I abandon this, then I am already dead."

Mahskevic gave a shout and shook his head vigorously. "Insanity!" he cried. "This is naught but insanity. And I'll not have it!"

"And you can not stop it," said Le'lorinel, and the elf started around the old man, but Mahskevic was quick to shift, again blocking the way.

"Do not underestimate—" Mahskevic started to say, but he stopped short, the tip of a dagger suddenly pressing against his throat.

"Take your own advice," Le'lorinel threatened. "What spells have you prepared this day? Battle spells? Not likely, I know, and even if you have a couple in your present repertoire, do you believe you will ever get the chance to cast them? Think hard, wizard. A few seconds is a long time."

"Le'lorinel," Mahskevic said as calmly as he could muster.

"It is only because of our friendship that I will put my weapons aside," the elf said quietly, and Mahskevic breathed more easily as the dagger went away. "I had hoped you would help me on my way, but I knew that as the time drew near, your efforts to aid me would diminish. And so I forgive you your abandonment, but be warned, I will not tolerate interference from anybody. Too long have I waited, have I prepared, and now the day is upon me. Wish me well, for our years together, if for nothing else."

Mahskevic considered it for a while, then grimly nodded. "I do wish you well," he said. "I pray you will find a greater truth in your heart than this and a greater road to travel than one of blind hatred."

Le'lorinel just walked away.

"He is beyond reason," came a familiar voice behind Mahskevic a few moments later, with the wizard watching the empty road where Le'lorinel had already gone out of sight. Mahskevic turned to see Tunevec standing there, quite at ease.

"I had hoped to dissuade him, as well," Tunevec explained. "I believed the three of us could have carved out quite an existence here."

"The two of us, then?" Mahskevic asked, and Tunevec nodded, for he and the wizard had already spoken of his apprenticeship.

"Le'lorinel is not the first elf I have heard grumble about this Drizzt Do'Urden," Tunevec explained as the pair walked back to the tower. "On those occasions when the rogue drow visited Alustriel in Silverymoon, there were more than a few citizens openly offering complaints, the light-skinned elves foremost among them. The enmity between the elves, light and dark, can not be overstated."

Mahskevic gave one longing glance back over his shoulder at the road Le'lorinel had walked. "Indeed," he said, his heart heavy.

With a profound sigh, the old wizard let go of his friend, of a large part of the last few years of his life.

⋈ ⋈ ⋈ ⋈ ⋈

On a rocky road many hundreds of miles away, Sheila Kree stood before a quartet of her crewmen.

One of her most trusted compatriots, Gayselle Wayfarer, her

deck commander for boarding parties, sat astride a small but strong chestnut mare. Though not nearly as thin or possessed of classic beauty as Bellany the Sorceress or the tall and willowy Jule Pepper, Gayselle was far from unattractive. Even though she kept her blond hair cropped short, there was a thickness and a luster to it that nicely complimented the softness of her blue eyes and her light complexion, a creaminess to her skin that remained despite the many days aboard ship. Gayselle, a short woman with the muscular stature to match her mount, was, perhaps, the most skilled with weapons of anyone aboard *Bloody Keel*, with the exception of Sheila Kree herself. She favored a short sword and dagger. The latter she could throw as precisely as anyone who'd ever served with Sheila Kree.

"Bellany wouldn't agree with this," Gayselle said.

"If the task is completed, Bellany will be glad for it," Sheila Kree replied.

She looked around somewhat sourly at Gayselle's chosen companions, a trio of brutal half-ogres. These three would be running, not riding, for no horse would suffer one of them on its back. It hardly seemed as if it would slow Gayselle down on her journey to Luskan's docks, where a small rowboat would be waiting for them, for their ogre heritage gave them a long, swift stride and inhuman endurance.

"You have the potions?" the pirate captain asked.

Gayselle lifted one fold of her brown traveling cloak, revealing several small vials. "My companions will look human enough to walk through the gates of Luskan and off the docks of Waterdeep," the rider assured her captain.

"If *Sea Sprite* is in . . ."

"We go nowhere near Deudermont's house," Gayselle completed.

Sheila Kree started another remark but stopped and nodded, reminding herself that this was Gayselle, intelligent and dependable, the second of her crew after Bellany to wear the brand. Gayselle understood not only the desired course for this, but any alternate routes should the immediate plan not be possible. She would get the job done, and Captain Deudermont and the other fools of *Sea Sprite* would understand that their hounding of Sheila Kree might not be a wise course to continue.

PART TWO

It has often struck me how reckless human beings tend to be. In comparison to the other goodly reasoning beings, I mean, for comparisons of humans to dark elves and goblins and other creatures of

TRACKING

selfish and vicious ends make no sense. Menzoberranzan is no safe place, to be sure, and most dark elves die long before the natural expiration of their corporeal bodies, but that, I believe, is more a matter of ambition and religious zeal, and also a measure of hubris. Every dark elf, in his ultimate confidence, rarely envisions the possibility of his own death, and when he does, he often deludes himself into thinking that any death in the chaotic service of Lolth can only bring him eternal glory and paradise beside the Spider Queen.

The same can be said of the goblinkin, creatures who, for whatever misguided reasons, often rush headlong to their deaths.

Many races, humans included, often use the reasoning of godly service to justify dangerous actions, even warfare, and there is a good deal of truth to the belief that dying in the cause of a greater good must be an ennobling thing.

But aside from the fanaticism and the various cultures of warfare, I find that humans are often the most reckless of the goodly reasoning beings. I have witnessed many wealthy humans venturing to Ten-Towns for holiday, to sail on the cold and deadly waters of Maer Dualdon, or to climb rugged Kelvin's Cairn, a dangerous prospect. They risk everything for the sake of minor accomplishment.

I admire their determination and trust in themselves.

I suspect that this willingness to risk is in part due to the short expected life span of the humans. A human of four decades risking his life could lose a score of years, perhaps two, perhaps three in extraordinary circumstances, but an elf of four decades would be risking several centuries of life! There is, then, an immediacy and urgency in being human that elves, light or dark, and dwarves will never understand.

And with that immediacy comes a zest for life beyond anything an elf or a dwarf might know. I see it, every day, in Catti-brie's fair face—this love of life, this urgency, this need to fill the hours and the days with experience and joy. In a strange paradox, I saw that urgency only increase when we thought that Wulfgar had died, and in speaking to Catti-brie about this, I came to know that such eagerness to experience, even at great personal risk, is often a experienced by humans who have lost a loved one, as if the reminder of their own impending mortality serves to enhance the need to squeeze as much living as possible into the days and years remaining.

What a wonderful way to view the world, and sad, it seems, that it takes a loss to correct the often mundane path.

What course for me, then, who might know seven centuries of life, even eight, perhaps? Am I to take the easy trail of contemplation and sedentary existence, so common to the elves of Toril? Am I to dance beneath the stars every night, and spend the days in reverie, turning inward to better see the world about me? Both worthy pursuits, indeed, and dancing under the nighttime sky is a joy I would never forsake. But there must be more for me, I know. There must be the pursuit of adventure and experience. I take my cue from Catti-brie and the other humans on this, and remind myself of the fuller road with every beautiful sunrise.

The fewer the lost hours, the fuller the life, and a life of a few decades can surely, in some measures, be longer than a life of several centuries. How else to explain the accomplishments of a warrior such as Artemis Entreri, who could outfight many drow veterans ten times his age? How else to explain the truth that the most accomplished wizards in the world are not elves but humans, who spend decades, not centuries, pondering the complexities of the magical Weave?

I have been blessed indeed in coming to the surface, in finding a companion such as Catti-brie. For this, I believe, is the mission of my existence, not just the purpose, but the point of life itself. What opportunities might I find if I can combine the life span of my heritage with the intensity of humanity? And what joys might I miss if I follow the more patient and sedate road, the winding road dotted with signposts reminding me that I have too much to lose, the road that avoids mountain and valley alike, traversing the plain, sacrificing the heights for fear of the depths?

Often elves forsake intimate relationships with humans, denying love, because they know, logically, that it can not be, in the frame of elven time, a long-lasting partnership.

Alas, a philosophy doomed to mediocrity.

We need to be reminded sometimes that a sunrise lasts but a few minutes.

But its beauty can burn in our hearts eternally.

—Drizzt Do'Urden

7
UNSEEMLY COMPANY

The guard blanched ridiculously, seeming as if he would simply fall over dead, when he noted the sylvan features and ebony skin of the visitor to Luskan's gate this rainy morning. He stuttered and stumbled, clenched his polearm so tightly in both hands that his knuckles turned as white as his face, and at last he managed to stammer out, "Halt!"

"We're not moving," Catti-brie replied, looking at the man curiously. "Just standing here, watching yerself sweating."

The man gave what could have been either a growl or a whimper, then, as if finding his heart, called out for support and boldly stepped in front of the pair, presenting his polearm defensively. "Halt!" he said again, though neither of them had started moving.

"He figured out ye were a drow," Catti-brie said dryly.

"He does not recognize that even a high elf's skin might darken under the sun," Drizzt replied with a profound sigh. "The curse of fine summer weather."

The guard stared at him, perplexed by the foolish words. "What do you want?" he demanded. "Why are you here?"

"To enter Luskan," said Catti-brie. "Can't ye be guessing that much yerself?"

"Enough of your ridicule!" cried the guard, and he thrust the polearm threateningly in Catti-brie's direction.

A black hand snapped out before the sentry could even register the movement, catching his weapon just below its metal head. "There is no need of any of this," Drizzt remarked, striding next to the trapped weapon to better secure his hold. "I, we, are no strangers to Luskan, nor, can I assure you, have we ever been less than welcomed."

"Well, Drizzt Do'Urden, bless my eyes!" came a call behind the startled sentry, a cry from one of a pair of soldiers rushing up to answer the man's cry. "And Catti-brie, looking less like a dwarf than e'er before!"

"Oh, put your weapon away, you fool, before this pair puts it away for you, in a holder you'd not expect and not much enjoy!" said the other of the newcomers. "Have you not heard of this duo before? Why, they sailed with *Sea Sprite* for years and brought more pirates in for trial than we've soldiers to guard them!"

The first sentry swallowed hard and, as soon as Drizzt let go of the polearm, hastily retracted it and skittered out of the way. "Your pardon," he said with an awkward bow. "I did not know . . . the sight of a . . ." He stopped there, obviously mortified.

"And how might you know?" Drizzt generously returned. "We have not been here in more than a year."

"I have only served for three months," the relieved sentry answered.

"And a pity to have to bury one so quickly," one of the soldiers behind him remarked with a hearty laugh. "Threatening Drizzt and Catti-brie! O, but that will get you in the ground right quick and make yer wife a weeping widow!"

Drizzt and Catti-brie accepted the compliments with a slight grin and a nod, trying to get past it. For the dark elf, compliments sat as uncomfortably as insults, and one of the natural side-products of hunting with Deudermont was a bit of notoriety in the port towns along the northern Sword Coast.

"So what blesses Luskan with your presence?" one of the more knowledgeable soldiers asked. His demeanor made both Drizzt and Catti-brie think they should know the man.

"Looking for an old friend," Drizzt answered. "We have reason to believe he might be in Luskan."

"Many folks in Luskan," the other seasoned soldier answered.

"A barbarian," Catti-brie explained. "A foot and more taller than me, with blond hair. If you saw him, you'd not likely forget him."

The closest of the soldiers nodded, but then a cloud crossed his face and he turned about to regard his companion.

"What's his name?" the other asked. "Wulfgar?"

Drizzt's excitement at hearing the confirmation was shallowed by the expressions worn by both soldiers, grave looks that made him think immediately that something terrible had befallen his friend.

"You have seen him," the drow stated, holding his arm out to calm Catti-brie, who had likewise noted the guards' concern.

"You'd best come with me, Master Drizzt," the older of the soldiers remarked.

"Is he in trouble?" Drizzt asked.

"Is he dead?" Catti-brie asked, stating the truth of what was on Drizzt's mind.

"*Was* in trouble, and I'd not be surprised one bit if he's now dead," the soldier answered. "Come along and I'll lead you to someone who can offer more answers."

They followed the soldier along Luskan's winding avenues,

moving toward the center of the city, and, finally, into one of the largest buildings in all the city, which housed both the jail and most of the city officials. The soldier, apparently a man of some importance, led the way without challenge from any of the many guards posted at nearly every corridor, up a couple of flights of stairs and into an area where every door marked the office of a magistrate.

He stopped in front of one that identified the office of Magistrate Bardoun, then, with a concerned look back at the pair, knocked loudly.

"Enter," came a commanding reply.

Two black-robed men were in the room, on opposite sides of a huge desk cluttered with papers. The closest, standing, looked every bit the part of one of Luskan's notorious justice-bringers, with hawkish features and narrow eyes all but hidden beneath long gray eyebrows. The man sitting behind the desk, Bardoun, obviously, was much younger than his counterpart, no more than thirty, certainly, with thick brown hair and matching eyes and a clean-shaven, boyish face.

"Begging your pardon, Magistrate," the soldier asked, his voice showing a nervous edge, "but I have here two heroes, Drizzt Do'Urden and Catti-brie, daughter of dwarf King Bruenor Battlehammer himself, come back to Luskan in search of an old friend."

"Do enter," Bardoun said in a friendly tone. His standing partner, though, put a scrutinizing glare over the two, particularly over the dark elf.

"Drizzt and Catti-brie sailed with Deudermont—" the soldier started to remark, but Bardoun stopped him with an upraised hand.

"Their exploits are well known to us," the magistrate said. "You may leave us."

The soldier bowed, offered a wink to the pair then exited, closing the door behind him.

"My associate, Magistrate Callanan," Bardoun introduced, and he stood up, motioning for the pair to come closer. "We will be of any help we may, of course," he said. "Though Deudermont has fallen on some disfavor among some of the magistrates, many of us greatly appreciate the work he and his brave crew have done in clearing the waters about our fair city of some dreadful pirates."

Drizzt glanced at Catti-brie, both of them surprised to hear that Captain Deudermont, as fine a man as ever sailed the Sword Coast, a man given a prized three-masted schooner by the Lords of Waterdeep to aid in his gallant work, had fallen upon any disfavor at all from officers of the law.

"Your soldier indicated that you might be able to help us in locating an old friend," Drizzt explained. "Wulfgar, by name. A large northman of fair complexion and light hair. We have reason to believe . . ." The drow stopped in mid-sentence, caught by the cloud that crossed Bardoun's face and the scowl suddenly worn by Callanan.

"If you are friends of that one, then perhaps you should not be in Luskan," Callanan remarked with a derisive snort.

Bardoun composed himself and sat back down. "Wulfgar is well known to us indeed," he explained. "Too well known, perhaps."

He motioned for Drizzt and Catti-brie to take the seats along the side of the small office, then told them the story of Wulfgar's entanglement with Luskan's law, of how the barbarian had been accused and convicted of trying to murder Deudermont—which Catti-brie interrupted by saying, "Impossible!"—and had been facing execution at Prisoner's Carnival, barely moments from death, when Deudermont himself had pardoned the man.

"A foolish move by the good captain," Callanan added. "One that brought him disfavor. We do not enjoy seeing a guilty man walk free of the Carnival."

"I know what you enjoy," Drizzt said, more harshly than he had intended.

The drow was no fan of the brutal and sadistic Prisoner's Carnival, nor did he carry many kind words for the magistrates of Luskan. When he and Catti-brie had sailed with Deudermont and they had taken pirate prisoners on the high seas, the couple had always prompted the captain to turn for Waterdeep instead of Luskan, and Deudermont, no fan of the vicious Prisoner's Carnival himself, had often complied, even if the larger city was a longer sail.

Recognizing the harshness in his tone, Drizzt turned to the relatively gentle Bardoun and said, "Some of you, at least."

"You speak honestly," Bardoun returned. "I do respect that, even if I do not agree with you. Deudermont saved your friend from execution, but not from banishment. He, along with his little friend were cast out of Luskan, though rumor has it that Morik the Rogue has returned."

"And apparently with enough influence so that we are instructed not to go and bring him back to our dungeons for breaking the exile," Callanan said with obvious disgust.

Morik the Rogue?" Catti-brie asked.

Bardoun waved his hand, indicating that this character was of no great importance. "A minor street thug," he explained.

"And he traveled with Wulfgar?"

"They were known associates, yes, and convicted together of the attempt upon Deudermont's life, along with a pair of pirates whose lives were not spared that day."

Callanan's wicked grin at Bardoun's remark was not lost on Drizzt, yet another confirmation to the dark elf of the barbarism that was Luskan's Prisoner's Carnival.

Drizzt and Catti-brie looked to each other again.

"Where can we find Morik?" the woman asked, her tone determined and offering no debate.

"In the gutter," Callanan answered. "Or the sewer, perhaps."

"You may try Half-Moon Street," Magistrate Bardoun added. "He has been known to frequent that area, particularly a tavern known as the Cutlass."

The name had a ring of familiarity to Drizzt, and he nodded as he remembered the place. He hadn't been there during his days with Deudermont, but well before that, he and Wulfgar had come through Luskan on their way to reclaim Mithral Hall. Together, they had gone into the Cutlass, where Wulfgar had started quite a brawl.

"That is where your friend Wulfgar made quite a reputation, as well," said Callanan.

Drizzt nodded, as did Catti-brie. "My thanks to you for the information," he said. "We will find our friend, I am sure." He bowed and started away, but stopped at the door as Bardoun called after him.

"If you do find Wulfgar, and in Luskan, do well by him and take him far, far away," the magistrate said. "Far away from here, and, for his own sake, far away from the rat, Morik the Rogue."

Drizzt turned and nodded, then left the room. He and Catti-brie went and got their own lodgings at a fine inn along one of the better avenues of Luskan, and spent the day walking about the city, reminiscing about old times and their previous journey through the city. The weather was fine for the season, with bright sun splashing about the leaves, beginning their autumnal color turn, and the city certainly had many places of great beauty. Together, then, walking and enjoying the sights and the weather, Drizzt and Catti-brie took no note of the gawks and the gasps, even the sight of several children running full speed away from the dark elf.

Drizzt couldn't be bothered by such things. Not with Catti-brie at his side.

The couple waited patiently for the fall of night, when they knew they had a better chance of finding someone like Morik the Rogue, and, it seemed, of finding someone like Wulfgar.

The Cutlass was not busy when the pair entered, soon after dusk, though it seemed to Drizzt as if a hundred sets of eyes had suddenly focused upon him, most notably, a glance both horrified and threatening from a skinny man seated at the bar, directly opposite the barkeep, whose rag stopped its movement completely as he too focused on the unexpected newcomer. When he had come into this place those years ago, Drizzt had remained off to the side, buried in the clamor and tumult of the busy, ill-lit tavern, his hood up and his head low.

Drizzt nodded to the barkeep and approached him directly. The skinny man gave a yelp and fell away, scrambling to the far end of the room.

"Greetings, good sir," Drizzt said to the barkeep. "I come here with no ill intentions, I assure you, despite the panic of your patron."

"Just Josi Puddles," the barkeep replied, though he, too, was obviously a bit shaken at the appearance of a dark elf in his establishment. "Don't pay him any attention." The man extended his hand, then retracted it quickly and wiped it on his apron before offering it again. "Arumn Gardpeck at your service."

"Drizzt Do'Urden," the drow replied, taking the hand in his own surprisingly strong grasp. "And my friend is Catti-brie."

Arumn looked at the pair curiously, his expression softening as if he came to truly recognize them.

"We seek someone," Drizzt started.

"Wulfgar," Arumn said with confidence, and he grinned at the wide-eyed expressions his response brought to the drow and the woman. "Aye, he told me of you. Both of you."

"Is he here?" Catti-brie asked.

"Been gone for a long time," the skinny man, Josi, said, daring to come forward. "Come back only once, to get Delly."

"Delly?"

"She worked here," Arumn explained. "Was always sweet on Wulfgar. He came back for her, and the three of them left Luskan—for Waterdeep, I'm guessing."

"Three?" Drizzt asked, thinking the third to be Morik.

"Wulfgar, Delly, and the baby," Josi explained.

"The baby?" both Drizzt and Catti-brie said together. They looked at each other incredulously. When they turned back to Arumn, he merely shrugged, having nothing to offer.

"That was months ago," Josi Puddles interjected. "Ain't heared a thing o' them since."

Drizzt paused, digesting it all. Apparently, Wulfgar would have quite a tale to tell when at last they found him—if he was still alive. "Actually, we came in here seeking one we were told might have information about Wulfgar," the drow explained. "A man named Morik."

There came a scuffle of scrambling feet from behind, and the pair turned to see a small, dark-cloaked figure moving swiftly out of the tavern.

"That'd be yer Morik," Arumn explained.

Drizzt and Catti-brie rushed outside, glancing up and down the nearly deserted Half-Moon Street, but Morik, obviously a master of shadows, was nowhere to be seen.

Drizzt bent down near the soft dirt just beyond the Cutlass's wooden porch, noting a boot print. He smiled at Catti-brie and pointed to the left, an easy trail for the skilled ranger to follow.

⚔ ⚔ ⚔ ⚔ ⚔

"Ye're a pretty laddie, ain't ye?" the grimy old lech said. He pushed Le'lorinel up against the wall, putting his smelly face right up against the elf's.

Le'lorinel looked past him, to the other four old drunkards, all of them howling with laughter as the old fool started fiddling with the rope he used as a belt.

He stopped abruptly and slowly sank to the floor before the elf, moving his suddenly trembling hands lower, to where the knee had just connected.

Le'lorinel came out from the wall, drawing a sword, putting the flat of it against the old wretch's head, and none too gently pushing him over to the floor.

"I came in asking a simple question," the elf explained to the others, who were not laughing any longer.

The old wretches, former sailors and pirates, glanced nervously from one to the other.

"Ye be a good laddie," one bald-headed man said, climbing to stand on severely bowed legs. "Tookie, there, he was just funning with ye."

"A simple question," Le'lorinel said again.

The elf had come into this dirty tavern along Luskan's docks showing the illusionary images E'kressa had prepared, asking about the significance of the mark.

"Not so simple, mayhaps," the bald-headed sea dog replied. "Ye're askin' about a mark, and many're wearin' marks."

"And most who are wearin' marks ain't looking to show 'em," another of the old men said.

Le'lorinel heard a movement to the side and saw the man, Tookie, rising fast from the floor and coming in hard. A sweep and turn, swinging the sword down to the side, not to slash the man—though Le'lorinel thought he surely deserved it—but to force him into an awkward, off-balance dodge, followed by a simple duck and step maneuver had the elf behind the attacker. A firm shove against Tookie's back had him diving forward to skid down hard to the floor.

But two of the others were there, one brandishing a curved knife used for scaling fish, another a short gaff hook.

Le'lorinel's right hand presented the sword defensively, while the elf's left hand went to the right hip, then snapped out.

The man with the gaff hook fell back, wailing and wheezing, a dagger deep in his chest.

Le'lorinel lunged forward, and the other attacker leaped back, presented his hands up before him in surrender, and let the curved knife fall to the floor.

"A simple question," the elf reiterated through gritted teeth, and the look in Le'lorinel's blue and gold eyes left no doubt among any in the room that this warrior would leave them all dead with hardly a thought.

"I ain't never seen it," the man who'd been holding the knife replied.

"But you are going to go and find out about it for me, correct?" Le'lorinel remarked. "All of you."

"Oh, yes, laddie, we'll get ye yer answers," another said.

The one still lying on the floor and facing away from Le'lorinel scrambled up suddenly and bolted for the door, bursting through and out into the twilight. Another rose to follow, but Le'lorinel stepped to the side, tore the dagger free from the dying man's chest and cocked it back, ready to throw.

"A simple question," Le'lorinel said yet again. "Find me my answer and I will reward you. Fail me and. . . ." The elf finished by turning to look at the man propped against the wall, laboring for breath now, obviously suffering in the last moments of his life.

Le'lorinel walked for the open door, pausing only long enough to wipe the dagger on the tunic of the man who'd attacked with the curved blade, finishing by sliding the knife up teasingly toward the man's throat, up and over his shoulder as the elf walked by.

✕ ✕ ✕ ✕ ✕

The small form came out of the alleyway in a blur of motion, spinning and swinging, a pair of silvery daggers in his hands.

His attack was nearly perfect, slicing in low at Drizzt's midsection with his left, then stopping short with a feint and launching a wide-arching chopping left, coming down at the side of the drow's neck.

Nearly perfect.

Drizzt saw the feint for what it was, ignored the first attack, and focused on the second. The dark elf caught Morik's hand in his own and as he did he turned the rogue's hand in so that Drizzt's fingers covered those of the rogue.

Morik neatly adjusted to the block, trying instead to finish his first stab, but Drizzt was too quick and too balanced, skittering with blazing speed, his already brilliant footwork enhanced by magical anklets. The drow went right under Morik's upraised arm, turning as he moved, then running right behind the rogue, twisting that arm and maneuvering out of the reach of the other stabbing dagger.

Morik, too, started to turn, but then Drizzt merely cupped the ends of his fingers and squeezed, compressing the top knuckles of Morik's hand and causing excruciating pain. The dagger fell to the ground, and Morik too went down to one knee.

Catti-brie had the rogue's other hand caught and held before he could even think of trying to retaliate again.

"Oh, please don't kill me," the rogue pleaded. "I did get the jewels . . . I told the assassin . . . I did follow Wulfgar . . . everything you said!"

Drizzt stared up at Catti-brie in disbelief, and he lessened his pressure on the man's hand and yanked Morik back to his feet.

"I did not betray Jarlaxle," Morik cried. "Never that!"

"Jarlaxle?" Catti-brie asked incredulously. "Who does he think we are?"

"A good question," Drizzt asked, looking to Morik for an answer.

"You are not agents of Jarlaxle?" the rogue asked. A moment later, his face beamed with obvious relief and he gave a little embarrassed chuckle. "But then, who . . ." He stopped short, his smile going wide. "You're Wulfgar's friends," he said, his smile nearly taking in his ears.

Drizzt let him go, and so did Catti-brie, and the man retrieved his fallen dagger and replaced both in his belt. "Well met!" he said exuberantly, reaching his hand toward them. "Wulfgar told me so much about the both of you!"

"It would appear that you and Wulfgar have a few tales of your own to tell," Drizzt remarked.

Morik chuckled again and shook his head. When it became apparent that neither the drow nor the woman were going to take the offered handshake, Morik brought his hand back in and wiped it on his hip. "Too many tales to tell!" he explained. "Stories of battle and love all the way from Luskan to Auckney."

"How do you know Jarlaxle?" Catti-brie asked. "And where is Wulfgar?"

"Two completely unrelated events, I assure you," Morik replied. "At least, they were when last I saw my large friend. He left Luskan some time ago, with Delly Curtie and the child he took from the foppish lord of Auckney."

"Kidnapped?" Drizzt asked skeptically.

"Saved," Morik replied. "A bastard child of a frightened young lady, certain to be killed by the fop or his nasty sister." He gave a great sigh. "It is a long and complicated tale. Better that you hear it from Wulfgar."

"He is alive?"

"Last I heard," Morik replied. "Alive and heading for . . . for Waterdeep, I believe. Trying to find Captain Deudermont, and hoping the captain would help him retrieve his lost warhammer."

Catti-brie blew a most profound and relieved sigh.

"How did he lose the warhammer?" Drizzt asked.

"The fool Josi Puddles stole it and sold it to Sheila Kree, a most disagreeable pirate," Morik answered. "Nasty sort, that pirate lady, but Wulfgar's found his heart again, I believe, and so I would not wish to be serving beside Sheila Kree!" He looked at Drizzt, who was staring at Catti-brie, and with both wearing their emotions in plain sight. "You thought he was dead," Morik stated.

"We found a highwayman, a highway*woman*, actually, wearing a brand that could only have come from Aegis-fang," Drizzt explained. "We know how dear that weapon was to Wulfgar and know that he was not in league with the bandit's former gang."

"Never did we think he'd have let the thing go, except from his dying grasp," Catti-brie admitted.

"I think we owe you a meal and a drink, at least," Drizzt said to Morik, whose face brightened at the prospect.

Together, the three walked back toward the Cutlass, Morik seeming quite pleased with himself.

"And you can tell us how you have come to know Jarlaxle," Drizzt remarked as they were entering, and Morik's shoulders visibly slumped.

The rogue did tell them of the coming of the dark elves to Luskan, of how he had been visited by henchmen of Jarlaxle and by the strange mercenary himself and told to shadow Wulfgar. He recounted his more recent adventures with the dark elves, after Wulfgar had departed Luskan and Morik's life, taking care to leave out the part about Jarlaxle's punishment once he had lost touch with the barbarian. Still, when he got to that particular part of the tale, Morik's hand went up reflexively for his face, which had been burned away by the nasty Rai-guy, a dark elf Morik despised with all his heart.

Catti-brie and Drizzt looked at each other throughout the tale with honest concern. If Jarlaxle was interested in their friend, perhaps Wulfgar was not so safe after all. Even more perplexing to them, though, was the question of why the dangerous Jarlaxle would be interested in Wulfgar in the first place.

Morik went on to assure the two that he'd had no dealings with Jarlaxle or his lieutenants in months and didn't expect to see any of them again. "Not since that human assassin showed up and told me to run away," Morik explained. "Which I did, and only recently came back. I'm smarter than to have that band after me, but I believe the human covered my trail well enough. He could not have gone back to them if they believed I was still alive, I would guess."

"Human assassin?" Drizzt asked, and he could guess easily enough who it might have been, though as to why Artemis Entreri would spare the life of anyone and risk the displeasure of mighty Bregan D'aerthe, the drow could not begin to guess. But that was a long tale, likely, and one that Drizzt hoped had nothing to do with Wulfgar.

"Where can we find Sheila Kree?" he asked, stopping Morik before he could really get going with his dark elf stories.

Morik stared at him for a few moments. "The high seas, perhaps," he answered. "She may have a favored and secret port—in fact, I believe I have heard rumors of one."

"You can find out for us?" Catti-brie asked.

"Such information will not come cheaply," Morik started to explain, but his words were lost in a great gulp when Drizzt, a friend of a rich dwarf king whose stake in Wulfgar's return was no less than his own, dropped a small bag bulging with coins on the table.

"Tomorrow night," the drow explained. "In here."

Morik took the purse, nodded, and went fast out of the Cutlass.

"Ye're thinking the rogue will return with information?" Catti-brie asked.

"He was an honest friend of Wulfgar's," Drizzt answered, "and he's too afraid of us to stay away."

"Sounds like our old friend got himself mixed up in a bit of trouble and adventure," Catti-brie remarked.

"Sounds like our old friend found his way out of the darkness," Drizzt countered, his smile beaming behind his dark features, his lavender eyes full of sparkling hope.

8
TEARING AT THE
WARRIOR'S SOUL

They found the merchant vessel listing badly, a fair portion of her sails torn away by chain-shot, and her crewmen—those who were still aboard—lying dead, sprawled across the deck. Deudermont and his experienced crew knew that others had been aboard. A ship such as this would normally carry a crew of at least a dozen and only seven bodies had been found. The captain held out little hope that any of the missing were still alive. An abundance of sharks could be seen in the water around the wounded caravel, and probably more than a few had their bellies full of human flesh.

"No more than a few hours," Robillard announced to the captain, catching up to Deudermont near to the damaged ship's tied-off wheel.

The pirates had wounded her, stripped her of her crew and her valuables, then set her on a tight course, circling in the water. In the stiff wind that had been blowing all day, Deudermont had been forced to order Robillard to further damage the merchant vessel, letting loose a lightning bolt to destroy the rudder, before he could allow *Sea Sprite* to even catch hold of the caravel.

"They would have taken a fair haul from her," Deudermont reasoned.

The remaining stocks in the merchant vessel's hold indicated that the ship, bound from Memnon, had been carrying a large cargo of fabrics, though the cargo log said nothing about any exotic or exceptional pieces.

"Minimal value goods," Robillard replied. "They had to take a substantial amount simply to make the scuttling and murder worth their time. If they filled their hold, they're obviously running for land." He paused and wetted a finger, then held it up. "And they've a favorable breeze for such a journey."

"No more favorable than our own," the captain said grimly. He called to one of his lieutenants, who was standing nearby ordering a last check for any survivors, to be followed by a hasty return to *Sea Sprite*.

The hunt was on.

✖ ✖ ✖ ✖ ✖

Standing not so far away from Captain Deudermont and Robillard, Wulfgar heard every word. He agreed with the assessment that the atrocity was barely hours old. With the strong wind, the fleet *Sea Sprite*, her holds empty, would quickly overtake the laden pirate, even if the pirate was making all speed for safe harbor.

The barbarian closed his eyes and considered the forthcoming battle, his first action since *Sea Sprite* had put back out from Waterdeep. This would be a moment of truth for Wulfgar, a time when his determination and strength of will would have to take command from his faltering fortitude. He looked around at the murdered merchant sailors, men slaughtered by bloodthirsty pirates. Those killers deserved the harsh fate that would likely find them soon, deserved to be sent to a cold and lonely death in the dark waters, or to be captured and returned to Waterdeep, even to Luskan, for trial and execution.

Wulfgar told himself that it was his duty to avenge these innocent sailors, that it was his responsibility to use his gods-given prowess as a warrior to help bring justice to a wild world, to help bring security to helpless and innocent people.

Standing there on the deck of the broken merchant caravel, Wulfgar tried to consciously appeal to every ennobling character- istic, to every ideal. Standing there in that place of murder, Wulfgar appealed to his instincts of duty and responsibility, to the altruism of his former friends—to Drizzt, who would not hesitate to throw himself in harm's way for the sake of another.

But he kept seeing Delly and Colson, standing alone against the harshness of the world, broken in grief and poverty.

A prod in the side alerted the barbarian to the scene about him, to the fact that he and the lieutenant who had poked him were the only remaining crewmen on the wounded caravel. He followed the lieutenant to the boarding plank and noted that Robillard was watching his every step.

Stepping back onto *Sea Sprite*, the barbarian took one last glance at the grisly scene on the merchant ship and burned the images of the dead sailors into his consciousness that he might recall it when the time came for action.

He tried very hard to suppress the images of Delly and Colson as he did, tried to remind himself of who he was and of who he must be.

✕ ✕ ✕ ✕ ✕

Using common sense and a bit of Robillard's magic, *Sea Sprite* had the pirate in sight soon after the next dawn. It seemed a formidable craft, a large three-master with a prominent second deck and catapult. Even from a distance, Deudermont could see many crewmen scrambling about the pirate's deck, bows in hand.

"Carling Badeen?" Robillard asked Deudermont, moving beside him near the prow of the swift-sailing schooner.

"It could be," the captain replied, turning to regard his thin friend.

Sea Sprite had been chasing Carling Badeen, one of the more notorious pirates of the Sword Coast, off and on for years. It appeared they'd finally caught up to the elusive cutthroat. By reputation, Badeen's ship was large but slow and formidably armored and armed, with a crack crew of archers and a pair of notorious wizards. The pirate Badeen himself was known to be one of the more bloodthirsty of the breed, and certainly the gruesome scene back at the merchant ship fit the pattern of Badeen's work.

"If it is, then we must be at our very best, or risk losing many crewmen," Robillard remarked.

Deudermont, his eye back against his spyglass, did not disagree.

"One error, like the many we have been making of late, could cost many of our crew their lives," the wizard pressed on.

Deudermont lowered the glass and regarded his cryptic friend, then followed Robillard's reasoning, and his sidelong glance, to Wulfgar, who stood at the starboard rail amidships.

"He has been shown his errors," Deudermont reminded.

"Errors that he logically understood he was making even as he was making them," Robillard countered. "Our large friend is not controlled by reason when these affairs begin, but rather by emotion, by fear and by rage. You appeal to his rational mind when you explain the errors to him, and on that level, your words do get through. But once the battle is joined, that rational mind, that level of logical progression, is replaced by something more primal and apparently uncontrollable."

Deudermont listened carefully, if somewhat defensively. Still, despite his hopes to the opposite, he could not deny his wizard friend's reasoning. Neither could he ignore the implications for the rest of his crew should Wulfgar act irrationally, interrupting Robillard's progression of the battle. Badeen's ship, after all, carried two wizards and a healthy number of dangerous archers.

"We will win this fight by sailing circles around the lumbering craft," Robillard went on. "We will need to be quick and responsive, and strong on the turn."

Deudermont nodded, for indeed *Sea Sprite* had employed maneuverability as its main weapon against many larger ships, often putting a broadside along a pirate's stern for a devastating archer rake of the enemy decks. Robillard's words, then, seemed fairly obvious.

"Strong on the turn," the wizard reiterated, and Deudermont caught on to what the wizard was really saying.

"You wish me to assign Wulfgar to the rudder crew."

"I wish you to do that which is best for the safety of every man aboard *Sea Sprite*," Robillard answered. "We know how to defeat a ship such as this one, Captain. I only ask that you allow us to do so in our practiced manner, without adding a dangerous variable to the mix. I am not going to deny that our Wulfgar is a mighty warrior, but unlike his friends who once sailed with us, he is unpredictable."

Robillard made to continue, but Deudermont stopped him with an upraised hand and a slight nod, an admission of defeat in this debate. Wulfgar had indeed acted dangerously in previous encounters, and doing that now, against this formidable pirate, could bring disaster.

Was Deudermont willing to risk that for the sake of a friend's ego?

He looked more closely at Wulfgar, the big man standing at the rail staring intently at their quarry, fists clenched, blue eyes blazing with inner fires.

✕ ✕ ✕ ✕ ✕

Wulfgar reluctantly climbed down into the hold—even more so when he realized he actually preferred to be down there. He had watched the captain's approach, coming to him from Robillard, but still Wulfgar had been surprised when Deudermont instructed him to go down into the aft hold where the battle rudder crew worked. Normally, *Sea Sprite*'s rudder worked off the wheel above, but when battle was joined the navigator at the wheel simply relayed his commands to the crew below, who more forcefully and reliably turned the ship as instructed.

Wulfgar had never worked the manual rudder before and hardly saw it as the optimal place to make use of his talents.

"Sour face," said Grimsley, the rudder crew chief. "Ye should be glad for bein' outta the way o' the wizards and bowmen."

Wulfgar hardly responded, just walked over and took up the heavy steering pole.

"He put ye down here for yer strength, I'm guessin'," Grimsley went on, and Wulfgar recognized that the grizzled old seaman was trying to spare his feelings.

The barbarian knew better. If Deudermont truly wanted to utilize his great strength in steering the ship, he would have put Wulfgar on the main tack lines above. Once, aboard the old *Sea Sprite* many years before, Wulfgar had brilliantly and mightily turned the ship, bringing her prow right out of the water, executing a seemingly impossible maneuver to win the day.

But now, it seemed, Deudermont would not even trust him at that task, would not allow him to even view the battle at all.

Wulfgar didn't like it—not one bit—but this was Deudermont's ship, he reminded himself. It was not his place to question the captain, especially with a battle looming before them.

The first shouts of alarm echoed down a few moments later. Wulfgar heard the concussion of a fireball exploding nearby.

"Pull her left to mark three!" Grimsley yelled.

Wulfgar and the one other man on the long pole tugged hard, lining the pole's front tip with the third mark on the wall to the left of center.

"Bring her back to left one!" Grimsley screamed.

The pair responded, and *Sea Sprite* cut back out of a steep turn.

Wulfgar heard the continuing shouts above, the hum of bowstrings, the swish of the catapult, and the blasts of wizardry. The sounds cut to the core of the noble barbarian's warrior identity.

Warrior?

How could Wulfgar rightly even call himself that when he could not be trusted to join in the battle, when he could not be allowed to perform the tasks he had trained for all his life? Who was he, then, he had to wonder, when companions—men of lesser fighting skill and strength than he—were doing battle right above him, while he acted the part of a mule and nothing more?

With a growl, Wulfgar responded to the next command of, "Two right!" then yanked back fiercely as Grimsley, following the frantic shouts from above, called for a dramatic cut to the left, as steep as *Sea Sprite* could make it.

The beams and rudder groaned in protest as Wulfgar forced the bar all the way to the left, and *Sea Sprite* leaned so violently that the man working the pole behind Wulfgar lost his balance.

"Easy! Easy!" Grimsley shouted at the mighty barbarian. "Ye're not to pitch the crew off the deck, ye fool!"

Wulfgar eased up a bit and accepted the scolding as deserved. He was hardly listening to Grimsley anyway, other than the specific commands the old sea dog was shouting. His attention was more to the sound of the battle above, the shrieks and the cries, the continuing roar of wizardry and catapult.

Other men were up there in danger, in his place.

"Bah, don't ye worry," Grimsley remarked, obviously noting the sour expression on Wulfgar's face, "Deudermont and his boys'll win the day, don't ye doubt!"

Indeed, Wulfgar didn't doubt that at all. Captain Deudermont and his crew had been successfully waging these battles since long before his arrival. But that wasn't what was tearing at Wulfgar's heart. He knew his place, and this wasn't it, but because of his own weakness of heart it was the only place Captain Deudermont could responsibly put him.

Above him, the fireballs boomed and the lightning crackled, the bowstrings hummed and the catapults launched their fiery loads with a great swish of sound. The battle went on for nearly an hour, and when the call was relayed through Grimsley that the crew could reattach the rudder to the wheel, the man working beside Wulfgar eagerly rushed up to the deck to survey the victory, right behind Grimsley.

Wulfgar stayed alone in the aft hold, sitting against the wall, too ashamed to show his face above, too fearful that someone had died in his stead.

He heard someone on the ladder a short while later and was surprised to see Robillard coming down, his dark blue robes hiked up so that he could manage the steps.

"Control is back with the wheel," the wizard said. "Do you not think you might be useful helping to salvage what we might from the pirate ship?"

Wulfgar stared at him hard. Even sitting, the barbarian seemed to tower over the wizard. Wulfgar was thrice the man's weight, with arms thicker than Robillard's skinny legs. By all appearances,

Wulfgar could snap the wizard into pieces with hardly an effort.

If Robillard was the least bit intimidated by the barbarian, he never once showed it.

"You did this to me," Wulfgar remarked.

"Did what?"

"Your words put me here, not those of Captain Deudermont," Wulfgar clarified. "You did this."

"No, dear Wulfgar," Robillard said venomously. "You did."

Wulfgar lifted his chin, his stare defiant.

"In the face of a potentially difficult battle, Captain Deudermont had no choice but to relegate you to this place," the wizard was happy to explain. "Your own insolence and independence demanded nothing less of him. Do you think we would risk losing crewmen to satisfy your unbridled rage and high opinion of yourself?"

Wulfgar shifted forward and went up to his feet, into a crouch as if he meant to spring out and throttle the wizard.

"For what else but such an opinion, unless it is sheer stupidity itself, could possibly have guided your actions in the last battles?" Robillard went on, seeming hardly impressed or nervous. "We are a team, well-disciplined and each with a role to play. When one does not play his prescribed part, then we are a weakened team, working in spite of each other instead of in unison. That we can not tolerate. Not from you, not from anyone. So spare me your insults, your accusations and your empty threats, or you may find yourself swimming."

Wulfgar's eyes did widen a bit, betraying his intentionally stoic posture and stare.

"And I assure you, we are a long way from land," Robillard finished, and he started up the ladder. He paused, though, and looked back to Wulfgar. "If you did not enjoy this day's battle, then perhaps you would be wise to remain behind after our next docking in Waterdeep.

"Yes, perhaps that would be the best course," Robillard went on after a pause, after assuming a pensive posture. "Go back to the land, Wulfgar. You do not belong here."

The wizard left, but Wulfgar did not start after him. Rather, the barbarian slumped back to the wall, sliding to a sitting position once again, thinking of who he once had been, of who he now was—an awful truth he did not wish to face.

He couldn't even begin to look ahead, to consider who he wished to become.

9
PATHS CROSSING . . .
ALMOST

L e'lorinel stalked down Dollemand Street in Luskan, the elf's stride revealing anxiety and eagerness. The destination was a private apartment, where the elf was to meet with a representative of Sheila Kree. It all seemed to be falling into place now, the road to Drizzt Do'Urden, the road to justice.

The elf stopped abruptly and wheeled about as two cloaked figures came out of an alley. Hands going to sword and dagger, Le'lorinel had to pause and take a deep breath, recognizing that these two were no threat. They weren't even paying the elf any heed but were simply walking on their way back down the street in the opposite direction.

"Too anxious," the elf quietly chided, easing the sword and dagger back into their respective sheaths.

With a last look at the pair as they walked away, Le'lorinel gave a laugh and turned back toward the apartment, resuming the march down the road for Drizzt Do'Urden.

⚔ ⚔ ⚔ ⚔ ⚔

Walking the other way down Dollemand Street, Drizzt and Catti-brie didn't even notice Le'lorinel as the elf spun on them, thinking them to be a threat. Had Drizzt not been wearing the hood of his cloak, his distinctive long, thick white hair might have marked him clearly for the vengeful elf.

The couple's strides were no less eager than Le'lorinel's, carrying them in the opposite direction, to a meeting with Morik the Rogue and news of Wulfgar. They found the rogue in the appointed place, a back table in Arumn Gardpeck's Cutlass. He smiled at their approach and lifted his foaming mug of beer in toast to them.

"Ye've got our information, then?" Catti-brie asked, sliding into a seat opposite the rogue.

"As much as can be found," Morik replied. His smile dimmed and he lifted the bag of coins Drizzt had given him to the table. "You might want to take some of it back," Morik admitted, pushing it out toward the pair.

"We shall see," Drizzt said, pushing it right back.

Morik shrugged but didn't reach for the bag. "Not much to be learned of Sheila Kree," he began. "I will be honest with you in saying that I'm not overly fond of even asking anyone about her. The only ones who truly know about her are her many commanders, all of them women, and none of them fond of men. Men who go asking too much about Kree usually wind up dead or running, and I have no desire for either course."

"But ye said ye did learn a bit," the eager Catti-brie prompted.

Morik nodded and took a long draw on his beer. "It's been rumored that she operates her own private, secret port somewhere north of Luskan, probably nestled in one of the many coves along the end of the Spine of the World. That would make sense, since she's rarely seen in Luskan of late and has never been known to sail the waters to the south. I don't think her ship has ever been seen in Waterdeep."

Drizzt looked at Catti-brie, the two sharing silent agreement. They had chased pirates with Deudermont for some time, mostly to the south off the docks of Waterdeep, and neither had ever heard of the pirate, Kree.

"What's her ship's name?" Catti-brie asked.

"*Bloody Keel*," Morik replied. "Well-earned name. Sheila takes great enjoyment in keelhauling her victims." He shuddered visibly and took another drink. "That is all I have," he finished, and he again pushed the bag of coins back toward Drizzt.

"And more than I expected," the drow replied, pushing it right back. This time, after a quick pause and a confirming look, Morik took it up and slipped it away.

"There is one more thing," the rogue said as the couple stood to leave. "From all reports, Sheila has not been seen much of late. It may well be that she is in hiding, knowing Deudermont to be after her."

"With her reputation and Wulfgar's hammer, don't ye think she'd try to take *Sea Sprite* on?" Catti-brie asked.

Morik laughed aloud before she ever finished asking the question. "Kree's no fool, and one would have to be a fool to go against *Sea Sprite* on the open waters. *Sea Sprite*'s got one purpose in being out there, and she and her crew do that task with perfect efficiency. Kree might have the warhammer, but Deudermont's got Robillard, and a nasty one he is! And Deudermont's got Wulfgar. No, Kree's laying low, and wise to be doing so. That might well work to your advantage, though."

He paused, making sure he had their attention, which he most certainly did.

"Kree knows the waters north of here better than anyone," Morik explained. "Better than Deudermont, certainly, who spends most of his time to the south. If she's in hiding the good captain will have a hard time finding her. I think it likely that *Sea Sprite* has many voyages ahead before they ever catch sight of Bloody Keel."

Again, Drizzt and Catti-brie exchanged curious looks. "Perhaps we should stay put in the city if we wish to find Wulfgar," the drow offered.

"*Sea Sprite* doesn't put in to Luskan much anymore," Morik interjected. "The ship's wizard is not so fond of the Hosttower of the Arcane."

"And Captain Deudermont has sullied his good name somewhat, has he not?" Catti-brie asked.

Morik's expression showed surprise. "Deudermont and his crew have been the greatest pirate hunters along the Sword Coast for longer than the memories of the eldest elves," he said.

"In freeing yerself and Wulfgar, I mean," Catti-brie clarified with an unintentional smirk. "We're hearing his action at Prisoner's Carnival wasn't looked on with favor by the magistrates."

"Idiots all," Morik mumbled. "But yes, Deudermont's reputation took a blow that day—the day he acted in the name of justice and not politics. He would have been better off personally in letting them kill us, but . . ."

"To his credit, he did not," Drizzt finished for him.

"Deudermont never liked the carnival," Catti-brie remarked.

"So it's likely that the captain has found a more favorable berth for his ship," Morik went on. "Waterdeep, I'd guess, since that's where he is best known—and known to keep a fairly fabulous house."

Drizzt looked to Catti-brie yet again. "We can be there in a tenday," he suggested, and the woman nodded her agreement.

"Well met, Morik, and thank you for your time," the drow said. He bowed and turned to leave.

"You are described in the same manner as a paladin might be, dark elf," Morik remarked, turning both friends back to him one last time. "Righteous and self-righteous. Does it not harm your reputation to do business with the likes of Morik the Rogue?"

Drizzt offered a smile that somehow managed to be warm, self-deprecating, and to show the ridiculousness of Morik's statement clearly, all at once. "You were a friend of Wulfgar's, by all I have heard. I name Wulfgar among my most trusted of companions."

"The Wulfgar you knew, or the one I knew?" Morik asked. "Perhaps they are not one and the same."

"Perhaps they are," Drizzt replied, and he bowed again, as did Catti-brie, and the pair departed.

⚔ ⚔ ⚔ ⚔ ⚔

Le'lorinel entered the small room at the back of the tavern tentatively, hands on dagger and sword. A woman—Sheila Kree's representative, Le'lorinel believed—sat across the room, not behind any desk, but simply against the wall, out in the open. Flanking her were two huge guards, brutes Le'lorinel figured had more than human blood running through their veins—a bit of orc, perhaps even ogre.

"Do come in," the woman said in a friendly and casual manner. She held up her hands to show the elf that she had no weapon. "You requested an audience, and so you have found one."

Le'lorinel relaxed, just a bit, one hand slipping down from the weapon hilt. A glance to the left and the right showed that no one was concealed in the small and sparsely furnished room, so the elf took a stride forward.

The right cross came out of nowhere, a heavy slug that caught the unsuspecting elf on the side of the jaw.

Only the far wall kept the staggering Le'lorinel from falling to the floor. The elf struggled against waves of dizziness and disorientation, fighting to find some center of balance.

The third guard, the largest of the trio, came visible, the concealing enchantment dispelled with the attack. Smiling evilly through a couple of crooked yellow teeth, the brute waded in with another heavy punch, this one blowing the air out of the stunned elf's lungs.

Le'lorinel went for dagger and sword, but the third punch, an uppercut, connected squarely under the elf's chin, lifting Le'lorinel into the air. The last thing Le'lorinel saw was the approach of the other two, one of them with its huge fists wrapped in chains.

A downward chop caught the elf on the side of the head, bringing a myriad of flashing explosions.

All went black.

⚔ ⚔ ⚔ ⚔ ⚔

"Information is not so high a price to pay," Val-Doussen said dramatically—as he said everything dramatically—waving his arms so that his voluminous sleeves seemed more like a raven's wings. "Is it so much that I ask of you?"

Drizzt dropped his head and ran his fingers through his thick white hair, glancing sidelong at Catti-brie as he did. The two had come to the Hosttower of the Arcane, Luskan's wizards guild, in hopes that they would find a mage traveling to Ten-Towns, one who might deliver a message to Bruenor. They knew the dwarf to be terribly worried, and the things they'd learned concerning Wulfgar, while not confirming that he was alive, certainly pointed in that positive direction.

They'd been directed to this black-robed eccentric, Val-Doussen, who'd been planning a trip to Icewind Dale for several tendays. They didn't think they were asking much of the wizard, though they were prepared to pay him, if necessary, but then the silver-haired and bearded wizard had taken a huge interest in Drizzt, particularly in the drow's origins.

He would deliver the information to Bruenor, as requested, but only if Drizzt would give him a dissertation on the dark elf society of Menzoberranzan.

"I have not the time," Drizzt said, yet again. "I am bound for the south, for Waterdeep."

"Might that our wizardly friend here can take us to Waterdeep in a hurry," Catti-brie put in on sudden inspiration, as Val-Doussen began to nervously tug at his beard.

Across the room, the other mage in attendance, one of the guild's leaders by the name of Cannabere, began waving his arms frantically, warding off the suggestion with a look of the purest alarm on his craggy old features.

"Well, well," Val-Doussen said, picking up on Catti-brie's suggestion. "Yes, that would require a bit of effort, but it can be done. For a price, of course, and a substantial one at that. Yes, let me think . . . I take you two to Waterdeep in exchange for a thousand gold coins and two days of tales of Menzoberranzan. Yes, yes, that might do well. And of course, I'll then go to Ten-Towns, as I had planned, and speak with Bruenor—but that for yet another day of dark elven tales."

He looked up at Drizzt, bright-eyed with eagerness, but the drow merely shook his head.

"I've no tales to tell," Drizzt remarked. "I left before I knew much of the place. In truth, I'm certain that many others, likely yourself included, know more of Menzoberranzan than I."

Val-Doussen's expression became a pout. "One day of stories, then, and I shall take your letter to Bruenor."

"No tales of Menzoberranzan," Drizzt replied firmly. He reached under the folds of his cloak and pulled forth the letter he'd prepared for Bruenor. "I will pay you twenty gold pieces—and that is a great sum for this small favor—for you to deliver this to a councilor in Brynn Shander, where you are going anyway, with the request that he relay it to Regis of Lonelywood."

"Small favor?" Val-Doussen asked dramatically.

"We have spent more time discussing this issue than it will take you to carry through with my request," Drizzt replied.

"I will have my stories!" the wizard insisted.

"From someone else," Drizzt answered. He rose to leave, Catti-brie right behind.

The couple nearly made it to the door before Cannabere called out, "He will do it."

Drizzt turned to regard the guildmaster, then the huffing Val-Doussen.

Cannabere looked to the flustered mage, as well, then nodded toward Drizzt. With a great sigh, Val-Doussen went over and took the note. As he began to hold out his hand for the payment, Cannabere added, "As a favor to you, Drizzt Do'Urden, and with our thanks for your work with *Sea Sprite*."

Val-Doussen grumbled again, but he snapped up the note in his hand and spun away.

"Perhaps I will weave a tale or two for you when we meet again," Drizzt said to placate him, as the wizard stormed from the room.

The drow looked to the guildmaster, who merely bowed politely, and Drizzt and Catti-brie went on their way, bound for Luskan's southern gate and the road to Waterdeep.

⚔ ⚔ ⚔ ⚔ ⚔

Tight cords dug deep lines into Le'lorinel's wrists as the elf sat upright on a hard, high, straight-backed wooden chair. A leather band even went about Le'lorinel's neck, holding the elf firmly in place, forcing a grimace.

One eye didn't open all the way, bloated and bruised from the beating, and both shoulders ached and showed purplish bruises, for the elf was no longer wearing a tunic, was no longer wearing many clothes at all.

As the elf's eyes adjusted, Le'lorinel noted that the same four— three brutish guards and a brown-haired woman of medium build—remained in the room. The guards were standing to the side, the woman sitting directly across the way, staring hard at the prisoner.

"My Lady is not fond of having people inquiring about her in public," the woman remarked, her eyes roaming Le'lorinel's finely muscled frame.

"Your lady can not distinguish between friend and foe," Le'lorinel, ever defiant, replied.

"Some things are difficult to distinguish," the woman agreed, and she smiled as she continued her scan.

Le'lorinel gave a derisive snicker, and the woman nodded to the side. A brutish guard was beside the prisoner in a moment, offering a vicious smack across the face.

"Your attitude will get you killed," the woman calmly stated.

Now it was Le'lorinel's turn to stare hard.

"You have been all around Luskan asking about Sheila Kree," the woman went on after a few moments. "What is it about? Are you with the authorities? With that wretch Deudermont perhaps?"

"I am alone, and without friends west of Silverymoon," Le'lorinel replied with equal calm.

"But with the name of a hoped-for contact you carelessly utter to anyone who will listen."

"Not so," the elf answered. "I spoke of Kree only to the one group, and only because I believed they could lead me to her."

Again the woman nodded, and again the brute smacked Le'lorinel across the face.

"*Sheila* Kree," the woman corrected.

Le'lorinel didn't audibly respond but did give a slight, deferential nod.

"You should explain, then, here and now, and parse your words carefully," the woman explained. "Why do you so seek out my boss?"

"On the directions of a seer," Le'lorinel admitted. "The one who created the sketch for me."

As the elf finished, the woman lifted the parchment that held the symbol of Aegis-fang, the symbol that had become so connected to Sheila Kree's pirate band.

"I come in search of another, a dangerous foe, and one who will seek out Kr—Sheila Kree," Le'lorinel explained. "I know not the time nor the place, but by the words of the seer, I will complete my quest to do battle with this rogue when I am in the company of Sheila Kree, if it is indeed Sheila Kree who now holds the weapon bearing that insignia."

"A dangerous foe?" the woman slyly asked. "Captain Deudermont, perhaps?"

"Drizzt Do'Urden," Le'lorinel stated clearly, seeing no reason to hide the truth—especially since any ill-considered words now could prove disastrous for the quest and for the elf's very life. "A dark elf, and friend to the one who once owned that weapon."

"A drow?" the woman asked skeptically, showing no obvious recognition of the strange name.

"Indeed," Le'lorinel said with a huff. "Hero of the northland. Beloved by many in Icewind Dale—and other locales."

The woman's expression became curious, as if she might have heard of such a drow, but she merely shrugged it away. "And he seeks Sheila Kree?" she asked.

It was Le'lorinel's turn to shrug—had the tight binding allowed for such a movement. "I know only what the seer told to me and have traveled many hundreds of miles to find the vision fulfilled. I intend to kill this dark elf."

"And what, then, of any relationship you begin with my boss?" the woman asked. "Is she merely a pawn for your quest?"

"She . . . her home, or fortress, or ship, or wherever it is she resides, is merely my destination, yes," Le'lorinel admitted. "As of now, I have no relationship with your captain. Whether that situation changes or not will likely have more to do with her than with me, since . . ." The elf stopped and glanced at the bindings.

The woman spent a long while studying the elf and considering the strange tale, then nodded again to her brutish guards, offering a subtle, yet clear signal to them.

One moved fast for Le'lorinel, drawing a long, jagged knife. The elf thought that doom had come, but then the brute stepped behind the chair and cut the wrist bindings. Another of the brutish guards came out of the shadows at the side of the room, bearing Le'lorinel's clothing and belongings, except for the weapons and the enchanted ring.

Le'lorinel looked to the woman, trying hard to ignore the disappointed scowls of the three brutes, and noted that she was wearing the ring—the ring Le'lorinel so desperately needed to win a battle against Drizzt Do'Urden.

"Give back the weapons, as well," the woman instructed the guards, and all three paused and stared at her incredulously—or perhaps just stupidly.

"The road to Sheila Kree is fraught with danger," the woman explained. "You will likely need your blades. Do not disappoint me in this journey, and perhaps you will live long enough to tell your tale to Sheila Kree, though whether she listens to it in full or merely kills you for the fun of it, only time will tell."

Le'lorinel had to be satisfied with that. The elf gathered up the clothes and dressed, trying hard not to rush, trying hard to remain indignant toward the rude guards all the while.

Soon they, all five, were on the road, out of Luskan's north gate.

10
DAMN THE WINTER

"From Drizzt," Cassius explained, handing the parchment over to Regis. "Delivered by a most unfriendly fellow from Luskan. A wizard of great importance, by his own measure, at least."

Regis took the rolled and tied note and undid the bow holding it.

"You will be pleased, I believe," Cassius prompted.

The halfling looked up at him skeptically. "You read it?"

"The wizard from Luskan, Val-Doussen by name—and he of self-proclaimed great intellect—forgot the name of the person I was supposed to give it to," Cassius explained dryly. "So, yes, I perused it, and from its contents it seems obvious that it's either for you or for Bruenor Battlehammer or both."

Regis nodded as if satisfied, though in truth he figured Cassius could have reasoned as much without ever reading the note. Who else would Drizzt and Catti-brie be sending messages to, after all? The halfling let it go, though, too concerned with what Drizzt might have to say. He pulled open the note, his eyes scanning the words quickly.

A smile brightened his face.

"Perhaps the barbarian remains alive," Cassius remarked.

"So it would seem," said the halfling. "Or at least, the brand we found on the woman does not mean what we all feared it might."

Cassius nodded, but Regis couldn't help but note a bit of a cloud passing over his features.

"What is it?" the halfling asked.

"Nothing."

"More than nothing," Regis reasoned, and he considered his own words that had brought on the slight frown. "The woman," he reasoned. "What of the woman?"

"She is gone," Cassius admitted.

"Dead?"

"Escaped," the elderman corrected. "A tenday ago. Councilor Kemp put her on a Targos fishing ship for indenture—a different ship than that on which he placed the other ruffians, for he knew she was the most dangerous by far. She leaped from the deck soon after the ship put out."

"Then she died, frozen in Maer Dualdon," Regis reasoned, for he knew the lake well and knew that no one could survive for long in the cold waters even in midsummer, let alone at this time of the year.

"So the crew believed," Cassius said. "She must have had some enchantment upon her, for she was seen emerging from the water a short distance from the western reaches of Targos."

"Then she is lying dead of exposure along the lake's southern bank," the halfling said, "or is wandering in a near-dead stupor along the water's edge."

Cassius was shaking his head through every word. "Jule Pepper is a clever one, it would seem," he said. "She is nowhere to be found, and clothing was stolen from a farmhouse to the west of the city.

Likely that one is long on the road out of Icewind Dale, and a glad farewell I offer her."

Regis wasn't thinking along those same lines. He wondered if Jule Pepper presented any threat to his friends. Jule knew of Drizzt, obviously and likely held a grudge against him. If she was returning to her old hunting band, perhaps she and the drow would cross paths once more.

Regis forced himself to calm down, remembering the two friends, Drizzt and Catti-brie, that he was fearing for. If Jule Pepper crossed paths with that pair, then woe to her, he figured, and he let it go at that.

"I must get to Bruenor," he said to Cassius. Regis snapped the parchment up tight in his hand and rushed out of the elderman's house, sprinting across Brynn Shander in the hopes that he might catch up to a merchant caravan he knew to be leaving for the dwarven mines that very morning.

Luck was with him, and he talked his way into a ride on a wagon full of grain bags. He slept nearly all the way.

Bruenor was in a foul mood when Regis finally caught up to him late that same night—a mood that had been common with the dwarf since Drizzt and Catti-brie had left Ten-Towns.

"Ye're bringing up weak stone!" the red-bearded dwarf king howled at a pair of young miners, their faces and beards black with dirt and dust. Bruenor held up one of the rock samples he had proffered from their small cart and crumbled it in one hand. "Ye're thinking there's ore worth taking in that?" he asked incredulously.

"A tough dig," remarked one of the younger dwarves, his black beard barely reaching the middle of his thick neck. "We're down the deepest hole, hanging upside down . . ."

"Bah, but ye're mixing me up for one who's caring to hear yer whining!" Bruenor roared. The dwarf king gritted his teeth, clenched his fists, and gave a great growl, trembling as if he was throwing all of the rage right out of his body.

"Me king!" the black-bearded dwarf exclaimed. "We'll go and get better stone!"

"Bah!" Bruenor snorted.

He turned and slammed his body hard against the laden cart, overturning it. As if that one explosion had released the tension, Bruenor stood there, staring at the overturned cart and the stones strewn about the corridor, stubby hands on hips. He closed his eyes.

"Ye're not needing to go back down there," he said calmly to the pair. "Ye go get yerselves cleaned and get yerselves some food. Ain't a thing wrong with most o' that ore—it's yer king who's needing a bit o' toughening, by me own eyes and ears."

"Yes, me king," both young dwarves said in unison.

Regis came up from the other side, then, and nodded to the pair, who turned and trotted away, mumbling.

The halfling walked up and put his hand on Bruenor's shoulder. The dwarf king nearly jumped out of his boots, spinning about, his face a mask of fury.

"Don't ye be doing that!" he roared, though he did calm somewhat when he saw that it was only Regis. "Ain't ye supposed to be in a council meeting?"

"They can get through it without me," the halfling replied, managing a smile. "I think you might need me more."

Bruenor looked at him curiously, so Regis just turned and led the dwarf's gaze down the corridor, to the departing pair. "Criminals?" the halfling asked sarcastically.

Bruenor kicked a stone, sending it flying against the wall, seeming again as if he was so full of rage and frustration that he would simply explode. The dark cloud passed quickly, though, replaced by a more general air of gloom, and the dwarf's shoulders slumped. He bowed his head and shook it slowly.

"I can't be losin' me boy again," he admitted.

Regis was beside him in an instant, one hand comfortingly placed on Bruenor's shoulder. As soon as the dwarf looked up at his buddy, Regis offered a wide smile and held the parchment up before him. "From Drizzt," the halfling explained.

The words had barely left Regis's mouth before Bruenor grabbed the parchment away and pulled it open.

"He and Catti-brie found me boy!" the dwarf howled, but he stopped short as he read on.

"No, but they found out how Wulfgar got separated from Aegis-fang," Regis was quick to add, for that, after all, had been the primary source of their concern that the barbarian might be dead.

"We're goin'," Bruenor declared.

"Going?" Regis echoed. "Going where?"

"To find Drizzt and Catti-brie. To find me boy!" the dwarf roared. He stormed away down the corridor. "We're leaving tonight, Rumblebelly. Ye'd best get yerself ready."

"But . . ." Regis started to reply. He stuttered over the beginnings of a series of arguments, the primary of which was the fact that it was getting late in the season to be heading out of Ten-Towns. Autumn was fast on the wane, and Icewind Dale had never been known for especially long autumn seasons, with winter seeming ever hungry to descend upon the region.

"We'll get to Luskan, don't ye worry, Rumblebelly!" Bruenor howled.

"You should take dwarves with you," Regis stammered, skittering to catch up. "Yes, sturdy dwarves who can brave the winter snows, and who can fight. . . ."

"Don't need me kin," Bruenor assured him. "I've got yerself beside me, and I know ye wouldn't be missing the chance to help me find me boy."

It wasn't so much what Bruenor had said as it was the manner in which he had said it, a flat declaration that left no hint at all that he would even listen to contrary arguments.

Regis sputtered out a few undecipherable sounds, then just huffed through a resigned sigh. "All of my supplies for the road are in Lonelywood," the halfling did manage to complain.

"And anything ye'll be needin' is right here in me caves," Bruenor explained. "We'll put through Brynn Shander on our way so ye can apologize to Cassius—he'll see to yer house and yer possessions."

"Indeed," Regis mumbled under his breath, and in purely sarcastic tones, for the last time he had left the region, as in all the times he had wandered out of Icewind Dale, he had returned to find that he had nothing left waiting for him. The folk of Ten-Towns were honest enough as neighbors, but perfectly vulturelike when it came to picking clean abandoned houses—even if they were only supposed to be abandoned for a short time.

True to Bruenor's word, the halfling and the dwarf were on the road that very night, rambling along under crystalline skies and a cold wind, following the distant lights to Brynn Shander. They arrived just before the dawn, and though Regis begged for patience Bruenor led the way straight to Cassius's house and banged hard on the door, calling out loudly enough to not only wake Cassius but a substantial number of his neighbors as well.

When a sleepy-eyed Cassius at last opened his door, the dwarf bellowed, "Ye got a few heartbeats!" and shoved Regis through.

And when, by Bruenor's count, the appropriated time had passed, the dwarf barged through the door, collected the halfling by the scruff of his neck, offered a few insincere apologies to Cassius, and pulled Regis out the door. Bruenor prodded him along all the way across the city and out the western gate.

"Cassius informed me that the fishermen are expecting a gale," Regis said repeatedly, but if Bruenor even heard him, the determined

149

dwarf wasn't showing it. "The wind and rain will be bad enough, but if it turns to snow and sleet. . . ."

"Just a storm," Bruenor said with a derisive snort. "Ain't no storm to stop me, Rumblebelly, nor yerself. I'll get ye there!"

"The yetis are out in force this time of year," Regis cautioned.

"Good enough for keeping me axe nice and sharp," Bruenor countered. "Hard-headed beasts."

The storm began that same night, a cold and biting, steady rain, pelting them more horizontally than vertically in the driving wind.

Thoroughly miserable and soaked to the bone, Regis complained continually, though he knew Bruenor, in the sheer volume of the wind, couldn't even hear him. The wind was directly behind them, at least, propelling them along at a great pace, which Bruenor pointed out often and with a wide smile.

But Regis knew better, and so did the dwarf. The storm was coming from the southeast, off the mountains, the most unlikely direction, and often the most ominous. In Icewind Dale, such storms, if they progressed as expected, were known as Nor'westers. If the gale made its way across the dale and to the sea, the cold northeasterly wind would hold it there, over the moving ice, sometimes for days on end.

The pair stopped at a farmhouse for the evening and were welcomed in, though told that they could sleep in the barn with the livestock and not in the main house. Huddled about a small fire, naked and with their clothes drying on a rafter above, Regis again appealed to Bruenor's common sense.

The halfling found that target a hard one to locate.

"Nor'wester," Regis explained. "Could storm for a tenday and could turn colder."

"Not a Nor'wester yet," the dwarf replied gruffly.

"We can wait it out. Stay here—or go to Bremen, perhaps. But to cross the dale in this could be the end of us!"

"Bah, it's just a bit o' rain," Bruenor grumbled. He bit a huge chunk off the piece of mutton their hosts had provided. "Seen worse—used to play in worse when I was but a boy in Mithral Hall. Ye should've seen the snows in the mountains out there, Rumblebelly. Twice a dwarf's height in a single fall!"

"And a quarter of that will stop us cold on the road," Regis answered. "And leave us frozen and dead in a place where only the yetis will ever find us."

"Bah!" Bruenor snorted. "No snow'll stop me from me boy, or I'm a bearded gnome! Ye can turn about if ye're wantin'—ye should be able to get to Targos easy enough, and they'll get ye across the lake to yer home. But I'm for going on, soon as I get me sleep, and I'm not for stopping until I see Luskan's gate, until I find that tavern Drizzt wrote about, the Cutlass."

Regis tried to hide his frown and just nodded.

"I'm not holdin' a bit o' yer choices against ye," Bruenor said. "If ye ain't got the heart for it, then turn yerself about."

"But you are going on?" Regis asked.

"All the way."

What Regis didn't have the heart for, despite what his common sense was screaming out at him, was abandoning his friend to the perils of the road. When Bruenor left the next day, Regis was right beside him.

The only change that next day was that the wind was now from the northwest instead of the southeast, blowing the rain into their faces, which made them all the more miserable and slowed their progress considerably. Bruenor didn't complain, didn't say a word, just bent low into the gale and plowed on.

And Regis went with him, stoically, though the halfling did position himself somewhat behind and to the left of the dwarf, using Bruenor's wide body to block a bit of the rain and the wind.

The dwarf did concede to a more northerly route that day, one that would bring them to another farmhouse along the route, a homestead that was quite used to having visitors. In fact, when the dwarf and halfling arrived, they met with another group who had started on their way to Luskan. They had pulled in two days before, fearing that the mud would stop their wagon wheels dead in their tracks.

"Too early in the season," the lead driver explained to the duo. "Ground's not frozen up yet, so we've no chance of getting through."

"Seems as if we'll be wintering in Bremen," another of the group grumbled.

"Happened before, and'll happen again," the lead driver said. "We'll take ye on with us to Bremen, if ye want."

"Not going to Bremen," Bruenor explained between bites of another mutton dinner. "Going to Luskan."

Every member of the other group glanced incredulously at each other, and both Bruenor and Regis heard the word "Nor'wester" mumbled more than once.

"Got no wagons to get stuck in the mud," Bruenor explained.

"Mud that'll reach more than halfway up yer little legs," said another, with a chuckle that lasted only as long as it took Bruenor to fix him with a threatening scowl.

The other group, even the lead driver, appealed to the pair to be more sensible, but it was Regis, not Bruenor, who finally said, "We will see you on the road. Next spring. We'll be returning as you're leaving."

That brought a great belly laugh out of Bruenor, and sure enough, before dawn the next day, before any members of the farm family or the other group had even opened their eyes, the dwarf and the halfling were on the road, bending into the cold wind. They knew they'd spent their last comfortable night for a long while, knew they'd have a difficult time even finding enough shelter to start a fizzling fire, knew that deep mud awaited them and possibly with deep snow covering it.

But they knew, too, that Drizzt and Catti-brie waited for them, and, perhaps, so did Wulfgar.

Regis did not register a single complaint that third day, nor the fourth, nor the fifth, though they were out of dry clothes and the wind had turned decidedly colder, and the rain had become sleet and snow. They plowed on, single file, Bruenor's sheer strength and determination plowing a trail ahead of Regis, though the mud grabbed at his every stride and the snow was piling as deep as his waist.

The fifth night they built a dome of snow for shelter and Bruenor did manage a bit of a fire, but neither could feel their feet any longer. With the current pace of the snowfall they expected to wake up to find the white stuff as deep as the horn on Bruenor's helmet.

"I shouldn't have taked ye along," Bruenor admitted solemnly, as close to an admission of defeat as Regis had ever heard from the indomitable dwarf. "Should've trusted in Drizzt and Catti-brie to bring me boy back in the spring."

"We're almost out of the dale," Regis replied with as much enthusiasm as he could muster. It was true enough. Despite the weather, they had made great progress, and the mountain pass was in sight, though still a day's march away. "The storm has kept the yetis at bay."

"Only because the damn things're smarter than us," Bruenor grumbled. He put his toes practically into the fire, trying to thaw them.

They had a difficult time falling asleep that night, expecting the wind and the storm to collapse the dome atop them. In fact, when Regis awoke in the darkness, everything seeming perfectly still—too still! He knew in his heart that he was dead.

He lay there for what seemed like days, when finally the snow dome above him began to lighten and even glow.

Regis breathed a sigh of relief, but where was Bruenor? The halfling rolled to his side and propped himself up on his elbows, glancing all about. In the dim light, he finally made out Bruenor's bedroll, tossed asunder. Before he could even begin to question the scene, he heard a commotion by the low tunnel to the igloo and sucked in his breath.

It was Bruenor coming through, and wearing less clothing than Regis had seen him in for several days.

"Sun's up," the dwarf said with a wide smile. "And the snow's fast melting. We best get our things and ourselves outta here afore the roof melts in on us!"

They didn't travel very far that day, for the warming weather fast melted the snows, making the mud nearly impossible to traverse. At least they weren't freezing anymore, though, and so they took the slowdown in good stride. Bruenor managed to find a dry spot for their camp, and they enjoyed a hearty meal and a fretful night filled with the sounds of wolves howling and yetis growling.

Still, they managed to find a bit of sleep, but when they awoke they had to wonder how good a thing that was. In the night a wolf, by the shape of the tracks, had come in and made off with a good deal of their supplies.

Despite loss and weariness, it was in good spirits that they made the beginning of the pass that day. No snow had fallen there, and the ground was stony and dry. They camped just within the protective walls of stone that night and were surprised when other lights appeared in the darkness. There was a camp of some sort higher up on the gorge's eastern wall.

"Well, go and see what that's all about," Bruenor bade Regis.

Regis looked at him skeptically.

"Ye're the sneak, ain't ye?" the dwarf said.

With a helpless chuckle, Regis picked himself up from the stone on which he had been enjoying his meal, gave a series of belches, and rubbed his full belly.

"Get all the wind outta ye afore ye try sneakin' up on our friends," the dwarf advised.

Regis burped again and patted his belly then, with a resigned sigh he always seemed to be doing around Bruenor, he turned and started off into the dark night, leaving the dwarf to do the clean-up.

The smell of venison cooking as he neared the encampment, climbing quietly up a steep rock face, made the halfling think that perhaps Bruenor had been right in sending him out. Perhaps they would find a band of rangers willing to share the spoils of their hunt, or a band of merchants who had ridden out of the dale before them, and would be glad to hire them on as guards for the duration of the journey to Luskan.

Lost in fantasies of comfort, so eager to get his mouth on that beautiful-smelling venison, Regis nearly pulled himself full over the ledge with a big smile. Caution got the better of the halfling, though, and it was a good thing it did. As he pulled himself up slowly, lifting to just peek over the ledge, he saw that these were not rangers and were not merchants, but orcs. Big, smelly, ugly, nasty orcs. Fierce mountain orcs, wearing the skins of yetis, tearing at the hocks of venison with abandon, crunching cartilage and bone, swearing at each other and jostling for every piece they tore off the cooking carcass.

It took Regis a few moments to even realize that his arms had gone weak, and he had to catch himself before falling off the thirty-foot cliff. Slowly, trying hard not to scream out, trying hard not to breathe too loudly, he lowered himself back below the lip.

In times past, that would have been the end of it, with Regis scrambling back down then running to Bruenor to report that there was nothing to be gained. But now, bolstered by the confidence that had come through his efforts on the road over the last few months, where he had worked hard to play an important role in his friends' heroics, and still stung by the nearly constant dismissal others showed to him when speaking of the Companions of the Hall, Regis decided it was not yet time to turn back. Far from it.

The halfling would get himself a meal of venison and one for Bruenor, too. But how?

The halfling worked himself around to the side, just a bit. Once out of the illumination of the firelight, he peeked over the ledge again. The orcs remained engrossed in their meal. One fight nearly broke out as two reached for the same chunk of meat, the first one even trying to bite the arm of the second as it reached in.

In the commotion that ensued, Regis went up over the ledge, staying flat on his belly and crawling behind a rock. A few moments later, with another squabble breaking out at the camp, the halfling picked a course and moved closer, and closer again.

"O, but now I've done it," Regis silently mouthed. "I'll get myself killed, to be sure. Or worse, captured, and Bruenor will get himself killed coming to fiznd me!"

The potential of that thought weighed heavily on the little halfling. The dwarf was a brutal foe, Regis knew, and these orcs would feel his wrath terribly, but they were big and tough, and there were six of them after all.

The thought that he might get his friend killed almost turned the halfling back.

Almost.

Eventually he was close enough to smell the ugly brutes, and, more importantly, to notice some of the particulars about them. Like the fact that one was wearing a fairly expensive bracelet of gold, with a clasp that Regis knew he could easily undo.

A plan began to take shape.

The orc with the bracelet had a huge chunk of deer, a rear leg, in that hand. The nasty creature brought it up to its chomping mouth, then brought it back down to its side, then up and down, repeatedly and predictably.

Regis waited patiently for the next struggle that orc had with the beast to its left, as he knew that it would, as they all were, one after the other. As the bracelet-wearing brute held the venison out to the right defensively, fending off the advance of the creature on its left, a small hand came up from the shadows, taking the bracelet with a simple flick of plump little fingers.

The halfling brought his hand down, but to the right and not back, taking his loot to the pocket of the orc sitting to the right of his victim. In it went, softly and silently, and Regis took care to hang the end of the chain out in open sight.

The halfling quickly went back behind his rock and waited.

He heard his victim start with surprise a moment later.

"Who taked it?" the orc asked in its own brutish tongue, some of which Regis understood.

"Take what?" blustered the orc to the left. "Yer got yerself the bestest piece, ye glutton!"

"Yer taked me chain!" the victimized orc growled. It brought the deer leg across, smacking the other orc hard on the head.

"Aw, now how's Tuko got it?" asked another of the group. Ironically, it was the one with the chain hanging out of its pocket. "Yer been keeping yer hand away from Tuko all night!"

Things calmed for a second. Regis held his breath.

"Yer right, ain't ye, Ginick?" asked the victimized orc, and from its sly tone, Regis knew that the dim-witted creature had spotted something.

A terrible row ensued, with Regis's victim leaping up and swinging the deer leg in both hands like a club, aiming for Ginick's head. The target orc blocked with a burly arm and came up hard, catching the other about the waist and bearing it right over poor

Tuko the other way. Soon all six were into it—pulling each other's hair, clubbing, punching, and biting.

Regis crept away soon after, enough venison in hand to satisfy a hungry dwarf and a hungrier halfling.

And wearing on his left wrist a newly acquired gold bracelet, one that had conveniently dropped from the pocket of a falsely accused orc thief.

II

DIVERGING ROADS

We'd've found a faster road with a bit of wizard's magic," Catti-brie remarked. It wasn't the first time the woman had good-naturedly ribbed Drizzt about his refusal to accept Val-Doussen's offer. "We'd be well on our way back, I'm thinking, and with Wulfgar in tow."

"You sound more like a dwarf every day," Drizzt countered, using a stick to prod the fire upon which a fine stew was cooking. "You should begin to worry when you notice an aversion to open spaces, like the road we now travel.

"No, wait!" the drow sarcastically exclaimed, as if the truth had just come to him. "Are you not expressing just such an aversion?"

"Keep waggin' yer tongue, Drizzt Do'Urden," Catti-brie muttered quietly. "Ye might be fine with yer spinning blades, but how are ye with catching a few stinging arrows?"

"I have already cut your bowstring," the drow casually replied, leaning forward and taking a sip of the steaming stew.

Catti-brie actually started to look over at Taulmaril, lying unstrung at the side of the fallen log on which she now sat. She put on a smirk, though, and turned back to her sarcastic friend. "I'm just thinking we might have missed *Sea Sprite* as she put out for her last run o' the season," Catti-brie said, seriously, this time.

Indeed, the wind had taken on a bit of a bite over the last few days, autumn fast flowing past. Deudermont often took *Sea Sprite* out at this time of the year to haunt the waters off Waterdeep for a couple of tendays before turning south to warmer climes and more active pirates.

Drizzt knew it, too, as was evident by the frown that crossed his angular features. That little possibility had been troubling him since he and Catti-brie had left the Hosttower, and made him wonder if his refusal of Val-Doussen's offer had been too selfish an act.

"All the fool mage wanted was a bit of talking," the woman went on. "A few hours of yer time would've made him happy and would have saved us a tenday of walking—and no, I'm not fearing the road or even bothered by it, and ye know it! There's no place in the world I'd rather be than on the road beside ye, but we've got others to think of, and it'd be better for Bruenor, and for Wulfgar, if we find him before he gets into too much more trouble."

Drizzt started to respond with a reminder that Wulfgar, if he was indeed with Deudermont and the crew of *Sea Sprite*, was in fine hands, was among allies at least as powerful as the Companions of the Hall. He held the words, though, and considered Catti-brie's argument more carefully, truly hearing what she was saying instead of reflexively formulating a defensive answer.

He knew she was right, that Wulfgar, that all of them, would be better off if they were reunited. Perhaps he should have spent a few hours talking to Val-Doussen.

"So just tell me why ye didn't," Catti-brie gently prompted. "Ye could've got us to Waterdeep in the blink of a wizard's eye, and

I'm knowing ye believe that to be a good thing. And yet ye didn't, so might ye be telling me why?"

"Val-Doussen is no scholar," Drizzt replied.

Catti-brie leaned in and took the spoon from him, then dipped it into the stew and, brushing her thick, long auburn hair back from her face, took a sip. She stared at Drizzt all the while, her inquisitive expression indicating that he should elaborate.

"His interest in Menzoberranzan is one of personal gain and nothing more," Drizzt remarked. "He had no desire for bettering the world, but only hoped that something I would tell him might offer him an advantage he could exploit."

Still Catti-brie stared at him, obviously not catching on. Even if Drizzt's words were true, why, given Drizzt's relationship with his wicked kin, did that even matter?

"He hoped I would unveil some of the mysteries of the drow," Drizzt continued, undaunted by his companion's expression.

"And even if ye did, from what I know of Menzoberranzan Val-Doussen couldn't be using yer words for anything more than his own doom," Catti-brie put in, and sincerely, for she had visited that exotic dark elf city, and she knew well the great power of the place.

Drizzt shrugged and reached for the spoon, but Catti-brie, smiling widely, pulled it away from him.

Drizzt sat back, staring at her, not sharing her smile. He was deep in concentration, needing to make his point. "Val-Doussen hoped to personally profit from my words, to use my tales for his own nefarious reasons, and at the expense of those my information delivered unto him. Be it my kin in Menzoberranzan, or Bruenor's in Mithral Hall, my actions would have been no less wicked."

"I'd not be comparing Clan Battlehammer to . . ." Catti-brie started.

"I am not," Drizzt assured her. "I speak of nothing more here than my own principles. If Val-Doussen sought information of a goblin settlement that he could lead a preemptive assault against them, I would gladly comply, because I trust that such a goblin settlement would soon enough cause tragedy to any living nearby."

"And didn't yer own kin come to Mithral Hall?" Catti-brie asked, following the logic.

"Once," Drizzt admitted. "But as far as I know, my kin are not on their way back to the surface world in search of plunder and mayhem."

"As far as ye know."

"Besides, anything I offered to Val-Doussen would not have prevented any dark elf raids in any case," Drizzt went on, stepping lightly so that Catti-brie could not catch him in a logic trap. "No, more likely, the fool would have gone to Menzoberranzan, alone or with others, in some attempt at grand thievery. That most likely would have done no more than to stir up the dark elves into murderous revenge."

Catti-brie started to ask another question, but just sat back instead, staring at her friend. Finally, she nodded and said, "Ye're making a bit o' assumptions there."

Drizzt didn't begin to disagree, audibly or with his body language.

"But I'm seeing yer point that ye shouldn't be mixing yerself up with those of less than honorable intent."

"You respect that?" Drizzt asked.

Catti-brie gave what might have been an agreeing nod.

"Then give me the spoon," the dark elf said more forcefully. "I'm starving!"

In response, Catti-brie moved forward and dipped the spoon into the pot, then lifted it toward Drizzt's waiting lips. At the last moment, the drow's lavender eyes closed against the steam, the woman pulled the spoon back to her own lips.

Drizzt's eyes popped open, his surprised and angry expression overwhelmed by the playful and teasing stare of Catti-brie. He went forward in a sudden burst, falling over the woman and knocking her right off the back of the log, then wrestling with her for the spoon.

Neither Drizzt nor Catti-brie could deny the truth that there was no place in all the world they would rather be.

✕ ✕ ✕ ✕ ✕

The walls climbed up around the small party, a combination of dark gray-brown cliff facings and patches of steeply sloping green grass. A few trees dotted the sides of the gorge, small and thin things, really, unable to get firm footing or to send their roots very deep into the rocky ground.

The place was ripe for an ambush, Le'lorinel understood, but neither the elf nor the other four members of the party were the least bit worried of any such possibility. Sheila Kree and her ruffians owned this gorge. Le'lorinel had caught the group's leader, the brown-haired woman named Genny, offering a few subtle signals toward the peaks. Sentries were obviously in place there.

There would be no calls, though, for none would be heard beyond a few dozen strides. In the distance, Le'lorinel could hear the constant song of the river that had cut this gorge, flowing underground now, under the left-hand wall as they made their way to the south. Directly ahead, some distance away, the surf thundered against the rocky coast. The wind blew down from behind them, filling their ears. The chilling wind of Icewind Dale escaped the tundra through this mountain pass.

Le'lorinel felt strangely comfortable in this seemingly inhospitable and forlorn place. The elf felt a sense of freedom away from the clutter of society that had never held much interest. Perhaps there would be more to this relationship with Sheila Kree, Le'lorinel mused. Perhaps after the business with Drizzt Do'Urden was finished, Le'lorinel could stay on with Kree's band, serving as a sentry in this very gorge.

Of course, that all hinged on whether or not the elf remained alive after an encounter with the deadly dark elf, and in truth, unless Le'lorinel could find some way to get the enchanted ring back from Genny, that seemed a remote possibility indeed.

Without that ring, would Le'lorinel even dare to go against the dark elf?

A shudder coursed the elf's spine, one brought on by thoughts and not the chilly wind.

The party moved past several small openings, natural vents for the caverns that served as Kree's home in the three-hundred-foot mound to the left, a series of caves settled above the present-day river. Down around a bend in the gorge, they came to a wide natural alcove and a larger cave entrance, a place where the river had once cut its way out through the limestone rock.

A trio of guards sat among the crags to the right-hand wall within, huddled in the shadows, throwing bones and chewing near-raw mutton, their heavy weapons close at hand. Like the three who had accompanied Le'lorinel to this place, the guards were huge, obviously a product of mixed parentage, human and ogre, and favoring the ogre side indeed.

They bristled at the approach of the band but didn't seem too concerned, and Le'lorinel understood that the sentries along the gorge had likely warned them of the intruders.

"Where is the boss?" Genny asked.

"Chogurugga in her room," one soldier grunted in reply.

"Not Chogurugga," said Genny "Sheila Kree. The real boss."

Le'lorinel didn't miss the scowl that came at the woman at that proclamation. The elf readily understood that there was some kind of power struggle going on here, likely between the pirates and the ogres.

One of the guards grunted and showed its nasty yellow teeth, then motioned toward the back of the cave.

The three accompanying soldiers took out torches and set them ablaze. On the travelers went, winding their way through a myriad of spectacular natural designs. At first, Le'lorinel thought running water was all around them, cascading down the sides of the tunnel in wide, graceful waterfalls, but as the elf looked closer the truth became evident. It was not water, but formations of rock left behind by the old river, limestone solidified into waterfall images still slick from the dripping that came with every rainfall.

Great tunnels ran off the main one, many winding up, spiraling, into the mound, others branching off at this level often forming huge, boulder-filled chambers. So many shapes assaulted the elf's outdoor sensibilities! Images of animals and weapons, of lovers entwined and great forests, of whatever Le'lorinel's imagination allowed the elf to see! Le'lorinel was a creature of the forest, a creature of the moon, and had never before been underground. For the very first time, the elf gained some appreciation of the dwarves and the halflings, the gnomes and any other race that chose the subterranean world over that of the open sky.

No, not *any* other race, Le'lorinel promptly reminded. Not the drow, those ebon-skinned devils of lightless chambers. Certainly there was beauty here, but beauty only reflected in the light of the torches.

The party moved on in near silence, save the crackle of the torches, for the floor was of clay, smooth and soft. They descended for some time along the main chamber, the primary riverbed of ages past, and moved beyond several other guard stations, sometimes manned by half-ogres, once by a pair of true ogres, and once by normal-looking men—pirates, judging from their dress and from the company they kept.

Le'lorinel took it all in halfheartedly then, too concerned with the forthcoming meeting, the all-important plea that had to be made to Sheila Kree. With Kree's assistance, Le'lorinel might find the end of a long, heart-wrenching road. Without Kree's favor, Le'lorinel would likely wind up dead and discarded in one of these side-passages.

And worse, to the elf's sensibilities, Drizzt Do'Urden would remain very much alive.

Genny turned aside suddenly, down a narrow side passage. Both Genny and Le'lorinel had to drop to all fours to continue on, crawling under a low overhang of solid stone. Their three larger companions had to get right down on their bellies and crawl. On the other side was a wide chamber of startling design, widening up and out to the left, its stalactite ceiling many, many feet above.

Genny didn't even look at it, though, but rather focused on a small hole in the floor, moving to a ladder that had been set into one wall. Down she went, followed by a guard, then Le'lorinel, then the other two.

Far down, perhaps a hundred steps, they came to another corridor and set off, arriving soon after in another cave. It was a huge cavern, open to the southwest, to the rocky bay and the sea beyond. Water poured in from many openings in the walls and ceiling, the river emptying into the sea.

In the cave sat *Bloody Keel*, moored to the western wall, with sailors crawling all over her repairing the rigging and hull damage.

"Now that you've seen this much, you would be wise to pray to whatever god you know that Sheila Kree accepts you," Genny whispered to the elf. "There are but two ways out of here, as a friend or as a corpse."

Looking at the ruffian crew scrambling all about the ship, cut-throats all, Le'lorinel didn't doubt those words for a moment.

Genny led the way out of another exit, this one winding back up into the mountain from the back of the docking cave. The passages smelled of smoke, and were torch-lit all the way, so the escorting guards doused their own torches and put them away. Higher and higher they climbed into the mountain, passing storerooms and barracks, crossing through an area that seemed to Le'lorinel to be reserved for the pirates, and another horribly smelly place that housed the ogre clan.

More than a few hungry gazes came the elf's way as they passed by the ravenous ogres, but none came close enough to even prod Le'lorinel. Their respect for Kree was tremendous, the elf recognized, simply from the fact that they weren't causing any trouble. Le'lorinel had enough experience with ogres to know that they were usually unruly and more than ready to make a meal of any smaller humanoid they encountered.

They came to the highest levels of the mound soon after, pausing in an open chamber lined by several doors. Genny motioned for the other four to wait there while she went to the center door of the room, knocked, and disappeared through the door. She returned a short while later.

"Come," she bade Le'lorinel.

When the three brutish guards moved to escort the elf, Genny held them at bay with an upraised hand. "Go get some food," the brown-haired woman instructed the half-ogres.

Le'lorinel glanced at the departing half-ogres curiously, not sure whether this signaled that Sheila Kree trusted Genny's word, or whether the pirate was simply too confident or too well-protected to care.

Le'lorinel figured it must be the latter.

Sheila Kree, dressed in nothing more than light breeches and a thin, sleeveless shirt, was standing in the room within, amongst piles of furs, staring out her window at the wide waters. She turned when Genny announced Le'lorinel, her smile bright on her freckled face, her green eyes shining under the crown of her tied-up red hair.

"I've been told ye're fearing for me life, elf," the pirate leader remarked. "I'm touched by yer concern."

Le'lorinel stared at her curiously.

"Ye've come to warn me of a dark elf, so says Genny," the pirate clarified.

"I have come to slay a dark elf," Le'lorinel corrected. "That my actions will benefit you as well is merely a fortunate coincidence."

Sheila Kree gave a great belly laugh and strode over to stand right in front of the elf, towering over Le'lorinel. The pirate's eyes roamed up and down Le'lorinel's slender, even delicate form. "Fortunate for yerself, or for me?"

"For both, I would guess," Le'lorinel answered.

"Ye must hate this drow more than a bit to have come here," Sheila Kree remarked.

"More than you can possibly imagine."

"And would ye tell me why?"

"It is a long tale," Le'lorinel said.

"Well, since winter's fast coming and *Bloody Keel*'s still in dock, it's looking like I've got the time," Sheila Kree said with another laugh. She swept her arm out toward some piles of furs, motioning for Le'lorinel to join her.

They talked for the rest of the afternoon, with Le'lorinel giving an honest, if slanted account of the many errors of Drizzt Do'Urden. Sheila Kree listened intently, as did Genny, as did a third woman, Bellany, who came in soon after the elf had begun the tale. All three seemed more than a little amused and interested, and as time went on, Le'lorinel relaxed even more.

When the tale was done, both Bellany and Genny applauded,

but just for a moment stopping and looking to Sheila for a cue.

"A good tale," the pirate leader decided. "And I find that I believe yer words. Ye'll understand that we've much to check on afore we let ye have a free run."

"Of course," Le'lorinel agreed, giving a slight bow.

"Ye give over yer weapons, and we'll set ye in a room," Sheila explained. "I've no work for ye right now, so ye can get yer rest from the long road." As she finished, the pirate held out her hand.

Le'lorinel considered things for just a moment, then decided that Kree and her associates—especially the one named Bellany, who Le'lorinel had concluded was a spellcaster, likely a sorceress—in truth made surrendering the weapons nothing more than symbolic. With a smile at the fiery pirate, the elf turned over the dagger and sword.

⚔ ⚔ ⚔ ⚔ ⚔

"I suppose you consider this humorous," Drizzt said dryly, his tone interrupted only by the occasional wheeze as he tried to draw breath.

He was lying on the ground, facedown in the dirt, with six hundred pounds of panther draped over him. He had called up Guenhwyvar to do some hunting while he and Catti-brie continued their mock battle over the stew, but then the woman had whispered something in Guen's ear, and the cat, obviously gender loyal, had brought Drizzt down with a great flying tackle.

A few feet away, Catti-brie was thoroughly enjoying her stew.

"Ye do look a bit ridiculous," she admitted between sips.

Drizzt scrambled, and almost slipped out from under the panther. Guenhwyvar dropped a huge paw on his shoulder, extracting long claws and holding him fast.

"Ye keep on with yer fighting and Guen'll have herself a meal," Catti-brie remarked.

Drizzt's lavender eyes narrowed. "There remains a small matter of repayment," he said quietly.

Catti-brie gave a snort, then moved down close to him, on her knees. She lifted a spoon full of stew and blew on it gently, then moved it out toward Drizzt, slowly, teasingly. It almost reached his mouth when the woman pulled it back abruptly, the spoon disappearing into her mouth.

Her smile went away fast, though, as she saw Guenhwyvar dissipating into a gray mist. The cat protested, but the dismissal of her master, Drizzt, could not be ignored.

Catti-brie darted off into the woods with Drizzt in fast pursuit.

He caught her with a leaping tackle a short distance away, bearing her to the ground beneath him, then using his amazing agility and deceptive strength to roll her over and pin her. The firelight was lost behind the trees and shrubs, the starlight and the glow of a half moon alone highlighting the woman's beautiful features.

"Ye call this repayment?" the woman teased when Drizzt was atop her, straddling her and holding her arms to the ground above her head.

"Only beginning," he promised.

Catti-brie started to laugh, but stopped suddenly, her look to Drizzt becoming serious, even concerned.

"What is it?" the perceptive drow asked. He backed off a bit, letting go of her arms.

"With any luck, we'll be finding Wulfgar," Catti-brie said.

"That is our hope, yes," the drow agreed.

"How're ye feeling about that?" the woman asked bluntly.

Drizzt sat up straighter, staring at her hard. "How should I feel?"

"Are ye jealous?" Catti-brie asked. "Are ye fearing that Wulfgar's return—if he should return with us, I mean—will change some things in yer life that ye're not wanting changed?"

Drizzt gave a helpless chuckle, overwhelmed by Catti-brie's straightforwardness and honesty. Something was beginning to burn between them, the drow knew, something long overdue yet still amazing and unexpected. Catti-brie had once loved Wulfgar, had even been engaged to marry him before his apparent demise in Mithral Hall, so what would happen if Wulfgar returned to them now—not the Wulfgar who had run away, the Wulfgar who had slapped Catti-brie hard—but the man they had once known, the man who had once taken Catti-brie's heart?

"Do I hope that Wulfgar's return will not affect our relationship in any negative way?" he asked. "Of course I do. And saying that, do I hope that Wulfgar returns to us? Of course I do. And I pray that he has climbed out of his darkness, back to the man we both once knew and loved."

Catti-brie settled comfortably and didn't interrupt, her interested expression prompting him to elaborate.

Drizzt began with a shrug. "I do not wish to live my life in a jealous manner," he said. "And I especially can not think in those terms with any of my true friends. My stake in Wulfgar's return is no less than your own. My happiness will be greater if once again the proud and noble barbarian I once adventured beside returns to my life.

"As for our friendship and what may come of it," Drizzt continued quietly, but with that same old self-assurance, that inner guidance that had walked the drow out of wicked Menzoberranzan and had carried him through so many difficult adventures and decisions ever since.

He gave a wistful smile and a shrug. "I live my life in the best manner I can," he said. "I act honestly and in good faith and with the hopes of good friendship, and I hope that things turn out for the best. I can only be this drow you see before you, whether or not Wulfgar returns to us. If in your heart and in mine, there is meant to be more between us, then it shall be. If not. . . ." He stopped and smiled and shrugged again.

"There ye go, with yer tongue wandering about again," Catti-brie said. "Did ye ever think ye should just shut up and kiss me?"

12

THE LAVENDER-EYED STATUE

"Pull quiet, you oafs," Gayselle softly scolded as the small skiff approached the imposing lights of Waterdeep harbor. "I hope to make shore without any notice at all."

The three oarsmen, half-ogres with burly muscles that lacked a gentle touch, grumbled amongst themselves but did try, with no success, to quiet the splash of the oars. Gayselle suffered through it, knowing they were doing the best they could. She would be glad when this business was ended, when she could be away from her present companions, whose names she did not know but who she'd nicknamed Lumpy, Grumpy, and Dumb-bunny.

She stayed up front of the skiff, trying to make out some markers along the shoreline that would guide her in. She had put into Waterdeep many, many times over the last few years and knew the place well. Most of all now, she wanted to avoid the long wharves and larger ships, wanted to get into the smaller, less observed and regulated docks, where a temporary berth could be bought for a few coins.

To her relief she noted that few of the guards were moving about the pier this dark evening. The skiff, even with the half-ogres' splashing, had little trouble gliding into the collection of small docks to the south of the long wharves.

Gayselle shifted back and reached to the nearest brute, Grumpy, holding out a satchel that held three small vials. "Drink and shift to human form," she explained. When Grumpy gave her a lewd smile as he took the satchel, she added, "A *male* human form. Sheila Kree would not suffer one of you to even briefly assume the form of a woman."

That brought some more grumbling from the brutes, but they each took a bottle and quaffed the liquid contents. One after another they transformed their physical features into those of human men.

Gayselle nodded with satisfaction and took a few long and steady breaths, considering the course before her. She knew the location of the target's house, of course. It was not far from the docks, set up on a hill above a rocky cove. They had to be done with this dark business quickly, she knew, for the polymorph potions would not last for very long, and the last thing Gayselle wanted was to be walking along Waterdeep's streets accompanied by a trio of half-ogres.

The woman made up her mind then and there that if the potions wore off and her companions became obvious as intruders, she would abandon them and go off on her own, deeper into the city, where she had friends who could get her back to Sheila Kree.

They set up the boat against one of the smaller docks, tying it off beside a dozen other similar boats quietly bumping the pier with the gentle ebb and flow of the tide. With no one about, Gayselle and her three "human" escorts moved with all speed to the north, off the docks and onto the winding avenues that would take them to Captain Deudermont's house.

⚔ ⚔ ⚔ ⚔ ⚔

Not so far away, Drizzt and Catti-brie walked through Waterdeep's northern gate, the drow easily brushing away the hard stares that came at him from nearly every sentry. One or two recognized him for who he was and said as much to their nervous companions, but it would take more than a few reassuring words to alleviate the average surface dweller's trepidation toward a drow elf.

It didn't bother Drizzt, for he had played through this scenario a hundred times before.

"They know ye, don't ye worry," Catti-brie whispered to him.

"Some," he agreed.

"Enough," the woman said flatly. "Ye canno' be expecting all the world to know yer name."

Drizzt gave a chuckle at that and shook his head in agreement. "And I know well enough that no matter what I may accomplish in my life, I will suffer their stares." He gave a sincere smile and a shrug. "Suffer is not the right word," he assured her. "Not any more."

Catti-brie started to respond but stopped short, her defiant words defeated by Drizzt's disarming smile. She had fought this battle for acceptance beside her friend for all these years, in Icewind Dale, in Mithral Hall and Silverymoon, and even here in Waterdeep, and in every city and town along the Sword Coast during the years they sailed with Deudermont. In many ways, Catti-brie understood at that telling moment, she was more bothered by the stares than was Drizzt. She forced herself to take his lead this time, to let the looks slide off her shoulders, for surely Drizzt was doing just that. She could tell from the sincerity of his smile.

Drizzt stopped and spun about to face the guards, and the nearest couple jumped back in surprise.

"Is *Sea Sprite* in?" the drow asked.

"*S-Sea Sprite?*" one stammered in reply. "In where? What?"

An older soldier stepped by the flustered pair. "Captain Deudermont is not yet in," he explained. "Though he's expected for a last stop at least before the winter sets in."

Drizzt touched his hand to his forehead in a salute of thanks, then spun back and walked off with Catti-brie.

※ ※ ※ ※ ※

Delly Curtie was in fine spirits this evening. She had this feeling that Wulfgar would soon return with Aegis-fang and that she and her husband could finally get on with their lives.

Delly wasn't quite sure what that meant. Would they return to Luskan and life at the Cutlass with Arumn Gardpeck? She didn't think so. No, Delly understood that this hunt for Aegis-fang was about more than the retrieval of a warhammer—had it been just that, Delly would have discouraged Wulfgar from ever going out in search of the weapon.

This hunt was about Wulfgar finding himself, his past and his heart, and when that happened, Delly believed, he would also find his way back home—his true home, in Icewind Dale.

"And we will go there with him," she said to Colson, as she held the baby girl out at arms' length.

The thought of Icewind Dale appealed to Delly. She knew the hardships of the region, knew all about the tremendous snows and powerful winds, of the goblins and the yetis and other perils. But to Delly, who had grown up on the dirty streets of Luskan, there seemed something clean about Icewind Dale, something honest and pure, and in any case, she would be beside the man she loved, the man she loved more every day. She knew that when Wulfgar found himself, their relationship would only grow stronger.

She began to sing, then, dancing gracefully around the room, swinging Colson about as she turned and skittered, this way and that.

"Daddy will be home soon," she promised their daughter, and, as if understanding, Colson laughed.

And Delly danced.

And all the world seemed beautiful and full of possibilities.

⚔ ⚔ ⚔ ⚔ ⚔

Captain Deudermont's house was indeed palatial, even by Waterdhavian standards. It was two stories tall, with more than a dozen rooms. A great sweeping stairway dominated the foyer, which also sported a domed alcove that held two grand wooden double doors, each decorated with the carving of one half of a three-masted schooner. When the doors were closed, the image of *Sea Sprite* was clear to see. A second staircase in back led to the drawing room that overlooked the rocky cove and the sea.

This was Waterdeep, the City of Splendors, a city of laws. But despite the many patrols of the fabled Waterdhavian Watch and the general civility of the populace, most of the larger houses, Deudermont's included, also employed personal guards.

Deudermont had hired two, former soldiers, former sailors, both of whom had actually served on *Sea Sprite* many years before. They were friends as much as hired hands, house guests as much as sentries. Though they took their job seriously, they couldn't help but be lax about their work. Every day was inevitably uneventful. Thus, the pair helped out with chores, working with Delly at repairing the shingles blown away by a sea wind, or with the nearly constant painting of the clapboards. They cooked and they cleaned. Sometimes they carried their weapons, and sometimes they did not, for they understood, and so did Deudermont, that they were there more as a preventative measure than anything else. The thieves of

Waterdeep avoided homes known to house guards.

Thus the pair were perfectly unprepared for what befell the House of Deudermont that dark night.

Gayselle was the first to Deudermont's front door, accompanied by one of the brutes who, using the polymorph potion, was doing a pretty fair imitation of the physical traits of Captain Deudermont. So good, in fact, that Gayselle found herself wondering if she had misnamed the brute Dumb-bunny. With a look around to see that the streets were quiet, Gayselle nodded to Lumpy, who was standing at the end of the walk, between the two hedgerows. Immediately, the brute began rubbing its feet on the stones, gaining traction and grinning wickedly.

One of the double doors opened to the knock, just three or four inches, for it was, as expected, secured with a chain. A clean-shaven, large man with short black hair and a brow so furrowed it seemed as if it could shield his eyes from a noonday sun, answered.

"Can I help you . . . ?"

His voice trailed off, though, as he scanned the man standing behind the woman, a man who surely resembled Captain Deudermont.

"I have brought the brother of Captain Deudermont," Gayselle answered. "Come to speak with his long-lost sibling."

The guard's eyes widened for just a moment, then he resumed his steely, professional demeanor. "Well met," he offered, "but I fear that your brother is not in Waterdeep at this time. Tell me where you will be staying and I will inform him as soon as he returns."

"Our funds are low," Gayselle answered quickly. "We have been on the road for a long time. We were hoping to find shelter here."

The guard thought it over for just a moment but then shook his head. His orders concerning such matters were uncompromising, despite this surprising twist, and especially so with a woman and her child as guests in the house. He started to explain, to tell them he was sorry, but that they could find shelter at one of several inns for a reasonable price.

Gayselle was hardly listening. She casually looked back down the walk, to the eager half-ogre. The pirate gave a slight nod, setting Lumpy into a charge.

"Perhaps you will then open your door for the third of my group," the woman said sweetly.

Again the guard shook his head. "I doubt—" he started to say, but then his words and his breath were stolen away as the half-ogre hit the doors in a dead run, splintering wood and tearing free the chain anchors. The guard was thrown back and to the floor, and the half-ogre stumbled in to land atop him.

In went Gayselle and the Deudermont impersonator, drawing weapons. The half-ogre willed away the illusionary image, dropping the human facade.

The guard on the floor started to call out, as he tried to scramble away from the half-ogre, but Gayselle was there, dagger in hand. With a swift and sure movement, she slashed open his throat.

The second guard came through the door at the side of the foyer. Then, his expression one of the purest horror, he sprinted for the stands.

Gayselle's dagger caught him in the back of the leg, hamstringing him. He continued on stubbornly, limping up the stairs and calling out. Dumb-bunny caught up to him and with fearful strength yanked him off the stairs and sent him flying back down to the bottom. The other half-ogre waited there.

Grumpy, still in human form, entered. He calmly closed the doors, though one no longer sat straight on its bent hinges.

⚔ ⚔ ⚔ ⚔ ⚔

Delly heard clearly the sour note from below that ended her song. Having grown up around ruffians, having seen and been involved in many, many brawls, the woman understood the gist of what was happening below.

"By the gods," she muttered, biting off a wail before it could give her and Colson away.

She hugged the child close to her and rushed to the door. She cracked it, peeked out, then swung it wide. She paused only long enough to kick off her hard shoes, knowing they would give her away, then padded quietly along the corridor between the wall and the banister. She hugged the wall, not wanting to be spotted from the foyer below, and that, she could tell from the noises—grunting and heavy punches—was where the intruders were. Had she been alone, she would have rushed down the stairs and joined in the fight, but with Colson in her arms, the woman's only thoughts were for the safety of her child.

Past the front stairs, Delly turned down a side passage and ran full out, cutting through Deudermont's personal suite to the back staircase. Down she went, holding her breath with every step, for she had no way of knowing if others might be in the house, perhaps even in the room below.

She heard a noise above her and understood that she had few options, so she pushed right through the door into the elaborate drawing room. One of the windows was open across the wide room. A chill breeze was blowing in, just catching the edge of one opened drape, fluttering it below the sash tie.

Delly considered the route. Those large windows overlooked a rocky drop to the cove. She cursed herself then for having discarded her shoes, but she knew in her heart that it made little difference. The climb was too steep and too treacherous—she doubted the intruders had gained access from that direction—and she didn't dare attempt it with Colson in her arms.

But where to go?

She turned for the room's main doors, leading to a corridor to the foyer. There were side rooms off that corridor, including the kitchen, which held a garbage chute. Thinking she and Colson could hide in there, she rushed to the doors and cracked them open—but slammed them immediately and dropped the locking bar across them when she saw the approach of hulking figures. She heard running steps on the other side, followed by a tremendous crash as someone hurled himself against the locked doors.

Delly glanced all around, to the stairs and the open window, not knowing where she should run. So flustered was she that she didn't even see another form slip into the room.

The doors got hit again and started to crack. Delly heard one powerful man pounding hard against the wood. The woman retreated.

Then came some running footsteps, and another threw himself against the doors. They burst open, a large hulking form going down atop the pile of kindling. A woman entered, flanked by one, and the second as the door-breaker stood up. They were two of the ugliest, most imposing brutes Delly Curtie had ever seen. She didn't know what they were, having had few experiences outside of Luskan, but from their splotchy greenish skin and sheer size she understood that they had to be some kind of giantkin.

"Well, well, pretty one," said the strange woman with a wicked smile. "You're not thinking of leaving before the party is over, are you?"

Delly turned for the stairs but didn't even start that way, seeing yet another of the brutes slowly descending, eyeing her lewdly with every step.

Delly considered the window behind her, the one that she and Wulfgar used to spend so many hours at, watching the setting sun or the reflection of the stars on the dark waters. She couldn't possibly get out and away without being caught, but she honestly considered that route anyway, thought of running full speed and throwing herself and Colson down onto the rocks, ending it quickly and mercifully.

Delly Curtie knew this type of ruffian and understood that she was surely doomed.

The woman and her two companions took a step toward her.

The window, Delly decided. She turned and fled, determined to leap far and wide to ensure a quick and painless end.

But the third giantkin had come down from the stairs by then, Delly's hesitation costing her the suicidal escape. The brute caught her easily with one huge arm, pinning her tightly to its massive chest.

It turned back, laughing, and was joined by the howls of its two ogre companions. The woman, though, seemed hardly amused. She stalked up to Delly, eyeing her every inch.

"You're Deudermont's woman, aren't you?" she asked.

"No," Delly answered honestly, but her sincerity was far from apparent in her tone, since she was trembling so with fear.

She wasn't so much afraid for herself as for Colson, though she knew that the next few moments of her life, likely the last few moments of her life, were going to be as horrible as anything she had ever known.

The strange woman calmly walked over to her, smiling. "Deudermont is your man?"

"No," Delly repeated, a bit more confidently.

The woman slapped her hard across the face, a blow that had Delly staggering back a step. A thug promptly pulled her forward, though, back into striking range.

"She's a tender one," the brute said with a lewd chuckle, and it gave Delly's arms a squeeze. "We plays with her 'fore we eats her!"

The other two in the room started laughing, one of them gyrating its hips crudely.

Delly felt her legs going weak beneath her, but she gritted her teeth and strengthened her resolve, realizing that she had a duty that went beyond the sacrifice that was soon to be forced upon her.

"Do as ye will with me," she said. "And I'll be making it good for ye, so long as ye don't hurt me baby."

The strange woman's eyes narrowed as Delly said that, the woman obviously not thrilled about Delly taking any kind of control at all. "You get your fun later," she said to her three companions, then she swiveled her head, scanning each in turn. "Now go and gather some loot. You wouldn't wish to face the boss without any loot, now would you?"

The brute holding Delly tensed at the words but didn't let her go. Its companions, however, scrambled wildly, falling all over each other in an attempt to satisfy their boss's demands.

"Please," Delly said to the woman. "I'm not a threat to ye and won't be any trouble. Just don't be hurting me babe. Ye're a woman, so ye know."

"Shut your mouth," the stranger interrupted harshly.

"Eats 'em both!" the giantkin holding Delly shouted, taking a cue from the woman's dismissive tone.

The woman came forward a step, hand upraised, and Delly flinched. But this slap went past her, striking the surprised brute. The woman stepped back, eyeing Delly once more.

"We will see about the baby," she said calmly.

"Please," Delly pleaded.

"For yourself, you're done with, and you know it," the woman went on, ignoring her. "But you tell us the best loot and we might take pity on the little one. I might even consider taking her in myself."

Delly tried hard not to wince at that wretched thought.

The stranger's smile widened as she leaned closer, regarding the child. "She can not be pointing us out to the watch, after all, now can she?"

Delly knew she should say something constructive at that point, knew that she should sort through the terror and the craziness of all of this and lead the woman on in the best direction for the sake of Colson. But it proved to be too much for her, a stymieing realization that she was soon to die, that her daughter was in mortal peril, and there was not a thing she could do about it. She stuttered and stammered and in the end said nothing at all.

The woman curled up her fist and punched Delly hard, right in the face. As Delly fell away, the stranger tore Colson from her arms.

Delly reached out even as she fell, trying to grab the baby back, but the big thug drove a heavy forearm across her chest, speeding her descent. She landed hard on her back, and the brute wasted no time in scrambling atop her.

A crash from the side granted her a temporary reprieve, all eyes turning to see one of the other brutes standing amidst a pile of broken dinnerware—very expensive dinnerware.

"Find something for carrying it, you fool!" the woman yelled at him. She glanced all about the room, finally settling her gaze on one of the heavy, long drapes, then motioned for the creature to be quick.

She gave a disgusted sigh, then stepped forward and kicked the brute that was still atop Delly hard in the ribs. "Just kill the witch and be done with it," she said.

The brute looked up at her, as defiant as any of them had yet been, and shook its head.

To Delly's dismay, the woman merely waved away the ugly creature, giving in.

Delly closed her eyes and tried to let her mind fly free of her body.

The thug that had dropped the dinnerware scrambled across the room to the drapery beside the open window and with one great tug, pulled it free. The brute started to turn back for the remaining dinnerware, but it stopped, regarding a curious sculpture revealed by removing the curtain. It was a full-sized elf figure, dressed in the garb of an adventurer and apparently made of some ebony material, black stone or wood. It stood with eyes closed and two ornate scimitars presented in a cross-chest pose.

"Huh?" the brute said.

"Huh?" it said again, reaching slowly to feel the smooth skin.

The eyes popped open, penetrating, lavender orbs that froze the giantkin in place, that seemed to tell the brute without the slightest bit of doubt that its time in this world was fast ending.

⚔ ⚔ ⚔ ⚔ ⚔

With a blur the creature hardly even registered, the "statue" exploded into motion, scimitars cutting left and right. Around spun the drow elf, gaining momentum for even mightier slashes. A double-cut, one scimitar following the other, opened the stunned half-ogre from shoulder to hip. A quick-step put the drow right beside the falling brute. He reversed his grip with his right hand and plunged one enchanted blade deeply into the half-ogre's back, severing its spine, then half-turned and hamstrung the beast—both legs—with a precise and devastating slash of the other blade.

Drizzt stepped aside as the dying half-ogre crumbled to the floor.

"You should probably get off of her," the drow said casually to the next brute, who was laying atop Delly, staring at Drizzt incredulously.

Before the pirate woman could even growl out, "Kill him!" the third half-ogre charged across the room at Drizzt, a course that

185

brought it right past the opened window. Halfway across, a flying black form intercepted the brute. Six hundred pounds of snapping teeth and raking claws stopped dead the half-ogre's progress toward Drizzt and launched it back toward the center of the room.

The brute flailed wildly, but the panther had too many natural weapons and too much sheer strength. Guenhwyvar snapped one forearm in her maw, then ripped her head back and forth, shattering the bone and tearing the flesh. All the while, the panther's front paws clawed repeatedly at the frantic brute's face, too quick for the other arm to block. Guen's powerful back legs found holds on the half-ogre's legs and torso, claws digging in, then tearing straight back.

The surviving half-ogre rolled off of Delly and onto its feet. It lifted its weapon, a heavy broadsword, and rushed the drow, thinking to cut Drizzt in half with a single stroke.

The slashing sword met only air as the agile drow easily sidestepped the blow, then poked Twinkle into the brute's belly and danced another step away.

The half-ogre grabbed at the wound, but only for a moment. It came on fast with a straightforward thrust.

The scimitar Icingdeath, in Drizzt's left hand, easily turned the broadsword to the side. Drizzt stepped forward beside the lunging brute and poked it hard again with Twinkle, this time the scimitar's tip scratching off a thick rib.

The half-ogre roared and spun, slashing mightily as it went, expecting to cut Drizzt in half. Again the blade cut only air.

The half-ogre paused, dumbfounded, for its opponent was nowhere to be seen.

"Strong, but slow," came the drow's voice behind it. "Terrible combination."

The half-ogre howled in fear and leaped to the side, but Icingdeath was quicker, slashing in hard at the side of its neck. The half-ogre took three running strides, hand going up to its torn neck, then stumbled to one knee, then to the ground, writhing in agony.

Drizzt started toward it to finish it off but changed direction and stopped cold, staring hard at the woman who had backed to the wall beside the room's broken doors. The baby girl was in her arms, with a narrow, deadly dagger pressed up against the child's throat.

"What business does a dark elf have in Waterdeep?" the woman asked, trying to sound calm and confident, but obviously shaken. "If you wish the house as your own target, I will leave it to you. I assure you I have no interest in speaking with the authorities." The woman paused and stared hard at Drizzt, a smile of recognition at last coming over her.

"You are no drow come from the lightless depths as part of a raid," the woman remarked. "You sailed with Deudermont."

Drizzt bowed to her and didn't even bother trying to stop the last half-ogre he had grievously wounded as it crawled toward the woman. Across the room, Guenhwyvar stalked about the wall, flanking the woman, leaving the other half-ogre torn and dead in a puddle of its own blood and gore.

"And who are you who comes unbidden to the House of Deudermont?" Drizzt asked. "Along with some less-than-acceptable companions."

"Give me Colson!" pleaded the second woman—who must have been Delly Curtie. She was still on the floor, propped on her elbows. "Oh, please. She has done nothing."

"Silence!" the pirate roared at her. She looked back at Drizzt, pointedly turning that nasty dagger over and over against the child's throat. "She will get her child back, and alive," the woman explained. "Once I am out of here, running free."

"You bargain with that which you only think you possess," Drizzt remarked, coming forward a step.

The half-ogre had reached its boss by that time. With great

effort, it worked itself into a kneeling position before her, climbing its arms up the wall and pulling itself to its knees.

Gayselle gave it one look, then her hand flashed, driving her dagger deep into the brute's throat. It fell away gasping, dying.

The woman, obviously no novice to battle, had the dagger back at the child's throat in an instant, a flashing movement that made Delly cry out and had both Drizzt and Guenhwyvar breaking for her briefly. But only briefly, for that dagger was in place too quickly, and there could be no doubt that she would put it to use.

"I could not take him with me and could not leave the big mouth behind," the woman explained as the drow looked at her dying half-ogre companion.

"As I can not let you leave with the child," the drow replied.

"But you can, for you have little choice," she announced. "I will leave this place, and I will send word as to where you can retrieve the uninjured babe."

"No," Drizzt corrected. "You will give the babe to her mother, then leave this place, never to return."

The woman laughed at the notion. "Your panther friend would catch me and pull me down before I made the street," she said.

"I give you my word," Drizzt offered.

Again, the woman laughed. "I am to take the word of a drow elf?"

"And I am to take the word of a thief and murderess?" Drizzt was quick to reply.

"But you have no choice, drow," the woman explained, lifting the baby closer to her face, looking at it with a strange, cold expression, and sliding the flat of the dagger back and forth over Colson's neck.

Delly Curtie whimpered again and buried her face in her hands.

"How are you to stop me, drow?" the woman teased.

Even as the words left her mouth, a streak like blue lightning shot across the room, over the prone form of Delly Curtie, cutting right beside the tender flesh of Colson, to nail the pirate woman right between the eyes, slamming her back against the wall and pinning her there.

Her arms flew out wide, jerking spasmodically, the baby falling from her grasp.

But not to the floor, for as soon as he heard that familiar bowstring, Drizzt dived into a forward roll, coming around right before the pinned woman and gently catching Colson in his outstretched hands. He stood up and stared at the pirate.

The woman was already dead. Her arms gave a few more jerking spasms, and she went limp, hanging there, skull pinned to the wall. She wasn't seeing or hearing anything of this world.

"Just like that," Drizzt told her anyway.

13
WINTER SETTLING

Never much liked this place," Bruenor grumbled as he and Regis stood at the north gate of Luskan. They had been held up for a long, long time by the curious and suspicious guards.

"They'll let us in soon," Regis replied. "They always get like this as the weather turns—that's when the scum floats down from the mountains, after all. And when the highwaymen wander back into the city, pretending as if they belonged there all along."

Bruenor spat on the ground.

Finally, the guard who'd first stopped them returned, along with another, older soldier.

"My friend says you've come from Icewind Dale," the older man remarked. "And what goods have you brought to sell over the winter?"

"I bringed meself, and that oughta be enough for ye," Bruenor grumbled. The soldier eyed him dangerously.

"We've come to meet up with friends who are on the road," Regis was quick to interject, in a calmer tone.

He stepped between Bruenor and the soldier, trying to diffuse a potentially volatile situation—for any situation involving Bruenor Battlehammer was volatile these days! The dwarf was anxious to find his lost son, and woe to any who hindered him on that road.

"I am a councilor in Ten-Towns," the halfling explained. "Regis of Lonelywood. Perhaps you have heard of me?"

The soldier, his bristles up from Bruenor's attitude, spat at the halfling's feet. "Nope."

"And my companion is Bruenor Battlehammer himself," Regis said, somewhat dramatically. "Leader of Clan Battlehammer in Ten-Towns. Once, and soon again to be, King of Mithral Hall."

"Never heard of that either."

"But oh, ye're gonna," Bruenor muttered. He started around Regis, and the halfling skittered to stay in his way.

"Tough one, aren't you?" the soldier said.

"Please, good sir, enough of this foolishness," Regis pleaded. "Bruenor is in a terrible way, for he has lost his son, who is rumored to be sailing with Captain Deudermont."

This brought a puzzled expression to the face of the old soldier. "Haven't heard of any dwarves sailing on *Sea Sprite*," he said.

"His son is no dwarf, but a warrior, proud and strong," Regis explained. "Wulfgar by name." The halfling thought that he was making progress here, but, at the mention of Wulfgar's name, the soldier took on a most horrified and outraged expression.

"If you're calling that oaf your son, then you are far from welcome in Luskan!" the soldier declared.

Regis sighed, knowing what was to come. The many-notched axe hit the ground at his feet. At least Bruenor wouldn't cut the man in half. The halfling tried to anticipate the dwarf's movements to keep between the two, but Bruenor casually picked him up and turned around, dropping Regis behind him.

"Ye stay right there," the dwarf instructed, wagging a gnarly, crooked finger in the halfling's face.

By the time the dwarf turned back around, the soldier had drawn his sword.

Bruenor regarded it and laughed. "Now, what was ye saying about me boy?" he asked.

"I said he was an oaf," the man said, after glancing around to make sure he had enough support in the area. "And there are a million other insults I could rightfully hurl at the one named Wulfgar, murderer and rogue among them!"

He almost finished the sentence.

He almost got his sword up in time to block Bruenor's missile— that missile being Bruenor's entire body.

※ ※ ※ ※ ※

Drizzt turned to see a ragged and dirty Catti-brie standing at the window, outside and leaning on the pane, grim-faced and with Taulmaril in hand.

"It took you long enough," the drow remarked, but his humor found no spot in Catti-brie—not so soon after the kill. She stared right past Drizzt, not even registering his words. Would such actions ever become less troubling to her?

A big part of the woman who was Catti-brie hoped they would not.

Delly Curtie sprang up from the floor and rushed at Drizzt, running to her crying child's call. The woman calmed as she neared, for the smiling dark elf held the unharmed, though obviously upset child out to her and gladly handed Colson over.

"It would have been easier if you came up right behind me," Drizzt said to Catti-brie. "We could have saved some trouble."

"Are these looking like elven-bred to ye?" the woman growled back, pointing to her eyes—human orbs far inferior in the low light of the Waterdeep night. "And are ye thinking this to be an easy climb?"

Drizzt shrugged, grinning still. After all, the rocky climb hadn't given him any trouble at all.

"Go back down, then," Catti-brie insisted. She threw one leg over the window and eased herself into the room, not moving quickly, for her pant leg was torn, her leg bleeding. "Come back up with yer eyes closed, and ye tell me how easy them wet rocks might be for climbing."

She stumbled into the room, moving forward a few steps before fully gaining her balance—and that put her right in front of Delly Curtie and the baby.

"Catti-brie," the woman said. Her tone, while friendly and grateful enough, showed that she was a bit uneasy with seeing Catti-brie here.

The woman from Icewind Dale gave a slight bow. "And ye're Delly Curtie, unless I'm missing me guess," she replied. "Me and me friend just came from Luskan, from the tavern of Arumn Gardpeck."

Delly gave a chuckle and seemed to breathe for the first time since the fighting began. She looked from Catti-brie to Drizzt, knowing them from the tales Wulfgar had told to her. "Never seen a drow elf before," she said. "But I've heard all about ye from me man."

Despite herself, Catti-brie started at that remark, her blue eyes widening. She looked at Drizzt and saw him regarding her knowingly. She just grinned, shook her head, and turned her sights back on Delly.

"From Wulfgar," Delly said evenly.

"Wulfgar is yer man?" Catti-brie asked bluntly.

"He's been," Delly admitted, chewing her bottom lip.

Catti-brie read the woman perfectly. She understood that Delly was afraid, not of any physical harm, but that the return of Catti-brie into Wulfgar's life would somehow endanger her relationship with him. But Delly was ambiguous, as well, Catti-brie understood, for she couldn't rightly be upset about the arrival of Catti-brie and Drizzt, considering the pair had just saved her and her baby from certain death.

"We have come to find him," Drizzt explained, "to see if it is time for him to come home, to Icewind Dale."

"He's not alone anymore, ye know," Delly said to the drow. "He's got . . ." She started to name herself, but stopped and presented Colson instead. "He's got a little one to take care of."

"So we heard, but a confusing tale, it seems," Catti-brie said, approaching. "Can I hold the girl?"

Delly pulled the still-crying child in closer. "She's afraid," she explained. "Best that she's with her ma."

Catti-brie smiled at her, offering an expression that was honestly warm.

Their joy at the rescue was muted somewhat when Drizzt left Delly and Catti-brie in the drawing room and confirmed just how bloodthirsty this band truly had been. He found the two house guards murdered in the foyer, one lying by the door, one on the stairs. He went out front of the house, then, and called out repeatedly, until there at last came a reply.

"Go and fetch the watch," Drizzt bade the neighbor. "A murder most terrible has occurred!"

The drow went back to Delly and Catti-brie. He found Delly sitting with the child, trying to stop her crying, while Catti-brie stood by the window, staring out, with Guenhwyvar curled up on the floor beside her.

"She's got quite a tale to tell us of our Wulfgar," Catti-brie said to Drizzt.

The drow looked at Delly Curtie.

"He's speaking of ye both often," Delly explained. "Ye should know the road he's walked."

"Soon enough, then," Drizzt replied. "But not now. The authorities should arrive momentarily." The dark elf glanced around the room as he finished, his gaze landing alternately on the bodies of the intruders. "Do you have any idea what might have precipitated this attack?" he asked Delly.

"Deudermont's made many enemies," Catti-brie reminded him from the window, not even turning about as she spoke.

"Nothing more than the usual," Delly agreed. "Lots who'd like Captain Deudermont's head, but nothing special is afoot that I'm knowing."

Drizzt paused before responding, thinking to ask Delly what she knew of this pirate who supposedly had Wulfgar's warhammer. He looked again at the fallen intruders, settling his gaze on the woman.

The pattern fit, he realized, given what he had learned from the encounter with Jule Pepper in Icewind Dale and from Morik the Rogue. He crossed the room, ignoring the noise of the authorities coming to the front door, and moved right beside the dead woman, who was still stuck upright against the wall, pinned by Catti-brie's arrow.

"What're ye doing?" Catti-brie asked as Drizzt tugged at the collar of the dead woman's bloody tunic. "Just pull the damned arrow out to drop her from the perch."

Catti-brie was obviously unnerved by the sight of the dead woman, the sight of her latest kill, but Drizzt wasn't trying to pull this one down. Far from it, her present angle afforded him the best view.

He took out one scimitar and used its fine edge to slice through the clothing a bit, enough so that he could pull the fabric down low over the back of the dead woman's shoulder.

The drow nodded, far from surprised.

"What is it?" Delly asked from her seat, where she had at last quieted Colson.

Catti-brie's expression showed that she was about to ask the same thing, but it shifted almost at once as she considered the angle with which Drizzt was viewing the woman and the knowing expression stamped upon his dark face. "She's branded," Catti-brie answered, though she remained across the room.

"The mark of Aegis-fang," Drizzt confirmed. "The mark of Sheila Kree."

"What does it mean?" asked a concerned Delly, and she rose out of her chair, moving toward the drow, hugging her child close like some living, emotional armor. "Does it mean that Wulfgar and Captain Deudermont have caught Sheila Kree, and so her friends're trying to hit back?" she asked, looking nervously from the drow to the woman at the window. "Or might it mean that Sheila's sunk *Sea Sprite* and now is coming to finish off everything connected with Captain Deudermont and his crew?" Her voice rose as she finished, an edge of anxiety bubbling over.

"Or it means nothing more than that the pirate has learned that Captain Deudermont is in pursuit of her, and she wished to strike the first blow," Drizzt replied, unconvincingly.

"Or it means nothing at all," Catti-brie added. "Just a coincidence."

The other two looked at her, but none, not even Catti-brie, believed that for a moment.

The door crashed open a moment later and a group of soldiers charged into the room. Some turned immediately for the dark elf, howling at the sight of a drow, but others recognized Drizzt, or at least recognized Delly Curtie and saw by her posture that the danger had passed. They held their companions at bay.

Catti-brie ushered Delly Curtie away, the woman bearing the child, and with Catti-brie calling Guenhwyvar to follow, while

Drizzt gave the authorities a full account of what had occurred. The drow didn't stop at that, but went on to explain the likely personal feud heightening between Sheila Kree and Captain Deudermont.

After he had secured a net of soldiers to stand guard about the house, Drizzt went upstairs to join the women.

He found them in good spirits, with Catti-brie rocking Colson and Delly resting on the bed, a glass of wine in hand.

Catti-brie nodded to the woman, and without further word, Delly launched into her tale of Wulfgar, telling Drizzt and Catti-brie all about the barbarian's decline in Luskan, his trial at Prisoner's Carnival, his flight to the north with Morik and the circumstances that had brought him the child.

"Surprised was I when Wulfgar came back to the Cutlass," Delly finished. "For me!"

She couldn't help but glance at Catti-brie as she said that, somewhat nervously, somewhat superiorly. The auburn-haired woman's expression hardly changed, though.

"He came to apologize, and oh, but he owed it to us all," Delly went on. "We left, us three—me man and me child—to find Captain Deudermont, and for Wulfgar to find Aegis-fang. He's out there now," Delly ended, staring out the west-facing window. "So I'm hoping."

"Sheila Kree has not met up with *Sea Sprite* yet," Drizzt said to her. "Or if she has, then her ship is at the bottom of those cold waters, and Wulfgar is on his way back to Waterdeep."

"Ye can not know that," Delly said.

"But we will find out," a determined Catti-brie put in.

⚔ ⚔ ⚔ ⚔

"The winter fast approaches," Captain Deudermont remarked to Wulfgar, the two of them standing at *Sea Sprite*'s rail as the ship sailed along at a great clip. They had seen no pirates over the past few tendays, and few merchant vessels save the last groups making the southern run out of Luskan.

Wulfgar, who had grown up in Icewind Dale and knew well the change of the season—a dramatic and swift change this far north—didn't disagree. He, too, had seen the signs, the noticeably chilly shift in the wind and the change of direction, flowing more from the northwest now, off the cold waters of the Sea of Moving Ice.

"We will not put in to Luskan, but sail straight for Waterdeep," Deudermont explained. "There, we will ready the ship for winter sailing."

"Then you do not intend to put in for the season," Wulfgar reasoned.

"No, but our route will be south out of Waterdeep harbor and not north," Deudermont pointedly explained. "Perhaps we will patrol off of Baldur's Gate, perhaps even farther south. Robillard has made it clear that he would prefer a busy winter and has mentioned the Pirate Isles to me many times."

Wulfgar nodded grimly, understanding more from Deudermont's leading tone than from his actual words. The captain was politely inviting him to debark in Waterdeep and remain there with Delly and Colson.

"You will need my strong arm," Wulfgar said, less than convincingly.

"We are not likely to find Sheila Kree south of Waterdeep," Deudermont said clearly. "*Bloody Keel* has never been known to sail south of the City of Splendors. She has a reputation for putting into dock, wherever that dock may be, for the winter months."

There, he had said it, plainly and bluntly. Wulfgar looked at him, trying hard to take no offense. Logically, he understood the captain's reasoning. He hadn't been of much help to *Sea Sprite's* efforts of late, he had to admit. While that only made him want to get right back into battle, he understood that Deudermont had more to worry about than the sensibilities of one warrior.

Wulfgar found it hard to get the words out of his mouth, but he graciously said, "I will spend the winter with my family. If you would allow us the use of your house through the season."

"Of course," said Deudermont. He managed a smile and gently patted Wulfgar on the shoulder, which meant that he had to reach up a considerable distance. "Enjoy these moments with your family," he said quietly and with great compassion. "We will seek out Sheila Kree in the spring, on my word, and Aegis-fang will be returned to its rightful owner."

Every fiber within Wulfgar wanted to refuse this entire scenario, wanted to shout out at Deudermont that he was not a broken warrior, that he would find his way back to the battle, with all of the fury, and, more importantly, with all of the discipline demanded by a crack crew. He wanted to explain to the captain that he would find his way clear, to assure the man that the warrior who was Wulfgar, son of Beornegar, was waiting to be freed of this emotional prison to find his way back.

But Wulfgar held back the thoughts. In light of his recent, dangerous failures in battle, it was not his place to argue with Deudermont but rather to graciously accept the captain's polite excuse to get him off the ship.

They would be in Waterdeep in a tenday's time, and there Wulfgar would stay.

⚔ ⚔ ⚔ ⚔ ⚔

Delly Curtie found Drizzt and Catti-brie packing their belongings, preparing to leave Deudermont's house early the next morning.

"*Sea Sprite* will likely return soon," she explained to the duo.

"Likely," Drizzt echoed. "But I fear there might already be news of a confrontation between Kree and *Sea Sprite*, farther in the north. We will go to Luskan, where we are to meet with some friends and follow a trail that will take us to Kree, or to Wulfgar."

Delly thought about it for just a moment. "Give me some time to pack and to ready Colson," she said.

Catti-brie was shaking her head before Delly ever finished the thought. "Ye'll slow us down," she said.

"If ye're going to Wulfgar, then me place is with yerself," the woman replied firmly.

"We're not knowing that we're going to Wulfgar," Catti-brie replied with all honesty and with measured calm. "It might well be that Wulfgar will soon enough be here, with *Sea Sprite*. If that's the truth, then better that ye're here to meet with him and tell him all that ye know."

"If you come with us, and *Sea Sprite* puts into Waterdeep, Wulfgar will be terribly worried about you," Drizzt explained. "You stay here—the watch will keep you and your child safe now."

Delly considered the pair for a few moments, her trepidation obvious on her soft features. Catti-brie caught it clearly and certainly understood.

"If we're first to Wulfgar, then we'll be coming with him back here," she said, and Delly relaxed visibly.

After a moment, the woman nodded her agreement.

Drizzt and Catti-brie left a short while later, after gaining assurances from the authorities that Deudermont's house, and Delly and Colson, would be guarded day and night.

"Our road's going back and forth," Catti-brie remarked to the drow as they made their way out of the great city's northern gate. "And all the while, Wulfgar's sailing out there, back and forth. We've just got to hope that our routes cross soon enough, though I'm thinking that he'll be landing in Waterdeep while we're walking into Luskan."

Drizzt didn't crack a smile at her humorous words and tone. He looked to her and stared intently, giving her a moment to reflect on the raid of the previous night, and the dangerous implications, then said grimly, "We've just got to hope that *Sea Sprite* is still afloat and that Wulfgar is still alive."

PART THREE

THE BLOODY TRAIL

Once again Catti-brie shows me that she knows me better than I know myself. As we came to understand that Wulfgar was climbing out of his dark hole, was truly resurfacing into the warrior he had once been, I have to admit a bit of fear, a bit of jealousy. Would he come back as the man who once stole Catti-brie's heart? Or had he, in fact, ever really done that? Was their planned marriage more a matter of convenience on both parts, a logical joining of the only two humans, matched in age and beauty, among our little band?

I think it was a little of both, and hence

my jealousy. For though I understand that I have become special to Catti-brie in ways I had never before imagined, there is a part of me that wishes no one else ever had. For though I am certain that we two share many feelings that are new and exciting to both of us, I do not like to consider the possibility that she ever shared such emotions with another, even one who is so dear a friend.

Perhaps especially one who is so dear a friend!

But even as I admit all this, I know that I must take a deep breath and blow all of my fears and jealousies away. I must remind myself that I love this woman, Catti-brie, and that this woman is who she is because of a combination of all the experiences that brought her to this point. Would I prefer that her human parents had never died? On the one hand, of course! But if they hadn't, Catti-brie would not have wound up as Bruenor's adopted daughter, would likely not have come to reside in Icewind Dale at all. Given that, it is unlikely that we would have ever met. Beyond that, if she had been raised in a traditional human manner, she never would have become the warrior that she now is, the person who can best share my sense of adventure, who can accept the hardships of the road with good humor and risk, and allow me to risk—everything!—when going against the elements and the monsters of the world.

Hindsight, I think, is a useless tool. We, each of us, are at a place in our lives because of innumerable circumstances, and we, each of us, have a responsibility, if we do not like where we are, to move along life's road, to find a better path if this one does not suit, or to walk happily along this one if it is indeed our life's way. Changing even the bad things that have gone before would fundamentally change who we now are, and whether or not that would be a good thing, I believe, is impossible to predict.

So I take my past experiences and let Catti-brie take hers and try to regret nothing for either. I just try to blend our current existence into something grander and more beautiful together.

What of Wulfgar, then? He has a new bride and a child who is neither his nor hers naturally. And yet, it was obvious from Delly Curtie's face, and from her willingness to give of herself if only the child would be unharmed that she loves the babe as if it was her own. I think the same must be true for Wulfgar because, despite the trials, despite the more recent behaviors, I know who he is, deep down, beneath the crusted, emotionally hardened exterior.

I know from her words that he loves this woman, Delly Curtie, and yet I know that he once loved Catti-brie as well.

What of this mystery, love? What is it that brings about this most elusive of magic? So many times I have heard people proclaim that their partner is their only love, the only possible completion to their soul, and surely I feel that way about Catti-brie, and I expect that she feels the same about me. But logically, is that possible? Is there one other person out there who can complete the soul of another? Is it really one for one, or is it rather a matter of circumstance?

Or do reasoning beings have the capacity to love many, and situation instead of fate brings them together?

Logically, I know the answer to be the latter. I know that if Wulfgar, or Catti-brie, or myself resided in another part of the world, we would all likely find that special completion to our soul, and with another. Logically, in a world of varying races and huge populations, that must be the case, or how, then, would true lovers ever meet? I am a thinking creature, a rational being, and so I know this to be the truth.

Why is it, then, that when I look at Catti-brie, all of those logical arguments make little sense? I remember our first meeting, when she was barely a young woman—more a girl, actually—and I saw her on the side of Kelvin's Cairn. I remember looking into her blue eyes on that occasion, feeling the warmth of her smile and the openness of her heart—something I had not much encountered since coming to the surface world—and feeling a definite bond there, a magic I could not explain. And as I watched her grow, that bond only strengthened.

So was it situation or fate? I know what logic says.

But I know, too, what my heart tells me.

It was fate. She is the one.

Perhaps situation allows for some, even most, people to find a suitable partner, but there is much more to it than finding just that. Perhaps some people are just more fortunate than others.

When I look into Catti-brie's blue eyes, when I feel the warmth of her smile and the openness of her heart, I know that I am.

—Drizzt Do'Urden

14
CONFIRMATION

Ye've been keeping yer eyes and ears on the elf?" Sheila Kree asked Bellany when the woman joined her in her private quarters that blustery autumn day.

"Le'lorinel is at work on *Bloody Keel*, attending to duties with little complaint or argument," the sorceress replied.

"Just what I'd be expectin' from a spy."

Bellany shrugged, brushing back her dark hair, her expression a dismissal of Sheila Kree's suspicions. "I have visited Le'lorinel privately and without permission. Magically, when Le'lorinel believed the room was empty. I have seen or heard nothing to make me doubt the elf's story."

"A dark elf," Sheila Kree remarked, going to the opening facing the sea, her red hair fluttering back from the whistling salty breeze that blew in. "A dark elf will seek us out, by Le'lorinel's own words." She half-turned to regard Bellany, who seemed as if she might believe anything at that moment.

"If this dark elf, this Drizzt Do'Urden, does seek us out, then we will be glad we have not disposed of that one," the sorceress reasoned.

Sheila Kree turned back to the sea, shaking her head as if it seemed impossible. "And how long should we be waitin' before we decide that Le'lorinel is a spy?" she asked.

"We can not keel-haul the elf while *Bloody Keel* is in dock anyway," Bellany said with a chuckle, and her reasoning brightened Sheila's mood as well. "The winter will not be so long, I expect."

It wasn't the first time these two had shared such a discussion. Ever since Le'lorinel had arrived with the wild tale of a dark elf and a dwarf king coming to retrieve the warhammer, which Sheila believed she had honestly purchased from the fool Josi Puddles, the boss and her sorceress advisor had spent countless hours and endless days debating the fate of this strange elf. And on many of those days, Bellany had left Sheila thinking that Le'lorinel would likely be dead before the next dawn.

And yet, the elf remained alive.

"A visitor, boss lady," came a guttural call from the door. A half-ogre guard entered, leading a tall and willowy black-haired woman, flanked by a pair of the half-ogre's kin. Both Sheila and Bellany gawked in surprise when they noted the newcomer.

"Jule Pepper," Sheila said incredulously. "I been thinking that ye must own half the Ten-Towns by now!"

The black-haired woman, obviously bolstered by the warm tone from her former boss, shook her arms free of the two brutes flanking her and walked across the room to share a hug with Sheila and one with Bellany.

"I was doing well," the highwaywoman purred. "I had a band of reasonable strength working under me, and on a scheme that seemed fairly secure. Or so I thought, until a certain wretched drow elf and his friends showed up to end the party."

Sheila Kree and Bellany turned to each other in surprise, the pirate boss giving an amazed snort. "A dark elf?" she asked Jule. "Wouldn't happen to be one named Drizzt Do'Urden, would it?"

✕ ✕ ✕ ✕ ✕

Even without the aid of wizards and clerics, without their magic spells of divination and communication, word traveled fast along the northern stretches of the Sword Coast, particularly when the news concerned the people living outside the restrictions and sensibilities of the law, and even more particularly when the hero of the hour was of a race not known for such actions. From tavern to tavern, street to street, boat to boat, and port to port went the recounting of the events at the house of Captain Deudermont, of how a mysterious drow elf and his two companions, one a great cat, throttled a theft and murder plot against the good captain's house. Few made the connection between Drizzt and Wulfgar or even between Drizzt and Deudermont, though some did know that a dark elf once had sailed on *Sea Sprite*. It was a juicy tale bringing great interest on its own, but for the folks of the city bowels, ones who understood that such attempts against a noble and heroic citizen were rarely self-contained things, the interest was even greater. There were surely implications here that went beyond the events in the famous captain's house.

So the tale sped along the coast, and even at one point did encounter some wizardly assistance in moving it along, and so the news of the events at the house long preceded the arrival of Drizzt and Catti-brie in Luskan, and so the news spread even faster farther north.

Sheila Kree knew of the loss of Gayselle before the dark elf crossed through Luskan's southern gate.

The pirate stormed about her private rooms, overturning tables and swearing profusely. She called a pair of half-ogre sentries in so that she could yell at them and slap them, playing out her frustrations for a long, long while.

Finally, too exhausted to continue, the red-haired pirate dismissed the guards and picked up a chair so that she could fall into it, cursing still under her breath.

It made no sense to her. Who was this stupid dark elf—the same one who had foiled Jule Pepper's attempts to begin a powerful band in Ten-Towns—and how in the world did he happen to wind up at Captain Deudermont's house at the precise time to intercept Gayselle's band? Sheila Kree closed her eyes and let it all sink in.

"Redecorating?" came a question from the doorway, and Sheila opened her eyes to see Bellany, a bemused smile on her face, standing at the door.

"Ye heard o' Gayselle?" Sheila asked.

The sorceress shrugged as if it didn't matter. "She'll not be the last we lose."

"I'm thinkin' that I'm hearing too much about a certain drow elf of late," Sheila remarked.

"Seems we have made an enemy," Bellany agreed. "How fortunate that we have been forewarned."

"Where's the elf?"

"At work on the boat, as with every day. Le'lorinel goes about any duties assigned without a word of complaint."

"There's but one focus for that one."

"A certain dark elf," Bellany agreed. "Is it time for Le'lorinel to take a higher step in our little band?"

"Time for a talk, at least," Sheila replied, and Bellany didn't have to be told twice. She turned around with a nod and headed off for the lower levels to fetch the elf, whose tale had become so much more intriguing with the return of Jule Pepper and the news of the disaster in Waterdeep.

✖ ✖ ✖ ✖ ✖

"When ye first came wandering in, I thought to kill ye dead and be done with ye," Sheila Kree remarked bluntly. The pirate nodded to her burly guards, and they rushed in close, grabbing Le'lorinel fast by the arms.

"I have not lied to you, have done nothing to deserve—" Le'lorinel started to protest.

"Oh, ye're to get what ye're deserving," Sheila Kree assured the elf. She walked over and grabbed a handful of shirt, and with a wicked grin and a sudden jerk, she tore the shirt away, stripping the elf to the waist.

The two half-ogres giggled. Sheila Kree motioned to the door at the back of the room, and the brutes dragged their captive off, through the door and into a smaller room, undecorated except for a hot fire pit near one wall and a block set at about waist height in the center.

"What are you doing?" Le'lorinel demanded in a tone that held its calm edge, despite the obvious trouble.

"It's gonna hurt," Sheila Kree promised as the half-ogres yanked the elf across the block, holding tight.

Le'lorinel struggled futilely against the powerful press.

"Now, ye tell me again about the drow elf, Drizzt Do'Urden," Sheila remarked.

"I told you everything, and honestly," Le'lorinel protested.

"Tell me again," said Sheila.

"Yes, do," came another voice, that of Bellany, who walked into the room. "Tell us about this fascinating character who has suddenly become so very important to us."

"I heard of the killings at Captain Deudermont's house," Le'lorinel remarked, grunting as the half-ogres pulled a bit too hard. "I warned you that Drizzt Do'Urden is a powerful enemy."

"But one ye're thinking ye can defeat," Sheila interjected.

"I have prepared for little else."

"And have ye prepared for the pain?" Sheila asked wickedly. Le'lorinel felt an intense heat.

"I do not deserve this!" the elf protested, but the sentence ended with an agonized scream as the glowing hot metal came down hard on Le'lorinel's back.

The sickly smell of burning skin permeated the room.

"Now, ye tell us all about Drizzt Do'Urden again," Sheila Kree demanded some time later, when Le'lorinel had come back to consciousness and sensibility. "Everything, including why ye're so damned determined to see him dead."

Still held over the block, Le'lorinel stared at the pirate long and hard.

"Ah, let the fool go," Sheila told the half-ogres. "And get ye gone, both of ye!"

The pair did as they were ordered, rushing out of the room. With great effort, Le'lorinel straightened.

Bellany thrust a shirt into the elf's trembling hands. "You might want to wait a while before you try to put that on," the sorceress explained.

Le'lorinel nodded and stretched repeatedly, trying to loosen the new scars.

"I'll be wanting to hear it all," Sheila said. "Ye're owing me that, now."

Le'lorinel looked at the pirate for a moment, then craned to see the new brand, the mark of Aegis-fang, the mark of acceptance and hierarchy in Sheila's band.

Eyes narrowed threateningly, teeth gritted with rage that denied the burning agony of the brand, the elf looked back at Sheila. "Everything, and you will come to trust that I will never rest until Drizzt Do'Urden is dead, slain by my own hands."

Later Sheila, Bellany, and Jule Pepper sat together in Sheila's room, digesting all that Le'lorinel had told them of Drizzt Do'Urden and his companions, who were apparently hunting Sheila in an effort to retrieve the warhammer.

"We are fortunate that Le'lorinel came to us," Bellany admitted.

"Ye thinking that the elf can beat the drow?" Sheila asked with a doubtful snort. "Damn drow. Never seen one. Never wanted to."

"I have no idea whether Le'lorinel has any chance at all against this dark elf or not," Bellany honestly answered. "I do know that the elf's hatred for Drizzt is genuine and deep, and whatever the odds, we can expect Le'lorinel to lead the charge if Drizzt Do'Urden comes against us. That alone is a benefit." As she finished, she turned a leading gaze over Jule Pepper, the only one of them to ever encounter Drizzt and his friends.

"I would hesitate to ever bet against that group," Jule said. "Their teamwork is impeccable, wrought of years fighting together, and each of them, even the runt halfling, is formidable."

"What o' these other ones, then?" the obviously nervous pirate leader asked. "What o' Bruenor the dwarf king? Think he'll bring an army against us?"

Neither Jule nor Bellany had any way of knowing. "Le'lorinel told us much," the sorceress said, "but the information is far from complete."

"In my encounter with them in Icewind Dale, the dwarf worked with his friends, but with no support from his clan whatsoever," Jule interjected. "If Bruenor knows the power of your band, though, he might decide to rouse the fury of Clan Battlehammer."

"And?" Sheila asked.

"Then we sail, winter storm or no," Bellany was quick to reply. Sheila started to scold her but noted that Jule was nodding her agreement, and in truth, the icy waters of the northern Sword

Coast in winter seemed insignificant against the threat of an army of hostile dwarves.

"When Wulfgar was in Luskan, he was known to be working for Arumn Gardpeck at the Cutlass," Jule, who had been in Luskan in those days, offered.

" 'Twas Arumn's fool friend who sold me the warhammer," Sheila remarked.

"But his running companion was an old friend of mine," Jule went on. "A shadowy little thief known as Morik the Rogue."

Sheila and Bellany looked to each other and nodded. Sheila had heard of Morik, though not in any detail. Bellany, though, knew the man fairly well, or had known him, at least, back in her days as an apprentice at the Hosttower of the Arcane. She looked to Jule, considered what she personally knew of lusty Morik, and understood what the beautiful, sensuous woman likely meant by the phrase "an old friend."

"Oh, by the gods," Sheila Kree huffed a few moments later, her head sagging as so many things suddenly became clear to her.

Both of her companions looked at her curiously.

"Deudermont's chasing us," Sheila Kree explained. "What'd'ye think he's looking for?"

"Do we know that he's looking for anything at all?" Bellany replied, but she slowed down as she finished the sentence, as if starting to catch on.

"And now Drizzt and his girlfriend are waiting for us at Deudermont's house," Sheila went on.

"So Deudermont is after Aegis-fang, as well," reasoned Jule Pepper. "It's all connected. But Wulfgar is not—or at least was not—with Drizzt and the others from Icewind Dale, so . . ."

"Wulfgar might be with Deudermont," Bellany finished.

"I'll be paying Josi Puddles back for this, don't ye doubt," Sheila said grimly, settling back in her seat.

215

"We know not where Wulfgar might be," Jule Pepper put in. "We do know that Deudermont will not likely be sailing anywhere north of Waterdeep for the next season, so if Wulfgar is with Deudermont . . ."

She stopped as Sheila growled and leaped up from her seat, pounding a fist into an open palm. "We're not knowing enough to make any choices," she grumbled. "We're needing to learn more."

An uncomfortable silence followed, at last broken by Jule Pepper. "Morik," the woman said.

Bellany and Sheila looked at her curiously.

"Morik the Rogue, as well-connected as any rogue on Luskan's streets," Bellany explained. "And with a previous interest in Wulfgar, as you just said. He will have some answers for us, perhaps."

Sheila thought it over for a moment. "Bring him to me," she ordered Bellany, whose magical powers could take her quickly to Luskan, despite the season.

Bellany nodded, and without a word she rose and left the room.

"Dark elves and warhammers," Sheila Kree remarked when she and Jule were alone. "A mysterious and beautiful elf visitor . . ."

"Exotic, if not beautiful," Jule agreed. "And I admit I do like the look. Especially the black mask."

Sheila Kree laughed at the craziness of it all and shook her head vigorously, her wild red hair flying all about. "If Le'lorinel survives this, then I'll be naming an elf among me commanders," she explained.

"A most mysterious and beautiful and exotic elf," Jule agreed with a laugh. "Though perhaps a bit crazy."

Sheila considered her with an incredulous expression. "Ain't we all?"

15
Sharing a Drink with a Surly Dwarf

I should've known better than to let the two of ye go running off on yer own," a blustering voice greeted loudly as Drizzt and Catti-brie entered the Cutlass in Luskan. Bruenor and Regis sat at the bar, across from Arumn Gardpeck, both looking a bit haggard still from their harrowing journey.

"I didn't think you would come out," Drizzt remarked, pulling a seat up beside his friends. "It is late in the season."

"Later than you think," Regis mumbled, and both Drizzt and Catti-brie turned to Bruenor for clarification.

"Bah, a little storm and nothing to fret about," the dwarf bellowed.

"Little to a mountain giant," Regis muttered quietly, and Bruenor gave a snort.

"Fix up me friend and me girl here with a bit o' the wine," Bruenor called to Arumn, who was already doing just that. As soon as the drinks were delivered and Arumn, with a nod to the pair, started away, the red-bearded dwarf's expression grew very serious.

"So where's me boy?" he asked.

"With Deudermont, sailing on *Sea Sprite*, as far as we can tell," Catti-brie answered.

"Not in port here," Regis remarked.

"Nor in Waterdeep, though they might put in before winter," Drizzt explained. "That would be Captain Deudermont's normal procedure, to properly stock the ship for the coming cold season."

"Then they'll likely sail south," Catti-brie added. "Not returning to Waterdeep until the spring."

Bruenor snorted again, but with a mouthful of ale, and wound up spitting half of it over Regis. "Then why're ye here?" he demanded. "If me boy's soon to be in Waterdeep, and not back for half a year, why ain't ye there seeing to him?"

"We left word," Drizzt explained.

"Word?" the dwarf echoed incredulously. "What word might that be? Hello? Well met? Keep warm through the winter? Ye durn fool elf, I was counting on ye to bring me boy back to us."

"It is complicated," Drizzt replied.

Only then did Catti-brie note that both Arumn Gardpeck and Josi Puddles were quietly edging closer, each craning an ear the way of the four friends. She didn't scold them, though, for she well understood their stake in all of this.

"We found Delly," she said, turning to regard the two of them in turn. "And the child, Colson."

"How fares my Delly?" asked Arumn, and Catti-brie didn't miss the fact that Josi Puddles was chewing his lip with anticipation. Likely that one was sweet on the girl, Catti-brie recognized.

"She does well, as does the little girl," Drizzt put in. "Though even as we arrived, we found them in peril."

All four of the listeners stared hard at those ominous words.

"Sheila Kree, the pirate, or so we believe," Drizzt explained.

"For some reason that I do not yet know, she took it upon herself to send a raiding party to Waterdeep."

"Looking for me boy?" Bruenor asked.

"Or looking to back off Deudermont, who's been chasing her all season," remarked Arumn, who was well versed in such things, listening to much of the gossip from the many sailors who frequented his tavern.

"One or the other, and so we have returned to find out which," Drizzt replied.

"Do we even know that *Sea Sprite* is still afloat?" Regis asked.

The halfling's eyes went wide and he bit his lip as soon as he heard the words coming out of his mouth, his wince showing clearly that he had realized, too late, that such a possibility as the destruction of the ship would weigh very heavily on the shoulders of Bruenor.

Still, it was an honest question to ask, and one that Drizzt and Catti-brie had planned on asking Arumn long before they arrived in Luskan. Both looked questioningly to the tavern-keeper.

"Heard nothing to say it ain't," Arumn answered, "But if Sheila Kree got *Sea Sprite*, then it could well be months before we knowed it here. Can't believe she did, though. Word among the docks is that none'd take on *Sea Sprite* in the open water."

"See what you can find out, I beg you," Drizzt said to him.

The portly tavern-keeper nodded and motioned to Josi to likewise begin an inquiry.

"I strongly doubt that Sheila Kree got anywhere near to *Sea Sprite*," Drizzt echoed, for Bruenor's benefit, and with conviction. "Or if she did, then likely it was the remnants of her devastated band that staged the raid against Captain Deudermont's house, seeking one last bit of retribution for the destruction of Sheila's ship and the loss of her crew. I sailed with Captain Deudermont for five years, and I can tell you that I never encountered a single ship that could out-duel *Sea Sprite*."

"Or her wizard, Robillard," Catti-brie added.

Bruenor continued to simply stare at the two of them hard, the dwarf obviously on the very edge of anxiety for his missing son.

"And so we're to wait?" he asked a few moments later. It was obvious from his tone that he wasn't thrilled with that prospect.

"The winter puts *Sea Sprite* out of the hunt for Sheila Kree's ship," Drizzt explained, lowering his voice so that only the companions could hear. "And likely it puts Sheila Kree off the cold waters for the season. She has to be docked somewhere."

That seemed to appease Bruenor somewhat. "We'll find her, then," he said determinedly. "And get back me warhammer."

"And hopefully Wulfgar will join us," Catti-brie added. "That he might be holdin' Aegis-fang once again. That he might be finding where he belongs and where the hammer belongs."

Bruenor lifted his mug of ale in a toast to that hopeful sentiment, and all the others joined in, each understanding that Catti-brie's scenario had to be considered the most optimistic and that a far darker road likely awaited them all.

In the subsequent discussion, the companions decided to spend the next few days searching the immediate area around Luskan, including the docks. Arumn and Josi, and Morik the Rogue once they could find him, were to inquire where they might about *Sea Sprite* and Sheila Kree. The plan would give Wulfgar a chance to catch up with them, perhaps, if he got the news in Waterdeep and that was his intent. It was also possible that *Sea Sprite* would come through Luskan on its way to Waterdeep. If that was to happen, it would be very soon, Drizzt knew, for the season was getting late.

Drizzt ordered a round for all four, then held back the others before they could begin their drinking. He held his own glass up in a second toast, a reaffirmation of Bruenor's first one.

"The news is brighter than we could have expected when first we left Ten-Towns," he reminded them all. "By all accounts, our friend is alive and with good and reliable company."

"To Wulfgar!" said Regis, as Drizzt paused.

"And to Delly Curtie and to Colson," Catti-brie added with a smile aimed right at Bruenor and even more pointedly at Drizzt. "A fine wife our friend has found, and a child who'll grow strong under Wulfgar's watchful eye."

"He learned to raise a son from a master, I would say," Drizzt remarked, grinning at Bruenor.

"And too bad it is that that one didn't know as much about raising a girl," Catti-brie added, but she waited until precisely the moment that Bruenor began gulping his ale before launching the taunt.

Predictably, the dwarf spat and Regis got soaked again.

⚔ ⚔ ⚔ ⚔ ⚔

Morik the Rogue wore a curious and not displeased expression when he opened the door to his small apartment to find a petite, dark-haired woman waiting for him.

"Perhaps you have found the wrong door," Morik graciously offered, his dark eyes surveying the woman with more than a little interest. She was a comely one, and she held herself with perfect poise and a flicker of intelligence that Morik always found intriguing.

"Many people would call the door of Morik the Rogue the wrong door," the woman answered. "But no, this is where I intended to be." She gave a coy little smile and looked Morik over as thoroughly as he was regarding her. "You have aged well," she said.

The implication that this enticing creature had known Morik in his earlier years piqued the rogue's curiosity. He stared at her hard, trying to place her.

"Perhaps it would help if I cast spells to shake our bed," the woman remarked. "Or multicolored lights to dance about us as we make love."

"Bellany!" Morik cried suddenly. "Bellany Tundash! How many years have passed?"

Indeed, Morik hadn't seen the sorceress in several years, not since she was a minor apprentice in the Hosttower of the Arcane. She had been the wild one! Sneaking out from the wizards' guild nearly every night to come and play along the wilder streets of Luskan. And like so many pretty women who had come out to play, Bellany had inevitably found her way to Morik's side and Morik's bed for a few encounters.

Amazing encounters, Morik recalled.

"Not so many years, Morik," Bellany replied. "And here I thought I was more special than that to you." She gave a little pout, pursing her lips in such a way as to make Morik's knees go weak. "I believed you would recognize me immediately and sweep me into your arms for a great kiss."

"A situation I must correct!" said Morik, coming forward with his arms out wide, a bright and eager expression on his face.

⚔ ⚔ ⚔ ⚔

Both Catti-brie and Regis retired early that night, but Drizzt stayed on in the tavern with Bruenor, suspecting that the dwarf needed to talk.

"When this business is finished, you and I must go to Waterdeep," the drow remarked. "It would do my heart good to hear Colson talk of her grandfather."

"Kid's talking?" Bruenor asked.

"No, not yet," Drizzt replied with a laugh. "But soon enough."

Bruenor merely nodded, seeming less than intrigued with it all.

"She has a good mother," Drizzt said after a while. "And we know the character of her father. Colson will be a fine lass."

"Colson," Bruenor muttered, and he downed half his mug of ale. "Stupid name."

"It is Elvish," Drizzt explained. "With two meanings, and seeming perfectly fitting. 'Col' means 'not', and so the name literally translates into 'not-son,' or 'daughter.' Put together, though, the name Colson means 'from the dark town'. A fitting name, I would say, given Delly Curtie's tale of how Wulfgar came by the child."

Bruenor huffed again and finished the mug.

"I would have thought you would be thrilled at the news," the drow dared to say. "You, who knows better than any the joy of finding a wayward child to love as your own."

"Bah," Bruenor snorted.

"And I suspect that Wulfgar will soon enough produce grandchildren for you from his own loins," Drizzt remarked, sliding another ale Bruenor's way.

"Grandchildren?" Bruenor echoed doubtfully, and he turned in his chair to face the drow directly. "Ain't ye assuming that Wulfgar's me own boy?"

"He is."

"Is he?" Bruenor asked. "Ye're thinking that a couple o' years apart mended me heart for his actions on Catti-brie." The dwarf snorted yet again, threw his hand up in disgust, then turned back to the bar, cradling his new drink below him, muttering, "Might be that I'm looking to find him so I can give him a big punch in the mouth for the way he treated me girl."

"Your worry has been obvious and genuine," Drizzt remarked. "You have forgiven Wulfgar, whether you admit it or not.

"As have I," Drizzt quickly added when the dwarf turned back on him, his eyes narrow and threatening. "As has Catti-brie. Wulfgar was in a dark place, but from all I've learned, it would seem that he has begun the climb back to the light."

Those words softened Bruenor's expression somewhat, and his ensuing snort was not as definitive this time.

"You will like Colson," Drizzt said with a laugh. "And Delly Curtie."

"Colson," Bruenor echoed, listening carefully to the name as he spoke it. He looked at Drizzt and shook his head, but if he was trying to continue to show his disapproval, he was failing miserably.

"So now I got a granddaughter from a son who's not me own, and a daughter o' his that's not his own," Bruenor said some time later, he and Drizzt having gone back to their respective drinks for a few reflective moments. "Ye'd think that one of us would've figured out that half the fun's in makin' the damn brats!"

"And will Bruenor one day sire his own son?" Drizzt asked. "A dwarf child?"

The dwarf turned and regarded Drizzt incredulously, but considered the words for a moment and shrugged. "I just might," he said. He looked back at his ale, his face growing more serious and a bit sad, Drizzt noticed. "I'm not a young one, ye know, elf?" he asked. "Seen the centuries come and go, and remember times when Catti-brie and Wulfgar's parents' parents' parents' parents hadn't felt the warming of their first dawn. And I feel old, don't ye doubt! Feel it in me bones."

"Centuries of banging stone will do that," Drizzt said dryly, but his levity couldn't penetrate the dwarf's mood at that moment.

"And I see me girl all grown, and me boy the same, and now he's got a little one . . ." Bruenor's voice trailed off and he gave a great sigh, then drained the rest of his mug, turning as he finished to face Drizzt squarely. "And that little one will grow old and die, and I'll still be here with me aching bones."

Drizzt understood, for he too, as a long-living creature, surely saw Bruenor's dilemma. When elves, dark or light, or dwarves befriended the shorter living races—humans, halflings, and gnomes—there came the expectancy that they would watch their friends grow old and die. Drizzt knew that one of the reasons elves and dwarves remained clannish to their own, whether they wanted to admit it or not, was because of exactly that, both races protecting themselves from the emotional tearing.

"Guess that's why we should be stickin' with our own kind, eh, elf?" Bruenor finished, looking slyly at Drizzt out of the corner of his eye.

Drizzt's expression went from sympathy to curiosity. Had Bruenor just warned him away from Catti-brie? That caught the drow off his guard, indeed! And rocked him right back in his seat, as he sat staring hard at Bruenor. Had he finally let himself see the truth of his feelings for Catti-brie just to encounter this dwarven roadblock? Or was Bruenor right, and was Drizzt being a fool?

The drow took a long, long moment to steady himself and collect his thoughts.

"Or perhaps those of us who hide from the pain will never know the joys that might lead to such profound pain," Drizzt finally said. "Better to—"

"To what?" Bruenor interrupted. "To fall in love with one of them? To marry one, elf?"

Drizzt still didn't know what Bruenor was up to. Was he telling Drizzt to back off, calling the drow a fool for even thinking of falling in love with Catti-brie?

But then Bruenor tipped his hand.

"Yeah, fall in love with one," he said with a derisive snort, but one Drizzt recognized that was equally aimed at himself. "Or maybe take one of 'em in to raise as yer own. Heck, maybe more than one!"

Bruenor glanced over at Drizzt, his toothy smile showing through his brilliant red whiskers. He lifted his mug toward Drizzt in a toast. "To the both of us, then, elf!" he boomed. "A pair o' fools, but smiling fools!"

Drizzt gladly answered that toast with a tap of his own glass. He understood then that Bruenor wasn't trying to subtly, in a dwarf sort of way, ward him off, but rather that the dwarf was merely making sure Drizzt understood the depth of what he had.

They went back to their drinking. Bruenor drained mug after mug, but Drizzt cradled that single glass of fine wine.

Many minutes passed before either spoke again, and it was Bruenor, cracking in a tone that seemed all seriousness, which made it all the funnier, "Hey, elf, me next grandkid won't be striped, will it?"

"As long as it doesn't have a red beard," Drizzt replied without missing a beat.

⚔ ⚔ ⚔ ⚔ ⚔

"I heard you were traveling with a great barbarian warrior named Wulfgar," Bellany said to Morik when the rogue finally woke up long after the following dawn.

"Wulfgar?" Morik echoed, rubbing the sleep from his dark eyes and running his fingers through his matted black hair. "I have not seen Wulfgar in many months."

He didn't catch on to the telling manner in which Bellany was scrutinizing him.

"He went south, to find Deudermont, I think," Morik went on, and he looked at Bellany curiously. "Am I not enough man for you?" he asked.

The dark-haired sorceress smirked in a neutral manner, pointedly not answering the rogue's question. "I ask only for a friend of mine," she said.

Morik's smile was perfectly crude. "Two of you, eh?" he asked. "Am I not man enough?"

Bellany gave a great sigh and rolled to the side of the bed, gathering up the bedclothes about her and dragging them free as she rose.

Only then, upon the back of her naked shoulder, did Morik take note of the curious brand.

"So you have not spoken with Wulfgar in months?" the woman asked, moving to her clothing.

"Why do you ask?"

The suspicious nature of the question had the sorceress turning about to regard Morik, who was still reclining on the bed, lying on his side and propped up on one elbow.

"A friend wishes to know of him," Bellany said, rather curtly.

"Seems like a lot of people are suddenly wanting to know about him," the rogue remarked. He fell to his back and threw one arm across his eyes.

"People like a dark elf?" Bellany asked.

Morik peeked out at her from under his arm, his expression answering the question clearly.

Wider went his eyes when the sorceress lifted the robe that was lying across one chair, and produced from beneath it a thin, black wand. Bellany didn't point it at him, but the threat was obvious.

"Get dressed, and quickly," Bellany said. "My lady will speak with you."

"Your lady?"

"I've not the time to explain things now," Bellany replied. "We've a long road ahead of us, and though I have spells to speed us along our way, it would be better if we were gone from Luskan within the hour."

Morik scoffed at her. "Gone to where?" he asked. "I have no plans to leave . . ."

His voice trailed off as Bellany came back over to the edge of the bed, placing one knee up on it in a sexy pose, and lowered her face, putting one finger across her pouting lips.

"There are two ways we can do this, Morik," she explained quietly and calmly—too calmly for the sensibilities of the poor, surprised rogue. "One will be quite pleasurable for you, I am sure, and will guarantee your safe return to Luskan, where your friends here will no doubt comment on the wideness and constancy of your smile."

Morik regarded the enticing woman for a few moments. "Don't even bother to tell me the other way," he agreed.

⚔ ⚔ ⚔ ⚔ ⚔

"Arumn Gardpeck has not seen him," Catti-brie reported, "nor have any of the other regulars at the Cutlass—and they see Morik the Rogue almost every day."

Drizzt considered the words carefully. It was possible, of course, that the absence of Morik—he was not at his apartment, nor in any of his familiar haunts—was nothing more than coincidence. A man like Morik was constantly on the move, from one deal to another, from one theft to another.

But more than a day had passed since the four friends had begun their search for the rogue, using all the assets at their disposal, including the Luskan town guard, with no sign of the man. Given what had happened in Waterdeep with the agents of Sheila Kree, and given that Morik was a known associate of Wulfgar, Drizzt was not pleased by this disappearance.

"You put word in at the Hosttower?" Drizzt asked Regis.

"Robbers to a wizard," the halfling replied. "But yes, they will send word to *Sea Sprite*'s wizard, Robillard, as soon as they can locate him. It took more than half a bag of gold to persuade them to do the work."

"I gived ye a whole bag to pay for the task," Bruenor remarked dryly.

"Even with my ruby pendant, it took more than half a bag of gold to persuade them to do the work," Regis clarified.

Bruenor just put his head down and shook it. "Well, that means ye got nearly half a bag o' me gold for safe-keeping, Rumblebelly," he took care to state openly, and before witnesses.

"Did the wizards say anything about the fate of *Sea Sprite?*" Catti-brie asked. "Do they know if she's still afloat?"

"They said they've seen nothing to indicate anything different," Regis answered. "They have contacts among the docks, including many pirates. If *Sea Sprite* went down anywhere near Luskan the celebration would be immediate and surely loud."

It wasn't much of a confirmation, really, but the other three took the words with great hope.

"Which brings us back to Morik," Drizzt said. "If the pirate Kree is trying to strike first to chase off Deudermont and Wulfgar, then perhaps Morik became a target."

"What connection would Deudermont hold with that rogue?" Catti-brie asked, a perfectly logical question and one that had Drizzt obviously stumped.

"Perhaps Morik is in league with Sheila Kree," Regis reasoned. "An informant?"

Drizzt was shaking his head before the halfling ever finished. From his brief meeting with Morik, he did not think that the man would do such a thing. Though, he had to admit, Morik was a man whose loyalties didn't seem hard to buy.

"What do we know of Kree?" the drow asked.

"We know she ain't nowhere near to here," Bruenor answered impatiently. "And we know that we're wasting time here, that bein' the case!"

"True enough," Catti-brie agreed.

"But the season is deepening up north," Regis put in. "Perhaps we should begin our search to the south."

"All signs are that Sheila Kree is put in up north," Drizzt was quick to answer. "The rumors we have heard, from Morik and from Josi Puddles, place her somewhere up there."

"Lotta coast between here and the Sea o' Moving Ice," Bruenor put in.

"So we should wait?" Regis quickly followed.

"So we should get moving!" Bruenor retorted just as quickly, and since both Drizzt and Catti-brie agreed with the dwarf's reasoning the four friends departed Luskan later that same day, only hours after Morik and Bellany had left the city. But the latter, moving with the enhancements of many magical spells, and knowing where they were going, were soon enough far, far away.

16
Unexpected Friendship

As usual, Wulfgar was the first one to debark *Sea Sprite* when the schooner glided into dock at one of Waterdeep's many long wharves. There was little spring in the barbarian's step this day, despite his excitement at the prospect of seeing Delly and Colson again. Deudermont's last real discussion with him, more than a tenday before, had put many things into perspective for Wulfgar, had forced him to look into a mirror.

He did not like the reflection.

He knew Captain Deudermont was his friend, an honest friend and one who had spared his life despite evidence that he, along with Morik, had tried to murder the man. Deudermont had believed in Wulfgar when no others would. He'd rescued Wulfgar from Prisoner's Carnival without even a question begging confirmation that Wulfgar had not been involved in any plot to kill him. Deudermont had welcomed Wulfgar aboard *Sea Sprite* and had altered the course of his pirate-hunting schooner many times in an effort to find the elusive Sheila Kree. Even with the anger bubbling within him from the image in the mirror Deudermont had pointedly held up before his eyes on the return journey to their home port, Wulfgar could not dispute the honesty embodied in that image.

Deudermont had told him the truth of who he had become, with as much tact as was possible.

Wulfgar couldn't ignore that truth now. He knew his days sailing with *Sea Sprite* were at their end, at least for the season. If *Sea Sprite* was going south, as was her usual winter route—and in truth, the only available winter route—then there was little chance of encountering Kree. And if the ship wasn't going to find Kree, then what point would there be in having Wulfgar aboard, especially if the barbarian warrior and his impulsive tactics were a detriment to the crew?

That was the crux of it, Wulfgar knew. That was the truth in the mirror. Never before had the proud son of Beornegar considered himself anything less than a warrior. Many times in his life, Wulfgar had done things of which he was not proud—nothing more poignantly than the occasion on which he had slapped Catti-brie. But even then, Wulfgar had one thing he could hold onto. He was a fighter, among the greatest ever to come out of Icewind Dale, among the most legendary to ever come out of the Tribe of the Elk, or any of the other tribes. He was the warrior who had united the tribes with strength of arm and conviction, the barbarian who had hurled his warhammer high to shatter the cavern's hold on the great icicle, dropping the natural spear onto the back of the great white wyrm, Icingdeath. He was the warrior who had braved the Calimport sun and the assassins, tearing through the guildhouse of a notorious ruffian to save his halfling friend. He was, above all else, the companion of Drizzt Do'Urden, a Companion of the Hall, part of a team that had fostered the talk of legend wherever it had gone.

But not now. Now he could not rightly hold claim to that title of mighty warrior, not after his disastrous attempts to battle pirates aboard *Sea Sprite*. Now his friend Deudermont—an honest and compassionate friend—had looked him in the eye and showed to him the truth, and a diminishing truth it was. Would Wulfgar find again the courageous heart that had guided him through his emotional crises? Would he ever again be that proud warrior who had united the tribes of Ten-Towns, who had helped reclaim Mithral Hall, who had chased a notorious assassin across Toril too rescue his halfling friend?

Or had Errtu stolen that from him forever? Had the demon truly broken that spirit deep within the son of Beornegar? Had the demon altered his identity forever?

As he walked across the city of Waterdeep, turning to the hillock containing Deudermont's house, Wulfgar could not truly deny the possibility that the man he had once been, the warrior he had once been, was now lost to him forever. He wasn't sure what that meant, however.

Who was he?

His thoughts remained inward until he almost reached the front door of Captain Deudermont's mansion, when the sharp, unfamiliar voice ordered him to halt and be counted.

Wulfgar looked up, his crystal-blue eyes scanning all about, noting the many soldiers standing about the perimeter of the house, noting the lighter colors of the splintered wood near the lock of the front doors.

Wulfgar felt his gut churning, his warrior instincts telling him clearly that something was terribly amiss, his heart telling him that danger had come to Delly and Colson. With a growl that was half rage and half terror, Wulfgar sprinted straight ahead for the house, oblivious to the trio of soldiers who rushed to bar the way with their great halberds.

"Let him pass!" came a shout at the last second, right before Wulfgar crashed through the blocking soldiers. "It's Wulfgar returned! *Sea Sprite* is in!"

The soldiers parted, the rearmost wisely rushing back to push open the door or Wulfgar would have surely shattered it to pieces. The barbarian charged through.

He skidded to an abrupt stop just in side the foyer, though, spotting Delly coming down the main stairway, holding Colson tight in her arms.

She stared at him, managing a weak smile until she reached the bottom of the stairs—and there she broke down, tears flowing freely, and she rushed forward, falling into Wulfgar's waiting arms and tender hug.

Time seemed to stop for the couple as they stood there, clenched, needing each other's support. Wulfgar could have stayed like that for hours, indeed, but then he heard the voice of Captain Deudermont's surprise behind him, followed by a stream of curses from Robillard.

Wulfgar gently pushed Delly back, and turned about as the pair entered. The three stood there, looking about blankly, and their stares were no less incredulous when Delly at last inserted some sense into the surreal scene by saying, simply, "Sheila Kree."

⚔ ⚔ ⚔ ⚔ ⚔

Deudermont caught up to Wulfgar later, alone, the barbarian staring out the window at the crashing waves far below. It was the same window through which Drizzt and Catti-brie had entered, to save Delly and Colson.

"Fine friends you left behind in Icewind Dale," the captain remarked, moving to stand beside Wulfgar and staring out rather than looking at the huge man. When Wulfgar didn't answer,

Deudermont did glance his way, and noted that his expression was pained.

"Do you believe you should have been here, protecting Delly and the child?" the captain said bluntly. He looked up as Wulfgar looked down upon him, not scowling, but not looking very happy, either.

"You apparently believe so," the barbarian quipped.

"Why do you say that?" the captain asked. "Because I hinted that perhaps you should not take the next voyage out of Waterdeep with *Sea Sprite*? What would be the point? You joined with us to hunt Sheila Kree, and we'll not find her in the south, where surely we will go."

"Even now?" Wulfgar asked, seeming a bit surprised. "After Kree launched this attack against your own house? After your two friends lay cold in the ground, murdered by her assassins?"

"We can not sail to the north with the winter winds beginning to blow," Deudermont replied. "And thus, our course is south, where we will find many pirates the equal to Sheila Kree in their murders and mayhem. But do not think that I will forget this attack upon my house," the captain added with a dangerous grimace. "When the warm spring winds blow, *Sea Sprite* will return and sail right into the Sea of Moving Ice, if necessary, to find Kree and pay her her due."

Deudermont paused and stared at Wulfgar, holding the look until the barbarian reciprocated with a stare of his own. "Unless our dark elf friend beats us to the target, of course," the captain remarked.

Again Wulfgar winced, and looked back out to sea.

"The attack was nearly a month ago," Deudermont went on. "Drizzt is likely far north of Luskan by now, already on the hunt."

Wulfgar nodded, but didn't even blink at the proclamation, and the captain could see that the huge man was truly torn.

"I suspect the drow and Catti-brie would welcome the companionship of their old friend for this battle," he dared to say.

"Would you so curse Drizzt as to wish that upon him?" Wulfgar asked in all seriousness. He turned an icy glare upon Deudermont as he spoke the damning words, a look that showed a combination of sarcasm, anger, and just a bit of resignation.

Deudermont matched that stare for just a few short moments, taking a measure of the man. Then he just shrugged his shoulders and said, "As you wish. But I must tell you, Wulfgar of Icewind Dale, self pity does not become you."

With that, the captain turned and walked out of the room, leaving Wulfgar alone with some very unsettling thoughts.

✠ ✠ ✠ ✠ ✠

"The captain said we can stay as long as we wish," Wulfgar explained to Delly that same night. "Through the winter and spring. I'll find some work—I am no stranger to a blacksmith's shop—and perhaps we can find our own home next year."

"In Waterdeep?" the woman asked, seeming quite concerned.

"Perhaps. Or Luskan, or anywhere else you believe would be best for Colson to grow strong."

"Icewind Dale?" the woman asked without hesitation, and Wulfgar's shoulders sagged.

"It is a difficult land, full of hardship," Wulfgar answered, trying to remain matter-of-fact.

"Full o' strong men," Delly added. "Full of heroes."

Wulfgar's expression showed clearly that he was through playing this game. "Full of cutthroats and thieves," he said sternly. "Full of folk running from the honest lands, and no place for a girl to grow to a woman."

"I know of one girl who grew quite strong and true up there," the indomitable Delly Curtie pressed.

Wulfgar glanced all around, seeming angry and tense, and Delly knew that she had put him into a box here. Given his increasingly surly expression, she had to wonder if that was a good thing, and was about to suggest that they stay in Waterdeep for the foreseeable future just to let him out of the trap.

But then Wulfgar admitted the truth, bluntly. "I will not return to Icewind Dale. That is who I was, not who I am, and I have no desire to ever see the place again. Let the tribes of my people find their way without me."

"Let yer friends find their way without ye, even when they're trying to find their way to help ye?"

Wulfgar stared at her for a long moment, grinding his teeth at her accusatory words. He turned and pulled off his shirt, as if the matter was settled, but Delly Curtie could not be put in her place so easily.

"And ye speak of honest work," she said after him, and though he didn't turn back, he did stop walking away. "Honest work like hunting pirates with Captain Deudermont? He'd give ye a fine pay, no doubt, and get ye yer hammer in the meantime."

Wulfgar turned slowly, ominously. "Aegis-fang is not mine," he announced, and Delly had to chew on her bottom lip so she didn't scream out at him. "It belonged to a man who is dead, to a warrior who is no more."

"Ye canno' be meaning that!" Delly exclaimed, moving right up to grab him in a hug.

But Wulfgar pushed her back to arms' length and answered her denial with an uncompromising glare.

"Do ye not even wish to find Drizzt and Catti-brie to offer yer thanks for their saving me and yer baby girl?" the woman, obviously wounded, asked. "Or is that no big matter to ye?"

Wulfgar's expression softened, and he brought Delly in and hugged her tightly. "It is everything to me," he whispered into her ear. "Everything. And if I ever cross paths with Drizzt and Catti-brie again, I will offer my thanks. But I'll not go to find them—there is no need. They know how I feel."

Delly Curtie just let herself enjoy the hug and let the conversation end there. She knew that Wulfgar was kidding himself, though. There was no way Drizzt and Catti-brie could know how he truly felt.

How could they, when Wulfgar didn't even know?

Delly didn't know her place here, to push the warrior back to his roots or to allow him this new identity he was apparently trying on. Would the return to who he once was break him in the process, or would he forever be haunted by that intimidating and heroic past if he settled into a more mundane life as a blacksmith?

Delly Curtie had no answers.

ᚷ ᚷ ᚷ ᚷ ᚷ

A foul mood followed Wulfgar throughout the next few days. He took his comfort with Delly and Colson, using them as armor against the emotional turmoil that now roiled within him, but he could plainly see that even Delly was growing frustrated with him. More than once, the woman suggested that perhaps he should convince Deudermont to take him with *Sea Sprite* when they put out for the south, an imminent event.

Wulfgar understood those suggestions for what they were, frustration on the part of poor Delly, who had to listen to his constant grumbling, who had to sit by and watch him get torn apart by emotions he could not control.

He went out of the house often those few days and even managed to find some work with one of the many blacksmiths operating in Waterdeep.

He was at that job on the day *Sea Sprite* sailed.

He was at that job the day after that when a very unexpected visitor walked in to see him.

"Putting those enormous muscles of yours to work, I see," said Robillard the wizard.

Wulfgar looked at the man incredulously, his expression shifting from surprise to suspicion. He gripped the large hammer he had been using tightly as he stood and considered the visitor, ready to throw the tool right through this one's face if he began any sort of spellcasting. For Wulfgar knew that *Sea Sprite* was long out of dock, and he knew, too, that Robillard was well enough known among the rabble of the pirate culture for other wizards to use magic to impersonate him. Given the previous attack on Deudermont's house, the barbarian wasn't about to take any chances.

"It is me, Wulfgar," Robillard said with a chuckle, obviously recognizing every doubt on the barbarian's face. "I will rejoin the captain and crew in a couple of days—a minor spell, really, to teleport me to a place I have set up on the ship for just such occasions."

"You have never done that before, to my knowledge," Wulfgar remarked, his suspicions holding strong, his grip as tight as ever on the hammer.

"Never before have I had to play nursemaid to a confused barbarian," Robillard countered.

"Here now," came a gruff voice. A grizzled man walked in, all girth, hair, and beard, his skin as dark as his hair from all the soot. "What're ye looking to buy or get fixed?"

"I am looking to speak with Wulfgar, and nothing more," Robillard said curtly.

The blacksmith spat on the floor, then wiped a dirty cloth across his mouth. "I ain't paying him to talk," he said. "I'm paying him to work!"

"We shall see," the wizard replied. He turned back to Wulfgar but the blacksmith stormed over, poking a finger the wizard's way and reiterating his point.

Robillard turned his bored expression toward Wulfgar, and the barbarian understood that if he did not calm his often-angry boss, he might soon be self-employed. He patted the blacksmith's shoulders gently, and with strength that mocked even that of the lifelong smith, Wulfgar guided the man away.

When Wulfgar returned to Robillard, his face was a mask of anger. "What do you want, wizard?" he asked gruffly. "Have you come here to taunt me? To inform me of how much better off *Sea Sprite* is with me here on land?"

"Hmm," said Robillard, scratching at his chin. "There is truth in that, I suppose."

Wulfgar's crystal-blue eyes narrowed threateningly.

"But no, my large, foolish . . . whatever you are," Robillard remarked, and if he was the least bit nervous about Wulfgar's dangerous posture, he didn't show it one bit. "I came here, I suppose, because I am possessed of a tender heart."

"Well hidden."

"Purposely so," the wizard replied without hesitation. "So tell me, are you planning to spend the entirety of the winter at Deudermont's house, working . . . here?" He finished the question with a derisive snort.

"Would you be pleased if I left the captain's house?" Wulfgar asked in reply. "Do you have plans for the house? Because if you do, then I will gladly leave, and at once."

"Calm down, angry giant," Robillard said in purely condescending tones. "I have no plans for the house, for as I already told you I will be rejoining *Sea Sprite* very soon, and I have no family to speak of left on shore. You should pay better attention."

"Then you simply want me out," Wulfgar concluded. "Out of the house and out of Deudermont's life."

"That is a completely different point," Robillard dryly responded. "Have I said that I want you out, or have I asked if you plan to stay?"

Tired of the word games, and tired of Robillard all together, Wulfgar gave a little growl and went back to his work, banging away on the metal with his heavy hammer. "The captain told me that I could stay," he said. "And so I plan to stay until I have earned enough coin to purchase living quarters of my own. I would leave now—I plan to hold no debts to any man—except that I have Delly and Colson to look after."

"Got that backward," Robillard muttered under his breath, but loud enough—and Wulfgar knew, intentionally so—so that Wulfgar could hear.

"Wonderful plan," the wizard said more loudly. "And you will execute it while your former friends run off, and perhaps get themselves killed, trying to retrieve the magical warhammer that you were too stupid to hold onto. Brilliant, young Wulfgar!"

Wulfgar stood up straight from his work, the hammer falling from his hand, his jaw dropping open in astonishment.

"It is the truth, is it not?" the unshakable wizard calmly asked.

Wulfgar started to respond, but had no practical words to use as armor against the brutal and straightforward attack. However he might parse his response, however he might speak the words to make himself feel better, the simple fact was that Robillard's observations were correct.

"I can not change that which has happened," the defeated barbarian said as he bent to retrieve his hammer.

"But you can work to right the wrongs you have committed,"

Robillard pointed out. "Who are you, Wulfgar of Icewind Dale? And more importantly, who do you wish to be?"

There was nothing friendly in Robillard's sharp tone or in his stiff and hawkish posture, his arms crossed defiantly over his chest, his expression one of absolute superiority. But still, the mere fact that the wizard was showing any interest in Wulfgar's plight at all came as a surprise to the barbarian. He had thought, and not without reason, that Robillard's only concern regarding him was to keep him off *Sea Sprite*.

Wulfgar's angry stare at Robillard gradually eased into a self-deprecating chuckle. "I am who you see before you," he said, and he presented himself with his arms wide, his leather smithy apron prominently displayed. "Nothing more, nothing less."

"A man who lives a lie will soon enough be consumed by it," Robillard remarked.

Wulfgar's smile became a sudden scowl.

"Wulfgar the smith?" Robillard asked skeptically, and he gave a snort. "You are no laborer, and you fool yourself if you think that this newest pursuit will allow you to hide from the truth. You were born a warrior, bred and trained a warrior, and have ever relished that calling. How many times has Wulfgar charged into battle, the song of Tempus on his lips?"

"Tempus," Wulfgar said with disdain. "Tempus deserted me."

"Tempus was with you, and your faith in the code of the warrior sustained you through your trials," Robillard strongly countered. "*All* of your trials."

"You can not know what I endured."

"I do not care what you endured," Robillard replied. His claim, and the sheer power in his voice, surely had Wulfgar back on his heels. "I care only for that which I see before me now, a man living a lie and bringing pain to all around him and to himself because he hasn't the courage to face the truth of his own identity."

"A warrior?" Wulfgar asked doubtfully. "And yet it is Robillard who keeps me from that very pursuit. It is Robillard who bids Captain Deudermont to put me off *Sea Sprite*."

"You do not belong on *Sea Sprite*, of that I am certain," the wizard calmly replied. "Not at this time, at least. *Sea Sprite* is no place for one who would charge ahead in pursuit of personal demons. We succeed because we each know our place against the pirates. But I know, too, that you do not belong here, working as a smith in a Waterdhavian shop. Take heed of my words here and now, Wulfgar of Icewind Dale. Your friends are walking into grave danger, and whether you admit it or not, they are doing so for your benefit. If you do not join with them now, or at least go and speak with them to alter their course, there will be consequences. If Drizzt Do'Urden and Catti-brie walk into peril in search of Aegis-fang, whatever the outcome, you will punish yourself for the rest of your life. Not for your stupidity in losing the hammer so much as your cowardice in refusing to join in with them."

The wizard ended abruptly and just stood staring at the barbarian, whose expression was blank as he digested the truth of the words.

"They have been gone nearly a month," Wulfgar said, his voice carrying far less conviction. "They could be anywhere."

"They passed through Luskan, to be sure," Robillard replied. "I can have you there this very day, and from there, I have contacts to guide our pursuit."

"You will join in the hunt?"

"For your former friends, yes," Robillard answered. "For Aegis-fang? We shall see, but it hardly seems my affair."

Wulfgar looked as if a gentle breeze could blow him right over. He rocked back and forth, from foot to foot, staring blankly.

"Do not refuse this opportunity," Robillard warned. "It is your one chance to answer the questions that so haunt you and your one chance to belay the guilt that will forever stoop your shoulders. I offer you this, but life's road is too wound with unexpected turns for you to dare hope that the opportunity will ever again be before you."

"Why?" Wulfgar asked quietly.

"I have explained my reasoning of your current state clearly enough, as well as my beliefs that you should now take the strides to correct your errant course," Robillard answered, but Wulfgar was shaking his head before the wizard finished the thought.

"No," the barbarian clarified. "Why you?" When Robillard didn't immediately answer, Wulfgar went on, "You offer to help me, though you have shown me little friendship and I have made no attempt to befriend you. Yet here you are, offering advice and assistance. Why? Is it out of your previous friendship with Drizzt and Catti-brie? Or is it out of your desire to be rid of me, to have me far from your precious *Sea Sprite?*"

Robillard looked at him slyly. "Yes," he answered.

17

Morik's View

He's a bit forthcoming for a prisoner, I'd say," Sheila Kree remarked to Bellany after an exhausting three hours of interrogation during which Morik the Rogue had volunteered all he knew of Wulfgar, Drizzt, and Catti-brie. Sheila had listened carefully to every word about the dark elf in particular.

"Morik's credo is self-preservation," Bellany explained. "Nothing more than that. He would put a dagger into Wulfgar's heart himself, if his own life demanded it. Morik will not be glad if Drizzt and Wulfgar come against us. He may even find ways to stay out of the fight and not aid us as we destroy his former companion. but he'll not risk his own life going against us. Nor will he jeopardize the promise of a better future he knows we can offer to him. That's just not his way."

Sheila could accept the idea of personal gain over communal loyalty readily enough. It was certainly the source of any loyalty her cutthroat band held for her. They were a crew she kept together only by threat and promise—only because they all knew their best personal gains could be found under the command of Sheila Kree. They likewise knew that if they tried to leave, they would face the wrath of the deadly pirate leader and her elite group of commanders.

Sitting at the side of the room, Jule Pepper was even more convinced of Morik's authenticity, mostly because of his actions since he'd arrived with Bellany in Golden Cove. Everything Morik had said had been in complete agreement with all she'd learned of Drizzt during her short stay in Ten-Towns.

"If the drow and Catti-brie intend to come after the warhammer, then we can expect the dwarf, Bruenor, and the halfling, Regis, to join with them," she said. "And do not dismiss that panther companion Drizzt carries along."

"Won't forget any of it," Sheila Kree assured her. "Makes me glad Le'lorinel came to us."

"Le'lorinel's appearance here might prove to be the most fortunate thing of all," Bellany agreed.

"Morik's going to fight the elf now?" the pirate leader asked, for Le'lorinel, so obsessed with Drizzt, had requested some private time with this newest addition to the hide-out, one who had just suffered firsthand experience against the hated dark elf.

Jule Pepper laughed aloud at the question. Soon after Jule had arrived at Golden Cove, Le'lorinel had spent hour after hour with her, making her mimic every movement she'd seen Drizzt make, even those unrelated to battle. Le'lorinel wanted to know the length of his stride, the tilt of his head when he spoke, anything at all about the hated drow. Jule knew Morik would likely show the elf nothing of any value, but knew, too, that Le'lorinel would make him repeat his actions and words again and again. Never had Jule seen anyone so perfectly obsessed.

"Morik is likely beside Le'lorinel even now, no doubt reenacting the sequence that got him caught by Drizzt and Catti-brie," Bellany answered with a glance at the amused Jule.

"Ye be watchin' them with yer magic," Sheila instructed the sorceress. "Ye pay attention to every word Le'lorinel utters, to every movement made toward Morik."

"You still fear that our enemies might have sent the elf as a diversion?" Bellany asked.

"Le'lorinel's arrival was a bit too convenient," Jule remarked.

"What I'm fearin' even more is that the fool elf'll go finding Drizzt and his friends afore they're finding us," Sheila explained. "That group might be spendin' tendays wandering the mountains without any sign o' Minster Gorge or Golden Cove, and I'm preferring that to having enemies that powerful walkin' right in."

"I'd like to raise a beacon to guide them in," Jule said quietly. "I owe that group and intend to see them paid back in full."

"To say nothing of the many magical treasures they carry," Bellany agreed. "I believe I could get used to such a companion as Guenhwyvar, and wouldn't you look fine, Sheila, wearing the dark elf's reportedly fabulous scimitars strapped about your waist?"

Sheila Kree nodded and smiled wickedly. "But we got to get that group on our own terms and not theirs," she explained. "We'll bring 'em in when we're ready for 'em, after the winter's softened them up a bit. We'll get Le'lorinel the fight that's been doggin' the stubborn fool elf for all these years and hope that Drizzt falls hard then and there. And if not, there'll be fewer of us left to split the treasure."

"Speaking of that," Jule put in, "I note that many of our ogre friends have gone out and about, hunting the countryside. We would do well, I think, to keep them close until this business with Drizzt Do'Urden is finished."

"Only a few out at a time," Sheila Kree replied. "I told as much to Chogurugga already."

Bellany left the room soon after, and she couldn't help but smile at the way things were playing out. Normally, the winters had been dreadfully uneventful, but now this one promised a good fight, better treasure, and more companionship in the person of Morik the Rogue than the young sorceress had known since her days as an apprentice back in Luskan.

It was going to be a fine winter.

But Bellany knew that Sheila Kree was right concerning Le'lorinel. If they weren't careful, the crazy elf's obsession with Drizzt could invite disaster.

Bellany went right to her chamber and gathered together the components she needed for some divination spells, tuning in to the wide and rocky chamber Sheila Kree had assigned to Le'lorinel, watching as the elf and Morik went at their weapon dance, Le'lorinel instructing Morik over and over again to tell everything he knew about this strange dark elf.

✠ ✠ ✠ ✠ ✠

"How many times must I tell you that it was no fight?" Morik asked in exasperation, holding his arms out and down to the side, a dagger in each hand. "I had no desire to continue when I learned the prowess of the drow and his friend."

"No desire to continue," Le'lorinel pointedly echoed. "Which means that you began. And you just admitted that you learned of the dark elf's prowess. So show me, and now, else I will show you *my* prowess!"

Morik tilted his head and smirked at the elf, dismissing this upstart's threat. Or at least, appearing to. In truth, Le'lorinel had Morik quite unsettled. The rogue had survived many years on the tough streets by understanding his potential enemies and friends. He instinctively knew when to fight, when to bluff, and when to run away.

This encounter was fast shifting into the third category, for Morik could get no barometer on Le'lorinel. The elf's obsession was beyond readable, he recognized, drifting into something nearing insanity. He could see that clearly in the sheer intensity of the elf's blue and gold eyes, staring out at him through that ridiculous black mask. Would Le'lorinel really attack him if he didn't give the necessary information, and, apparently, in a manner that Le'lorinel could accept? He didn't doubt that for a moment, nor did he doubt that he might be overmatched. Drizzt Do'Urden had defeated his best attack routine with seeming ease, and had begun a counter that would have had Morik dead in seconds if the drow had so desired, and if Le'lorinel could pose an honest challenge to Drizzt . . .

"You wish him dead, but why?" the rogue asked.

"That is my affair and not your own," Le'lorinel answered curtly.

"You speak to me in anger, as if I can not or would not help you," Morik said, forcing a distinct level of calm into his voice. "Perhaps there's a way—"

"This is my fight and not your own," came the response, as sharp as Morik's daggers.

"Ah, but you alone, against Drizzt and his friends?" the rogue reasoned. "You may begin a brilliant and winning attack against the drow only to be shot dead by Catti-brie, standing calmly off to the side. Her bow—"

"I know all of Taulmaril and of Guenhwyvar and all the others," the elf assured him. "I will find Drizzt on my own terms and defeat him face to face, as justice demands."

Morik gave a laugh. "He is not such a bad fellow," he started to say, but the feral expression growing in Le'lorinel's eyes advised him to alter that course of reasoning. "Perhaps you should go and find a woman," the rogue added. "Elf or human—there seem to be many attractive ones about. Make love, my friend. That is justice!"

The expression that came back at Morik, though he had never

expected agreement, caught him by surprise, so doubtful and incredulous did it seem.

"How old are you?" Morik pressed on. "Seventy? Fifty? Even less? It is so hard to tell with you elves, and yes, I am jealous of you for that. But you are undeniably handsome, a delicate beauty the women will enjoy. So find a lover, my friend. Find two! And do not risk the centuries of life you have remaining in this battle with Drizzt Do'Urden."

Le'lorinel came forward a step. Morik fast retreated, subtly twisting his hands to prepare to launch a dagger into the masked face of his opponent, should Le'lorinel continue.

"I can not live!" the elf cried angrily. "I will see justice done! The mere notion of a dark elf walking the surface, feigning friendship and goodness offends everything I am and everything I believe. This dupe that is Drizzt Do'Urden is an insult to all of my ancestors, who drove the drow from the surface world and into the lightless depths where they belong."

"And if Drizzt retreated into the lightless depths, would you then pursue him?" Morik asked, thinking he might have found a break in the elf's wall of reasoning.

"I would kill every drow if that power was in my hands," Le'lorinel sneered in response. "I would obliterate the entire race and be proud of the action. I would kill their matrons and their murderous raiders. I would drive my dagger into the heart of every drow child!"

The elf was advancing with every sentence, and Morik was wisely backing, staying out of dangerous range, holding his hands up before him, daggers still ready, and patting the air in an effort to calm this brewing storm.

Finally Le'lorinel stopped the approach and stood glaring at him. "Now, Morik, are you going to show me the action that occurred between you and Drizzt Do'Urden, or am I to test your battle mettle personally and use it as a measure of the prowess of Drizzt Do'Urden, given what I already know about your encounter?"

Morik gave a sigh and nodded his compliance. Then he positioned Le'lorinel as Drizzt had been that night in the Luskan alley and took the elf through the attack and defense sequence.

Over and over and over and over, at Le'lorinel's predictable insistence.

✕ ✕ ✕ ✕ ✕

Bellany watched the entire exchange with more than a bit of amusement. She enjoyed watching Morik's fluid motions, though she couldn't deny that Le'lorinel was even more beautiful in battle than he, with greater skill and grace. Bellany laughed aloud at that, given Morik's errant perceptions.

When the pair at last finished the multiple dances, Bellany heard Morik dare to argue, "You are a fine fighter, a wonderful warrior. I do not question your abilities, friend. But I warn you that Drizzt Do'Urden is good, very good. Perhaps as good as anyone in all the northland. I know that not only from my brief encounter with him, but from the tales that Wulfgar told me during our time together. I see that your rage is an honest one, but I implore you to reconsider this course. Drizzt Do'Urden is very good, and his friends are powerful indeed. If you follow through with this course, he will kill you. And what a waste of centuries that would be!"

Morik bowed, turned, and quickly headed away, moving, Bellany suspected, toward her room. She liked that thought, for watching the play between Morik and Le'lorinel had surely excited her, and she decided she would not correct the rogue. Not soon, at least.

This was too much fun.

✕ ✕ ✕ ✕ ✕

Morik did indeed consider going to see Bellany as he departed Le'lorinel's sparring chamber. The elf had more amused him than shaken him—Morik saw him as a complete fool, wasting every potential enjoyment and experience in life in seeking this bloody vow of vengeance against a dark elf better left alone. Whether Drizzt was a good sort or a bad one wasn't really the issue, in Morik's view. The simple measure of the worth of Le'lorinel's quest was the question of whether or not Drizzt was seeking the elf. If he was, then Le'lorinel would do well to strike first, but if he was not, then the elf was surely a fool.

Drizzt was not looking for the elf. Morik knew that instinctively. Drizzt had come seeking information about Wulfgar and about Aegis-fang but had said nothing about any elf named Le'lorinel, or about any elf at all. Drizzt wasn't hunting Le'lorinel, and likely, he didn't even know that Le'lorinel was hunting him.

Morik turned down a side corridor, moving to an awkwardly set wooden door. With great effort, he managed to push it open and moved through it to an outside landing high up on the cliff face, perhaps two hundred feet from the crashing waves far below.

Morik considered the path that wound down around the rocky spur that would take him to the floor of the gorge on the other side of the mound and to the trails that would lead him far away from Sheila Kree. He could probably get by the sentries watching the gorge with relative ease, could probably get far, far away with little effort.

Of course, the storm clouds were gathering in the northwest, over the Sea of Moving Ice, and the wind was cold. He'd have a hard time making Luskan before the season overwhelmed him, and it wouldn't be a pleasant journey even if he did make it. And of course, Bellany had already shown that she could find him in Luskan.

Morik grinned as he considered other possible routes. He wasn't exactly sure where he was—Bellany had used magic to bounce them from place to place on the way there—but he suspected he wasn't very far from a potential shelter against the winter.

"Ah, Lord Feringal, are you expecting visitors?" the rogue whispered, but he was laughing with every word, hardly considering the possibility of fleeing to Auckney—if he could even figure out where Auckney was, relative to Golden Cove. Without the proper attire, it would not be easy for the rogue Morik to assume again the identity of Lord Brandeburg of Waterdeep, an alias he had once used to dupe Lord Feringal of Auckney.

Morik was laughing at the thought of wandering away into the wintry mountains, and the notion was far from serious. It was just comforting for Morik to know he could likely get away if he so desired.

With that in mind, Morik wasn't surprised that the pirates had given him fairly free reign. If they offered to put him back in Luskan and never bother him again, he wasn't sure he would take them up on it. Life there was tough, even for one of Morik's cunning and reputation, but life in the cove seemed easy enough, and certainly Bellany was going out of her way to make it pleasant.

But what about Wulfgar? What about Drizzt Do'Urden and Catti-brie?

Morik looked out over the cold waters and seriously considered the debts he might owe to his former traveling companion. Yes, he did care about Wulfgar, and he made up his mind then and there, that if the barbarian did come against Golden Cove in an effort to regain Aegis-fang, then he would do all that he could to convince Sheila Kree and particularly Bellany to try to capture the man and not to destroy him.

That would be a more difficult task concerning Drizzt, Morik knew, considering his recent encounter with the crazy Le'lorinel, but Morik was able to shrug that possibility away easily enough.

In truth, what in the world did Morik the Rogue owe to Drizzt Do'Urden? Or to Catti-brie?

The little dark-haired thief stretched and hugged his arms close to his chest to ward the cold wind. He thought of Bellany and her warm bed and started off for her immediately.

✠ ✠ ✠ ✠ ✠

Le'lorinel stood sullenly in the sparring chamber after Morik had gone, considering his last words.

Morik was wrong, Le'lorinel knew. The elf didn't doubt his assessment of Drizzt's fighting prowess. Le'lorinel knew well the tales of Drizzt's exploits. But Morik did not understand the years of preparation for this one fight, the great extremes to which Le'lorinel had gone to be in a position to defeat Drizzt Do'Urden.

But Le'lorinel could not easily dismiss Morik's warning. This fight with Drizzt would indeed happen, the elf repeated silently, fingering the ring that contained the necessary spells. Even if it went exactly as Le'lorinel had prepared and planned, it would likely end in two deaths, not one.

So be it.

18
WHERE TRAIL AND SMOKE COMBINE

The four companions, wearing layers of fur and with blood thickened from years of living in the harshness of Icewind Dale, were not overly bothered by the wintry conditions they found waiting for them not so far north of Luskan. The snow was deep in some places, the trails icy in others, but the group plodded along. Bruenor led Catti-bric and Regis, plowing a trail with his stout body, with Drizzt guiding them from along the side.

Their progress was wonderful, given the season and the difficult terrain, but of course Bruenor found a reason to grumble. "Damn twinkly elf don't even break the crust!" he muttered, crunching through one snow drift that was more than waist high, while Drizzt skipped along on the crusty surface of the snow, half-skating, half-running. "Gotta get him to eat more and put some meat on them skinny limbs!"

Behind the dwarf, Catti-brie merely smiled. She knew, and so did Bruenor, that Drizzt's grace was more a measure of balance than of weight. The drow knew how to distribute his weight perfectly, and because he was always balanced, he could shift that weight to his other foot immediately if he felt the snow collapsing beneath him. Catti-brie was about Drizzt's height and was even a bit lighter than him, but there was no way she could possibly move as he did.

Because he was atop the snow instead of plowing through it, Drizzt was afforded a fine vantage point of the rolling white lands all around. He noted a trail not far to the side—a recent one, where someone or something had plodded along, much as Bruenor was doing now.

"Hold!" the drow called. Even as he spoke, Drizzt noted another curious sight, that of smoke up ahead, some distance away, rising in a thin line as if from a chimney. He considered it for just a moment, then glanced back to the trail, which seemed to be going in that general direction. He wondered if the two were somehow connected. A trapper's house, perhaps, or a hermit.

Figuring that the friends could all use a bit of rest, Drizzt made good speed for the trail. They had been out from Luskan for nearly a tenday, finding good shelter only twice, once with a farmer the first night and another night spent in a cave.

Drizzt wasn't as hopeful for shelter when he arrived at the line in the snow and saw footprints more than twice the size of his own.

"What'd'ye got, elf?" Bruenor called.

Drizzt motioned for the group to be quiet and for them to come and join him.

"Big orcs, perhaps," he remarked when they were all there. "Or small ogres."

"Or barbarians," Bruenor remarked. "Them folk got the biggest feet I ever seen on a human."

Drizzt examined one clear print more carefully, bending over to put his eyes only a few inches from it. He shook his head. "These are too heavy, and those who made them wore hard boots, not the doeskin Wulfgar's people would wear," he explained.

"Ogres, then," said Catti-brie. "Or big orcs."

"Plenty of those in these mountains," Regis put in.

"And heading for that line of smoke," Drizzt explained, pointing ahead to the thin plume.

"Might be their kinfolk making the smoke," Bruenor reasoned. With a wry grin, the dwarf turned to Regis. "Get to it, Rumblebelly."

Regis blanched, thinking then that perhaps he had done too well with that last orc camp, when he and Bruenor were making their way to Luskan. The halfling wasn't going to shy from his responsibilities, but if these were ogres, he'd be sorely overmatched. And Regis knew that ogres favored halfling as one of their most desired meals.

When Regis came out of his contemplation, he noted that Drizzt was looking at him, smiling knowingly, as if he'd read the halfling's every thought.

"This is no job for Regis," the dark elf said.

"He done it on the way to Luskan," Bruenor protested. "Done it well, too."

"But not in this snow," Drizzt replied. "No thief would be able to find appropriate shadows in this white-out. No, let us go in together to see what friends or enemies we might find."

"And if they are ogres?" Catti-brie asked. "Ye thinking we're overdue for a fight?"

Drizzt's expression showed clearly that the notion was not an unpleasant one, but he shook his head. "If they do not concern us, then better that we do not concern them," he said. "But let us learn what we might—it may be that we will find shelter and good food for the night."

Drizzt moved off to the side and a little ahead, and Bruenor led the way along the carved trail. The dwarf brought out his large axe, slapping its handle across his shield hand, and set his one-horned helmet firmly on his head, more than ready for a fight. Behind him, Catti-brie set an arrow to Taulmaril and tested the pull.

If these were ogres or orcs and they happened to have a decent shelter constructed, then Catti-brie fully expected to be occupying that shelter long before nightfall. She knew Bruenor Battlehammer too well to think that the dwarf would ever walk away from a fight with either of those beasts.

✗ ✗ ✗ ✗ ✗

"Yer turn to get the firewood," Donbago snarled at his younger brother, Jeddith. He pushed the young man toward the tower door. "We'll all be frozen by morning if ye don't bring it!"

"Yeah, I know," the younger soldier grumbled, running a hand through his greasy hair and scratching at some lice. "Damn weather. Shouldn't be this cold yet."

The other two soldiers in the stone tower grumbled their agreement. Winter had come early, and with vigor, to the Spine of the World, sweeping down on an icy wind that cut right through the stones of the simple tower fortress to bite at the soldiers. They did have a fire burning in the hearth, but it was getting thin, and they didn't have enough wood to get through the night. There was plenty to be found, though, so none of them were worried.

"If ye help me, we'll bring enough to get it blazing," Jeddith observed, but Donbago grumbled about taking his turn on the tower top watch, and headed for the stairs even as Jeddith started for the outside door.

A breeze whistling in through the opened door pushed Donbago along as he made the landing to the second floor, to find the other two soldiers of the remote outpost.

"Well, who's up top?" Donbago scolded.

"No one," answered one of the pair, scaling the ladder running up from the center of the circular floor to the center of the ceiling. "The trapdoor's frozen stuck."

Donbago grumbled and moved to the base of the ladder, watching as his companion for the sentry duty banged at the metal trapdoor. It took them some time to break through the ice, and so Donbago wasn't on the rooftop and didn't have to watch helplessly as Jeddith, some thirty feet from the tower door, bent over to retrieve some deadwood, oblivious to the hulking ogre that stepped out from behind a tree and crushed his skull with a single blow from a heavy club.

Jeddith went down without a sound, and the marauder dragged him out of sight.

The brute working at the back of the tower was noisier, throwing a grapnel attached to a heavy rope at the tower's top lip, but its tumult was covered by the banging on the metal trapdoor.

Before Donbago and his companion had the door unstuck, the half-ogre grabbed the knotted rope in its powerful hands and walked itself right up the nearly thirty feet of the tower wall, heaving itself to the roof.

The brute turned about, reaching for a large axe it had strapped across its back, even as the door banged open and Donbago climbed through.

With a roar, the half-ogre leaped at him, but it wound up just bowling the man aside. Fortune was with Donbago, and the half-ogre's axe got hooked on the heavy strapping. Still, the man went flying down hard against the tower crenellation, his breath blasting away.

Gasping, Donbago couldn't even cry out a warning as his companion climbed onto the roof. The half-ogre tore its axe free.

Donbago winced and grimaced as the brute cut his companion nearly in half. Donbago drew his sword and forced himself to his feet and into a charge. He let his rage be his guide as he closed on the brute, saw his companion, his friend, half out of the trapdoor, squirming in the last moments of his life. A seasoned warrior, Donbago didn't let the image force him into any rash movements. He came in fast and furiously, but in a tempered manner, launching what looked like a wild swing then retracting the sword just enough so that the brute's powerful parry whistled past without hitting anything.

Now Donbago came forward with a stab, and another, driving the brute back and opening its gut.

The half-ogre wailed and tried to retreat, but lost its footing on the slippery stone and went down hard.

On came Donbago, leaping forward with a tremendous slash, but even as his sword descended, the half-ogre's great leg kicked up, connecting solidly and launching the man into a head-over-heels somersault. His blow still landed, though, and the ragged half-ogre had to work hard to regain its footing.

Donbago was up before it, stabbing and slashing. He kept looking from his target to his dead friend, letting the rage drive him on. Even as the ogre attacked he scored a deep strike. Still, in his offensive stance, he couldn't get aside, and he took a glancing blow from that awful axe. Then he took a heavy punch in the face, one that shattered his nose, cracked the bones in both his cheeks, and sent him skidding back hard into the wall.

He slumped there, telling himself that he had to shake the black spots out of his eyes, had to get up and in a defensive posture, telling himself that the brute was falling over him even then, and that he would be crushed and chopped apart.

With a growl that came from deep in his belly, the dazed and bleeding Donbago forced himself to his feet, his sword before him in a pitiful attempt to ward what he knew would be a killing blow.

But the half-ogre wasn't there. It stood, or rather knelt on one knee by the open trapdoor, clutching at its belly, holding in its entrails, the look on its ugly face one of pure incredulity and pure horror.

Not wanting to wait until the beast decided if the wound was mortal or not, Donbago rushed across the tower top and smashed his sword repeatedly on the half-ogre's upraised arm. When that arm was at last knocked aside, the man continued to bash with every ounce of strength and energy, again spurred on by the sight of his dead companion and by the sudden fear that his brother—

His brother!

Donbago cried out and bashed away, cracking the beast's skull, knocking it flat to the stone. He bashed away some more, long after the half-ogre stopped moving, turning its ugly head to pulp.

Then he got up and staggered to the open hatch, trying to pull his torn friend all the way through. When that didn't work, Donbago pushed the man inside instead, holding him as low as he could so that the fall wouldn't be too jarring to the torn corpse.

Sniffling away the horror and the tears, Donbago called out for the others to secure the tower, called out for someone to go and find his brother.

But he heard the fighting from below and knew that no one was hearing him.

Without the strength to rush down to join them, Donbago considered his other options and worried, too, that other brutes might be climbing up behind him.

He started to turn away from the trapdoor and the spectacle of his dead friend in the room below, but stopped as he saw another of the soldiers rush up the stairs to make the landing at the side of the second level.

"Ogres!" the man cried, stumbling for the ladder. He made it to the base, almost, but then a half-ogre appeared on the landing behind him and launched a grapnel secured to a chain. It hooked over the man's shoulder even as he grabbed the ladder.

Donbago yelled out and started to go down after him, but with a single mighty jerk, an inhumanly powerful tug, the half-ogre tore the man from the ladder, so instantly, so brutally, that Donbago had to blink away the illusion that the man had simply disappeared.

Or part of him had, at least, for still holding the ladder below him was the man's severed arm.

Donbago looked over to the landing just in time to see the man's last moments as the half-ogre pummeled him down to the stone floor. Then the brute looked up at Donbago, smiling wickedly.

The battered Donbago rolled away from the trapdoor and quickly turned the metal portal over and closed it, then rolled on top of it using his body as a locking bar.

A glance at the dead ogre on the tower top reminded him of his vulnerability up there. Hearing no noise from below other than the distant fighting, Donbago leaped up and ran to the back lip of the tower, pulling free the grapnel. He took it with him as he dived back to cover the trapdoor, pulling the rope up the tower's side from there.

A few moment's later, he felt the first jarring blow from beneath him, a thunderous report that shook the teeth in his mouth.

⚔ ⚔ ⚔ ⚔ ⚔

Drizzt noted that the tower door was ajar, and noted, too, the crimson stain on the snow near some trees not far away. Then he heard the shout from the tower top.

He motioned for his friends to be alert and ready, then sprinted off to the side, flanking the tower, trying to get a measure of what was happening and where he would best fit into the battle.

Catti-brie and Bruenor stayed on the ogre trail, but moved

more cautiously then, motioning to Drizzt. To the drow's surprise, Regis did not remain with the pair. The halfling ran off to the left, flanking the tower the other way. He plowed through the snow, then finally reached a patch of wind-blown stone and sprinted off from shadow to shadow, keeping low and moving swiftly, heading around the back.

Drizzt couldn't suppress a grin, thinking that Regis was typically trying to find an out-of-the-way hiding spot.

That smile went away almost immediately, though, as the drow came to understand that the threat was imminent, that indeed battle was already underway. He saw a man, his tunic and face bloody, sprint out of the open tower door and rush off to the side, screaming for help.

A hulking form, a large and ugly ogre, chased after him in close pursuit, its already bloody club raised high.

The man had a few step lead, but that wouldn't last in the deep snow, Drizzt knew. The ogre's longer and stronger legs would close the gap fast, and that club. . . .

Drizzt turned away from the tower in pursuit of the pair. He managed to offer a quick hand signal to Bruenor and Catti-brie, showing them his intent and indicating that they should continue on to the tower. He ran on, his light steps keeping him atop the snow pack.

At first Drizzt feared that the ogre would get to the fleeing man first, but the man put on a burst of speed and dived headlong over the side of a ridge, tumbling away in the snow.

The ogre stopped at the ridge, and Drizzt yelled out. The brute seemed more than happy to spin about and fight this newest challenger. Of course, the eager gleam in the ogre's eye melted away, and the stupid grin became an expression of surprise indeed when the ogre recognized that this newest challenger was not another human, but a drow elf.

Drizzt went in hard, scimitars whirling, hoping to make a quick kill. Then he could see to the wounded man, and he could get back to the tower and help his friends.

But this brute was no ordinary ogre. This was a seasoned warrior, nine feet of muscle and bone with the agility to maneuver its heavy spiked club with surprising deftness.

Drizzt's eagerness nearly cost him dearly, for as he came ahead, scimitars twirling in oppositional arcs, the quick-footed ogre stepped back just out of range and brought its club across with a tremendous sweep, taking one scimitar along with it. Drizzt was barely able to keep a grip on the weapon. If he'd dropped it, he might never find it in the deep snow.

Drizzt managed not only to get his second blade, in his right hand, out of the way of the blow, but he got in a stab that bloodied the ogre's trailing forearm. The brute accepted the sting, though, in exchange for slipping through its real attack. Lifting its heavy leg and following the sweep of the club with a mighty kick, it caught Drizzt on the shoulder and launched him a dozen spinning feet through the air to crash down into the snow.

The drow recognized his error, then, and was only glad that he had made the error out in the open, where he could fast recover. If he had gotten kicked like that inside the tower, he figured he'd now be little more than a red stain on the stone wall.

⚔ ⚔ ⚔ ⚔

They saw the drow's signal, but neither Bruenor nor Catti-brie were about to abandon Drizzt as he chased off after the ogre—until they heard the cry for help, as pitiful a wail as either had ever heard, coming from inside the tower.

"Ye keep yer damned shots higher than me head!" Bruenor yelled to his girl, and the dwarf bent his shoulders low and rambled on for the tower door, gaining speed, momentum, and fury.

Catti-brie worked hard to keep up, just a few feet behind, Taulmaril in hand, leveled and ready.

There was nothing subtle or quiet about the dwarf's charge, and predictably, Bruenor was met at the doorway by another hulking form. The dwarf's axe chopped hard. Catti-brie's arrow slammed the brute in the chest. Those two blows, combined with the sturdy dwarf's momentum got Bruenor crashing into the main area of the tower's lowest floor.

This opponent, a half-ogre and a tough one at that, wasn't finished. It managed a counterstrike with its club, bouncing a mighty hit off Bruenor's shoulder.

"Ye got to do better than that!" the dwarf bellowed, though in truth, the blow hurt.

Smiling in spite of the pain, Bruenor swiped his axe across. The half-ogre stumbled out of reach but came back forward for a counter too soon. Bruenor's backhand caught it flat against the ribs, stealing its momentum and its intended attack.

The half-ogre staggered, giving Bruenor the time to set his feet properly and begin again. The next hit wasn't with the flat of the axe, but with the jagged, many-notched head, a swipe that cut a slice right down the battered brute's chest.

Before Bruenor could begin to celebrate the apparent victory, though, a second half-ogre leaped out from the stairway, slamming into its mortally wounded companion and taking both of them crashing over Bruenor, burying the dwarf beneath nearly a ton of flesh and bone.

The dwarf needed Catti-brie sorely at that point, but a call from above told him that, perhaps, so did someone else.

⚔ ⚔ ⚔ ⚔ ⚔

At the back of the tower, in close to the base of the wall and listening intently, Regis heard Bruenor's charge. He didn't have any great urge to go around with the dwarf, though, for Bruenor's tactics were straightforward, muscle against muscle, trading punch for punch.

Joining in that strategy against ogres, Regis wouldn't last beyond the first blow.

A cry from above jarred the halfling. He started to climb hand over hand, picking holds in the cold, cracked stone. By the time he was halfway up, his poor fingers were scraped and bleeding, but he kept going, moving with deceiving swiftness, picking his holds expertly and nearing the top.

He heard a yell and a crash, then some heavy scuffling. Up he went with all speed, and he nearly slipped and fell, catching himself at the very last moment—and with more than a little luck.

Finally he put his hand on the lip of the tower top and peeked over. What he saw almost made him want to leap right off.

⚔ ⚔ ⚔ ⚔ ⚔

Poor Donbago, crying out repeatedly, only wanted to hold the portal shut, to close his eyes and will all of this horror away. He was a seasoned fighter and had seen many battles and had lost many friends.

But not his brother.

He knew in his heart that Jeddith was down, and likely dead. He knew in his heart that the tower was lost, and that there would be no escape. Perhaps if he just lay there long enough, using his body to block the trapdoor, the brutes would go away. He knew, after all, that ogres were not known for persistence or for cunning.

Most were not, at least.

Donbago hardly noticed the warmth at first, though he did smell the burning leather. He didn't understand—until a sharp pain erupted in his back. Reflexively, the man rolled, but he stopped at once, realizing that he had to hold the door shut.

He tried going back, but the metal was hot—so hot!

The ogres below must have been heating it with torches.

Donbago jumped atop the door, hoping his boots would insulate him from the heat. He heard a scream as one of his companions exited the tower, and, a few moments later, a roar from below, by the front door.

He was hopping, his boots smoking. He looked around frantically, searching for something he could use to place over the door, a loose stone in the crenellation, perhaps.

He went flying away as an ogre below leveled a tremendous blow to the door. A second strike, before Donbago could scramble back, had the portal bouncing open. A brute came through with amazing speed, obviously boosted to the roof by a companion.

Donbago, waves of pain still spreading from his broken face, leaped into the fray immediately and furiously, thinking of his brother with every mad strike. He scored a couple of hits on the ogre, which seemed truly surprised by his ferocity, but then its companion was up beside it. Two heavy clubs swatted at him, back and forth.

He ducked, he dodged, he didn't even try to parry the too-powerful blows, and his desperate offensive posture allowed him to manage another serious stab at the first brute, sending it sprawling to the stone.

Donbago got hit, knocked to his back, his sword flying, and before he even realized what had happened, the valiant soldier felt a strong hand grab his ankle.

In an instant, he was scooped aloft, hanging upside down at the end of a mighty ogre's arm.

Drizzt rolled across the snow, not fighting the momentum but enhancing it, allowing the ogre's kick to take him as far from his formidable opponent as possible. He wanted to get up and face the ogre squarely, to take a better measure and put this fight back on more recognizable ground. He believed that his underestimation of his opponent alone had cost him that hit, that he had erred greatly.

He was surprised again when he at last tucked his feet under him and started to rise, to find that the ogre had kept up with him and was even then coming in for another furious attack.

The brute was moving too fast—too far beyond what Drizzt, no novice to battling ogres, would have expected from one of its lumbering kind.

In came the club, swatting down to the left, forcing the drow to dodge right. The ogre halted the swing quickly and put the club up and over, taking it up in both hands like someone splitting wood might, and slamming it straight down at the new position Drizzt was settling into, with more force than one of Drizzt's stature could possibly hope to block or even deflect.

Drizzt dived into a roll back to the left, coming up facing to the side and rushing fast in retreat, putting some ground between himself and the brute. He spun at the ready, almost expecting this surprising foe to be upon him once again.

This time, though, the ogre had remained in place. It grinned as it regarded Drizzt, then pulled a ceramic flask from its belt—a belt that already showed several open loops, Drizzt noted—and popped it into its mouth, chewing it up to get at the potion.

Almost immediately, the ogre's arms began to bulge with heightened strength, with the strength of a great giant.

Drizzt actually felt better now that he had sorted out the riddle. The ogre had taken a potion of speed, obviously, and now one of strength, and likely others of enhancing magical properties. Now the drow understood, and now the drow could better anticipate.

Drizzt lamented that Guenhwyvar had been with him the night before, that he had used up the magic of the figurine for the time being. He could not recall the panther, and now, it seemed, he could use the help.

In came the ogre, swatting its club all about, howling with rage and with the anticipation of this sweet kill. Drizzt had to drop low to his knees, else that victory would have come quickly for the brute.

But now Drizzt had a plan. The ogre was moving more quickly than it was used to moving, and its great strength would send its club out with tremendous, often unbreakable momentum. Drizzt could use that against the beast, perhaps, could utilize misdirection as a way of having the ogre off-balance and with apparent openings.

Up came the drow, skittering to the side—or seeming to then cutting back and rushing straight ahead, scoring a solid hit on the ogre's leg as he waded past.

He continued and dived ahead, turning as he came up to face his foe, expecting to see the blood turning bright red near that torn leg.

The ogre was hardly bleeding, as if something other than its skin had absorbed the bulk of that wicked scimitar strike.

Drizzt's mind whirled through the possibilities. There were potions, he had heard, that could do such things, potions offering varying degrees of added heroism.

"Ah, Guen," the drow lamented, for he knew that he was in for quite a fight.

⚔ ⚔ ⚔ ⚔ ⚔

The dwarf wondered if he would simply suffocate under the press of the two heavy bodies, particularly the dead weight of the one he had defeated. He squirmed and tucked his legs, then worked to find some solid footing and pushed ahead with all his strength, his short, bunched muscles straining mightily.

He got his head out from under the fallen brute's hip, but then had to duck right back underneath as the second brute, still lying atop the dying one, slapped down at him with a powerful grasping hand.

The ogre finger-walked that hand underneath in pursuit of the dwarf, and with his own arms still pinned down beside him, Bruenor couldn't match the grab.

So he bit the hand instead, latching on like an angry dog, gnashing his teeth, and crunching the brute's knuckles.

The half-ogre howled and pulled back, but the dwarf's mighty jaw remained clamped. Bruenor held on ferociously. The brute crawled off its dying companion, twisting about to gain some leverage, then lifted the fallen ogre's hip and tugged hard, pulling the dwarf out on the end of its arm.

The brute lifted its other arm to smack at the dwarf, but once free, Bruenor didn't hesitate. He grabbed the trapped forearm in both hands and, still biting hard, ran straight back, turning about and twisting the arm as he went behind the half-ogre.

"Got one for ye!" the dwarf yelled, finally releasing his bite, for he had the half-ogre off-balance then, momentarily helpless and lined up for the open doorway. Bruenor drove ahead with all his strength and leverage, forcing the brute into a quick-step. With a great heave, the dwarf got the brute to the doorway and through it.

Where Catti-brie's arrow met it, square in the chest.

The half-ogre staggered backward, or started to, for as soon as he had let the thing go, Bruenor quick-stepped back a few steps, rubbed his heavy boots on the stone for traction, and rushed forward, leaping as the half-ogre staggered back to slam hard into the brute's lower back.

The brute stumbled out through the door, where another arrow hit it hard in the chest.

It fell to its knees grasping at the two shafts with trembling hands.

Catti-brie shot it again, right in the face.

"More on the stairs!" Bruenor yelled out to her. "Come on, girl, I need ye!"

Catti-brie started forward, ready to rush right in past the brute she had just felled, but then came another cry from above. She looked up to see a squirming, whimpering man hanging out over the tower's edge, a huge half-ogre holding him by the ankles.

Up came Taulmaril, leveling at the brute's face, for Catti-brie figured that the man might well survive the fall into the snow, which was piled pretty deep on this side of the tower, but knew that he had no chance of surviving his current captor.

But the half-ogre saw her as well, and, with a wicked grin, brought up its own weapon—a huge club—and lined up for a hit that would surely break the squirming man apart.

Catti-brie reflexively cried out.

⚔ ⚔ ⚔ ⚔ ⚔

At the back of the tower top, Regis heard that cry. Looking that way he understood that the poor soldier was in a precarious predicament. But the halfling couldn't get to the brute in time, and even if he did, what could he and his tiny mace do against something of that monster's bulk?

The second half-ogre, wounded by the soldier's valiant fight but not down, was on the move again to join its companion. It rushed across the tower top, oblivious to the halfling peering over the rim.

Purely on instinct—if he had thought about it, the halfling would have more likely simply passed out from fear than made the move—Regis pulled himself over the lip and scrambled forward half running, half diving, skidding low right between the running half-ogre's leading heel and trailing toe.

The brute tripped up, its kick as it stumbled forward jolting and battering the poor halfling and lifting Regis into a short flight.

Out of control, the half-ogre gained momentum, falling headlong into its companion's broad back.

⚔ ⚔ ⚔ ⚔ ⚔

Catti-brie saw no choice but to take her chances on the shot, much as she had done against the pirate holding Delly in Captain Deudermont's house.

The half-ogre apparently anticipated just that and delayed its swing at the man and ducked back instead, the arrow streaking harmlessly into the air before it.

Catti-brie winced, thinking the man surely doomed. Before she could even reach to set another arrow, though, the half-ogre came forward suddenly, way over the tower lip. It let go of the man, who dropped, screaming, into the snow. It too went over, hands flailing helplessly.

⚔ ⚔ ⚔ ⚔ ⚔

Gasping for his lost breath, his ribs sorely bruised, the battered halfling struggled to his feet and faced the half-ogre he had tripped even as the brute turned to regard him ominously. Its look was one of pure menace, promising a horrible death.

With a growl, it took a long step toward the halfling.

Regis considered his little mace, a perfectly insignificant weapon against the sheer mass and strength of this brute, then sighed and tossed it to the ground. With a tip of his hood, the halfling turned around and ran for the back of the tower, crying out with every running step. He understood the drop over that lip. It was a good thirty feet, and the back side of the tower, unlike the front, was nearly clear, wind-blown stone.

Still, the halfling never slowed. He leaped up and rolled over the edge. Without slowing, roaring in rage with every step, the half-ogre dived over right behind.

⚔ ⚔ ⚔ ⚔ ⚔

The lower vantage point for Bruenor proved an advantage as he charged at the half-ogre standing on the curving stairway. The brute slammed its club straight down at the dwarf but Bruenor got his fine shield—emblazoned with the "foaming mug" standard of Clan Battlehammer—up over his head and angled perfectly. The dwarf was strong enough of arm to accept and deflect the blow.

The half-ogre wasn't as fortunate against the counter, a mighty sweep of Bruenor's fine axe that cracked the brute's ankle, snapping bone and digging a deep, deep gash. The half-ogre howled in pain and reached down reflexively to grab at the torn limb. Bruenor moved against the wall and leaped up three steps, putting him one above the bending half-ogre. The dwarf turned and braced, planting his shield against the brute as it started to turn to face him. Bruenor shoved out with all his strength, his short, muscled legs driving hard.

The half-ogre went off the stairs. It wasn't a long fall, but one that proved disastrous, for as the brute tried to hold its balance it landed hard on the broken ankle. It fell over on its side with a howl.

Its blurry vision cleared a moment later, and it looked back to see a flying red-bearded dwarf coming its way, mouth opened in a primal roar, face twisted with eager rage, and that devilish axe gripped in both hands.

The dwarf snapped his body as he impacted, driving the axe in hard and heavy, cleaving the half-ogre's head in half.

"Bet that hurt," Bruenor grumbled, pulling himself to his feet.

He looked at the gore on his axe and winced, then just shrugged and wiped it on the dead beast's dirty fur tunic.

⚔ ⚔ ⚔ ⚔ ⚔

Drizzt skittered back against a tree, then ducked and rolled around it to avoid a thundering smash.

The ogre's club smacked hard against the young tree and proved the stronger, cracking the living wood apart.

Drizzt groaned aloud as he considered the toppling tree, picturing what his own slender form might have looked like had he not dodged aside. He had no time to ponder at length, though, for the ogre, moving with enhanced speed and wielding its heavy club with ease with its giant-strength muscles, was fast in pursuit. It leaped the falling tree and swung again.

Drizzt fell to the snow flat on his face, the club whistling right above him. With amazing speed and grace, the drow put his legs under him and leaped straight up over the ogre's fast backhand, which came down diagonally from the side to smack the spot where Drizzt had just been lying. In the air, the drow had little weight behind the strikes, but he worked his scimitars in rapid alternating stabs, popping their points into the ogre's broad chest.

The drow landed lightly and went right back into the air, twisting as he did so that he rolled over the side-cutting club. As he landed he reversed the momentum of his somersault and drove one blade hard into the ogre's belly. Again, he didn't score nearly as much of a wound as he would have expected, but he didn't pause to lament the fact. He spun around the ogre's hip, reversed his grip on the blade in his right hand, and stabbed it out and hard into the back of the ogre's treelike leg.

Drizzt sprinted straight ahead, leaping another fallen tree and spinning around a pair of oaks, turning to face his predictably charging opponent.

The ogre chased him around the two oaks, but Drizzt held an advantage, for he could cut between the close-growing trees while the huge brute had to circle both. He went to the outside through a couple of rotations, letting the ogre fall into a set pace, then darted between the trees and came around fast and hard before the brute could properly turn and set its defenses.

Again the drow scored a pair of hits, one a stab, the other a slash. As he came across with his right hand, he followed through with the motion, turning a complete circle then sprinting ahead once more, the howling ogre in fast pursuit.

And so it went for many minutes, Drizzt using a hit and retreat strategy, hoping to tire the ogre, hoping that the potions, likely temporary enhancements, would run their course.

Drizzt scored again and again with minor hits, but he knew that this was no contest of finesse, where the better fighter would be awarded the victory by some neutral judges. This was a battle to the end, and while he looked beautiful with his precision movements and strikes, the only hit that would matter would be the last one. Given the ogre's sheer power, given the images burned into the drow's mind as yet another tree splintered and toppled under the weight of the brute's blow, Drizzt understood that the first solid hit he took from the creature would likely be the last hit of the fight.

The drow went full speed over one snowy ridge, diving down

in a roll on his back and sliding to the bottom. He came up fast, spinning to face the pursuit. The drow was looking to score another hit, perhaps, or more likely, in this unfavorable place, to simply run away.

But the ogre wasn't there, and Drizzt understood that it had used its heightened speed and heightened strength in a different manner when he heard the brute touch down behind him.

The ogre had leaped off the top of the ridge, right over the sliding and turning drow.

Drizzt realized his mistake.

✕ ✕ ✕ ✕ ✕

The surprised half-ogre landed flat on its back a few feet out from the tower and from the captive it had dropped, but was moving immediately, hardly seeming hurt, scrambling to its feet.

Catti-brie led her charge with another streaking arrow, a gut shot, then she threw her bow aside and drew out Khazid'hea. The eager sword prompted her telepathically to cut the beast apart.

The brute clutched at its belly wound with one hand and reached out at her with the other, as if to try to catch her charge. The flash of Khazid'hea ended that possibility, sending stubby fingers flying all about.

Catti-brie went in with fury, taking the advantage and never offering it back, slashing her fine-edged sword to and fro and hardly slowing enough to even bother to line up her strikes.

She didn't have to, not with this sword.

The half-ogre's heavy clothing and hide armor parted as if it was thin paper, and bright lines of red striped the creature in a matter of moments.

The half-ogre managed one punch out at her, but Khazid'hea was there, intercepting the punch with its sharp edge, splitting the half-ogre's hand and riding that cut right up through its thick wrist.

How the beast howled!

But that cry was silenced a moment later when Catti-brie slashed Khazid'hea across up high, taking out the brute's throat. Down went the half-ogre, and Catti-brie leaped beside it, her sword slashing repeatedly.

"Girl!" Bruenor cried, half in terror and half in surprise when he exited the tower to see his adopted daughter covered in blood. He ran to her and nearly got cut in half as she swung around, Khazid'hea flashing.

"It's the damn sword!" Bruenor cried at her, falling back and throwing his arms up defensively.

Catti-brie stopped suddenly, staring at her fine blade with shock.

Bruenor was right. In her moment of anger and terror at seeing the man fall from the tower, in her moment of guilt blaming herself for the man's fall because of her missed bowshot, the viciously sentient sword Khazid'hea had found its way into her thoughts yet again, prodding her into a frenzy.

She laughed aloud, helplessly. Her white teeth looked ridiculous, shining out from her bloodied face. She slapped the sword's blade down into the snow.

"Girl?" Bruenor asked cautiously.

"I'm thinking that we could both use a bath," Catti-brie said to him, obviously in control again.

⚔ ⚔ ⚔ ⚔ ⚔

Regis, hanging on the edge of the tower top, wondered if the half-ogre even understood its mistake as it flew out over him, limbs flailing wildly on its fast descent to the stony ground. The brute hit with a muffled groan, and bounced once or twice.

The halfling pulled himself back over the tower top and looked down to see the half-ogre stubbornly trying to regain its footing. It stumbled once and went back down, but then tried to rise again.

Regis retrieved his little mace and took aim. He whistled down to the half-ogre as he let fly, timing it perfectly so that the brute looked up just in time to catch the falling weapon right in the face. There came a sharp report, like metal hitting stone, and the half-ogre stood there for a long while, staring up at Regis.

The halfling sucked in his breath, hardly believing that the mace, falling from thirty feet, hadn't done more damage.

But it had. The brute went down hard and didn't get up.

A shiver coursed up Regis's little spine, and he paused long enough to consider his actions in this battle, to consider that he had gotten involved at all when he really didn't have to. The halfling tried very hard not to look at things that way, tried to remind himself repeatedly that he had acted in accordance with the tenets of his group of friends, his dear, trusted companions, who would risk their lives without a second thought to help those in dire need.

Not for the first time, and not for the last, Regis wondered if he would be better off finding a new group of friends.

⚔ ⚔ ⚔ ⚔ ⚔

Drizzt could only guess from which direction the ogre's mighty swing would come, and he understood that if he guessed wrong, he'd be leaping right into the oncoming blow. In the split second he had to react, it all sorted out, his warrior instincts replaying the ogre's fighting style, telling him clearly that the ogre had initiated every attack with a right-to-left strike.

So Drizzt went left, his magical anklets speeding his feet into a desperate run.

And the club swatted in behind him, clipping him as he turned and leaped, launching him into a long, twisting tumble. The snow padded his fall, but when he came up he found that he was only holding one scimitar. His right arm had gone completely numb and his shoulder and side were exploding with pain. The drow glanced down and winced. His shoulder had clearly been dislocated, pushed back from its normal position.

Drizzt didn't have long, for the ogre was coming on in pursuit—though, the drow noted with some hope, not as quickly as it had been moving.

Drizzt skittered away, turning as he went and literally throwing himself backward into a tree, using the solidity of the tree to pop his shoulder back into place. The wave of agony turned his stomach and brought black spots spinning before his eyes. He nearly swooned, but knew that if he gave into that momentary weakness, the ogre would break him apart.

He rolled around the tree and stumbled away, buying himself more time. He knew then, by how easily he could distance himself from the brute, that at least one of the potions had worn off.

Every step was bringing some measure of relief to Drizzt. The ache in his shoulder had lessened already, and he found that he could feel his fingers again. He took a circuitous route that led him back to his fallen scimitar, with the dumb ogre, apparently thinking that it had the fight won, following fast in pursuit.

Drizzt stopped and turned, his lavender eyes boring into the approaching brute. Just before the combatants came together, their gazes met, and the ogre's confidence melted away.

There would be no underestimation by the dark elf this time.

Drizzt came ahead in a fury, holding the ogre's stare with his own. His scimitars worked as if of their own accord, in perfect harmony and with blazing speed—too quickly for the ogre, its magical speed worn away and its giant strength diminishing, to possibly keep up. The brute tried to take an offensive posture instead, swinging wildly, but Drizzt was behind it before it ever completed the blow. That other potion, the one that had someone made the ogre resistant to the drow's scimitar stings, was also dissipating.

This time, both Twinkle and Icingdeath dug in, one taking a kidney, the other hamstringing the brute.

Drizzt worked in a fury but with controlled precision, rushing all around his opponent, stabbing and slashing, and always at a vital area.

The victorious drow put his scimitars away soon after, his right arm going numb again now that the adrenaline of battle was subsiding. Swaying with every step, and cursing himself for taking such an enemy as that for granted, he made his way back to the tower. There he found Bruenor and Regis sitting by the open door, both looking battered, and Catti-brie covered head to toe in blood, standing nearby, tending to a dazed and wounded man.

"A fine thing it'll be if we all wind up killed to death in battle afore we ever get to the pirate Kree," Bruenor grumbled.

19

WULFGAR'S CHOICE

Jeddith wasn't dead. Following Donbago's directions, after he had recovered his wits from the fall, Catti-brie and Regis found his brother behind some brush not far from the tower. His head was bloody and aching. They wrapped some bandages tight around the wound and tried to make him as comfortable as possible, but it became obvious that the dazed and delirious man would need to see a healer, and soon.

He's alive," Catti-brie announced to the man as she and Regis ushered him back to where Donbago sat propped against the tower.

Tears streamed down Donbago's face. "Me thanks," he said over and over again. "Whoever ye are, me thanks for me brother's life and me own."

"Another one's alive inside the tower," Bruenor announced, coming out. "Ye finally waked up, eh?" he asked Donbago, who was nodding appreciatively.

"And we got one o' them stupid half-ogres alive," Bruenor added. "Ugly thing."

"We have to get this one to a healer, and quick," Catti-brie explained as she and Regis managed to ease the half-conscious Jeddith down beside his brother.

"Auckney," Donbago insisted. "Ye got to get us to Auckney."

Drizzt came through the door and heard the man clearly. He and Catti-brie exchanged curious glances, knowing the name well from the tale Delly Curtie had told them of Wulfgar and the baby.

"How far a journey is Auckney?" the drow asked Donbago.

The man turned to regard Drizzt, and his eyes popped open wide. He seemed as if he would just fall over.

"He gets that a lot," Regis quipped, patting Donbago's shoulder. "He'll forgive you."

"Drow?" Donbago asked, trying to turn to regard Regis, but seeming unable to tear his eyes from the spectacle of a dark elf.

"Good drow," Regis explained. "You'll get to like him after a while."

"Bah, an elf's an elf!" Bruenor snorted.

"Yer pardon, good drow," Donbago stammered, obviously at a loss, his emotions torn between the fact that this group had just saved his life and his brother's, and all he'd ever known about the race of evil dark elves.

"No pardon is needed," Drizzt replied, "but an answer would be appreciated."

Donbago considered the statement for a few moments, then bobbed his head repeatedly. "Auckney," he echoed. "A few days and no more, if the weather holds."

"A few days if it don't," said Bruenor. "Good enough then. We got two to carry and a half-ogrie to drag along by the crotch."

"I think the brute can walk," Drizzt remarked. "He's a bit heavy to drag."

Drizzt fashioned a pair of litters out of blankets and sticks he retrieved from nearby, and the group left soon after. As it turned out, the half-ogre wasn't too badly wounded. That was a good thing, for while Bruenor could drag along Jeddith, the drow's injured shoulder would not allow him the strength to pull the other litter. They made the prisoner do it, with Catti-brie walking right behind, Taulmaril strung and ready, an arrow set to its string.

The weather did hold, and the ragged band, battered as they were, made strong headway, arriving at the outskirts of Auckney in less than three days.

✕ ✕ ✕ ✕ ✕

Wulfgar blinked repeatedly as the multicolored bubbles popped and dissipated in the air around him. Never fond of, and not very familiar with the ways of magic, the barbarian had to spend a long while reorienting himself to his new surroundings, for no longer was he in the grand city of Waterdeep. One structure, a uniquely designed tower whose branching arms made it look like a living tree, confirmed to Wulfgar that he was in Luskan now, as Robillard had promised.

"I see doubt clearly etched upon your face," the wizard remarked sourly. "I thought we had agreed—"

"You agreed," Wulfgar interrupted, "with yourself."

"You do not believe this to be the best course for you, then?" Robillard asked skeptically. "You would prefer the company of Delly Curtie back in the safety of Waterdeep, back in the security of a blacksmith's shop?"

The words surely stung the barbarian, but it was Robillard's condescending tone that really made Wulfgar want to throttle the skinny man. He didn't look at the wizard, fearing that he would simply spit in Robillard's face. He wasn't really afraid of a fight with the formidable wizard, not when he was this close, but if one did ensue and he did break Robillard in half, he'd have a long walk indeed back to Waterdeep.

"I will not go through this again with you, Wulfgar of Icewind Dale," Robillard remarked. "Or Wulfgar of Waterdeep, or Wulfgar of wherever you think Wulfgar should be from. I have offered you more than you deserve from me already, and more than I would normally offer to one such as you. I must be in a fine and generous mood this day."

Wulfgar scowled at him, but that only made Robillard laugh aloud.

"You are in the exact center of the city," Robillard went on. "Through the south gate lies the road to Waterdeep and Delly, and your job as a smith. Through the north gate, the road back to your friends and what I believe to be your true home. I suspect that you'll find the south road an easier journey by far than the north, Wulfgar son of Beornegar."

Wulfgar didn't respond, didn't even return the measuring stare Robillard was now casting over him. He knew which road the wizard believed he should take.

"I have always found those who take the easier road, when they know they should be walking the more difficult one, to be cowards," Robillard remarked. "Haven't you?"

"It is not as easy as you make it sound," Wulfgar replied quietly.

"It is likely far more difficult than ever I could imagine," the wizard said. For the first time, Wulfgar detected a bit of sympathy in his voice. "I know nothing of that which you have endured, nothing of the pains that have so weakened your heart. But I know who you were, and know who you now are, and I can say with more than a little confidence that you are better off walking into darkness and dying than trying to hide behind the embers of a smithy's hearth.

"Those are your choices," the wizard finished. "Farewell,

wherever you fare!" With that Robillard began waving his arms again, casting another spell.

Wulfgar, distracted and looking to the north, didn't notice until it was too late. He turned to see the multicolored bubbles already filling the air around the vanishing wizard. A sack appeared where the wizard had been standing, along with a large axelike bardiche. It was a rather unwieldy weapon, but one that resembled the great warhammer in design and style of fighting, at least, and one that could deal tremendous damage. He knew without even looking that the sack likely contained supplies for the road.

Wulfgar was alone, as much so as he had ever been, standing in the exact center of Luskan, and he remembered then that he was not supposed to be in this place. He was an outlaw in Luskan, or had been. He could only hope that the magistrates and the guards did not have so long a memory.

But which way to go, the barbarian wondered. He turned several circles. It was all too confusing, all too frightening, and Robillard's dire words haunted him with every turn.

Wulfgar of Icewind Dale exited Luskan's northern gate soon after, trudging off alone into the cold wilderness.

⚔ ⚔ ⚔ ⚔ ⚔

It was under the glare of one surprised and horrified expression after another that the friends made their way through the small village of Auckney and into the castle of Lord Feringal and Lady Meralda. Donbago, well enough to walk easily by that time, guided them in and warded away any who grabbed at weapons at the sight of the half-ogre, to say nothing of the dark elf.

Donbago talked them through a mob of soldiers led by a growling gnome guard at the door. The gnome put the others into efficient motion, helping Donbago scurry poor delirious Jeddith off to the healer and dragging the half-ogre down into the dungeons, beating the brute with every step.

The fierce gnome, Liam Woodgate, then led the five to an inner room and introduced them to an old, hawkish-looking man named Temigast.

"Drizzt Do'Urden," Temigast echoed, nodding with recognition as he spoke the name. "The ranger of Ten-Towns, I have heard. And you, good dwarf, are you not the King of Mithral Hall?"

"Was once and will be again, if me friends here don't get me killed to death," Bruenor replied.

"Might we meet with yer lord and lady?" Catti-brie asked. While Regis and Bruenor looked at her curiously, Drizzt, who also wanted to get a glimpse of this woman who had mothered the child Wulfgar was now raising as his own, smiled.

"Liam will show you to a place where you can properly clean and dress for your audience," Steward Temigast explained. "When you are ready, the audience with the Lord and Lady of Auckney will be arranged.

While Bruenor barely splashed some of the water over him, grumbling that he looked good enough for anyone, Drizzt and Regis thoroughly washed. In another room, Catti-brie not only took a most welcomed soapy bath, but then spent a long while trying on many of the gorgeous gowns that Lady Meralda had sent down to her.

Soon after, the four were in the grand audience hall of Castle Auck, standing before Lord Feringal, a man in his thirties with curly black hair and a thick, dark goatee, and Lady Meralda, younger and undeniably beautiful woman, with raven hair and creamy skin and a smile that brightened the whole of the huge room.

And while the Lord of Auckney was scowling almost continually, Meralda's smile didn't dissipate for a moment.

"I suppose that you now desire a reward," asked the third in attendance, a shrewish, heavyset woman seated to Feringal's left and just a bit behind, which, in the tradition of the region, marked her as Feringal's sister.

Behind the four road-weary companions, Steward Temigast cleared his throat.

"Ye thinking ye got enough gold for us to even notice?" Bruenor growled back at her.

"We have no need of coin," Drizzt interjected, trying to keep things calm. Bruenor had just suffered a bath, after all, and that always put the already surly dwarf into an even more foul mood. "We came here merely to return Donbago and two wounded men to their homes, as well as to deliver the prisoner. We would ask, though, that if you garner any information from the brute that might concern a certain notorious pirate by the name of Sheila Kree, you would pass it along. It is Kree we are hunting."

"Of course we will share with ye whatever we might learn," the Lady Meralda replied, cutting short her husband, whatever he meant to say. "And more. Whatever ye're needing, we're owing."

Drizzt didn't miss the scowl from the woman at the side, and he knew it to be both her general surliness and the somewhat common manner in which the Lady of Auckney spoke.

"Ye can stay the winter through, if ye so choose," Meralda went on.

Feringal looked at her, at first with surprise, but then in agreement.

"We might find an empty house about the town for—" the woman behind started to say.

"We will put them up right here in the castle, Priscilla," the Lady of Auckney declared.

"I hardly think—" Priscilla started to argue.

"In yer own room if I hear another word from ye," Meralda said, and she threw a wink at the four friends.

"Feri!" Priscilla roared.

"Shut up, dear sister," said Feringal, in an exasperated tone that showed the friends clearly that he often had to extend such sentiments his troublesome sister's way. "Do not embarrass us before our most distinguished guests—guests who rescued three of my loyal soldiers and avenged our losses at the hands of the beastly ogres."

"Guests who've got tales to tell of faraway lands and dragon's hoards," Meralda added with a gleam in her green eyes.

"Only the night, I fear," said Drizzt. "Our road will be winding and long, no doubt. We are determined to find and punish the pirate Kree before the spring thaw—before she can put her ship back out into the safety of the open seas and bring more mischief to the waters off Luskan."

Meralda's disappointment was obvious, but Feringal nodded, seeming to hardly care whether they stayed or left.

The Lord and Lady of Auckney put on a splendid feast that night in honor of the heroes, and Donbago was able to attend as well, bringing with him the welcomed news that both his brother and the other man were faring better and seemed as if they would recover.

They ate—Bruenor and Regis more than all the others combined—and they laughed. The companions, with so many miles beneath their weathered and well-worn boots, told tales of faraway lands as Lady Meralda had desired.

Much later, Catti-brie managed to toss a wink and nod to Drizzt, guiding him into a small side room where they could be alone. They fell onto a couch, side by side, beneath a bright tapestry cheaply sketched but with rich colors.

"Ye think we should tell her about the babe?" Catti-brie asked, her hand settling on Drizzt's slender, strong forearm.

"That would only bring her pain, after the initial relief, I fear," the drow replied. "One day, perhaps, but not now."

"Oh, ye must join us!" Meralda interrupted, coming through the door to stand beside the pair. "King Bruenor is telling the best o' tales, one of a dark dragon that stole his kingdom."

"One we're knowing all too well," Catti-brie replied with a smile.

"But it would be impolite not to hear it again," said Drizzt, rising. He took Catti-brie's hand and pulled her up, and the two started past Meralda.

"So do ye think ye'll find him?" the Lady of Auckney asked as they walked by.

The pair stopped and turned as one to regard her.

"The other one of yer group," Meralda explained. "The one who went to reclaim Mithral Hall with ye, by the dwarf's own words." She paused and stared hard at both of them. "The one ye call Wulfgar."

Drizzt and Catti-brie stood silent for a moment, the woman so obviously on the edge of her nerves here, biting her lip and looking to the drow for a cue.

"It is our hope to find him, and find him whole," Drizzt answered quietly, trying not to involve the whole room in this conversation.

"I've an interest . . ."

"We know all about it," Catti-brie interjected.

Lady Meralda stood very straight, obviously fighting to keep herself from swaying.

"The child grows strong and safe," Drizzt assured her.

"And what did they name her?"

"Colson."

Meralda sighed and steadied herself. A sadness showed in her green eyes, but she managed a smile a moment later. "Come," she said quietly. "Let us go and hear the dwarf's tale."

✖ ✖ ✖ ✖ ✖

"The prisoner will be hung as soon as we find a rope strong enough to hold it," Lord Feringal assured the group early the next morning, when they had gathered at the foyer of Castle Auckney, preparing to leave.

"The beast fancies itself a strong one," the man went on with a snicker. "But how it whimpered last night!"

Drizzt winced, as did Catti-brie and Regis, but Bruenor merely nodded.

"The brute was indeed part of a larger band," Feringal explained. "Perhaps pirates, though the stupid creature didn't seem to understand the word."

"Perhaps Kree," the drow said. "Do you have any idea where the raiding band came from?"

"South coast of the mountain spur," Feringal answered. "We could not get the ogre to admit it openly, but we believe it knows something of Minster Gorge. It will be a difficult hike in winter, with the passes likely full of snow."

"Difficult, but one worth taking," Drizzt replied.

Lady Meralda entered the room then, seeming no less beautiful in the early morning light than she had the night before. She regarded Drizzt and Catti-brie each in turn, offering a grateful smile.

And both the woman and the drow noted, too, that Feringal couldn't hide his scowl at the silent exchange. The wounds here were still too raw, and Feringal had obviously recognized Wulfgar's name from Bruenor's tale the night before, and that recognition had pained him greatly.

No doubt, the frustrated Lord of Auckney had taken that anger out on the half-ogre prisoner.

The four friends left Castle Auckney and the kingdom that same morning, though clouds had gathered in the east. There was no fanfare, no cheers for the departing heroes.

Just Lady Meralda, standing atop the parapet between the gate towers, wrapped in a heavy fur coat, watching them go.

Even from that distance, Drizzt and Catti-brie could see the mixture of pain and hope in her green eyes.

Part Four

The Hunt For Meaning

The weather was terrible, the cold biting at my fingers, the ice crusting my eyes until it pained me to see. Every pass was fraught with danger—an avalanche waiting to happen, a monster ready to spring. Every night was spent in the knowledge that we might get buried within whatever shelter we found—if we were even lucky enough to find shelter—unable to claw our way out, certain to die.

Not only was I in mortal danger, but so were my dearest friends.

Never in my life have I been more filled with joy.

For a purpose guided our steps, every one through the deep and driving snow. Our goal was clear, our course correct. In traversing the snowy mountains in pursuit of the pirate Kree and the warhammer Aegis-fang, we were standing for what we believed in, were following our hearts and our spirits.

Though many would seek short cuts to the truth, there is no way around the simplest of tenets: hardship begets achievement and achievement begets joy—true joy, and the sense of accomplishment that defines who we are as thinking beings. Often have I heard people lament that if only they had the wealth of the king, then they could be truly happy, and I take care not to argue the point, though I know they are surely wrong. There is a truth I will grant that, for the poorest, some measure of wealth can allow for some measure of happiness, but beyond filling the basic needs, the path to joy is not paved in gold, particularly in gold unearned.

Hardly that! The path to joy is paved in a sense of confidence and self-worth, a feeling that we have made the world a little bit better, perhaps, or that we fought on for our beliefs despite adversity. In my travels with Captain Deudermont, I dined with many of the wealthiest families of Waterdeep, I broke bread with many of the children of the very rich. Deudermont himself was among that group, his father being a prominent landowner in Waterdeep's southern district. Many of the current crop of young aristocrats would do well to hold Captain Deudermont up as an example, for he was unwilling to rest on the laurels of the previous generation. He spotted, very young, the entrapment of wealth without earning. And so the good captain decided at a young age the course of his own life, an existence following his heart and trying very hard to make the waters of the Sword Coast a better place for decent and honest sailors.

Captain Deudermont might die young because of that choice to serve, as I might because of my own, as Catti-brie might beside me. But the simple truth of it is that, had I remained in Menzoberranzan those decades ago, or had I chosen to remain safe and sound in Ten-Towns or Mithral Hall at this time, I would already, in so many ways, be dead.

No, give me the road and the dangers, give me the hope that I am striding purposefully for that which is right, give me the sense of accomplishment, and I will know joy.

So deep has my conviction become that I can say with confidence that even if Catti-brie were to die on the road beside me, I would not backtrack to that safer place. For I know that her heart is much as my own on this matter. I know that she will—that she must—pursue those endeavors, however dangerous, that point her in the direction of her heart and her conscience.

Perhaps that is the result of being raised by dwarves, for no race on all of Toril better understands this simple truth of happiness better than the growling, grumbling, bearded folk. Dwarven kings are almost always among the most active of the clan, the first to fight and the first to work. The first to envision a mighty underground fortress and the first to clear away the clay that blocks the cavern in which it will stand. The tough, hard-working dwarves long ago learned the value of accomplishment versus luxury, long ago came to understand that there are riches of spirit more valuable by far than gold—though they do love their gold!

So I find myself in the cold, windblown snow, and the treacherous passes surrounded by enemies, on our way to do battle with an undeniably formidable foe.

Could the sun shine any brighter?

—Drizzt Do'Urden

20

EVICTION NOTICE

The people of Faerûn's northern cities thought they understood the nature of snowstorms and the ferocity of winter but in reality, no person who hadn't walked the tundra of Icewind Dale or the passes of the Spine of the World during a winter blizzard could truly appreciate the raw power of nature unleashed.

Such a storm found the four friends as they traversed one high pass southeast of Auckney.

Driven by fierce and frigid winds that had them leaning far forward just to prevent being blown over, icy, stinging snow crashed against them more than fell over them. That driving wind shifted constantly among the alternating cliff faces, swirling and changing direction, denying them any chance of finding a shielding barricade, and always seeming to put snow in their faces no matter which way they turned. They each tried to formulate a plan and had to shout out their suggestions at the top of their lungs, putting lips right against the ear of the person with whom they were trying to communicate.

In the end, any hope of a plan for achieving some relief had to rely completely upon luck—the companions needed to find a cave, or at least a deep overhang with walls shielding them from the most pressing winds.

Drizzt bent low on the white trail and placed his black onyx figurine on the ground before him. With the same urgency he might have used if a tremendous battle loomed before him, the dark elf called to Guenhwyvar. Drizzt stepped back, but not too far, and waited for the gray mist to appear, swirling and gradually forming into the shape of the panther, then solidifying into the cat itself. The drow bent low and communicated his wishes, and the panther leaped away, padding off through the storm, searching the mountain walls and the many side passes that dipped down from the main trail.

Drizzt started away as well, on the same mission. The other three companions, though, remained tight together, defensively huddled from the wind and other potential dangers. That proximity alone prevented complete disaster when one great gust of wind roared up, knocking Catti-brie to one knee and blowing the poor halfling right over backward. Regis tumbled and scrambled, trying to find his balance, or at least find something to hold onto.

Bruenor, sturdy and steady, grabbed his daughter by the elbow and hoisted her up, then pushed her off in the direction of the scrambling halfling. Catti-brie reacted immediately, diving out over the lip of the trail's crest, pulling Taulmaril off her shoulder, falling flat to her belly and reaching the bow out toward the skidding, sliding halfling.

Regis caught the bow and held on a split second before he went tumbling over the side of the high trail, a spill that would have had him bouncing down hundreds of feet to a lower plateau and would have likely dropped an avalanche on his head right behind him. It only took a couple of minutes for Catti-brie to extract the halfling from the open face, but by the time she yanked him in he was covered white with snow and shivering terribly.

"We canno' stay out here," the woman yelled to Bruenor, who came stomping over. "The storm'll be the death of us!"

"The elf'll find us something!" the dwarf yelled. "Him or that cat o' his!"

Catti-brie nodded. Regis tried to nod as well, but his shivering only made the motion look ridiculous. All three knew that they were fast running out of options. All three understood that Drizzt and Guenhwyvar had better find them some shelter.

And soon.

⚔ ⚔ ⚔ ⚔ ⚔

Guenhwyvar's roar came as the most welcome sound Drizzt Do'Urden had heard in a long, long time. He peered through the blinding sheets of blowing white, to see the huge black panther atop a windblown jag of stone, ears flat back, face masked with icy white snow.

Drizzt half skipped and half fell along a diagonal course that kept the mighty wind somewhat behind him as he made his way to Guenhwyvar.

"What have you found?" he asked the cat when he arrived just below her, peering up.

Guenhwyvar roared again and leaped away. The drow rushed to follow, and a few hundred feet down a side trail piled deep with snow, the pair came under a long overhang of rock. Drizzt nodded, thinking that this would provide some shelter, at least, but then Guenhwyvar prodded him and growled. She moved into the shelter, toward the very back, which remained shadowed. The panther was moving and peering more intently, the drow understood, for there, in the back of the sheltered area, Drizzt spotted a fair-sized crack at the base of the stone wall.

The dark elf padded over, quickly and silently, and kneeled down to the crack, taking heart as his keen eyes revealed to him that there was indeed an even more sheltered area within, a cave or a passage. Hardly slowing, reminding himself that his friends were still out in the blizzard, Drizzt dived into the opening head first, squirming to get his feet under him as he came to a lower landing.

He was in a cave, large and with many rocky shelves and boulders. The floor was clay, mostly, and as he allowed his vision to shift into the heat-seeing spectrum of the Underdark dwellers, he did indeed note a heat source, a fire pit whose contents had been very recently extinguished.

So, the cave was not unoccupied, and given their locale and the tremendous storm blowing outside, Drizzt would have been honestly surprised if it had been.

He spotted the inhabitants a moment later, moving along the shadows of the far wall, their warmer bodies shining clearly to him. He knew at once that they were goblins, and he could well imagine that there were more than a few in this sheltered area.

Drizzt considered going back outside, retrieving his friends, and taking the cave as their own. Working with their typical efficiency, the companions should have little trouble with a small gang of goblins.

But the drow paused, and not out of fear for his friends. What of the morality involved? What of the companions walking into another creature's home and expelling it into the deadly weather? Drizzt recalled another goblin he had once met in his travels, long before and far away, a creature who was not evil. These goblins, so far out and so high up in nearly impassable mountains, might have never encountered a human, an elf, a dwarf, or any other of the goodly reasoning races. Was it acceptable, then, for Drizzt and his friends to wage war on them in an attempt to steal their home?

"Hail and well met," the drow called in the goblin tongue, which he had learned during his years in Menzoberranzan. Though the dialect of the goblins of the deep Underdark was vastly different from that of their surface cousins, he could communicate with them well enough.

The surprise on the goblin's face when it discovered that the intruder was not an elf, but a dark elf, was obvious indeed as the creature neared—or started to approach, only to skitter back, its sickly yellowish eyes wide with shock.

"My friends and I need shelter from the storm," Drizzt explained, standing calm and confident, trying to show neither hostility nor fear. "May we join you?"

The goblin stuttered too badly to even begin a response. It turned around, panic-stricken, to regard one of its companions. This second goblin, larger by far and likely, Drizzt surmised from his understanding of goblin culture, a leader in the tribe, stepped out from the shadows.

"How many?" it croaked at Drizzt.

Drizzt regarded the goblin for a few moments, noted that its dress was better than that of its ugly fellows, with a tall lumberjack's cap and golden ear-cuffs on both ears.

"Five," the drow replied.

"You pay gold?"

"We pay gold."

The large goblin gave a croaking laugh, which Drizzt took as an agreement. The drow pulled himself back out of the cave, set Guenhwyvar as a sentry, and rushed off to find the others.

It wasn't hard for Drizzt to predict Bruenor's reaction when he told the dwarf of the arrangement with their new landlords.

"Bah!" the dwarf blustered. "If ye're thinking that I'm givin' one piece o' me gold coins to the likes o' smelly goblins, then ye're thinkin' with the brains of a thick rock, elf! Or worse yet, ye're thinking like a smelly goblin!"

"They have little understanding of wealth," Drizzt replied with all confidence. He pointedly led the group away as he continued the discussion, not wanting to waste any time at all out in the freezing cold. Regis in particular was starting to look worse for wear, and was constantly trembling, his teeth chattering. "A coin or two should suffice."

"Ye can put copper coins over their eyes when I cleave 'em down!" Bruenor roared in reply. "Some folks do that."

Drizzt stopped, and stared hard at the dwarf. "I have made an arrangement, rightly or wrongly, but it is one that I expect you to honor," he explained. "We do not know if these goblins are deserving of our wrath, and whatever the case if we simply walk in and put them out of their own home then are we any better than they?"

Bruenor laughed aloud. "Been drinking the holy water again, eh, elf?" he asked.

Drizzt narrowed his lavender eyes.

"Bah, I'll let ye lead on this one," the dwarf conceded. "But be knowing that me axe'll be right in me hand the whole time, and if any stupid goblin makes a bad move or says a stupid thing, the place'll get a new coat o' paint—*red* paint!"

Drizzt looked at Catti-brie, expecting support, but the expression he saw there surprised him. The woman, if anything, seemed to be favoring Bruenor's side of this debate. Drizzt had to wonder if he might be wrong, had to wonder if he and his friends should have just walked in and sent the goblins running.

The dark elf went back into the cave first, with Guenhwyvar right behind. While the sight of the huge panther set more than a few goblins back on their heels, the sight of the next visitor—a red-bearded dwarf—had many of the humanoid tribe howling in protest, pointing crooked fingers, waving their fists, and hopping up and down.

"You drow, no dwarf!" the big goblin protested.

"Duergar," Drizzt replied. "Deep dwarf." He nudged Bruenor and whispered out of the corner of his mouth, "Try to act gray."

Bruenor turned a skeptical look his way.

"Dwarf!" the goblin leader protested.

"Duergar," Drizzt retorted. "Do you not know the duergar? The deep dwarves, allies of the drow and the goblins of the Underdark?"

There was enough truth in the dark elf's statement to put the goblin leader off his guard. The deep dwarves of Faerûn, the duergar, often traded and sometimes allied with the drow. In the Underdark, the duergar had roughly the same relationship with the deep goblins as did the drow, not so much a friendship as tolerance. There were goblins in Menzoberranzan, many goblins. Someone had to do the cleaning, after all, or give a young matron a target that she might practice with her snake whip.

Regis was the next one in, and the goblin leader squealed again.

"Young duergar," Drizzt said before the protest could gain any momentum. "We use them as decoys to infiltrate halfling villages."

"Oh," came the response.

Last in was Catti-brie, and the sight of her, the sight of a human, brought a new round of whooping and stomping, finger-pointing and fist waving.

"Ah, prisoner!" the goblin leader said lewdly.

Drizzt's eyes widened at the word and the tone, at the goblin leader's obvious intentions toward the woman. The drow recognized his error. He had refused to accept that Nojheim, the exceptional goblin he'd met those years before, was something less than representative of his cruel race. Nojheim was a complete anomaly, unique indeed.

"What'd he say?" asked Bruenor, who wasn't very good at understanding the goblin dialect.

"He said the deal is off," Drizzt replied. "He told us to get out."

Before Bruenor could begin to question what the drow wanted to do next, Drizzt had his scimitars in hand and began stalking across the uneven floor.

"Drizzt?" Catti-brie called to the drow. She looked to Bruenor, hardly seeing him in the dim light.

"Well, they started it!" the dwarf roared, but his bluster ended abruptly, and he called out to the dark elf, in less than certain terms, "Didn't they?"

"Oh, yes," came the drow's reply.

"Put up a torch for me girl, Rumblebelly!" Bruenor said with a happy howl, and he slapped his axe hard against his open hand and rushed forward. "Just shoot left, girl, until ye can see! Trust that I'll be keepin' meself to the right!"

A pair of goblins rushed in at Drizzt, one from either side. The drow skittered right, turned, and went into a sudden dip, thrusting both scimitars out that way. The goblin, holding a small spear, made a fine defensive shift and almost managed to parry one of the blades.

Drizzt retracted and swung back around the other way, turning right past his friends and letting his right hand lead in a vicious cross. He felt the throb in his injured shoulder, but that remark by the goblin leader, "prisoner," that inference that it would be happy to spend some time playing with Catti-brie, gave him the strength to ignore the pain.

The goblin coming in at him ducked the first blade and instinctively lifted its spear up to parry, should Drizzt dip that leading scimitar lower.

The second crossing scimitar took out its throat.

A third creature charged in on that goblin's heels and was suddenly lying atop its dead companion, taken down by a quick-step and thrust, the bloodied left-hand scimitar cutting a fast line to its heart, while Drizzt worked the right-hand blade in tight circles around the thrusting sword of a fourth creature.

"Damn elf, ye're taking all the fun!" Bruenor roared.

He rushed right past Drizzt, thinking to bury his axe into the skull of the goblin parrying back and forth with the dark elf. A black form flew past the dwarf, though, and launched the goblin away, pinning it under six hundred pounds of black fur and raking claws.

The cave lit suddenly with a sharp blue light, then another, as Catti-brie put her deadly bow to work, sending off a line of lightning-streaking arrows. The first shots burrowed into the stone wall to the cave's left side, but each offered enough illumination for her to sort out a target or two.

By the third shot, she got a goblin, and each successive shot either found a deadly mark or zipped in close enough to have goblins diving all about.

The three friends pressed on, cutting down goblins and sending dozens of the cowardly creatures running off before them.

Catti-brie kept up a stream of streaking arrows to the side, not really scoring any hits now, for all of the goblins over there were huddled under cover. Her efforts were not in vain, though, for she was keeping the creatures out of the main fight in the cave's center.

Regis, meanwhile, made his way around the other wall, creeping past boulders, stalagmites, and huddling goblins. He noted that the goblins were disappearing sporadically through a crack in the back of the cave and that the leader had already gone in.

Regis waited for a lull in the goblin line, then slipped into the deeper darkness of the inner tunnels.

The fight was over in a short time, for in truth, other than the initial three goblins' charge at Drizzt, it never was much of a fight.

Goblins worked harder at running away than at defending themselves from the mighty intruders—some even threw their kinfolk into the path of the charging dwarf or leaping panther.

It ended with Drizzt and Bruenor simultaneously stabbing and chopping a goblin as it tried to exit at the back of the cave.

Bruenor yanked back on his axe, but the embedded blade didn't disengage and he wound up hoisting the limp goblin right over his shoulder.

"Big one got through," the dwarf grumbled, seeming oblivious to the fact that he was holding a dead goblin on the end of his axe. "Ye going after it?"

"Where is Regis?" came Catti-brie's call from the cave entrance.

The pair turned to see the woman crouching just before the entrance slope, lighting a torch.

"Rumblebelly ain't good at following directions," Bruenor griped. "I told him to do that!"

"I didn't need it with me bow," Catti-brie explained. "But he ran off." She called out loudly, "Regis?"

"He ran away," Bruenor whispered to Drizzt, but that just didn't sound right—to either of them—after the halfling's brave work on the roads outside of Ten-Towns and his surprisingly good performance against the ogres. "I'm thinking them ogres scared the fight outta him."

Drizzt shook his head, slowly turning to scan the perimeter of the cave, fearing more that Regis had been cut down than that he had run off.

They heard their little friend a few moments later, whistling happily as he exited the goblin escape tunnel. He looked at Drizzt and Bruenor, who stared at him in blank amazement, then tossed something to Drizzt.

The drow caught it and regarded it, and his smile widened indeed.

A goblin ear, wearing a golden cuff.

The dwarf and the dark elf looked at the halfling incredulously.

"I heard what he said," Regis answered their stares. "And I do understand goblin." He snapped his little fingers in the air before the stunned pair and started across the cave toward Catti-brie. He stopped a few strides away, though, turned back, and tossed the second ear to Drizzt.

"What's gettin' into him?" Bruenor quietly asked the drow when Regis was far away.

"The adventurous spirit?" Drizzt asked more than stated.

"Ye could be right," said Bruenor. He spat on the ground. "He's gonna get us all killed, or I'm a bearded gnome."

The five, for Guenhwyvar remained throughout the night, waited out the rest of the storm in the goblin cave. They found a pile of kindling at the side of the cave, along with some rancid meat they didn't dare cook, and Bruenor set a blazing fire near the outside opening. Guenhwyvar stood sentry while Drizzt, Catti-brie, and Regis deposited the goblin bodies far down the passageway. They ate, and they huddled around the fire. They took turns on watch that night, sleeping two at a time, though they didn't really expect the cowardly goblins to return anytime soon.

⚔ ⚔ ⚔ ⚔ ⚔

Many miles to the south and east of the companions, another weary traveler didn't have the luxury of comrades who could stand watch while he slept. Still, not expecting that many enemies would be out and about on a stormy night such as this, Wulfgar did settle back against the rear wall of the covered nook he chose as his shelter and closed his eyes.

He had dug out this nook, and so he was flanked left and right by walls of solid snow, with the rock wall behind and a rising snow wall before him. He knew that even if no monsters or wild animals would likely find him, he had to take his sleep in short bursts, for if he didn't regularly clear some of the snow from the front, he ran the risk of being buried alive, and if he didn't occasionally throw another log on the fire, he'd likely freeze to death on this bitter night.

These were only minor inconveniences to the hearty barbarian, who had been raised from a babe on the open tundra of brutal Icewind Dale, who had been weaned with the bitter north wind singing in his ears.

And who had been hardened in the fiery swirls of Errtu's demonic home.

The wind sang a mournful song across the small opening of Wulfgar's rock and snow shelter, a long and melancholy note that opened the doorway to the barbarian's battered heart. In that cave, in that storm, and on that windy note, Wulfgar's thoughts were sent back across the span of time.

He recalled so many things about his childhood with the Tribe of the Elk, running the open and wild tundra, following the footsteps of his ancestors in hunts and rituals that had survived for hundreds of years.

He recalled the battle that had brought him to Ten-Towns, an aggressive attack by his warrior people upon the settlers of the villages. There an ill-placed blow on the head of a particularly hardheaded dwarf had led to young Wulfgar's defeat—and that defeat had landed young Wulfgar squarely in the tutelage and indenture of one Bruenor Battlehammer, the surly, gruff, golden-hearted dwarf who Wulfgar would soon enough come to know as a father. That defeat on the battlefield had brought Wulfgar to the side of Drizzt and Catti-brie, had set him on the road that had guided the later years of his youth and the early years of his adulthood. That same road, though, had landed Wulfgar in that most awful of all places, the lair of the demon Errtu.

Outside, the wind mourned and called to his soul, as if asking him to turn away now on his road of memories, to reject all thoughts of Errtu's hellish lair.

Warning him, warning him . . .

But Wulfgar, as tormented by his self-perception as he was by the tortures of Errtu, would not turn away. Not this time. He embraced the awful memories. He brought them into his consciousness and examined them fully and rationally, telling himself that this was as it had been. Not as it should have been, but a simple reality of his past, a memory that he would have to carry with him.

A place from which he should try to grow, and not one from which he should reflexively cower.

The wind wailed its dire warnings, calling to him that he might lose himself within that pit of horror, that he might be going to dark places better left at rest. But Wulfgar held on to the thoughts, carried them through to the final victory over Errtu, out on the Sea of Moving Ice.

With his friends beside him.

That was the rub, the forlorn barbarian knew. *With his friends beside him!* He had forsaken his former companions because he had believed that he must. He had run away from them, particularly from Catti-brie, because he could not let them come to see what he had truly become, a broken wretch, a shell of his former glory.

Wulfgar paused in his contemplation and tossed the last of his logs onto the fire. He adjusted the stones he had set under the blaze, rocks that would catch the heat and hold it for some time. He prodded one stone away from the fire and rolled it under his bedroll, then worked it down under the fabric so that he could comfortably rest atop it.

He did just that and felt the new heat rising beneath, but the new-found comfort could not eliminate or deflect the wall of questions.

"And where am I now?" the barbarian asked of the wind, but it only continued its melancholy wail.

It had no answers, and neither did he.

⚔ ⚔ ⚔ ⚔ ⚔

The next morning dawned bright and clear, with the brilliant sun climbing into a cloudless eastern sky, sending the temperatures to comfortable levels and beginning the melt of the previous day's blizzard.

Drizzt regarded the sight and the warmth with mixed feelings, for while he and all the others were glad to have some feeling returning to their extremities, they all knew the dangers that sunshine after a blizzard could bring to mountain passes. They would have to move extra carefully that day, wary of avalanches with every step.

The drow looked back to the cave, wherein slept his three companions, resting easily, hoping to continue on their way. With any luck, they might make the coast that very day and begin the search in earnest for Minster Gorge and Sheila Kree.

Drizzt looked around and realized they would need considerable luck. Already he could hear the distant rumblings of falling snow.

⚔ ⚔ ⚔ ⚔ ⚔

Wulfgar punched and thrashed his way out of the overhang that had become a cave, that had become a snowy tomb, crawling out and stretching in the brilliant morning sunlight.

The barbarian was right on the edge of the mountains, with the terrain sloping greatly down to the south toward Luskan and with towering, snow-covered peaks all along the northern horizon. He noted, too, with a snort of resignation, that he had apparently been on the edge of the rain/snow line of the blizzard's precipitation, for those sloping hillsides south of him seemed more wet than deep with snow, while the region north of him was clogged with powder.

It was as if the gods themselves were telling him to turn back.

Wulfgar nodded. Perhaps that was it. Or perhaps the storm had been no more than an analogy of the roads now facing him in his life. The easy way, as it would have been out of Luskan, was to the south. That road called to him clearly, showing him a path where he could avoid the difficult terrain.

The hearty barbarian laughed at the symbolism of it all, at the way nature herself seemed to be pushing him back toward that more peaceful and easy existence. He hoisted his pack and the unbalanced bardiche he carried in Aegis-fang's stead and trudged off to the north.

21
WASTED CHARMS

I have business to attend to in Luskan," Morik complained. "So many things I have set in place—connections and deals—and now, because of you and your friends, all of that will be for naught."

"But you will enjoy the long winter's night," Bellany said with a wicked grin. She curled seductively on the pile of furs.

"That is of no . . . well, there is that," Morik admitted, shaking his head. "And my protest has nothing to do with you—you do understand that."

"You talk way too much," the woman replied, reaching for the small man.

"I . . . I mean, no this cannot be! Not now. There is my business—"

"Later."

"Now!"

Bellany grinned, rolled over, and stretched. Morik's protests had to wait for some time. Later on, though, the rogue from Luskan was right back at it, complaining to Bellany that her little side trip here was going to cost him a king's treasure and more.

"Unavoidable," the sorceress explained. "I had to bring you here, and winter came early."

"And I am not allowed to leave?"

"Leave at your will," Bellany replied. "It is a long, cold road—do you think you'll survive all the way back to Luskan?"

"You brought me here, you take me back."

"Impossible," the sorceress said calmly. "I can not teleport such distances. That spell is beyond me. I could conjure the odd magical portal for short distances perhaps, but not enough to skip our way to Luskan. And I do not like the cold, Morik. Not at all."

"Then Sheila Kree will have to find a way to take me home," Morik declared, pulling his trousers on—or at least trying to. As he brought the pants up over his ankles, Bellany waved her hand and cast a simple spell to bring about a sudden breeze. The gust was strong enough to push the already off-balance Morik backward, causing him to trip and fall.

He rolled and put his feet under him, rising, stumbling back to his knees, then pulling himself up and turning an indignant stare over the woman.

"Very humorous," he said grimly, but as soon as he spoke the words, Morik noted the look on Bellany's face, one that showed little humor.

"You will go to Sheila Kree and demand that she take you home?" the sorceress asked.

"And if I do?"

"She will kill you," Bellany stated. "Sheila is not overly fond of you, my friend, and in truth she desires you gone from here as much as you desire to be gone. But she'll spare no resources to do that, unless it is the short journey for one of her pet ogres to toss your lifeless body into the frigid ocean waters.

"No, Morik, understand that you would do well to remain unobtrusive and quietly out of Sheila's way," Bellany went on. *"Bloody Keel* will sail in the spring, and likely along the coast. We'll put you ashore not so far from Luskan, perhaps even in port, if we can be certain Deudermont's not lying in wait for us there."

"I will be a pauper by then."

"Well, if you are still rich, and wish to die that way, then go to Sheila with your demands," the sorceress said with a laugh. She rolled over, wrapping herself in the furs, burying even her head to signal Morik that this conversation was at its end.

The rogue stood there staring at his lover for a long while. He liked Bellany—a lot—and believed that a winter of cuddling beside her wouldn't be so bad a thing. There were several other women there as well, including a couple of quite attractive ones, like Jule Pepper. Perhaps Morik might find a bit of challenge this season!

The rogue shook that thought out of his head. He had to be careful with such things, while in such tight and inescapable quarters beside such formidable companions. Woe to him if he angered Bellany by making a play for Jule. He winced as he considered the beating this beautiful sorceress might put on him. Morik had never liked wizards of any type, for they could see through his disguises and stealth and could blast him away before he ever got close to them. To Morik's way of thinking, wizards simply didn't fight fair.

Yes, he had to be careful not to evoke any jealousies.

Or perhaps that was it, Morik mused, considering Sheila's obvious disdain. Perhaps the fiery pirate didn't approve of Bellany's companion because she was trapped here as well, and with no one to warm her furs.

A wry smile grew on Morik's face as he watched the rhythmic breathing of sleeping Bellany.

"Ah, Sheila," he whispered, and he wondered if he would even want to go home after spending some time with the captain, wondered if he might not find an even greater prosperity right here.

✕ ✕ ✕ ✕ ✕

Chogurugga stalked about her huge room angrily, throwing furniture and any of the smaller ogres and half-ogres who were too slow to get out of her way.

"Bathunk!" the ogress wailed repeatedly. "Bathunk, where you be?" The ogress's prized son had gone out from the home to lead a raiding party, an expedition that was supposed to last only three or four days, but now nearly a tenday had passed, with no word from the young beast.

"Snow deep," said a composed Bloog from the side of the room, lying back on a huge hammock—a gift from Sheila Kree—his massive legs hanging over, one on either side.

Chogurugga raced across the room, grabbed the side of the hammock, and dumped Bloog onto the stone floor. "If me learn that you hurt—"

"Bathunk go out," Bloog protested, keeping his calm, though whether that was because he didn't want to lash out at his beautiful wife or because he didn't want to laugh at her hysteria, the ogress could not tell. "Him come back or him not. Bloog not go out."

The logic, simple enough for even Chogurugga to grasp, did not calm the ogress, but turned her away from Bloog at least. She rushed across the room, wailing for Bathunk.

In truth, her son had been late in returning from raiding parties many times, but this time was different. It wasn't just the fierce storm that had come up. This time, Chogurugga sensed that something was terribly amiss. Disaster had befallen her beloved Bathunk.

He wouldn't be coming home.

The ogress just knew it.

Morik grinned widely and pulled a second goblet, another beautiful silver and glass piece, out of the small belt pouch on his right hip, placing it in front of Sheila Kree on the table between them.

Sheila regarded him with an amused expression and a nod, bidding him to continue.

Out of the pouch next came a bottle of Feywine—itself much too big to fit in the small pouch, let alone beside a pair of sizeable goblets.

"What else ye got in yer magical pouch, Morik the Rogue?" Sheila asked suspiciously. "Does Bellany know ye got that magic about ye?"

"Why would it concern her, dear, beautiful Sheila?" Morik asked, pouring a generous amount of the expensive liquor into Sheila's cup and a lesser amount into his own. "I am no threat to anyone here. A friend and no enemy."

Sheila smirked, then brought her goblet up so fast for a big swallow that some wine splashed out the sides of the drinking vessel and across her ruddy face. Hardly caring, the pirate banged the goblet back to the table, then ran an arm across her face.

"Would any enemy e'er say different?" she asked, simply. "Don't know o' many who'd be calling themselfs a foe when they're caught."

Morik chuckled. "You do not approve of Bellany bringing me here."

"Have I ever given ye a different feeling?"

"Nor do you approve of Bellany's interest in my companionship," Morik dared to say.

When Sheila winced slightly and shifted in her seat, Morik knew he'd hit a nerve. Bolstered by the thought that Sheila's gruffness toward him might be nothing more than jealousy—and to confident Morik's way of thinking, why should it not be?—the rogue lifted his goblet out toward the pirate leader in toast.

"To a better understanding of each other's worth," he said, tapping Sheila's cup.

"And a better understanding of each other's desires," the pirate replied, her smirk even wider.

Morik grinned as well, considering how he might turn this one's fire into some wild pleasures.

He didn't get what he bargained for.

Morik staggered out of Sheila's room a short while later, his head throbbing from the left hook the pirate had leveled his way while still wearing that smirk of hers. Confused by Sheila's violent reaction to his advance—Morik had sidled up to her and gently brushed the back of his hand across her ruddy cheek—the rogue muttered a dozen different curses and stumbled across the way toward Bellany's room. Morik wasn't used to such treatment from the ladies, and his indignation was clear to the sorceress as she opened the door and stood there, blocking the way.

"Making love with a trapped badger?" the grinning Bellany asked.

"That would have been preferable," Morik replied and tried to enter the room. Bellany, though, kept her arm up before him, blocking the way.

Morik looked at her quizzically. "Surely you are not jealous."

"You seem to have a fair estimation of your worth to so definitely know that truth," she replied.

Morik started to respond, but then the insult registered, and he stopped and gave a little salute to the woman.

"Jealous?" Bellany asked skeptically. "Hardly that. I would have thought you'd have bedded Jule Pepper by now, at least. You do surprise me with your taste, though. I didn't think you were Sheila Kree's type, nor she yours."

"Apparently your suspicions are correct," the rogue remarked, rubbing his bruised temple. He started ahead again, and this time Bellany let him move past her and into the room. "I suspect *you* would have had more luck in wooing that one."

"Took you long enough to figure that one out," Bellany replied, closing the door as she entered behind the rogue.

Morik fell upon a bed of soft furs and rolled to cast a glance at the grinning sorceress. "A simple word of warning?" he asked. "You could not have done that for me beforehand?"

"And miss the fun?"

"You did not miss much," said Morik, and he held his arms out toward her.

"Do you need your wound massaged?" Bellany asked, not moving. "Or your pride?"

Morik considered the question for just a moment. "Both," he admitted, and, her smile widening even more, the sorceress approached.

"This is the last time I will warn you," she said, slipping onto the bed beside him. "Tangle with Sheila Kree, and she will kill you. If you are lucky, I mean. If not, she'll likely tell Chogurugga that you have amorous designs over her."

"The ogress?" asked a horrified Morik.

"And if your coupling with that one does not kill you, then Bloog surely will."

Bellany edged in closer, trying to kiss the man, but Morik turned away, any thoughts of passion suddenly flown.

"Chogurugga," he said, and a shudder coursed his spine.

22

ONE STEP AT A TIME

With the freezing wind roaring in at him from the right, Wulfgar plodded along, ducking his shoulder and head against the constant icy press. He was on a high pass, and though he didn't like being out in the open, this windblown stretch was the route with by far the least remaining snow. He knew that enemies might spot him from a mile away, a dark spot against the whiteness, but knew he also that unless they were aerial creatures—and ones large enough to buck the wintry blow—they'd never get near to him.

What he was hoping for was that his former companions might spot him. For how else might he find them in this vast, up-and-down landscape, where vision was ever limited by the next mountain peak and where distances were badly distorted? Sometimes the next mountain slope, where individual trees could be picked out, might seem to be a short march, but was in reality miles and miles away, and those with often insurmountable obstacles, a sharp ravine or unclimbable facing, preventing Wulfgar from getting there without a detour that would take days.

How did I ever hope to find them? the barbarian asked himself, and not for the first, or even the hundredth time. He shook his head at his own foolishness in ever walking through Luskan's north gate on that fateful morning, and again at continuing into the mountains after the terrific storm when the south road seemed so much more accessible.

"And would I not be the fool if Drizzt and the others have sought out shelter, a town through which they can spend the winter?" the barbarian asked himself, and he laughed aloud.

Yes, this was about as hopeless as seemed possible, seeking his friends in a wilderness so vast and inhospitable, in conditions so wild that he might pass within a few yards of them without ever noticing them. But still, when he considered it in context, the barbarian realized he was not foolish, despite the odds, that he had done what he needed to do.

Wulfgar paused from that high vantage point and looked all around him at the valleys, at the peak looming before him, and at one expanse of fur trees, a dark green splash against the white-sided mountain, down to the right.

He decided he would go there, under the cover of those trees, making his way to the west until he came to the main mountain pass that would take him back into Icewind Dale. If he found his former companions along the way, then all the better. If not, he would continue along to Ten-Towns and stay there until Drizzt and the others came to him, or until the spring, if they did not arrive, when he could sign on with a caravan heading back to Waterdeep.

Wulfgar shielded his eyes from the glare and the blowing snow and picked his path. He'd have to continue across the open facing to the larger mountain, then make his way down its steep western side. At least there were trees along that slope, against which he could lean his weight and slow his descent. If he tried to go down from this barren area and got into a slide, he'd tumble a long way indeed.

Wulfgar put his head down again and plowed on, leaning into the wind.

That lean cost him when he stepped upon one stone, which sloped down to the right much more than it appeared. His furry boot found little traction on the icy surface, and the overbalanced Wulfgar couldn't compensate quickly enough to belay the skid. Out he went, feet first, to land hard on his rump. He was sliding, his arms flailing wildly in an effort to find a hold.

He let go of the large, unwieldy bardiche, tossing the weapon a bit to the side so it didn't tumble down onto his head behind him. He couldn't slow and was soon bouncing more than sliding, going into a headlong roll and clipping one large stone that turned him over sideways. The straps on his pack fell loose, one untying, the other tearing free. He left it behind, its flap opening and a line of his supplies spilling out behind it as it slid.

Wulfgar continued his twisting, bouncing descent and left the pack, the bardiche, and the top of the pass, far behind.

⚔ ⚔ ⚔ ⚔ ⚔

"He's hurt!" Captain Deudermont said, his voice rising with anxiety as he watched the barbarian's long and brutal tumble.

He and Robillard were in his private quarters aboard *Sea Sprite*, staring into a bowl of enchanted water the wizard was using to scrye out the wandering barbarian. Robillard was not fond of such divination spells, nor was he very proficient with them, but he had secretly placed a magical pin under the folds of Wulfgar's silver wolf-furred clothing. That pin, attuned to the bowl, allowed even Robillard, whose prowess was in evocation and not divination, to catch a glimpse of the distant man.

"Oaf," Robillard quietly remarked.

They watched silently, Deudermont chewing his lip, as Wulfgar climbed to his feet at the bottom of the long slide. The barbarian leaned over to one side, favoring an injured shoulder. As he walked about, obviously trying to sort out the best path back to his equipment, the pair noted a pronounced limp.

"He'll not make it back up without aid," Deudermont said.

"Oaf," Robillard said again.

"Look at him!" the captain cried. "He could have turned south, as you predicted, but he did not. No, he went out to the north and into the frozen mountains, a place where few would travel, even in the summer and even in a group, and fewer still would dare try alone."

"That is the way of nature," Robillard quipped. "Those who would try alone likely have and thus are all dead. Fools have a way of weeding themselves out of the bloodlines."

"You wanted him to go north," the captain pointedly reminded. "You said as much, and many times. And not so that he would fall and die. You insisted that if Wulfgar was a man deserving of such friends as Drizzt and Catti-brie, that he would go in search of them, no matter the odds.

"Look now, my curmudgeonly friend," Deudermont stated, waving his arm out toward the water bowl, to the image of stubborn Wulfgar.

Obviously in pain but just grimacing it away, the man was scrambling inch by inch to scale back up the mountainside. The barbarian didn't stop and cry out in rage, didn't punch his fist into the air. He just picked his path and clawed at it without complaint.

Deudermont eyed Robillard as intently as the wizard was then eyeing the scrying bowl. Finally, Robillard looked up. "Perhaps there is more to this Wulfgar than I believed," the wizard admitted.

"Are we to let him die out there, alone and cold?"

Robillard sighed, then growled and rubbed his hands forcefully across his face, so that his skinny features glowed bright red. "He has been nothing but trouble since the day he arrived on Waterdeep's long dock to speak with you!" Robillard snarled, and he shook his head. "Nay, even before that, in Luskan, when he tried to kill—"

"He did not!" Deudermont insisted, angry that Robillard had reopened that old wound. "That was neither Wulfgar nor the little one named Morik."

"So you say."

"He suffers hardships without complaint," the captain went on, again directing the wizard's eyes to the image in the bowl. "Though I hardly think Wulfgar considers such a storm as this even a hardship after the torments he likely faced at the hands of the demon Errtu."

"Then there is no problem here."

"But what now?" the captain pressed. "Wulfgar will never find his friends while wandering aimlessly through the wintry mountains."

Deudermont could tell by the ensuing sigh that Robillard understood him completely.

"We spotted a pirate just yesterday," the wizard remarked, a verbal squirm if Deudermont had ever heard one. "Likely we will do battle in the morning. You can not afford—"

"If we see the pirate again and you have not returned, or if you are not yet prepared for the fight, then we will shadow her. As we can outrun any ship when we are in pursuit, so we can when we are in retreat."

"I do not like teleporting to unfamiliar places," Robillard grumbled. "I may appear too high, and fall."

"Enact a spell of flying or floating before you go, then."

"Or too low," Robillard said grimly, for that was ever a possibility, and any wizard who wound up appearing at the other end of a teleport spell too low would find pieces of himself scattered amongst the rocks and dirt.

Deudermont had no answer for that other than a shrug, but it wasn't really a debate. Robillard was only complaining anyway, with every intention of going to the wounded man.

"Wait for me to return before engaging any pirates," the wizard grumbled, fishing through his many pockets for the components he would need to safely—as safely as possible, anyway—go to Wulfgar. "If I do return, that is."

"I have every confidence."

"Of course you do," said Robillard.

Captain Deudermont stepped back as Robillard moved to a side cabinet and flung it open, removing one of Deudermont's own items, a heavy woolen blanket. Grumbling continually, the wizard began his casting, first a spell that had him gently floating off of the floor, and another that seemed to tear the fabric of the air itself. Many multicolored bubbles surrounded the wizard until his form became blurred by their multitude—and he was gone, and there were only bubbles, gradually popping and flowing together so that the air seemed whole again.

Deudermont rushed forward and stared into the watery bowl, catching the last images of Wulfgar before Robillard's divining dweomer dissipated.

He saw a second form come onto the snowy scene.

⚔ ⚔ ⚔ ⚔ ⚔

Wulfgar started to slip yet again, but growled and fell flat, reaching his arm up and catching onto a jag in the little bare stone he could find. His pulled with his powerful arm, sliding himself upward.

"We will be here all afternoon if you continue at that pace," came a familiar voice from above.

The barbarian looked up to see Robillard standing atop the pass, a heavy brown blanket wrapped around him, over his customary wizard robes.

"What?" the astonished Wulfgar started to ask, but with his

surprise came distraction, and he wound up sliding backward some twenty feet to crash heavily against a rocky outcrop.

The barbarian pulled himself to his feet and looked back up to see Robillard, the bardiche in hand, floating down the mountain slope. The wizard scooped a few of Wulfgar's other belongings on the way, dropped them to Wulfgar, and swooped about, flying magically back and forth until he had collected all of the spilled possessions. That job completed, he landed lightly beside the huge man.

"I hardly expected to see you here," said Wulfgar.

"No less than I expected to see you," Robillard answered. "I predicted that you would take the south road, not the north. Your surprising fortitude even cost me a wager I made with Donnark the oarsman."

"Should I repay you?" Wulfgar said dryly.

Robillard shrugged and nodded. "Another time, perhaps. I have no desire to remain in this godsforsaken wilderness any longer than is necessary."

"I have my possessions and am not badly injured," Wulfgar stated. He squared his massive shoulders and thrust out his chin defiantly, more than ready to allow the wizard to leave.

"But you have not found your friends," the wizard explained, "and have little chance of ever doing so without my help. And so I am here."

"Because you are my friend?"

"Because Captain Deudermont is," Robillard corrected, and with a huff to deny the wry grin that adorned the barbarian's ruddy and bristled face.

"You have spells to locate them?" Wulfgar asked.

"I have spells to make us fly up above the peaks," Robillard corrected, "and others to get us quickly from place to place. We will soon enough take account of every creature walking the region. We can only hope that your friends are among them."

"And if they are not?"

"Then I suggest that you return with me to Waterdeep."

"To *Sea Sprite*?"

"To Waterdeep," Robillard forcefully repeated.

Wulfgar shrugged, not wanting to argue the point—one that he hoped would be moot. He believed that Drizzt and the others had come in search of Aegis-fang, and if that was the case he expected that they would still be there, alive and well.

He still wasn't sure if he had chosen correctly that day back in Luskan, still wasn't sure if he was ready for this, if he wanted this. How would he react when he saw them again? What would he say to Bruenor, and what might he do if the dwarf, protective of Catti-brie to the end, simply leaped at him to throttle him? And what might he say to Catti-brie? How could he ever look into her blue eyes again after what he had done to her?

Those questions came up at him forcefully at that moment, now that it seemed possible that he would actually find the companions.

But he had no answers for those questions and knew that he would not be able to foresee the confrontation, even from his own sensibilities.

Wulfgar came out of his contemplation to see Robillard staring at him, the wizard wearing as close to an expression of empathy as Wulfgar had ever seen.

"How did you get this far?" Robillard asked.

Wulfgar's expression showed that he did not understand.

"One step at a time," Robillard answered his own question. "And that is how you will go on. One step at a time will Wulfgar trample his demons."

Robillard did something then that surprised the big man as profoundly as he had ever been, he reached up and patted Wulfgar on the shoulder.

23
And In Walked . . .

I'm thinking that we might be crawling back to that fool Lord Feringal and his little land o' Auckney," Bruenor grumbled when he crept back into the small cave the group had used for shelter that night after the storm had abated. The weather was better, to be sure, but Bruenor understood the dangers of avalanches, and the sheer volume of snow that had fallen the night before stunned him. "Snow's deeper than a giant's crotch!"

"Walk atop it," Drizzt remarked with a wry grin.

But in truth none of them, not even the drow, was much in the mood for smiling. The snow had piled high all through the mountains, and the day's travel had been shortened, as Drizzt had feared, by the specter of avalanches. Dozens cascaded down all around them, many blocking passes that would force the companions to wander far afield. This could mean a journey of hours, perhaps days, to circumvent a slide-filled pass that should have taken them but an hour to walk through.

"We ain't gonna find 'em, elf," Bruenor said bluntly. "They're deep underground, don't ye doubt, and not likely to stick their smelly heads above ground until the spring. We ain't for finding them in this."

"We always knew it would not be easy," Catti-brie reminded the dwarf.

"We found the group raiding the tower, and they pointed us in the right direction," Regis piped in. "We'll need some more luck, to be sure, but did we not know that all along?"

"Bah!" Bruenor snorted. He kicked a fairly large stone, launching it into a bouncing roll to crash into the side wall of the small cave.

"Surrender the hammer to them?" Drizzt asked Bruenor in all earnestness.

"Or get buried afore we e'er get near 'em?" the dwarf replied. "Great choices there, elf!"

"Or return to Auckney and wait out the winter," Regis offered. "Then try again in the spring."

"When *Bloody Keel* will likely be sailing the high seas," reminded Catti-brie. "With Sheila Kree and Aegis-fang long gone from these shores."

"We go south, then," reasoned Bruenor. "We find Deudermont and sign on to help with his pirate-killin' until we catch up to Kree. Then we take me hammer back and put the witch on the bottom o' those high seas—and good enough for her!"

A silence followed, profound and unbroken for a long, long time. Perhaps Bruenor was right. Perhaps hunting for the warhammer now wouldn't bring them anything but disaster. And if anyone among them had the right to call off the search for Aegis-fang, it was certainly Bruenor. He had crafted the hammer, after all, and had given it to Wulfgar. In truth, though, none of them, not even Regis, who was perhaps the most removed from the situation, wanted to let go of that warhammer, that special symbol of what Wulfgar had once been to all of them.

Perhaps it made sense to wait out the wintry season, but Drizzt couldn't accept the logical conclusion that the weather had made the journey simply too dangerous to continue. The drow wanted this done with, and soon. He wanted to finally catch up to Wulfgar, to retrieve both Aegis-fang and the lost symbol of all they had once been, and the thought of sitting around through several months of snow would not settle comfortably on his slender shoulders. Looking around, the drow realized that the others, even Bruenor—perhaps even particularly Bruenor, despite his typical blustering—were feeling much the same way.

The drow walked out of the cave, scrambling up the wall of snow that had drifted in front of the entrance. He ran to the highest vantage point he could find, and despite the glare that was surely stinging his light-sensitive eyes, he peered all around, seeking a course to the south, to the sea, seeking some way that they could continue.

He heard someone approaching from behind a short time later and from the sound of the footfalls knew it to be Catti-brie. She was walking with a stride that was somewhere between Drizzt's light-stepping and Bruenor's plowing technique.

"Lookin' as bad to me in going back as in going ahead," the woman said when she moved up beside Drizzt. "Might as well be going ahead, then, by me own thinking."

"And will Bruenor agree? Or Regis?"

"Rumblebelly's making much the same case to Bruenor inside right now," Catti-brie remarked, and Drizzt turned to regard her. Always before, Regis would have been the very first to abandon the road to adventure, the very first to seek a way back to warm comfort.

"Do you remember when Artemis Entreri impersonated Regis?" Drizzt asked, his tone a clear warning.

Catti-brie's blue eyes widened in shock for just a moment, until

Drizzt's expression clearly conveyed that he was only kidding. Still, the point that something was very different with Regis was clearly made, and fully taken.

"Ye'd think that the goblin spear he caught on the river in the south would've put him even more in the fluffy chair," Catti-brie remarked.

"Without the magical aid from that most unlikely source, he would have lost his arm, at least," Drizzt reminded, and it was true enough.

When Regis had been stabbed in the shoulder, the friends simply could not stop the bleeding. Drizzt and Catti-brie were actually in the act of preparing Regis's arm for amputation, which they figured to be the only possible chance they had for keeping the halfling alive, when Jarlaxle's drow lieutenant, in the guise of Cadderly, had walked up and offered some magical healing.

Regis had been quiet through the remainder of that adventure, the road to Jarlaxle's crystal tower and Drizzt's fight with Entreri, and the long and sullen road all the way back to Icewind Dale. The friends had seen many adventures together, and in truth, that last one had seen the worst outcome of all. The Crystal Shard was lost to the dangerous leader of Bregan D'aerthe. It had also been easily the most painful and dangerous for Regis personally, and yet for some reason Drizzt and Catti-brie could not fathom, that last adventure had apparently sparked something within Regis. It had become evident almost immediately after their return to Ten-Towns. Not once had Regis tried to dodge out of the companions' policing of the dangerous roads in and out of the region, and on those few occasions when they had encountered monsters or high-waymen, Regis had refused to sit back and let his skilled friends handle the situation.

And here he was, trying to convince Bruenor to plow on through the inhospitable and deadly mountains, when the warm hearth of

Lord Feringal's castle sat waiting behind them.

"Three against one, then," Catti-brie said at length. "We'll be going ahead, it seems."

"With Bruenor grumbling every step of the way."

"He'd be grumbling every step of the way if we turned back, as well."

"There is a dependability there."

"A reminder of times gone past and a signal of times to come," Catti-brie replied without missing a beat, and the pair shared a needed, heartfelt laugh.

When they went back into the deep, high cave they found Bruenor hard at work in packing up the camp, rolling blankets into tight bundles, while Regis stirred the pot over the still-blazing fire.

"Ye seein' a road worth trying?" Bruenor asked.

"Ahead or back . . . it is much the same," Drizzt answered.

"Except if we go ahead, we'll still have to come back," Bruenor reasoned.

"Go on, I say," Catti-brie offered. "We're not to find our answers in the sleepy town of Auckney, and I'm wanting answers before the spring thaw."

"What says yerself, elf?" Bruenor asked.

"We knew that the road would be dangerous and inhospitable before we ever set out from Luskan," Drizzt answered. "We knew the season then, and this snowfall is hardly unusual or unexpected."

"But we hoped to find the stupid pirate afore this," the dwarf put in.

"Hoped, but hardly expected," Drizzt was quick to reply. He looked to Catti-brie. "I, too, have little desire to spend the winter worrying about Wulfgar."

"On, then," Bruenor suddenly agreed. "And let the snow take us. And let Wulfgar spend the winter worrying about us!" The dwarf ended with a stream of curses, muttering under his breath in that typical Bruenor fashion. The other three in the cave shared a few knowing winks and smiles.

The low hum of Bruenor's grumbles shifted, though, into a more general humming noise that filled all the air and caught the attention of all four.

In the middle of the cave, a blue vertical line appeared, glowing to a height of about seven feet. Before the friends could begin to call out or react, that line split apart into two of equal height, and those two began drifting apart, a horizontal blue line atop them.

"Wizard door!" Regis cried, rolling to the side, scrambling for the shadows, and taking out his mace.

Drizzt dropped the figurine of Guenhwyvar to the floor, ready to call out to the panther. He drew forth his scimitars, moving beside Bruenor to face the growing portal directly, while Catti-brie slipped a few steps back and to the side, stringing and drawing her bow in one fluid motion.

The door formed completely, the area within the three defining lines buzzing with a lighter blue haze.

Out stepped a form, dressed in dark blue robes. Bruenor roared and lifted his many-notched axe, and Catti-brie pulled back, ready to let fly.

"Robillard!" Drizzt called, and Catti-brie echoed the name a split second later.

"Deudermont's wizard friend?" Bruenor started to ask.

"What are you doing here?" the drow asked, but his words fell away as a second form came through the magical portal behind the wizard, a huge and hulking form.

Regis said it first, for the other three, especially Bruenor, couldn't seem to find a single voice among them. "Wulfgar?"

24

Ðrow-Sign

The unearthly wail, its notes primal and agonized, echoed off the stone walls of the cavern complex, reverberating into the very heart of the mountain itself.

The tips of Le'lorinel's sword and dagger dipped toward the floor. The elf stopped the training session and turned to regard the room's open door and the corridor beyond, where that awful cry was still echoing.

"What is it?" Le'lorinel asked as a form rushed by. Jule Pepper, the elf, who sprinted to catch up, guessed.

Down the winding way Le'lorinel went, pursuing Jule all the way to the complex of large chambers immediately below those of Sheila Kree and her trusted, brand-wearing compatriots, and into the lair of Chogurugga and Bloog.

Le'lorinel had to dodge aside upon entering, as a huge chair sailed by to smash against the stone. Again came that terrible cry—Chogurugga's shriek. Looking past the ogress, Le'lorinel understood it to be a wail of grief.

For there, in the middle of the floor, lay the bloated body of another ogre, a young and strong one. Sheila Kree and Bellany stood over the body beside another ogre who was kneeling, its huge, ugly head resting atop the corpse. At first, Le'lorinel figured it to be Bloog, but then the elf spotted the gigantic ogre leader, looking on from the wall behind them. It didn't take Le'lorinel long to figure out that the mask of anguish that Bloog wore was far from genuine.

It occurred to Le'lorinel that Bloog might have done this.

"Bathunk! Me baby!" Chogurugga shrieked with concern very atypical for a mother ogress. "Bathunk! Bathunk!"

Sheila Kree moved to talk to the ogress, perhaps to console her, but Chogurugga went into another flailing fit at that moment, lifting a rock from the huge fire pit and hurling it to smash against the wall—not so far from the ducking Bloog, Le'lorinel noted.

"They found Bathunk's body near an outpost to the north," Bellany explained to Jule and Le'lorinel, the sorceress walking over to them. "A few were killed, it seems. That one, Pokker, thought it prudent to bring back Bathunk's body." As she explained, she pointed to the ogre kneeling over the body.

"You sound as if he shouldn't have," Jule Pepper remarked.

Bellany shrugged as if it didn't matter. "Look at the wretch," she whispered, nodding her chin toward the wild Chogurugga. "She'll likely kill half the ogres in Golden Cove or get herself killed by Bloog."

"Or by Sheila," Jule observed, for it seemed obvious that Sheila Kree was fast losing patience with the ogress.

"There is always that possibility," Bellany deadpanned.

"How did it happen?" asked Le'lorinel.

"It is not so uncommon a thing," Bellany answered. "We lose a few ogres every year, particularly in the winter. The idiots simply can't allow good judgment to get in the way of their need to squash people. The soldiers of the Spine of the World communities are veterans all, and no easy mark, even for monsters as powerful and as well-outfitted as Chogurugga's ogres."

While Bellany was answering, Le'lorinel subtly moved toward Bathunk's bloated corpse. Noting that it seemed as if Shcila had Chogurugga momentarily under control then, the elf dared move even closer, bending low to examine the body.

Le'lorinel found breathing suddenly difficult. The cuts on the body were many, were beautifully placed and were, in many different areas, curving. Curving like the blades of a scimitar. Noting one bruise behind Bathunk's hip, the elf gently reached down and edged the corpse a bit to the side. The mark resembled the imprint of a delicately curving blade, much like the blades Le'lorinel had fashioned for Tunevec during his portrayal of a certain dark elf.

Le'lorinel looked up suddenly, trying to digest it all, recognizing clearly that no ordinary soldier had downed this mighty ogre.

The elf nearly laughed aloud then—a desire only enhanced when Le'lorinel noticed that Bloog was sniffling and wiping his eyes as if they were teary, which they most surely were not. But another roar from behind came as a clear reminder that a certain ogress might not enjoy anyone making light of this tragedy.

Le'lorinel rose quickly and walked back to Jule and Bellany, then kept right on moving out of the room, running back up the passageway to the safety of the upper level. There, the elf gasped and laughed heartily, at once thrilled and scared.

For Le'lorinel knew that Drizzt Do'Urden had done this thing, that the drow was in the area—not so far away if the ogre could carry Bathunk back in this wintry climate.

"My thanks, E'kressa," the elf whispered.

Le'lorinel's hands went instinctively for sword and dagger, then came together in front, the fingers of the right hand turning the enchanted ring about its digit on the left. After all these years, it was about to happen. After all the careful planning, the studying of Drizzt's style and technique, the training, the consultations with some of the finest swordsmen of northern Faerûn to find ways to counter the drow's maneuvers. After all the costs, the years of labor to pay for the ring, the partners, and the information.

Le'lorinel could hardly draw breath. Drizzt was near. It had to have been that dangerous dark elf who had felled Bathunk.

The elf stalked about the room then went out into the corridor, stalking past Bellany's room and Sheila's, to the end of the hall and the small chamber where Jule Pepper had set up for the winter.

The three women arrived a few moments later, shaking their heads and making off-color jokes about Chogurugga's antics, with Sheila Kree doing a fair imitation of the crazed ogress.

"Quite an exit," Bellany remarked. "You missed the grandest show of all."

"Poor Chogurugga," said Jule with a grin.

"Poor Bloog, ye mean," Sheila was quick to correct, and the three had a laugh.

"All right, ye best be telling me what ye're knowing about it," Sheila said to Le'lorinel when the elf didn't join in the mirth, when the elf didn't crack the slightest of smiles, intensity burning behind those blue and gold orbs.

"I was here when Bathunk was killed, obviously," Le'lorinel reminded.

Bellany was the first to laugh. "You know something," the sorceress said. "As soon as you went to Bathunk's corpse . . ."

"Ye think it was that damned drow who did it to Bathunk," Sheila Kree reasoned.

Le'lorinel didn't answer, other than to keep a perfectly straight, perfectly grim countenance.

"Ye do!"

"The mountains are a big place, with many dangerous

adversaries," Jule Pepper put in. "There are thousands who could have done this to the foolish young ogre."

Before Le'lorinel could counter, Bellany said, "Hmm," and walked out in front of the other two, one delicate hand up against her pursed lips. "But you saw the wounds," the sorceress reasoned.

"Curving wounds, like the cuts of a scimitar," Le'lorinel confirmed

"A sword will cut a wound like that if the target's falling when he gets it," Sheila put in. "The wounds don't tell ye as much as ye think."

"They tell me all I need to know," Le'lorinel replied.

"They were well placed," Jule reasoned. "No novice swordsman cut down Bathunk.

"And I know Chogurugga gave him many of the potions you delivered to her," she added to Bellany.

That made even Sheila lift her eyebrows in surprise. Bathunk was no ordinary ogre. He was huge, strong, and well trained, and some of those potions were formidable enhancements.

"It was Drizzt," Le'lorinel stated with confidence. "He is nearby and likely on his way to us."

"So said the diviner who delivered you here," said Bellany, who knew the story well.

"E'kressa the gnome. He sent me to find the mark of Aegis-fang, for that mark would bring Drizzt Do'Urden."

Jule and Bellany looked to each other, then turned to regard Sheila Kree, who was standing with her head down, deep in thought.

"Could've been the soldiers at the tower," the pirate leader said at length. "Could've been reinforcements from one of the smaller villages. Could've been a wandering band of heroes, or even other monsters, trying to claim the prize the ogres had taken."

"Could've been Drizzt Do'Urden," interjected Jule, who had first-hand experience with the dangerous drow and his heroic friends.

337

Sheila looked at the tall, willowy woman and nodded, then turned her gaze over Le'lorinel. "Ye ready for him—if it is him and if he is coming this way?"

The elf stood straight and tall, head back, chest out proudly. "I have prepared for nothing else in many years."

"If he can take down Bathunk, he'll be a tough fight, don't ye doubt," the pirate leader added.

"We will all be there to aid in the cause," Bellany pointed out, but Le'lorinel didn't seem thrilled at that prospect.

"I know him as well as he knows himself," the elf explained. "If Drizzt Do'Urden comes to us, then he will die."

"At the end of your blade," Bellany said with a grin.

"Or at the end of his own," the ever-cryptic Le'lorinel replied.

"Then we'll be hoping that it's Drizzit," Sheila agreed. "But ye canno' be knowing. The towers in the mountains are well guarded. Many o' Chogurugga's kinfolk've been killed in going against them, or just in working the roads. Too many soldiers about and too many hero-minded adventurers. Ye canno' be knowing it's Drizzt or anyone else."

Le'lorinel let it go at that. Let Sheila think whatever Sheila wanted to think.

Le'lorinel, though, heard again the words of E'kressa.

Le'lorinel knew that it was Drizzt, and Le'lorinel was ready. Nothing else—not Sheila, not Drizzt's friends, not the ogres—mattered.

25
COMING TO TERMS

"Wulfgar," Regis said again, when no one reacted at all to his first remark.

The halfling looked around to the others, trying to read their expressions. Catti-brie's was easy enough to discern. The woman looked like she could be pushed over by a gentle breeze, looked frozen in shock at the realization that Wulfgar was again standing before her.

Drizzt appeared much more composed, and it seemed to Regis as if the perceptive drow was consciously studying Wulfgar's every move, that he was trying to get some honest gauge as to who this man standing before him truly was. The Wulfgar of their earlier days, or the one who had slapped Catti-brie?

As for Bruenor, Regis wasn't sure if the dwarf wanted to run up and hug the man or run up and throttle him. Bruenor was trembling—though out of surprise, rage, or simple amazement, the halfling couldn't tell.

And Wulfgar, too, seemed to be trying to read some hint of the truth of Bruenor's expression and posture. The barbarian, his stern gaze never leaving the crusty and sour look of Bruenor Battlehammer, gave a deferential nod the halfling's way.

"We have been looking for you," Drizzt remarked. "All the way to Waterdeep and back."

Wulfgar nodded, his expression holding steady, as if he feared to change it.

"It may be that Wulfgar has been looking for Wulfgar, as well," Robillard interjected. The wizard arced an eyebrow when Drizzt turned to regard him directly.

"Well, we found you—or you found us," said Regis.

"But ye think ye found yerself?" Bruenor asked, a healthy skepticism in his tone.

Wulfgar's lips tightened to thin lines, his jaw clenching tightly. He wanted to cry out that he had—he prayed that he had. He looked to them all in turn, wanting to explode into a wild rush that would gather them all up in his arms.

But there he found a wall, as fluid and shifting as the smoke of Errtu's Abyss, and yet through which his emotions seemed not to be able to pass.

"Once again, it seems that I am in your debt," the barbarian managed to say, a perfectly stupid change of subject, he knew.

"Delly told us of your heroics," Robillard was quick to add. "All of us are grateful, needless to say. Never before has anyone so boldly gone against the house of Deudermont. I assure you that the perpetrators have brought the scorn of the Lords of Waterdeep upon those they represented."

The grand statement was diminished somewhat by the knowledge of all in the audience that the Lords of Waterdeep would not likely come to the north in search of those missing conspirators. The Lords of Waterdeep, like the lords of almost every large city, were better at making proclamations than at carrying through with action.

"Perhaps we can exact that vengeance for the Lords of Waterdeep, and for Captain Deudermont as well," Drizzt offered with a sly expression turned Robillard's way. "We hunt for Sheila Kree, and it was she who perpetrated the attack on the captain's house."

"I have delivered Wulfgar to you to join in that hunt."

Again all eyes fell over the huge barbarian, and again, his lips thinned with the tension. Drizzt saw it clearly and understood that this was not the time to burst the dam that was holding back Wulfgar's, and thus all of their feelings. The drow turned to regard Catti-brie, and the fact that she didn't blink for several long moments told him much about her fragile state of mind.

"But what of Robillard?" the dark elf asked suddenly, thinking to deflect, or at least delay the forthcoming flood. "Will he not use his talents to aid us?"

That caught the wizard off guard, and his eyes widened. "He already did!" he protested, but the weakness of the argument was reflected in his tone.

Drizzt nodded, accepting that. "And he can do so much more, and with ease."

"My place is with Captain Deudermont and *Sea Sprite*, who are already at sea hunting pirates, and were, in fact, in pursuit of one such vessel even as I flew off to collect Wulfgar," Robillard explained, but the drow's smile only widened.

"Your magical talents allow you to search far and wide in a short time," Drizzt explained. "We know the approximate location of our prey, but with the ups and downs of the snow-covered mountains, they could be just beyond the next rise without our ever knowing it."

"My skills have been honed for shipboard battles, Master Do'Urden," Robillard replied.

"All we ask of you is aid in locating the pirate clan, if they are, as we believe, holed up on the southwestern edge of the mountains. Certainly if they've put their ship into winter port, they're near the water. How much more area can you scout, and how much grander the vantage point, with enchantments of flying and the like?"

Robillard thought the words over for a few moments, brought a hand up, and rubbed the back of his neck. "The mountains are vast," he countered.

"We believe we know the general direction," Drizzt answered.

Robillard paused a bit longer, then nodded his head. "I will search out a very specific region, giving you just this one afternoon," he said. "Then I must return to my duties aboard *Sea Sprite*. We've a pirate in chase that I'll not let flee."

"Fair enough," Drizzt said with a nod.

"I will take one of you with me," the wizard said. He glanced around, his gaze fast settling on Regis, who was by far the lightest of the group. "You," he said, pointing to the halfling. "You will ride with me on the search, learn what you may, then guide your friends back to the pirates."

Regis agreed without the slightest hesitation, and Drizzt and Catti-brie looked at each other with continued surprise.

The preparations were swift indeed, with Robillard gathering up one of the empty packs and bidding Regis to follow him outside. He warned the halfling to don more layers of clothing to battle the cold winds and the great chill up high, then cast an enchantment upon himself.

"Do you know the region Drizzt spoke of?" he asked.

Regis nodded and the wizard cast a second spell, this one over the halfling, shrinking him down considerably in size. Robillard plucked the halfling up and set him in place in the open pack, and off the pair flew, into the bright daylight.

"Quarterling?" Bruenor asked with a chuckle.

"Lookin' more like an eighthling," Catti-brie answered, and the two laughed.

The levity didn't seem to sink in to Wulfgar, nor to Drizzt who, now that the business with Robillard was out of the way, understood that it was time for them to deal with a much more profound issue, one they certainly could not ignore if they were to walk off together into danger with any hope of succeeding.

※ ※ ※ ※ ※

He saw the world as a bird might, soaring past below him as the wizard climbed higher and higher into the sky, finding wind currents that took them generally and swiftly in the desired direction, south and to the sea.

At first, Regis considered how vulnerable they were up there, black spots against a blue sky, but as they soared on the halfling lost himself in the experience. He watched the rolling landscape, coming over one ridge of a mountain, the ground beyond falling away so fast it took the halfling's breath away. He spotted a herd of deer below and took comfort in their tiny appearance, for if they were that small, barely distinguishable black spots, then how small he and Robillard must seem from the ground. How easy for them to be mistaken for a bird, Regis realized, especially given the wizard's trailing, flowing cape.

Of course, the sudden realization of how high they truly were soon incited other fears in Regis, and he grabbed on tightly to the wizard's shoulders.

"Lessen your pinching grasp!" Robillard shouted against the wind, and Regis complied, just a tiny bit.

Soon the pair were out over cold waters, and Robillard brought them down somewhat, beneath the line of the mountaintops. Below, white water thrashed over many looming rocks and waves thundered against the stony shore, a war that had been raging for millennia. Though they were lower in the sky, Regis couldn't help but tighten his grip again.

A thin line of smoke ahead alerted the pair to a campfire and Robillard immediately swooped back in toward shore, cutting up behind the closest peaks in an attempt to use them as a shield against the eyes of any potential sentries. To the halfling's surprise and relief, the wizard set down on a bare patch of stone.

"I must renew the spell of flying," Robillard explained, "and enact a couple more." The wizard fumbled in his pouch for various components, then began his spellcasting. A few seconds later, he disappeared.

Regis gave a little squeak of surprise and alarm.

"I am right here," Robillard's voice explained.

The halfling heard him begin casting again—the same spell, Regis recognized—and a moment later Regis was invisible too.

"You will have to feel your way back into my pack as soon as I am done renewing the spell of flying," the wizard's voice explained, and he began casting again.

Soon the pair were airborne once more, and though he knew logically that he was safer because he was invisible, Regis felt far less secure simply because he couldn't see the wizard supporting him in his flight. He clung with all his might as Robillard zoomed them around the mountains, finding lower passes that led in the general direction of the smoke they'd seen. Soon that smoke was back in sight yet again, only this time the pair were flying in from the northwest instead of the southwest.

As they approached, they came to see that it was indeed sentries. There was a pair of them, one a rough-looking human and the other a huge, muscled brute—a short ogre perhaps, or a creature of mixed human and ogre blood. The two huddled over a meager fire on a high ridge, rubbing their hands and hardly paying attention to their obvious duty overlooking a winding pass in a gorge just beyond their position.

"The prisoners we captured mentioned a gorge," Regis said to the wizard, loudly enough for Robillard to hear.

In response, Robillard swooped to the north and followed the ridge up to the end of the long gorge. Then he swung around and flew the halfling down the descending, swerving line of the ravine. It had obviously once been a riverbed that wound down toward the sea between two long walls of steep stone, two, maybe three hundred feet tall. The base was no more than a hundred feet wide at its widest point, the expanse widening as the walls rose so that from cliff top to cliff top was several hundred feet across in many locations.

They passed the position of the two sentries and noted another pair across the way, but the wizard didn't slow long enough for Regis to get a good look at this second duo.

Down the wizard and his unenthusiastic passenger went, soaring along, the gorge walls rolling past at a pace that had the poor halfling's thoughts whirling. Robillard spotted yet another ogre-looking sentry, but the halfling, too dizzy from the ride, didn't even look up to acknowledge the wizard's sighting.

The gorge rolled along for more than a thousand feet, and as they rounded one last bend, the pair came in sight of the wind-whipped sea. To the right, the ground broke away into various piles of boulders and outcroppings—a jagged, blasted terrain. To the left, at the base of the gorge, loomed a large mound perhaps four or five hundred feet high. There were openings along its rocky side, including a fairly large cave at ground level.

Robillard went past this, out to the sea, then turned a swift left to encircle the south side of the mound. Many great rocks dotted the seascape, a veritable maze of stone and danger for any ships that might dare it. Other mounds jutted out even more than this one all about the coast, further obscuring it from any seafaring eyes.

And there, in the south facing at sea level, loomed a cave large enough for a masted ship to enter.

Robillard went past it, rising as he continued to circle. Both he and Regis noted a pathway then, beginning to the side of the ocean level cavern and rising as it encircled the mountain to the east. Climbing up past the eastern face, the pair saw one door, and could easily imagine others along that often-shielded trail.

Robillard went up over the eastern face, continuing back to the north and cutting back down into the gorge. To the halfling's surprise and trepidation, the wizard put down at the base of the mound, right beside the cave opening, which was large enough for a pair of wagons to drive through side by side.

The wizard held onto the invisible halfling, pulling him along into the cave. They heard the gruff banter of three ogres as soon as they went in.

"There might be a better way into the complex for yourself and the drow," the wizard suggested in a whisper.

The halfling nearly jumped in the air at the sound of the voice right beside him. Regis composed himself quickly enough not to squeal out and alert the guards.

"Stay here," Robillard whispered, and he was gone.

And Regis was all alone, and though he was invisible he felt very small and very vulnerable indeed.

✠ ✠ ✠ ✠ ✠

"You nearly killed me with the first throw of the warhammer!" Drizzt reminded, and he and Catti-brie both smiled when the drow's words brought a chuckle to Wulfgar's grim visage.

They were discussing old times, fond recollections initiated by Drizzt in an effort to break the ice and to draw Wulfgar out of his understandable shell. There was nothing comfortable about this reunion, as was evidenced by Bruenor's unrelenting scowl and Wulfgar's obvious tension.

They were recounting the tales of Drizzt and Wulfgar's first battle together, in the lair of a giant named Biggrin. The two had been training together, and they understood their relative styles, and at many junctures those styles had meshed into brilliance. But indeed, as Drizzt clearly admitted, at some points more luck than teamwork or skill had been involved.

Despite Bruenor's quiet and continuing scowl, the drow went on with tales of the old days in Icewind Dale, of the many adventures, of the forging of Aegis-fang—at which both Bruenor and Wulfgar winced noticeably—of the journey to Calimport to rescue Regis and the trip back to the north and east to find and reclaim Mithral Hall. Even Drizzt was surprised at the sheer volume of the tales, of the depth of the friendship that had been. He started to talk of the coming of the dark elves to Mithral Hall, the tragic encounter that had taken Wulfgar away from them, but he stopped, reconsidering his words.

"How could such bonds have been so fleeting?" the drow asked bluntly. "How could even the intervention of a demon have sundered that which we all spent so many years constructing?"

"It was not the demon Errtu," Wulfgar said, even as Catti-brie started to respond.

The other three stared at the huge man, for these were his first words since Drizzt had begun the tales.

"It was the demon Errtu implanted within me," Wulfgar explained. He paused and moved to the side, facing Catti-brie directly instead of Drizzt. He gently took the woman's hands in his own. "Or the demons that were there before . . ."

His voice broke apart, and he looked up, moisture gathering in his crystal-blue eyes. Stoically, Wulfgar blinked it away and looked back determinedly at the woman.

"I can only say that I am sorry," he said, his normally resonant voice barely a whisper.

Even as he spoke the words, Catti-brie reached up and wrapped him in a great hug, burying her face in his huge shoulder. Wulfgar returned that hug a thousand times over, bending his face into the woman's thick auburn hair.

Catti-brie turned her face to the side, to regard Drizzt, and the drow was smiling and nodding, as pleased as she that this first in what would likely be a long line of barriers to the normal resumption of their friendship had been so thrown down.

Catti-brie stepped back a moment later, wiping her own eyes and regarding Wulfgar with a warm smile. "Ye've a fine wife there in Delly," she said. "And a beautiful child, though she's not yer own."

Wulfgar nodded to both, seeming very pleased at that moment, seeming as if he had just taken a huge step in the right direction.

His grunt was as much in surprise as in pain, then, when he got slammed suddenly in the side. A heavy punch staggered him to the side. The barbarian turned to see a fuming Bruenor standing there, hands on hips.

"Ye ever hit me girl again and I'll be making a fine necklace outta yer teeth, boy! Ye want to be callin' yerself me son, and ye don't go hitting yer sister!"

The way he put it was perfectly ridiculous, of course, but as Bruenor stomped past them and out of the cave the three left behind heard a little sniffle and understood that the dwarf had reacted in the only way his proud sensibilities would allow, that he was as pleased by the reunion as the rest of them.

Catti-brie walked over to Drizzt, then, and casually but tellingly draped her arm across his back. Wulfgar at first seemed surprised, at least as much so as when Bruenor had slugged him. Gradually, though, that look of surprise melted into an expression completely accepting and approving, the barbarian offering a wistful smile.

"The road before us becomes muddled," Drizzt said. "If we are together, and contented, need we go to find Aegis-fang now, against these obstacles?"

Wulfgar looked at him as if he didn't believe what he was hearing. The barbarian's expression changed, though, and quickly, as he seemed to almost come to agree with the reasoning.

"Ye're bats," Catti-brie answered Drizzt, in no uncertain terms.

The drow turned a surprised and incredulous look over her, given her vehemence.

"Don't ye be taking me own word," the woman said. "Ask him." As she finished, she pointed back behind the drow, who turned to see Bruenor stomping back in.

"What?" the dwarf asked.

"Drizzt was thinking that we might be better off leaving the hammer for now," Catti-brie remarked.

Bruenor's eyes widened and for a moment it seemed as if he would launch himself at the drow. "How can ye . . . ye durn fool elf . . . why . . . w-what?" he stammered.

Drizzt patted his hand in the air and offered a slight grin, while subtly motioning for the dwarf to take a look at Wulfgar. Bruenor continued to sputter for a few more moments before catching on, but then he steadied himself, hands on hips, and turned on the barbarian.

"Well?" the dwarf bellowed. "What're ye thinking, boy?"

Wulfgar took a deep breath as the gazes of his four friends settled over him. They placed him squarely in the middle of it all, which was where he belonged, he understood, for it was his action that had cost him the hammer, and since it was his hammer his word should be the final say on the course before them.

But what a weight that decision carried.

Wulfgar's thoughts swirled through all the possibilities, many of them grim indeed. What if he led the companions to Sheila Kree only to have the pirate band wipe them out? Or even worse, he figured, suppose one or more of his friends died, but he survived? How could he possibly live with himself if that . . .

Wulfgar laughed aloud and shook his head, seeing the trap for what it was.

"I lost Aegis-fang through my own fault," he admitted, which of course everyone already knew. "And now I understand the error—my error. And so I will go after the warhammer as soon as I may, through sleet and snow, against dragons and pirates alike if need be. But I can not make you, any of you, join with me. I would not blame any who turned back now for Ten-Towns, or for one of the smaller towns nestled in the mountains. I will go. That is my duty and my responsibility."

"Ye think we'd let ye do it alone?" Catti-brie remarked, but Wulfgar cut her short.

"And I welcome any aid that you four might offer, though I feel that I am hardly deserving of it."

"Stupid words," Bruenor huffed. " 'Course we're going, ye big dope. Ye got yer face into the soup, and so we're pullin' it out."

"The dangers—" Wulfgar started to respond.

"Ogries and stupid pirates," said Bruenor. "Ain't nothing tough there. We'll kill a few and send a few more running, get yer hammer back, and be home afore the spring. And if there's a dragon there . . ." Bruenor paused and smiled wickedly. "Well, we'll let ye kill it yerself!"

The levity was perfectly timed, and all of the companions seemed to be just that again, four friends on a singular mission.

"And if ye ever lose Aegis-fang again," Bruenor roared on, pointing a stubby finger Wulfgar's way, "I'll be buryin' ye afore I go get it back!"

Bruenor's tirade seemed as if it would ramble on, but a voice from outside silenced him and turned all heads that way.

Robillard and Regis entered the small cave.

"We found them," Regis said before the wizard could begin. The halfling stuffed his stubby thumbs under the edges of his heavy woolen vest, assuming a proud posture. "We went right in, past the ogre guards and—"

"We don't know if it is Sheila Kree," Robillard interrupted, "but it seems as if we've found the source of the ogre raiding party—a large complex of tunnels and caverns down by the sea."

"With a cave on the water large enough for a ship to sail into," Regis was quick to add.

"You believe it to be Kree?" Drizzt asked, staring at the wizard as he spoke.

"I would guess," Robillard answered with only the slightest hesitation. "*Sea Sprite* has pursued what we think was Kree's ship into these waters on more than one occasion, then simply lost her. We always suspected that she had a hidden port, perhaps a cave. The complex at the end of that gorge to the south would support that."

"Then that is where we must go," Drizzt remarked.

"I can not carry you all," Robillard explained. "Certainly that one is too large to hang on my back as I fly." He pointed to Wulfgar.

"You know the way?" the drow asked Regis.

The halfling stood very straight, seeming as if he was about to salute the drow. "I can find it," he assured Drizzt and Robillard.

The wizard nodded. "A day's march, and no more," he said. "And thus, your way is clear to you. If . . ." He paused and looked at each of them in turn, his gaze at last settling on Wulfgar. "If you don't choose to pursue this now, *Sea Sprite* would welcome you all in the spring, when we might find a better opportunity to retrieve the lost item from Sheila Kree."

"We go now," Wulfgar said.

"Won't be no Kree to chase, come spring," Bruenor snickered, and to accentuate his point, he pulled forth his battle-axe and slapped it across his open palm.

Robillard laughed and nodded his agreement.

"Good Robillard," Drizzt said, moving to stand before the wizard, "if you and *Sea Sprite* see *Bloody Keel* on the high seas, hail her before you sink her. It might well be us, bringing the pirateer into port."

Robillard laughed again, all the louder. "I do not doubt you," he said to Drizzt, patting the drow on the shoulder. "Pray, if we do meet on the open water, that you and your friends do not sink us!"

The good-natured humor was much appreciated, but it didn't last. Robillard walked past the dark elf to stand before Wulfgar.

"I have never come to like you," he said bluntly.

Wulfgar snorted—or started to, but he caught himself and let the wizard continue. Wulfgar expected a berating that perhaps he deserved, given his actions. The barbarian squared himself and set his shoulders back, but made no move to interrupt.

"But perhaps I have never really come to know you," Robillard admitted. "Perhaps the man you truly are is yet to be found. If so, and you do find the true Wulfgar, son of Beornegar, then do come back to sail with us. Even a crusty old wizard, who has seen too much sun and smelled too much brine, might change his mind."

Robillard turned to wave to the others, but looked back, turning a sly glance over Wulfgar. "If that matters to you at all, of course," he said, and he seemed to be joking.

"It does," Wulfgar said in all seriousness, a tone that stiffened the wizard and the friends with surprise.

An expression that showed startlement, and a pleasant one, widened on Robillard's face. "Farewell to you all, then," the wizard said with a great bow. He ended by launching directly and smoothly into a spell of teleportation, the air around him bubbling like multicolored boiling water, obscuring his form.

And he was gone, and it was just the five of them.

As it had once been.

26
LEADING WITH THEIR FACES

The sky had grayed again, threatening yet another wintry blast, but the friends, undaunted, started out from their latest resting spot full of hope and spirit, ready to do battle against whatever obstacles they might find. They were together again, and for the first time since Wulfgar's unexpected return from the Abyss it seemed comfortable to them all. It seemed . . . right.

When Wulfgar had first returned to them—in an icy cave on the Sea of Moving Ice in the midst of their raging battle against the demon Errtu—there had been elation, of course, but it had been an uncomfortable thing on many levels. It was a shock and a trial to readjust to this sudden new reality. Wulfgar had returned from the grave, and all the grief the other four friends had thought settled had suddenly been unearthed, resolution thrown aside.

Elation had led to many uncomfortable but much-needed adjustments as the friends had tried to get to know each other again. That led to disaster, to Wulfgar's moodiness, to Wulfgar's outrage, and to the subsequent disbanding of the Companions of the Hall. But now they were together again.

They fell into a comfortable rhythm in their determined march, with Bruenor leading the main group, plowing the trail with his sturdy body. Regis came next, noting the mountain peaks and guiding the dwarf. Then came Wulfgar, the heavy bardiche on his shoulder, using his height to scan the trail ahead and to the sides.

Catti-brie, a short distance back, brought up the rear of the four, bow in hand, on the alert and keeping track of the drow who was constantly flanking them, first on one side and then the other. Drizzt had not brought up Guenhwyvar from the Astral Plane—in fact, he had handed the figurine controlling the panther over to Catti-brie—because the longer they could wait, the more rested the great cat would be. And the drow had a feeling he would be needing Guenhwyvar before this was ended.

Soon after noon, with the band making great progress and the snow still holding back, Catti-brie noted a hand signal from Drizzt, who was ahead and to the left.

"Hold," she whispered to Wulfgar, who relayed the command to the front.

Bruenor pulled up, breathing hard from his trudging. He lifted the axe off his back and dropped the head to the snow, leaning on the upright handle.

"Drizzt approaches," said Wulfgar, who could easily see over the snowy berm and the drifts on the path ahead.

"Another trail," the drow explained when he appeared above the berm. "Crossing this one and leading to the west."

"We should go straight south from here," Regis reminded.

Drizzt shook his head. "Not a natural trail," he explained.

"Tracks?" asked Bruenor, seeming quite eager. "More ogres?"

"Different," said Drizzt, and he motioned for them all to follow him.

Barely a hundred yards ahead, they came upon the second trail. It was a pressed area of snow cutting across their current trail, moving along the sloping ground to the east. There, continuing across an expanse of deep, blown snow, the friends saw a lower area full of slush and with a bit of steam still rising from it.

"What in the Nine Hells done that?" asked Bruenor.

"Polar worm," Drizzt explained.

Bruenor spat , Regis shivered, and Catti-brie stood a bit straighter, suddenly on her guard. They all had some experience with the dreaded remorhaz, the great polar worms. Enough experience, certainly, to know that they each had little desire to battle one again.

"No foe I wish to leave behind us," the drow explained.

"So ye're thinking we should go and fight the damned thing?" Bruenor asked doubtfully.

Drizzt shook his head. "We should figure out where it is, at least. Whether or not we should kill the creature will depend on many things."

"Like how stupid we really are," Regis muttered under his breath. Only Catti-brie, who was standing near to him, heard. She looked at him with a smile and a wink, and the halfling only shrugged.

Hardly waiting for confirmation, Drizzt rushed up to take the point. He was far ahead, creeping along the easier path carved out by the strange and powerful polar worm, a beast that could superheat its spine to vaporize snow and, the drow reminded himself, vaporize flesh. They found the great beast only a few hundred yards off the main path, down in a shallow dell, devouring the last of a mountain goat it had caught in the deep snow. The mighty creature's back glowed from the excitement of the kill and feast.

"The beast will not bother with us," Wulfgar remarked. "They feed only rarely and once sated, they seek no further prey."

"True enough," Drizzt agreed, and he led them back to the main trail.

A few light flakes were drifting through the air by that point, but Regis bade them not to worry, for in the distance he noted a peculiar mountain peak that signaled the northern tip of Minster Gorge.

The snow was still light, no more than a flurry, when the five reached the trail on the side of the peak, with Minster Gorge winding away to the south before them. Regis took command, explaining the general layout of the winding run, pointing out the expected locations of sentries, left and right, and leading their gazes far, far to the south where the white-capped top of one larger mound could just be seen. Carefully, the halfling again diagrammed the place for the others, explaining the outer, ascending path running past the sea facing and around to the east on that distant mound. That path, he explained, led to at least one door set into the mound's side.

Regis looked to Drizzt, nodded, and said, "And there is another, more secret way inside."

"Ye thinking we'd be better splitting apart?" Bruenor asked the halfling doubtfully. He turned to aim his question at Drizzt as well, for it was obvious that Regis's reminder had the drow deep in thought.

Drizzt hesitated. Normally, the Companions of the Hall fought together, side by side, and usually to devastating effect. But this was no normal attack for them. This time, they were going against an entrenched fortress, a place no doubt secure and well defended. If he could take the inner corridors to some behind-the-lines vantage point, he might be able to help out quite a bit.

"Let us discern our course one step at a time," the drow finally said. "First we must deal with the sentries, if there are any."

"There were a few when I flew by with Robillard," said Regis. "A pair, at least, on either side of the gorge. They didn't seem to be in any hurry to leave."

"Then we must take alternate paths to avoid them," Wulfgar put in. "For if we strike at a band on one side, the band opposite will surely alert all the region before we ever get near to them."

"Unless Catti-brie can use her bow . . ." Regis started to say, but the woman was shaking her head, looking doubtfully at the expanse between the high gorge walls.

"We can not leave these potential enemies behind us," the drow decided. "I will go to the right, while the rest of you go to the left."

"Bah, there's a fool's notion," snorted Bruenor. "Ye might be killin' a pair o' half-ogries, elf—might even take out a pair o' full-ogries—but ye'd not do it in time to stop them from yelling for their friends."

"Then we have to disguise the truth of the attack across the way," Catti-brie said.

When the others turned to her, they found her wearing a most determined expression. The woman looked back to the north and west.

"Worm's not hungry," she explained. "But that don't mean we can't get the damn thing angry."

⚔ ⚔ ⚔ ⚔ ⚔

"Ettin?" one of the half-ogre guards on the eastern rim of the gorge asked.

Scratching its lice-ridden head, the half-ogre stared in amazement as the seven-foot-tall creature approached. It sported two heads, so it seemed to be of the ettin family, but one of those heads looked more akin to a human with blond hair, and the other had the craggy, wrinkled features and thick red hair and beard of a dwarf.

"Huh?" asked the second sentry, moving to join its companion.

"Ain't no ettins about," the third called from the warm area beside the fire.

"Well there's one coming," argued the first.

And indeed, the two-headed creature was coming on fast, though it presented no weapon and was not advancing in any threatening manner. The half-ogres lifted their respective weapons anyway and called for the curious creature to halt.

It did so, just a few strides away, staring at the sentries with a pair of positively smug smiles.

"What you about?" asked one half-ogre.

"About to get outta the way!" the red-haired head exclaimed.

The half-ogres' chins dropped considerably a moment later when the huge human—for it was indeed a human!—threw aside the blanket and the red-haired dwarf leaped off his shoulder, rolling to the left. The human, too, took off, sprinting to the right. Coming fast behind the splitting pair, bearing down on their original position, and thus bearing down on the stunned half-ogres, came a rolling line of steam.

The brutes screamed. The polar worm broke through the snow cap and reared, towering over them.

"That ain't no ettin, ye fools!" screeched the half-ogre by the fire. With typical loyalty for its wild nature, it leaped up and ran off to the south along the ravine edge and toward the cavern complex.

Or tried to, for three strides away, a blue-streaking arrow like a bolt of lightning slammed it in the hip, staggering it. The slowed beast, limping and squealing, didn't even see the next attack. The red-haired dwarf crashed in, body-slamming it, then chopping away with his nasty, many-notched axe. For good measure, the dwarf spun around and smashed his shield so hard into the slumping brute's face that he left an impression of a foaming mug on the half-ogre's cheek.

⚔ ⚔ ⚔ ⚔ ⚔

Regis heard the commotion behind him and took comfort in it as he worked his way along the side of the ravine across the way, working for handholds just below the rim, out of sight of the guards on that side. He and Drizzt had left the other three, picking their way to the western wall. Then Regis and the drow had split up, with the drow taking an inland route around the back of the sentry position. Regis, a plan in mind, had gone along the wall.

The halfling was well aware from the smirk Drizzt had given him when they'd split up, that Drizzt didn't expect much from him in the fight, that the drow believed he was just finding a place to hide. But Regis had a very definite plan in mind, and he was almost to the spot to execute it, a wide overhang of ice and snow.

He worked his way under it, staying against the stone wall, and began chipping away at the overhang's integrity with his small mace.

He glanced back across the gorge to see the polar worm rear again, a half-ogre thrashing about in its mouth. Regis winced in sympathy for the brute as the polar worm rolled its head back and let go of the half-ogre, rolling it over the horned head and down onto the glowing, superheated spine of the great creature. How the agonized half-ogre thrashed!

Further along, Regis spotted Bruenor, Wulfgar, and Catti-brie sprinting down to the south, getting as far away from the polar worm and the three wounded—and soon to be dead—half-ogres as possible.

The halfling paused, hearing commotion above. The guards on his side recognized the disaster across the way.

"Help!" Regis called out a moment later, and all above him went quiet.

"Help!" he called again.

He heard movement, heard the ice pack crunch a bit, and knew that one of the stupid brutes was moving out onto the overhang.

"Hey, yer little rat!" came the roar a moment later, as the half-ogre's head poked down. The creature was obviously lying flat atop the overhang, staring at Regis incredulously and reaching for him.

"Break . . . break," Regis demanded, smacking his mace up at the ice pack with all the strength he could muster. He had to stop the pounding and dodge aside when the brute's hand snapped at him, nearly getting him.

The half-ogre crept even lower. The ice pack creaked and groaned in protest.

"Gotcha!"

The brute's declaration became a wail of surprise and terror as the ice pack broke free, taking the half-ogre with it down the side of the ravine.

"Do you now?" Regis asked the fast-departing beast.

"Yup," came an unexpected response from above, and Regis slowly looked up to see the second sentry glaring down at him, spear in hand, and with Regis well within stabbing distance. The halfling thought of letting go, then, of taking his chances on a bouncing ride down the side of the ravine, but the half-ogre stiffened suddenly and hopped forward, then tried to turn but got slashed across the face. Over it went, plummeting past the halfling, and Drizzt was in its stead, lying flat and reaching down for Regis.

The halfling grabbed the offered hand, and Drizzt pulled him up.

"Five down," said Regis, his excitement bubbling over from the victory his information had apparently delivered. "See? I had the count right. Four, maybe five—and right where I told you they would be!"

"Six," Drizzt corrected, leading the halfling's gaze back a ways to another brute lying dead in a widening pool of bright red blood. "You missed one."

Regis stared at it for a moment, mouth hanging open, and, deflated, he only shrugged.

Surveying the scene, the pair quickly surmised that none of these two groups would give them any further trouble. Across the way, the three were dead, the white worm tearing at their bodies, and the two that had gone over the edge had bounced, tumbled, and fallen a long, long way. One of them was lying very still at the bottom of the gorge. The other, undoubtedly nearby its broken companion, was buried under a deep pile of snow and ice.

"Our friends went running down the edge of the ravine," Regis explained, "but I don't know where they went."

"They had to move away from the gorge," Drizzt reasoned, seeming hardly concerned. They had discussed this very possibility before bringing the white worm from its feast. The drow pointed down along the gorge to where a sizeable number of huge ogres and half-ogres were running up the ravine. The companions had hoped to dispatch these sentries without alerting the main base, but they had understood from the beginning that such might be the case—that's why they had used the white worm.

"Come," Drizzt bade the halfling. "We will catch up with our friends, or they with us, in due time." He started away to the south, staying as near to the edge of the gorge as he safely could.

They heard the ogre posse pass beneath them soon after, and Drizzt veered back to the edge, then moved down a bit farther and went right over, picking his way down a less steep part of the ravine.

Regis huffed and puffed and worked hard but somehow managed to keep up. Soon, the halfling and the drow were standing on the floor of the gorge, the posse far away to the north, the mound that housed the main complex just to the south and with the cave opening quite apparent.

"Are you ready?" Drizzt asked Regis.

The halfling swallowed hard, not so thrilled about moving off with the dangerous Drizzt alone. He far preferred having Bruenor and Wulfgar standing strong before him and having Catti-brie covering him with that deadly bow of hers, but it was obvious that Drizzt wasn't about to let this opportunity to get right inside the enemies' lair go by.

"Lead on," Regis heard himself saying, though he could hardly believe the words as they came out of his mouth.

⚔ ⚔ ⚔ ⚔

The four leaders of Sheila Kree's band all came out of their rooms together, hearing the shouts from below and from outside the mound complex.

"Chogurugga dispatched a group to investigate," Bellany informed the others. The sorceress's room faced north, the direction of the tumult, and included a door to the outside landing.

"Ye go and do the same," Sheila Kree told her. "Get yer scrying pool up and see what's coming against us."

"I heard yells about a white worm," the sorceress replied.

Sheila Kree shook her head, her fiery red hair flying wildly. "Too convenient," she muttered as she ran out of the room and down the curving, sloping passage leading to Chogurugga and Bloog's chamber, with Jule Pepper right behind her.

Le'lorinel made no move, though, just stood in the corridor, nodding knowingly.

"Is it the drow?" Bellany asked.

The elf smiled and retreated back into the private room, shutting the door.

Standing alone in the common area, Bellany just shook her head and took a deep breath and considered the possibilities if it turned out to be Drizzt Do'Urden and the Companions of the Hall who were now coming against them. The sorceress hoped it was indeed a white worm that had caused the commotion, whatever the cost of driving the monster away.

She went back into her chamber and set up for some divining spells, thinking to look out over the troubled area to the north and to look in on Morik, just to check on where his loyalties might truly lie.

✕ ✕ ✕ ✕ ✕

A few moments later, Le'lorinel slipped back out and headed down the same way Sheila and Jule had gone.

Chogurugga's chamber was in complete chaos, with the ogress's two large attendants rushing around, strapping on armor pieces and hoisting heavy weapons. Chogurugga stood quietly on the side of the room in front of an opened wardrobe, its shelves filled with potion bottles. Chogurugga mulled them over one at a time, pocketing some and separating the others into two bunches.

At the back of the room, Bloog remained in the hammock, the ogre's huge legs hanging over, one on either side. If Bloog was the slightest bit worried by the commotion, the lazy brute didn't show it.

Le'lorinel went to him. "He will find you," the elf warned. "It was foreseen that the drow would come for the warhammer."

"Drow?" the big ogre asked. "No damn drow. White worm."

"Perhaps," Le'lorinel replied with a shrug and a look that told Bloog implicitly that the elf hardly believed all the commotion was being caused by such a creature as that.

"Drow?" the ogre asked, and Bloog suddenly seemed a bit less cock-sure.

"He will find you."

"Bloog crunch him down!" the ogre shouted, rising, or at least trying to, though the movement nearly spilled him out of the unsteady hammock. "No take Bloog's new hammer! Crunch him down!"

"Crunch who?" Chogurugga called from across the way, and the ogress scowled, seeing Le'lorinel close to Bloog.

"Not as easy as that, mighty Bloog," the elf explained, pointedly taking no note of ugly Chogurugga. "Come, my friend. I will show you how to best defeat the dark elf."

Bloog looked from Le'lorinel to his scowling mate, then back to the delicate elf. With an expression that told Le'lorinel he was as interested in angering Chogurugga as he was in learning what he might about the drow, the giant ogre pulled himself out of the hammock and hoisted Aegis-fang to his shoulder. The mighty weapon was dwarfed by the creature's sheer bulk and muscle that it looked more like a carpenter's hammer.

With a final glance to Chogurugga, just to make sure the volatile ogress wasn't preparing a charge, Le'lorinel led Bloog out of the room and back up the ramp, going to the northern end of the next level and knocking hard on Bellany's door.

"What is he doing up here?" the sorceress asked when she answered the knock a few minutes later. "Sheila would not approve."

"What have you learned?" Le'lorinel asked.

A cloud passed over Bellany's face. "More than a white worm," she confirmed. "I have seen a dwarf and a large man moving close to our position, running hard."

"Bruenor Battlehammer and Wulfgar, likely," Le'lorinel replied. "What of the drow?"

Bellany shrugged and shook her head.

"If they have come, then so has Drizzt Do'Urden," Le'lorinel insisted. "The fight out there is likely a diversion. Look closer!"

Bellany scowled at the elf, but Le'lorinel didn't back down.

"Drizzt Do'Urden might already be in the complex," the elf added.

That took the anger off of Bellany's face, and she moved back into her room and shut the door. A moment later, Le'lorinel heard her casting a spell and watched with a smile as the wood on Bellany's door seemed to swell a bit, fitting the portal tightly into the jamb.

Fighting hard not to laugh out loud, as much on the edge of nerves as ever before, Le'lorinel motioned for Bloog to follow and moved to a different door.

⚔ ⚔ ⚔ ⚔ ⚔

Regis put his cherubic face up against the stone and didn't dare to breathe. He heard the rumble of the next pair of brutes, along with the snarl of a more human voice, as they came past his and Drizzt's position, heading up the gorge to check on their companions.

The halfling took some comfort in the fact that Drizzt was hiding right beside him—until he managed to turn his face that way to find that the drow was gone.

Panic welled in Regis. He could hear the cursing trio of enemies right behind him.

"Too bloody cold to be chasin' shadows!" the human snarled.

"Big wormie," said one of the ogres.

"And that makes it better?" the human asked sarcastically. "Leave the ugly thing alone, and it'll slither away!"

"Big worm killed Bonko!" the other ogre said indignantly.

The human started to respond—likely to dismiss the importance of a dead ogre, Regis realized, but apparently he thought the better of it and just cursed under his breath.

They went right past the halfling's position, and if they'd come any closer, they surely would have brushed right against Regis's rear end.

The halfling didn't breathe easier until their voices had faded considerably, and still he stood there in the shadows, hugging the wall.

"Regis," came a whisper, and he looked up to see Drizzt on a ledge above him. "Come along and be quick. It's clear into the cave."

Mustering all the courage he could find, the halfling scrambled up, taking the drow's offered hand. The pair skittered along the thin ridge, behind a wall of blocking boulders to the corner of the large cave.

Drizzt peeked around, then skittered in, pulling Regis along behind him.

The cave narrowed into a tunnel soon after, running level and branching in two or three places. The air was smoky, with torches lining the walls at irregular intervals, their dancing flames illuminating the place with wildly elongating and shrinking shadows.

"This way," Regis said, slipping past the drow at one fork, and moving down to the left. He tried to recall everything Robillard had told him about the place, for the wizard had done a thorough scan of the area and had even found his way up into the complex a bit.

The ground sloped down in some places, up in others, though the pair were generally descending. They came through darker rooms where there was no torchlight, and other chambers filled with stalagmites breaking up the trail, and with stalactites leering down at them threateningly from above. Many shelves lined the walls, rolling back to marvelous rock formations or with sheets of water-smoothed rock that seemed to be flowing. Many smaller tunnels ran off at every conceivable angle.

Soon Regis slowed, the sound of guttural voices becoming audible ahead of them. The halfling turned on Drizzt, an alarmed expression on his face. He pointed ahead emphatically, to where the corridor circled left and back to the right, ascending gradually.

Drizzt caught the signal and motioned for Regis to wait a moment, then slipped ahead into the shadows, moving with such grace, speed, and silence that Regis blinked many times, wondering if his friend had just simply disappeared. As soon as his amazement diminished, though, the halfling remembered where he was and took note of the fact that he was now alone. He quickly skittered into the shadows off to the side.

The drow returned a short while later, to Regis's profound relief, and with a smile that showed he had found the desired area. Drizzt led him around a bend and up a short incline, then up a few steps that were part natural, part carved, into a chamber that widened off to the left along a broken, rocky plateau about chest high to the drow.

The voices were much closer now, just up ahead and around the next bend. Drizzt leaped up to the left, then reached back and pulled Regis up beside him.

"Lots of loose stone," the drow quietly explained. "Take great care."

They inched across the wider area, staying as tight to the wall as possible until they came to one area cleared of stony debris. Drizzt bent down against the wall there and stuck his hand into a small alcove, pulling it back out and rubbing his fingers together.

Regis nodded knowingly. Ash. This was a natural chimney, the one Robillard had described to him on the flight back to the friends, the one he had subsequently described to Drizzt.

The drow went in first, bending his body perfectly to slide up the narrow hole. Before he could even consider the course before him, before he could even pause to muster his courage, Regis heard the sound of many voices moving along the corridor back behind him.

In he went, into the absolute darkness, sliding his hands and finding holds, blindly propelling himself up behind the drow.

⚔ ⚔ ⚔ ⚔ ⚔

For Drizzt, it was suddenly as if he was back in the Underdark, back in the realm of the hunter, where all his senses had to be on the very edge of perfection if he was to have any chance of survival. He heard so many sounds then: the distant dripping of water, a grating of stone on stone, shouts from below and in the distance, all echoing through cracks in the stone. He could *feel* that noise in his sensitive fingertips as he continued his climb, slowing only because he understood that Regis couldn't possibly keep up. Drizzt, a creature of the Underdark where natural chutes were common, where even a halfling's fine night vision would be perfectly useless, could move up this narrow chute as quickly as Regis could trot through a starlit meadow.

The drow marveled in the texture of the stone, feeling the life of this mound, once teeming with rushing water. The smoothness of the edges made the ascent more comfortable, and the walls were uneven enough so that the smoothness didn't much adversely affect climbing.

He moved along, silently, alert.

"Drizzt," he heard whispered below, and he understood that Regis had come to an impasse.

The drow backed down, finally lowering his leg so that Regis could grab on.

"I should have stayed with the others," the halfling whispered when he at last got over the troublesome rise.

"Nonsense," the drow answered. "Feel the life of the mountain about you. We will find a way to be useful to our friends here, perhaps pivotal."

"We do not even know if the fight will come in here."

"Even if it does not, our enemies will not expect us in here, behind them. Come along."

And so they went, higher and higher inside the mountain. Soon they heard the booming voices of huge humanoids, growing louder and louder as they ascended.

A short, slightly descending tunnel branched off the chute, with some heat rising, and the booming voices coming in loud and clear with it.

Drizzt waited for Regis to get up level with him in this wider area, then he moved along the side passage, coming to an opening above the low-burning embers of a wide hearth.

The opening of that hearth was somewhat higher than the bottom of the angling tunnel, so Drizzt could see into the huge room beyond, where three ogres, one an exotic, violet-skinned female, were rushing around, strapping on belts and testing weapons.

To the side of the room, Drizzt clearly marked another well-worn passage, sloping upward. The drow backed up to where Regis was waiting.

"Up," he whispered.

He paused and pulled off his waterskin, wetted the top of his shirt and pulled it over the bottom half of his face to ward off the smoke. Helping Regis do likewise, Drizzt started away.

Barely thirty feet higher, the pair came to a hub of sorts. The main chute continued upward, but five side chambers broke off at various heights and angles, with heat and some smoke coming back at the pair. Also, these side tunnels were obviously hand cut, and fashioned by smaller hands than those of an ogre.

Drizzt motioned for Regis to slowly follow, then crept along the tunnel he figured was heading most directly to the north.

The fire in this hearth was burning brighter, though fortunately the wood was not very wet and not much smoke was coming up.

Also, the angle of the chimney to the hearth was steeper, and so Drizzt could not see into the room beyond.

The drow spent a moment tying his long hair back and wetting it, then he knelt, took a deep breath, and went over head first, creeping like a spider down the side of the chute until he could poke his face out under the top lip of the hearth, the flames burning not far below him and with sparks rising up and stinging him.

This room appeared very different from the chamber of the ogres below. It was full of fine furniture and carpets, and with a lavish bed. A door stood across the way, partly opened and leading into another room. Drizzt couldn't make out much in there, but he did discern a few tables, covered with equipment like one might see in an alchemical workshop. Also, across that second room loomed another door, heavier in appearance, and with daylight creeping in around it.

Now he was intrigued, but out of time, for he had to retreat from the intense heat.

He got back to Regis at the hub and described what he had seen.

"We should go outside and try to spot the others," the halfling suggested, and Drizzt was nodding his agreement when they heard a loud voice echo along one of the other side passages.

"Bloog crunch! No take Bloog's new hammer!"

Off went the drow, Regis following right behind. They came to another steep chute at another hearth, this one hardly burning. Drizzt inverted and poked his head down.

There stood an ogre, a gigantic, ugly, and angry beast, swinging Aegis-fang easily at the end of one arm. Behind it, talking to the ogre in soothing tones, stood a slender elf swordsman.

Without even waiting for Regis, the drow flipped himself over to the fireplace, straddling the embers for a moment, then boldly striding out into the room.

⚔ ⚔ ⚔ ⚔ ⚔

The three friends ran along the ridge at full speed, veering away from the lip when they heard the ruckus of ogre reinforcements charging out from the mound below. They had to veer even farther from the straight path when a second group of beasts came off the mound above the ridge line, charging up through the snow.

"Probably many more within," Catti-brie remarked.

"More the reason to go!" snarled Bruenor.

"Drizzt and Regis are likely already nearing the place, if not already in," Wulfgar added.

The woman, bow in hand, motioned forward.

"Ye gonna call up that cat?" Bruenor asked.

Catti-brie glanced at her belt, where she had set the figurine of Guenhwyvar. "As we near," she answered. Bruenor only nodded, trusting her implicitly, and rushed off after Wulfgar.

Up ahead, Wulfgar ducked suddenly as another ogre leaped off the mound, across a short ravine to the sloping ridge line, the brute coming at him with a great swing of a heavy club.

Easily dodging, Wulfgar kicked out and slashed, cutting a deep gash in back of the brute's shoulder. The ogre started to turn, but then lurched wildly as Bruenor came in hard, smashing his axe through the brute's kneecap.

Down it went, howling.

"Finish it, girl!" Bruenor demanded, running past, running for the mound. The dwarf skittered to a stop, though, foiled by the ravine separating the mound from the slope, which was too far across for him to jump.

Then Bruenor had to dive to the side as a rock sailed at him from a position along the side of that mound, just up above him.

Wulfgar came past, roaring "Tempus!" and making the leap

across the ravine. The barbarian crashed along some rocks, but settled himself quickly onto a narrow trail winding its way up along the steep slope.

"Should've thrown me first," Bruenor grumbled, and he dived aside again as another rock crashed by.

The dwarf did pick out a path that would get him to the winding trail, but he knew he would be far behind Wulfgar by that point. "Girl! I need ye!" he howled.

He turned back to see the fallen ogre shudder again as another arrow buried itself deep into its skull.

Catti-brie rushed up, falling to one knee and setting off a stream of arrows at the concealed rock-thrower. The brute popped up once more, rock high over its head, but it fell away as an arrow sizzled past.

Catti-brie and Bruenor heard the roars of battle as Wulfgar reached the brute. Off ran the dwarf, while Catti-brie dropped the onyx figurine to the ground, called for the cat, then put her bow right back to work.

For on a ledge high above Wulfgar's position, a new threat had arrived, a group of archers firing bows instead of hurling boulders.

⚔ ⚔ ⚔ ⚔ ⚔

"Is it them?" Morik the Rogue asked, pushing against the unyielding door of Bellany's private chambers. He looked up at the swelled wood and understood that the sorceress had magically sealed it. "Bellany?"

In response, the door seemed to exhale and shrink to normal size, and Morik crept through.

"Bellany?"

"I believe your friend and his companions have come to retrieve the warhammer," came a voice from right in front of Morik. He nearly jumped out of his boots, for he could not see the woman standing before him.

"Wizards," he muttered as he settled down. "Where is Sheila Kree?"

There came no answer.

"Did you just shrug?" the rogue surmised.

Bellany's ensuing giggle told him she had.

"What of you, then?" Morik asked. "Are you to hide up here, or join in the fray?"

"Sheila instructed me to divine the source of the commotion, and so I have," the invisible sorceress answered.

A smile widened on Morik's face. He understood well what Bellany's cryptic answer meant. She was waiting to see who would win out before deciding her course. The rogue's respect for the sorceress heightened considerably at that moment.

"Have you another such enchantment?" he asked. "For me?"

Bellany was spellcasting before he ever finished the question. In a few moments Morik, too, vanished from sight.

"A minor enchantment only," Bellany explained. "It will not last for long."

"Long enough for me to find a dark hole to hide in," Morik answered, but he ended short, hearing sounds from outside, farther down the mountainside.

"They are fighting out along the trail," the sorceress explained.

A moment later, Bellany heard the creak from the other room and saw an increase in light as Morik moved through the outer door. The sorceress went to the side of the room, then heard a cry of surprise from across the way— from Le'lorinel's room.

27

BLIND VENGEANCE

"Crunch! Crunch!" the huge ogre roared, speaking to the elf and waving Aegis-fang.

"Slash, slash," came a remark behind the brute, spinning it around in surprise.

"Huh?"

The elf moved out around the side of the ogre and froze in place, staring hard at the slender dark figure who had come into the room.

Slowly Drizzt reached up and pulled his wet shirt down from in front of his face.

The ogre staggered, eyes bulging, but the drow was no longer even looking at the brute. He was staring hard at the elf, at the pair of blue, gold-flecked eyes staring out at him from behind the holes in a thin black mask, regarding him with haunting familiarity and intense hatred.

The ogre stammered over a couple more words, finally blurting, "Drow!"

"And no friend," said the elf. "Crunch him."

Drizzt, his scimitars still sheathed, simply stared at the elf, trying to figure out where he had seen those eyes before, where he had seen this elf before. And how had this one known right away that he was an enemy, almost as if expecting him?

"He has come to take your hammer, Bloog," the elf said teasingly.

The ogre exploded into motion, its roar shaking the stone of the walls. It grabbed up the hammer in both hands and chopped mightily at the drow. Or tried to, for Aegis-fang arced up behind the brute to slam hard into the low ceiling, cracking free a chip that dropped onto Bloog's head.

Drizzt didn't move, didn't take his intense stare off the elf, who was making no move against him, or even toward him.

Bloog roared again and stooped a bit. He tried again to crush the drow flat, this time with the hammer clearing the low ceiling and coming over in a tremendous swat.

Drizzt, who was standing somewhat sideways to the brute, hopped and did a sidelong somersault at the ogre, inside the angle of the blow. Even as the drow came around, he drew out his scimitars then landed lightly and bore into Bloog, stabbing several times and offering one slash before skittering out to the side opposite the elf.

The ogre retracted Aegis-fang easily with one arm, while he tried to grab at the drow with his free hand.

Drizzt was too quick for that, and as Bloog reached out in pursuit, the drow, who was skittering backward and still looking at the ogre, launched a double slash at the exposed hand.

Bloog howled and pulled his bloody hand in, but came forward in a sudden and devastating rush, Aegis-fang whipping wildly.

Drizzt dropped down to the floor, scrambled forward, came back up and rolled around the ogre's bulk, scoring a vicious double slash against the back of Bloog's hip as he passed. He stopped short, though, and rushed back expecting a charge from the elf, who now held a fine sword and dagger.

But the elf only laughed at him, and continued to stare.

"Bloog crunch you down!" the stubborn ogre roared, bouncing off the wall with a turn and charging back at Drizzt.

Aegis-fang whipped out, right and left, but Drizzt was in his pure fighting mode now, certainly not underestimating this monster—not with Aegis-fang in his grasp and not after he had nearly lost to a smaller ogre out by the tower.

The drow ducked the first swing, then ducked the second, and both times the drow managed to score small stings against the ogre's huge forearms.

Bloog swung again, and again Drizzt dropped to the floor. Aegis-fang smashed against the stone of the hearth, bringing a surprised squeak from Regis—who was still inside the chimney—that made Drizzt wince in fear.

Drizzt went forward hard, but the ogre didn't back from the twin stabbing scimitars, accepting the hit in exchange for a clear shot at the drow's puny head.

The whipping backhand with Aegis-fang, coming across and down, almost got Drizzt, almost smashed his skull to little bits.

He stabbed again, and hard, and rushed out to the side, but the ogre hardly seemed hurt, though his blood was running from many wounds.

Drizzt had to wonder how many hits it would take to bring this monster down.

Drizzt had to wonder how much time he had before others rushed in to the ogre's aid.

Drizzt had to wonder when that elf, seeming so very confident, would decide to join in.

⚔ ⚔ ⚔ ⚔ ⚔

Screaming to Tempus, his god of battle, the former guiding light in his warrior existence, the son of Beornegar charged along the winding trail. Sometimes the path was open to his right and sometimes blocked by low walls of stone. Sometimes the mountain on his left was steep and sheer, other times it sloped gradually, affording him a wider view of the mound.

And affording archers hiding among the higher rocks clear shots at him.

But Wulfgar ran on, coming to a place where the path leveled out. Around a bend ahead, in a larger area, he heard the ogre rock-thrower. With a silent prayer to Tempus, the barbarian charged right in, howling when the brute saw him, ducking when the surprised ogre hurled its boulder at him.

Seeing the boulder fly above the mark, the ogre reached for a heavy club, but Wulfgar was too fast for the brute to get its weapon ready. And the barbarian was too enraged, too full of battle-lust, for the ogre to accept the bardiche hit. The weapon pounded home with tremendous force, driving deep into the ogre's chest, sending it back against the wall, where it slumped in the last moments of its life.

But as Wulfgar leaped back, he understood that he was in trouble. For in that mighty hit, he felt the bardiche handle crack apart. It didn't splinter completely, but Wulfgar knew that the integrity of the weapon had been severely compromised. Worse still, a rock at the back of the clearing, against the mountain, suddenly rolled aside, revealing a passageway. Out poured another half-ogre, roaring and charging. A small and ugly man came out beside it, with a red-haired, powerful-looking woman behind them.

An arrow skipped off the stone right beside the backing

barbarian, and he understood that he had to stay closer to the mountain wall in this exposed place.

He bore in on the half-ogre, then stopped fast as the brute lowered its head and shoulder and tried to barrel over him. How glad Wulfgar was at that moment that he had been trained by Drizzt Do'Urden, that he had learned the subtleties and wisdom of angled deflection instead of just shrugging off every hit and responding in kind. He slipped to the side a single step, leaving his leg out in front of the overbalancing brute, then turned as the half-ogre stumbled past, planting the butt of his weapon behind the half-ogre's armpit and shoving with all his strength.

Wulfgar took some relief as the brute barreled forward, right over the lip of the front side of the clearing, tumbling over the rocks there. He didn't know how far down the mountainside the brute might be falling, but he understood that it was out of the fight for a while, at least.

And a good thing that was, for the human pirate was right there, stabbing with a nasty sword, and Wulfgar had to work furiously to keep that biting tip at bay. Worse, the red-haired woman bore in, her sword working magnificently, rolling around the blocking bardiche and forcing Wulfgar back with a devilish thrust.

She was good. Wulfgar recognized that at once. He knew it would take all his energy if he was to have any hope. So the barbarian took a chance, stepping forward suddenly and accepting a slight stab from the man on his side.

That stab had little energy, though, for as the man started to attack, Wulfgar let go of his weapon with his right hand and punched straight out, connecting on the pirate's face even as his smile started to widen. Before his sword could slip deeply into the barbarian's side, the pirate was flying away, crumpling to the stone.

Then it was Wulfgar and Sheila Kree—Wulfgar recognized that this was indeed the pirate leader. How he wished she was holding

Aegis-fang instead of this fine-edged sword. How he would have loved to summon the warhammer from her hand at that moment, then turn it back against her!

As it was, the barbarian had to work furiously to keep the warrior pirate at bay, for Sheila was surely no novice to battle. She stabbed and slashed, spun a complete circle and dived her sword in at Wulfgar's neck. The barbarian found himself forced back out into the open and took another hit as an arrow slashed down across his shoulder.

Sheila's smile widened.

A large ogre came out of the opening in the mountainside. Another roar came from above, and yet another from behind Wulfgar and not so far down the mountain—the half-ogre he had tripped up, he knew, on its way back.

"I need you!" the desperate barbarian cried out to his friends, but the wind stole the momentum from that call.

He knew that Catti-brie and Bruenor, wherever they were, would not likely hear him. He felt the bardiche handle cracking even more in his hand, and believed that the weapon would break apart in his hands with the next hit.

He forced his way forward again, skipping to his left, trying to delay the ogre's entry into the fray for as long as possible. But then he saw yet another form come out of the opening, another human pirate, it seemed, and he knew that he was doomed.

⚔ ⚔ ⚔ ⚔ ⚔

Drizzt scored and scored again, using the tight quarters and the low ceiling against the huge ogre. This one would have proven a much tougher opponent outdoors, the drow knew, especially with Aegis-fang in hand. But in here, now that he had the ogre's speed sorted out, the drow was too quick and too experienced.

Wound after wound opened up on the howling Bloog, and the ogre started calling for the elf to jump in and help.

And that elf did come forward, and Drizzt prepared a new strategy he had just worked out for keeping the ogre between him and this newest opponent. Before the drow could implement that strategy, though, the ogre lurched suddenly. A new and deeper wound appeared behind Bloog's hip, and the elf smiled wickedly.

Drizzt looked at the elf with amazement, and so did the ogre.

And the elf promptly drove the sword in again. The ogre howled and spun, but Drizzt was right there, his scimitar taking the beast deep in the kidney.

Back and forth it went, the two skilled warriors picking away while poor Bloog turned back and forth, never recovering from that initial surprise and the deep wound.

Soon enough, the big ogre went down hard and lay still.

Drizzt stood staring at the elf from across the large body. His scimitar tips lowered toward the floor, but he had them ready, unsure of this one's motives and intent.

"Perhaps I am a friend," the elf said, in a tone that was mocking and insincere. "Or perhaps I just wanted to kill you myself and grew impatient with Bloog's pitiful efforts against you."

Drizzt was circling then, and so was the elf, moving about Bloog's body, keeping it between as a deterrent to the potential foe.

"It would seem as if only you can answer which of the possibilities it might be."

The elf snorted derisively. "I have waited for this moment for years, Drizzt Do'Urden," came the surprising response.

Drizzt took a deep breath. This was as challenger here, perhaps someone who had studied his abilities and reputation and had prepared against him. This was not one to take lightly—he had seen the warrior's graceful movements against Bloog—but the drow suddenly remembered that he had more at stake here than this one fight, that he had others counting on him.

"This is not the time for a personal challenge," he said.

"This is exactly the time," the elf answered. "As I have arranged!"

"Regis!" Drizzt called.

The drow burst forward, putting both scimitars in one hand, grabbing Aegis-fang with the other, and tossing it into the hearth. The halfling leaped down to grab it up, pausing only to see the first exchange as the elf leaped in at Drizzt, sword and dagger flashing.

But Drizzt was away in the blink of an eye, scimitars out and ready, balanced in a perfect defensive posture.

Regis knew that he had no place in this titanic struggle, so he gathered up the warhammer and climbed back up the chimney, then moved down the other side passage toward the apparently empty room they had already scouted.

✗ ✗ ✗ ✗ ✗

The wind was just right, and so Catti-brie heard Wulfgar's desperate call for help after all. She knew he was in trouble, could hear the fighting up above, could see the half-ogre scrambling, almost back to the ledge.

But the woman, who had leaped across the ravine to the winding trail, was held in place by a barrage of arrows coming down at her.

Guenhwyvar had finally taken form by then, but before Catti-brie could even offer a command to the panther, an arrow drove down into the cat. Guenhwyvar, with a great roar, leaped away.

Catti-brie worked furiously then, using every opportunity to pop back out from the mountainside and let fly a devastating missile.

Her arrow blasted through stone, and given the cry of pain and surprise, apparently scored a hit on one of the archers. But they were many, and she was stuck and could not get to Wulfgar.

She did manage to slip out and let fly at the half-ogre that was stubbornly climbing back to Wulfgar's position, her missile slamming the creature in the hip and sending it into a slide back down the slope.

But Catti-brie took an arrow for her efforts, the missile biting into her forearm. She fell back against the wall with a cry. The woman clutched at the shaft gingerly, then steeled her gaze and her grip. Growling away the agony, she pushed the arrow through. Catti-brie reached for her pack, pulling forth a bandage and tightly wrapping the arm.

"Bruenor, where are you?" she said quietly, fighting against despair.

It occurred to her as more than a passing possibility that they had all come together again just to be sundered apart, and permanently.

"Oh, get to him, Guen," the woman quietly begged, tying off the bandage and wincing away the pain as she set another arrow.

✕ ✕ ✕ ✕ ✕

He fought brilliantly, purely on instinct, without rage and without fear. But he got hit again and again, and though no one wound was serious, Wulfgar knew that it was only a matter of time—a very short amount of time—before they overcame him. He sang out to Tempus, thinking it fitting, hoping it acceptable to the god, that he be singing that name as he died.

For surely this was the end for the son of Beornegar, with the red-haired pirate and the ogre pressing him, with his weapon falling apart in his hands, with a third opponent swiftly moving in.

No one could get to him in time.

He was glad, at least, that he might die honorably, in battle.

He took a stinging hit from the red-haired pirate, then had to pivot fast to block the ogre, and knew even as he turned that it was over. He had just left an opening for Sheila Kree to cut him down.

He glanced back to see the fatal blow.

Wulfgar, content for the first time in so many years, smiled.

⚔ ⚔ ⚔ ⚔ ⚔

Shouts of surprise from above clued Catti-brie, and she dared to leap out into the open.

There, above her, mighty Guenhwyvar charged the archers nest, taking arrow after stinging arrow, but never veering and never slowing. The archers were standing then, and so the woman wasted no time in putting an arrow into the side of one's head, then taking down another.

She took aim for a third, but held the shot, for Guenhwyvar leaped in among the nest then, scattering the band. One man tried to scramble up the back side, farther up the mountain, but a great black paw caught him in the back of his leg and tore him back down.

Another man leaped over the rim of the nest, falling and bouncing, preferring to the fall to the grim fate at the claws of the panther. He tried desperately to control his descent and finally managed to settle on a stone.

Right in Catti-brie's sights.

He died quickly, at least.

⚔ ⚔ ⚔ ⚔ ⚔

Sheila Kree had him dead, obviously so, and her sword dived in at Wulfgar's exposed flank.

But the pirate leader had to pull back before ever hitting the mark, for a pair of legs wrapped around her waist, and a pair of daggers stabbed in viciously at the sides of her neck.

The veteran pirate bent forward, flipping the cunning assassin over her.

"Morik, ye dog!" she cried as the rogue went into a roll that stood him up right beside Wulfgar, bloody daggers in hand.

Sheila stumbled backward, taking some comfort as more of her fighters passed her by.

"Kill 'em both!" she screamed as she staggered back into the cave complex.

"Like old times, eh?" Morik said to the stunned Wulfgar, who was already back to fending the ogre attacker.

Wulfgar could hardly respond. He just shook his head at the unexpected reprieve.

"Like old times?" Morik said again, as he fell into a fight with a pair of dirty pirates.

"We didn't win many of the fights in the old times," Wulfgar poignantly reminded him, for the odds had far from evened.

⚔ ⚔ ⚔ ⚔ ⚔

Drizzt worked his scimitars in a flurry of spinning parries, gradually turning them and altering his angle, moving his defensive posture into one more offensive, and forcing the elf back.

"Well done," the elf congratulated, skipping over one of fallen Bloog's legs.

"I do not even know your name, yet you bear me this hatred," the drow remarked.

The elf laughed at him. "I am Le'lorinel. That is the only name you need to hear."

Drizzt shook his head, staring at those intense eyes, somewhat recognizing them, but unable to place them.

And he was back into the fray, as Le'lorinel leaped forward, blades working furiously.

A sword came at Drizzt's head and he picked it off with an upraised scimitar. Le'lorinel turned the sword under the drow's curving blade and came ahead with a left-hand thrust of the dagger, a brilliant move.

But Drizzt was better. He accepted the cunning turn of the blades and instead of trying to move his second blade in front to deflect the dagger, he rolled to his right, driving his scimitar in toward the center, pushing the sword across and forcing his opponent to shift and alter the dagger thrust.

The drow's second blade came around with a sweep, driving against the elf's side.

The blade bounced off. Drizzt might as well have tried to slash through stone.

The drow rushed out, eyeing the turning and smiling Le'lorinel. He knew the enchantment immediately, for he had seen wizards use it. Was this elf a spellsword, then, a warrior trained in both the arcane and martial arts?

Drizzt hopped fallen Bloog's bloody chest, making a fast retreat to the back of the room, near to the hearth

Le'lorinel continued to smile and held up one hand, whispering something Drizzt did not hear. The ring flared, and the elf moved even faster, hastened by yet another enchantment.

Oh, yes, this one was indeed prepared.

⚔ ⚔ ⚔ ⚔

Regis dropped Aegis-fang down onto the burning logs, then scrambled as low as he could, rolled over so that he was going down head first, and caught the lip of the hearth and swung himself out. He was glad, as his feet kicked through the flames, that he was wearing heavy winter boots instead of walking in his typical barefoot manner.

The halfling scanned the room, seeing it much as Drizzt had described. He reached back and pulled Aegis-fang from the fire, then started across the room, to the partially opened door.

He went through silently, coming into a smaller chamber, this one some sort of alchemical workshop. There loomed the other door, with daylight streaming in around it.

The halfling ran for it, grabbed the handle, and tugged it open.

Then he was hit by a series of stinging, burning bursts against his hip and back. With a squeal, Regis scrambled out onto a natural balcony, but one that left him nowhere to run. He saw the fighting almost directly below him, so he threw the warhammer as far as he could, which wasn't very far, and cried out for Wulfgar.

Regis scrambled back, not even watching the hammer's bouncing descent. He saw the sorceress then, her invisibility enchantment dispelled. She stared at him from the side of the room, her hands working in the midst of casting yet another spell.

Regis yelped and ran out of the room into the main chamber, heading first for the hearth, then veering for another door.

The air around him grew thick with drifting strands of sticky, stringlike material. The halfling changed course yet again, making for the hearth, hoping its flames would burn this magical webbing away. He never got close, though, his strides shortened, his momentum stolen.

He was caught, encased in magical webbing that was holding him fast and was so thick around him he couldn't even breathe.

And the sorceress was there, in front of him, on the outside of the webbing barely a few inches away. She lifted a hand, holding a shining dagger up to Regis's face.

⚔ ⚔ ⚔ ⚔ ⚔

Another archer went down. Ignoring the burning pain and tightness in her arm, Catti-brie set another arrow to her bow.

More archers had appeared above Guenhwyvar. As the woman took aim on that position, she noted another movement in a more dangerous place, a ledge high up above where Wulfgar was fighting.

Catti-brie whirled and nearly fired.

It was Regis, falling back—and Aegis-fang, falling down!

Catti-brie held her breath, thinking that the warhammer would bounce all the way down to the sea, but it caught suddenly and held in place on a small ledge up above and to the side.

"Call for it!" she screamed repeatedly.

With a glance to the lower archer ledge, where she knew Guenhwyvar was still engaged, she ran along the trail.

⚔ ⚔ ⚔ ⚔ ⚔

Drizzt made the hearth and skidded down to one knee, dropping Icingdeath to the stone floor and reaching into the glowing fireplace. Out his arm pumped, then back in, then out again, launching a barrage of missiles at Le'lorinel. One hit, then another. The elf blocked a third, a spinning stick, but the missile broke apart across the elf's blade, each side spinning in to score a hit.

None of them were serious, none of them would have been even without the stoneskin defense, but every one, every strike upon the elf, removed a bit more of the defensive enchantment.

"Very wise, drow!" Le'lorinel congratulated, and on the elf warrior came, sword flashing for the stooping drow.

Drizzt grabbed his blade and started up, then dropped back to the floor and kicked out, his foot barely hitting Le'lorinel's shin.

Then Drizzt had to roll to the side and over backward to his feet, against the wall. His scimitars came up immediately, ringing with parry after parry as Le'lorinel launched a series of strong attacks his way.

✗ ✗ ✗ ✗ ✗

The bardiche was falling apart in his hands by then, as Wulfgar worked against the ogre.

To the side, Morik, too, found himself hard-pressed by a pair of pirates, both wielding vicious-looking cutlasses.

"We can't win!" the rogue cried.

"Then why did you help me?" Wulfgar countered.

Morik found his next words caught in his throat. Why indeed had he gone against Sheila Kree? Even when he had come visible again, on the ramp descending from Chogurugga's chamber, it would not have been difficult for him to find a shadowy place to sit out the fight. Cursing himself for what he now had to consider a foolhardy decision, the rogue leaped ahead, daggers slashing. He landed in a turn that sent his dark cloak flying wide.

"Run away!" he cried out, leaving the cloak behind as a pair of slashing cutlasses came against it. He skittered behind Wulfgar, moving between a pair of huge boulders and heading up the trail.

Then he came back onto the small clearing, shouting, "Not that way!" Yet another ogre was in fast pursuit.

Wulfgar groaned as this new foe seemed to be entering the fray— and another, he noted, seeing movement beside Morik.

But that was no ogre.

Bruenor Battlehammer leaped up onto the rock as Morik passed underneath. Axe in both hands and down behind him, the dwarf took aim as the oblivious ogre came by in fast pursuit.

Crack!

The hit resounded like splitting stone, and everyone on the clearing stopped their fighting for just a moment to regard the wild-eyed red-haired dwarf standing atop the stone, his axe buried deeply into the skull of an ogre that was only still upright because the mighty dwarf was holding it there, trying to tug the axe back out.

"Ain't that a beautiful sound?" Bruenor called to Wulfgar.

Wulfgar shook his head and went back into defensive action against the ogre, and now with the two pirates joining in. "Took you long enough!" he replied.

"Quit yer bitchin'!" Bruenor yelled back. "Me girl's seen yer hammer, ye durn fool! Call for it, boy!"

The ogre in front of Wulfgar stepped back to get some charging room, roared defiantly, and lifted its club, coming on hard.

Wulfgar threw his ruined bardiche at the beast, who blocked it with its chest and arm and tossed the pieces aside.

"Oh, brilliant!" complained Morik, who was back behind Wulfgar, coming around to engage the two pirates.

But Wulfgar wasn't even listening to the complaint or to the threats from the enraged ogre. He was yelling out instead, trusting Bruenor's word.

"What you to do now, puny one?" the ogre said, though its expression changed considerably as it finished the question. A finely crafted warhammer appeared in Wulfgar's waiting grasp.

"Catch this one," the barbarian remarked, letting fly.

As it had with the cracked bardiche, the ogre tried to accept the blow with its chest and its arm, tried to just take the hit and push the warhammer aside.

But this was no cracked bardiche.

The ogre had no idea why it was sitting against the wall then, unable to draw breath.

His hand up high in the air, Wulfgar called out again for the hammer.

And there it was, in his grasp, warrior and weapon united.

A cutlass came in at him from the side, along with a cry of warning from Morik.

Wulfgar snapped his warhammer down, blasting the thrusting cutlass away. With perfect balance, as if the warhammer was an extension of his own arm, Wulfgar turned the weapon and swung it out hard.

The pirate flew away.

The other turned and ran, but Morik had him before he reached the opening, stabbing him down.

Another ogre exited the cave and glared threateningly at nearby Morik, but a blue streak cut between the barbarian and the rogue, knocking the brute back inside.

The friends turned to see Catti-brie standing there, bow in hand.

"Guen's got them up above," the woman explained.

"And Rumblebelly's up there too, and likely needin' us!" howled Bruenor, motioning for them.

They ran on up the path, winding farther around the mountain. They came to another level, wide area with a huge door facing them, set into the mountain.

"Not that one," Morik tried to explain. "Big ogres . . ."

The rogue shut up as Bruenor and Wulfgar fell over the door, hammer and axe chopping, splintering the wood to pieces.

In the pair went.

Chogurugga and her attendants were waiting.

⚔ ⚔ ⚔ ⚔ ⚔

Their weapons rang against each other repeatedly, a blur of motion, a constant sound. Hastened by the enchantment, Le'lorinel matched Drizzt's blinding speed, but unlike the drow, the elf was not used to such lightning reflexive action.

Scimitar right, scimitar left, scimitar straight ahead, and Drizzt scored a hard stab against Le'lorinel's chest that would have finished the elf had it not been for the stonelike dweomer.

"How many more will it stop?" the drow asked, growing more confident now as his routines slipped around Le'lorinel's defenses. "We need not do this."

But the elf showed no sign of letting up.

Drizzt slashed out with his right, then spun as Le'lorinel, parrying, went into a circuit to the right as well, both coming together out of their respective spins with a clash of four blades.

Drizzt turned his blade over the elf's, driving Le'lorinel's down. When the elf predictably stabbed ahead, the drow leaped into a somersault right over the attack, landing on his feet and falling low as the sword swished over his head. Drizzt slashed out, scoring on Le'lorinel's hip, then kicked out as the elf retreated, clipping a knee.

Le'lorinel squeaked in pain and stumbled back a few steps.

The enchantment was defeated. The next scimitar hit would draw blood.

"There is no need for this," Drizzt graciously said.

Le'lorinel glared at him, and smiled again. Up came the ring, and with a word from the elf, it flashed again.

Drizzt charged, wanting to beat whatever trick might be coming next.

But Le'lorinel was gone, vanished from sight.

Drizzt skidded to a stop, eyes widening with surprise. On instinct, he reached within himself to his own magical powers, his innate drow abilities, and summoned a globe of darkness about him, one that filled the room and put him back on even footing with the invisible warrior.

Just as Le'lorinel had expected he would. For now, with the ring's fourth enchantment—the most insidious of the group—the invisible elf's form was outlined again in glowing fires.

Drizzt moved in, spinning and launching slashing attack routines, as he had long ago learned when fighting blindly. Every attack was also a parry, his scimitars whirling out wide from his body.

And he listened, and he heard the shuffle of feet.

He was on the spot in an instant and took heart when his blade rang against a blocking sword, awkwardly held.

The elf had miscalculated, he believed, had altered the fight into one in which the experienced drow held a great advantage.

He struck with wide-reaching blows, coming in from the left and the right, keeping his opponent before him.

Right and left again, and Drizzt turned suddenly behind his second swing, spinning and slashing with the right as he came around.

The victory was his, he knew, from the position of the blocking sword and dagger, the elf caught flatfooted and without defense.

His scimitar drove against Le'lorinel's side, tearing flesh.

But at precisely the same instant, Drizzt, too, got hit in the side.

Unable to retract or slow his blow, Drizzt had to finish the move, the scimitar bouncing off of a rib, tearing a lung and cutting back out across the front of the elf's chest.

And the same wound burrowed across the drow's chest.

Even as the pain exploded within him, even as he stumbled back, tripping over Bloog's leg and falling hard to the floor against the wall, Drizzt understood what had happened, recognized the fire shield enchantment, a devilish spell that inflicted damage upon anyone striking the spell-user.

He lay there, one lung collapsing, his lifeblood running out freely.

Across the way, Le'lorinel, dying as Drizzt was dying, groaned.

28
NOT WITHOUT LOSS

With equal intensity, Bruenor and Wulfgar charged into the large cave. Wulfgar headed to the side to intercept a pair of large, armored ogres while Bruenor went for the most exotic of the three, an ogress with light violet skin wearing a huge shining helmet and wielding a enormous scythe.

Morik came in behind the ferocious pair, tentatively, and making no definite strides to join the battle.

More eager behind him came Catti-brie. She had an arrow flying almost immediately, staggering one of the two ogres closing on Wulfgar.

That blast gave the barbarian all the momentum he needed. He drove hard against the other brute, Aegis-fang pounding repeatedly. The ogre blocked and blocked again, but the third chop hit it on the breastplate and sent it staggering backward.

Wulfgar bore in, smashing away.

The ogre's wounded companion tried to move back into the fight, but Catti-brie hit it with a second arrow, and a third. Howling with rage and pain, the brute turned and charged the door instead.

"Brilliant," Morik groaned, and he cried out as a large form brushed past him, sending him sprawling.

Guenhwyvar hit the charging, arrow-riddled ogre head on. She leaped onto its face, clawing, raking, and biting. The brute stood straight, its momentum lost, and staggered backward, its face erupting in fountains of blood.

"Good girl," said Catti-brie, and she turned and fired up above Bruenor, nailing the ogress, then drew out Khazid'hea. She paused and glanced back at Morik, who was standing against the wall, shaking his head.

"Well done," he muttered, in obvious disbelief.

They were indeed an efficient group!

⚔ ⚔ ⚔ ⚔ ⚔

The magical darkness lifted.

Drizzt sat against the wall. Across from him sat Le'lorinel, in almost the exact posture and with a wound identical to the drow's.

Drizzt stared at his fallen opponent, his eyes widening. Thin magical flames still licked at Le'lorinel's skin, but Drizzt hardly noted them. For the wound, torn through Le'lorinel's leather vest and across the front, revealed a breast—a female breast!

And Drizzt understood so very much, and knew those eyes so much better, and knew who this truly was even before Le'lorinel reached up and pulled the mask off her face.

An elf, a Moon elf, once a little child whom Drizzt had saved from drow raiders. An elf driven to rage by the devastation of the drow on that fateful, evil day, when she was bathed in the blood of her own murdered mother to convince the dark elves that she, too, was already dead.

"By the gods," the drow rasped, his voice weak for lack of air.

"You are dead, Drizzt Do'Urden," the elf said, her voice equally weak and faltering. "My family is avenged."

Drizzt tried to respond, but he could not begin to find the words. In this short time, how could he possibly explain to Le'lorinel that he had not participated in that murder, that he had saved her at great personal peril, and most importantly, that he was sorry, so very sorry, for what his evil kin had done.

He stared at Le'lorinel, bearing her no ill will, despite the fact that her misguided actions and blind vengeance had cost them both their very lives.

⚔ ⚔ ⚔ ⚔

Chogurugga was doing well against the mighty Bruenor Battlehammer, her potion-enhanced muscles, potion-enhanced speed, and potion-enhanced defenses more than holding their own against the dwarf.

Bruenor just growled and cursed, swatting powerfully, taking hits that would fell most opponents and shrugging them off with dwarven toughness then boring on, his axe slashing in.

He was losing, though, and he knew it, but then Catti-brie's arrow sizzled in above him, driving into the ogress's chest and sending her staggering backward.

"Oh, good girl!" the dwarf roared, taking the advantage to charge forward and press the offensive.

But even as he got there the ogress had yet another vial in hand and up to her lips, swallowing its contents in one great gulp.

Even as Bruenor closed, starting the battle once more, the ogress's wounds began to bind.

The dwarf growled in protest. "Damn healing potion!" he howled, and he got a hit in against Chogurugga's thigh, opening a gash.

Immediately, Chogurugga had another vial, one similar

to the last, off of her belt and moving up to her lips. Bruenor cursed anew.

A black form sailed above the dwarf, slamming into the ogress and latching on.

Chogurugga flailed as Guenhwyvar tore at her face, front claws holding fast, fangs biting and tearing, back claws raking wildly.

The ogress dropped the vial, which hit the floor but did not break, and dropped her weapon as well. The ogress grabbed at the cat with both hands, trying to pull Guenhwyvar away.

The panther's hooked claws held tight, which meant that throwing Guenhwyvar aside would mean tearing her face right off. And of course Bruenor was right there, smashing the ogress's legs and midsection with mighty, vicious chops.

Bruenor heard a crash to the side, and Catti-brie was beside him, her powerful sword slicing easily through Chogurugga's flesh and bone.

The ogress toppled to the floor.

The two companions and Guenhwyvar turned about just as Wulfgar's hammer caved in the last ogre's skull, the brute falling right over its dead partner.

"This way!" Morik called from an exit across the wide room, with a corridor beyond heading farther up into the complex.

Bruenor paused to wait for his girl as Catti-brie stooped to retrieve Chogurugga's fallen vial.

"When I find out who's selling this stuff to damn ogres, I'll chop him up!" the frustrated dwarf declared.

Across the room, Morik bit his lower lip. He knew who it was, for he had seen Bellany's alchemical room.

Up went the companions, to the level corridor with five doors that marked Sheila Kree's complex. A groan from the side brought them immediately to one door, which Bruenor barreled through with dwarven subtlety.

There lay Drizzt, and there lay the elf, both mortally wounded.

Catti-brie came in right behind, moving immediately for Drizzt, but the drow stopped her with an upheld hand.

"Save her," he demanded, his voice very weak. "You must."

And he slumped.

⚔ ⚔ ⚔ ⚔ ⚔

Wulfgar stood at the door, horrified, but Morik didn't even slow at that particular room, but rather ran across the hall to Bellany's chambers. He burst through, and even as he was entering he prayed that the wizard hadn't trapped the portal.

The rogue skidded to a stop just inside the threshold, hearing a shriek. He turned to see a halfling extracting himself from a magical web.

"Who are you?" Regis asked, then quickly added, "See what I have?" He pulled open his shirt, lifting out a ruby pendant for Morik to see.

"Where is the sorceress?" Morik demanded, not even noticing the tantalizing gemstone.

Regis pointed to the open outer door and the balcony beyond, and Morik sprinted out. The halfling glanced down, then, at his enchanted ruby pendant and scratched his head, wondering why it hadn't had its usual charming effect. Regis was glad that this small man was too busy to be bothered with him.

⚔ ⚔ ⚔ ⚔ ⚔

Catti-brie paused, taken aback by the sincerity and demand in Drizzt's voice as he had given her the surprising instructions. The woman turned toward the fallen elf, whose breathing was as shallow as Drizzt's, who seemed, as did Drizzt, as if each breath might be her last.

"The Nine Hells ye will!" Bruenor roared, rushing to her and tearing the vial away.

Sputtering a string of curses, the dwarf went right to Drizzt and poured the healing liquid down his throat.

The drow coughed and almost immediately began to breathe easier.

"Damn it all!" Catti-brie cried, and she ran across the room to the fallen elf, lifting her head gently with her hands, staring into those eyes.

Empty eyes.

Even as Drizzt opened his eyes once more, Le'lorinel's spirit fled her body.

"Come quickly!" said Regis, arriving at the door. The halfling paused, though, when he saw Drizzt lying there so badly wounded.

"What'd'ye know, Rumblebelly?" Bruenor said after a moment's pause.

"S-sorceress," Regis stammered, still staring at Drizzt. "Um . . . Morik's chasing her." Never turning his eyes, he pointed across the way.

Wulfgar started off and Bruenor called to Catti-brie as she fell to her knees beside the drow, "Get yer bow out there! They'll be needing ye!"

The woman hesitated for a long while, staring helplessly at Drizzt, but Bruenor pushed her away.

"Go, and be quick!" he demanded. "I ain't one for killing wizards. Yer bow's better for that."

Catti-brie rose and ran out of the room.

"But holler if ye see another ogre!" the dwarf shouted behind her.

⚔ ⚔ ⚔ ⚔ ⚔

Bellany cursed under her breath as she gingerly picked her way along the mountainside to come in sight of the coast, only to see *Bloody Keel* riding the receding tide out of the cave. Her deck bristled with pirates, including, prominently, Sheila Kree, wounded but undaunted, shouting orders from the deck.

Bellany fell into her magical powers immediately, beginning to cast a spell that would transport her to the deck. She almost finished the casting, was uttering the very last words and making the final motions, when she was grabbed from behind.

Horrified, the sorceress turned her head to see Morik the Rogue, grim-faced and holding her fast.

"Let me go!" she demanded.

"Do not," Morik said, shaking his head. "Do not, I beg."

"You fool, they will kill me!" Bellany howled, trying hard to pull away. "I could have slain you, but I did not! I could have killed the halfling, but . . ."

Her voice trailed away over those last few words, though, for the huge form of a barbarian warrior came bounding around the mountainside.

"What have you done to me?" the defeated woman asked Morik.

"Did you not let the halfling live?" the rogue reasoned.

"More than that! I cut him out," Bellany answered defiantly. She went silent, for Wulfgar was there, towering over her.

"Who is this?" the enraged barbarian demanded.

"An observer," Morik answered, "and nothing more. She is innocent."

Wulfgar narrowed his eyes, staring hard at both Bellany and Morik, and his expression showed that he hardly believed the rogue.

But Morik had saved his life this day, and so he said nothing.

Wulfgar's eyes widened and he stepped forward as he noted the ship, sails unfurling, gliding out past the rocks. He leaped out to another rock, gaining a better vantage point, and lifted Aegis-fang as if he meant to hurl it at the departing ship.

But *Bloody Keel* was long out of even his range.

Catti-brie joined the group next, and wasted no time in putting up Taulmaril, leveling the bow at *Bloody Keel*'s deck.

"The red-haired one," Morik instructed. Bellany elbowed him hard in the ribs and scowled at him deeply.

Indeed, Catti-brie already had a bead drawn on Sheila Kree, the pirate easy to spot on the ship's deck.

But the woman paused and lifted her head from the bow for a wider view. She took note of the many waves breaking over submerged rocks, all about the escaping pirate, and understood well the skill needed to take a ship out through those dangerous waters.

Catti-brie leveled her bow again, scouring the deck.

When she found the wheel, and the crewman handling it, she let fly.

The pirate lurched forward, then slid down to the decking, taking the wheel over to the side as he went.

Bloody Keel cut a sharp turn, crewmen rushing desperately from every angle to grab the wheel.

Then came the crunch as the ship sailed over a jagged reef, and the wind in the sails kept her going, splintering the hull all the way.

Many were thrown from the ship with the impact. Others leaped into the icy waters, the ship disintegrating beneath them. Still others grabbed a rail or a mast and held on for dear life.

Amidst it all stood Sheila Kree. The fiery pirate looked up at the mountainside, up at Catti-brie, in defiance.

And she, too, went into the cold water, and *Bloody Keel* was no more than kindling, scattering in the rushing waters.

Few would escape that icy grip, and those who did, and those who never got onto the ship in the first place—ogre, half-ogre, and human alike—had no intention of engaging the mighty friends again.

The fight for Golden Cove was won.

EPILOGUE

They buried the elf who called herself Le'lorinel in the clay, in the cave complex, as near to the exit and the outside air and the starry night sky as possible.

Drizzt didn't help with the digging, for his vicious wound was far from healed, but he watched it, every moment. And when they had put the elf, Ellifain by her true name, in the cold ground and had covered her with damp and cold clay, Drizzt Do'Urden stood there, staring helplessly.

"It should not have been like this," the drow said quietly to Catti-brie, who was standing beside him, supporting him.

"I heard that in yer voice," the woman replied. "When ye told me to save her."

"And so I wish that you had."

"Ye durn fool!" came a rocky voice from the side. "Get yerself healed quick so I can pound yer face!"

Drizzt turned to Bruenor, matching the dwarf's scowl.

"Ye think we'd've done that?" Bruenor demanded. "Do ye really?

Ye think we'd've let ye die to save the one that killed ye?"

"You do not understand . . ." Drizzt tried to explain, his lavender orbs wet with tears.

"And would ye have saved the damned elf instead of me?" the fiery dwarf bellowed. "Or instead of me girl? Ye say yes, elf, and I'll be wiping yer blood from me axe!"

The truth of that statement hit home to Drizzt, and he turned helplessly to Catti-brie.

"I would not have given her the potion," the woman said definitively. "Ye caught me by surprise, to be sure, but I'd've been back to ye with the brew in a moment."

Drizzt sighed and accepted the inevitable truth of that, but still, this whole thing seemed so very unfair to him, so very wrong. He had encountered Ellifain before this, and not so many years ago, in the Moonwood on his way back to the Underdark. The elf had come after him them with murderous rage, but her protective clan had held her back and had ushered Drizzt on his way. And Drizzt, though he knew that her anger was misplaced, could do nothing to persuade her or calm her.

And now this. She had come after him because of what his evil kin had done to her mother, to her family, and to her.

Drizzt sighed at the irony of it all, his heart surely broken by this sad turn of fate. If Ellifain had revealed herself to him truly, he never would have found the strength to lift his blades against her, even if she came at him to kill him.

"I had no choice," Drizzt said to Catti-brie, his voice barely a whisper.

"The elf killed herself," the woman replied. Bruenor, coming over to join his friends, agreed wholeheartedly.

"She should be alive, and healing from those wounds she felt those decades ago," the drow said.

To the side, Bruenor gave a loud snort. "Yerself's the one who should be alive," the dwarf bellowed. "And so ye are."

Drizzt looked at him and shrugged.

"Ye'd have gived the potion to me," the dwarf insisted quietly, and Drizzt nodded.

"But it saddens me," the drow explained.

"If it didn't, ye'd be less a friend of mine," Bruenor assured him.

Catti-brie held Drizzt close and kissed him on the cheek.

He didn't look at her, though, just stood there staring at the new grave, his shoulders slumped with the weight of the world.

※ ※ ※ ※ ※

The five companions, along with Morik and Bellany, left Golden Cove a tenday later, when the weather broke clear.

They knew they were fighting time in trying to get out of the mountains, but with Bellany's magical help they made the main pass through the Spine of the World, leading north to Icewind Dale and south to Luskan, soon enough.

And there they parted ways, with Morik, Bellany, and Wulfgar heading south, and the other four turning north back for Ten-Towns.

Before they split apart, though, Wulfgar promised his friends that he would be home soon.

Home. Icewind Dale.

※ ※ ※ ※ ※

Spring was in full bloom before Wulfgar, Delly, and Colson came through Luskan again, heading north for Icewind Dale.

The family paid a visit to the Cutlass, to Arumn and Josi, and to Bellany and Morik, who had taken up together in Morik's apartment—one made more comfortable by far by the workings of the sorceress.

Wulfgar didn't stay long in Luskan, though, his wagon rolling out the front gate within two days. For the warrior, knowing again who he was, was indeed anxious to be home with his truest friends.

Delly, too, was anxious to see this new home, to raise Colson in the clear, crisp air of fabled Icewind Dale.

As night was settling over the land, the couple noted a blazing campfire in the distance, just off the road, and since there were farmhouses all around in this civilized region, they rolled up without fear.

They smelled the encampment's occupants before they could make out the individual forms, and though Delly whispered, "goblins," Wulfgar knew better.

"Dwarves," he corrected.

Since this particular group apparently hadn't bothered to set any sort of a sentry, Wulfgar and Delly moved right into their midst, near to the campfire, before any of the dwarves cried out in surprise or protest. After a moment's hesitation, with many vicious-looking, many-bladed, many-hooked weapons rising up in the air, the most unpleasant, smelly, and animated dwarf either of the humans had ever seen bounded up before them. He still wore his armor, though it was obvious that the camp had been set hours before, and what armor that was! Razor-sharp edges showed everywhere, along with many small spikes.

"Wulfie!" bellowed Thibbledorf Pwent, raucous leader of the famed Gutbuster Brigade of Mithral Hall. "I heared ye wasn't dead!" He gave a huge, gap-toothed grin as he finished and slugged Wulfgar hard. "Tougher than the stone, ain't ye?"

"Why are you here?" the surprised barbarian asked, not thrilled to see this particular old friend.

Wulfgar had lived beside Thibbledorf in Mithral Hall those years ago and had watched the amazing training of the famed Gutbusters, a group of wild and vicious thugs. One of Thibbledorf's infamous battle tactics was to leap onto a foe and begin shaking wildly, his nasty armor cutting the enemy to pieces.

"Going to Icewind Dale," Thibbledorf explained. "Got to get to King Bruenor."

Wulfgar started to ask for the dwarf to expand on that, but he held the words as the title Thibbledorf had just laid upon Bruenor's powerful shoulders hit him clearly.

"King?"

Thibbledorf lowered his eyes, a movement that had all the other Gutbusters, a dozen or so, leaping up and falling to one knee. All of them save the leader gave a deep, monotone intonation, a long and low hum.

"Praise Moradin in taking Gandalug Battlehammer," Thibbledorf said solemnly. "The King of Mithral Hall is no more. The king before him is king again—Bruenor Battlehammer of the clan that bears his name. Long life and good beer to King Bruenor!"

He ended with a shout, and all the Gutbusters leaped up into the air. They resembled a field of bouncing rocks, punching their fists, most covered with spiked gauntlets, into the air.

"King Bruenor!" they all roared.

"What's it mean?" Delly whispered to Wulfgar.

"It means we should not get too comfortable in Ten-Towns," the barbarian answered. "For we'll be on the road again, do not doubt. A long road to the east, to Mithral Hall."

Delly looked around at the Gutbusters, who were dancing in couples, chanting "King Bruenor!" and ending each call with a shallow hop and a short run that brought each couple crashing together.

"Well, at least our own road north'll be safer now," the woman remarked. "If a bit more fragrant."

Wulfgar started to nod, but then saw Thibbledorf crash together forehead to forehead with one poor Gutbuster, laying the dwarf out cold. Thibbledorf shook his head to clear the dizziness, his lips flapping wildly. When he saw what he'd done, he howled all the louder and charged at another—who took up the challenge and roared and charged.

And went flying away into the peaceful land of sleeping Gutbusters.

Thibbledorf howled all the louder and hopped about, looking for a third victim.

"Safer? We shall see," was all that Wulfgar could say to Delly.

FORGOTTEN REALMS

The *New York Times* BEST-SELLING AUTHOR

RICHARD BAKER

BLADES OF THE MOONSEA

". . . it was so good that the bar has been raised.
Few other fantasy novels will hold up to it, I fear."
—Kevin Mathis, d20zines.com on *Forsaken House*

Book I
Swordmage

Book II
Corsair

Book III
Avenger
March 2010

Enter the Year of the Ageless One!

EBERRON

DRACONIC PROPHECIES

JAMES WYATT

From acclaimed author and award-winning game designer James Wyatt, an adventure that will shake the world of EBERRON®.

STORM DRAGON
AVAILABLE NOW IN PAPERBACK

DRAGON FORGE
AVAILABLE NOW IN PAPERBACK

DRAGON WAR
IN HARDCOVER AUGUST 2009

KEITH BAKER'S
THORN of BRELAND

As a child, Nyrielle Tam dreamed of being a soldier. Instead, she became a spy, a saboteur, and when necessary, an assassin.

She became Thorn, Dark Lantern of Breland.

THE
QUEEN OF
STONE
Available Now

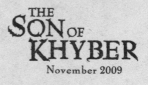

THE
SON OF
KHYBER
November 2009

THE
FADING
DREAM
October 2010